STEALTH

Two muffled explosions shook Dunne's aircraft and the fire warning light for his right engine filled the dark cockpit with a bright red glow. His heart rate went into overdrive as he saw the tailpipe temperature of his right engine increase into the red lined danger zone. He shut it down and punched the fire extinguisher button.

"Mayday! Frosty, I have to abort! Your target!"

She was only a few miles behind the target. She could see the transport's running lights and red strobe. She activated her master arming switch and opened the bomb-bay doors. Her right hand was wrapped around the control stick, her forefinger positioned over the FIRE button. *"God, give me strength to make the right decision,"* she prayed.

Her finger refused to move . . .

Other Avon Books by
M. E. Morris

BIOSTRIKE

STEALTH

M.E. MORRIS

AVON BOOKS ◆ NEW YORK

VISIT OUR WEBSITE AT
http://AvonBooks.com

STEALTH is an original publication of Avon Books. This work has never before appeared in book form. This work is a novel. Any similarity to actual persons, events, or locales is purely coincidental.

AVON BOOKS
A division of
The Hearst Corporation
1350 Avenue of the Americas
New York, New York 10019

Copyright © 1996 by M. E. Morris
Published by arrangement with the author
Library of Congress Catalog Card Number: 96-96413
ISBN: 0-380-78488-2

First Avon Books Printing: November 1996

AVON TRADEMARK REG. U.S. PAT. OFF. AND IN OTHER COUNTRIES, MARCA REGISTRADA, HECHO EN U.S.A.

Printed in the U.S.A.

RA   10 9 8 7 6 5 4 3 2 1

For the grandchildren: Colleen, Eric, Kristen, Patrick, Timmy, Sean, Mary, Phillip, Ginny, Krista, Jordy, Charla, Robby, Melissa, Elizabeth, Kaley, McKenzie, and those to come.

Writing is never a lonely profession when an author enjoys the confidence and support of fellow professionals who evaluate and market his/her work. In this case, I could ask for no better associates than my agent, Jane Dystel, and my editor, Tom Colgan. Also a hearty tip of my hat is due to copyeditor Kate Liba, a most competent and thorough person.

Glossary

ASROC	anti-submarine rocket
ASW	anti-submarine warfare
bingo	proceed to designated alternate airfield
CACC	carrier air control center
CAG	carrier air group commander (World War II designation, even though it now applies to carrier air wing commander)
CICO	combat information center officer
CTS	China Travel Service
DME	distance measuring equipment
DOD	Department of Defense
FBW	fly-by-wire aircraft control system
GPS	global positioning satellites
IFF	Identification: friend or foe
ILS	instrument landing system
LSO	landing signal officer
NATOPS	Naval Aviation Training and Operational Procedure Standards
OOD	Officer of the Deck
PAX	Patuxent River Naval Air Station
PIM	position of intended movement
RAM	radar absorbent material
RIO	radar intercept officer
SAR	search and rescue
SECDEF	Secretary of Defense
SSM	surface-to-surface missile

TAC	tactical
TDY	temporary duty
TLQ	temporary living quarters
VFR	visual flight rules
VH	helicopter ASW air squadron
VS	fixed-wing ASW air squadron

STEALTH

Prologue ━━━━━━━━━━━━━━━

Seoul, South Korea
September 26, dawn

The Soviet-built Tu-22M Backfire, wearing the red star within two thin red and blue circles insignia of the Korean People's Army Air Forcè, raced along at near treetop level just twenty kilometers north of the already bustling city of Seoul. The supersonic bomber had laboriously flown a ball-busting Mach .9 ground-terrain following profile and the crew was reaching its peak in anticipation, despite the early morning turbulence that jostled them about like pebbles in a rock polishing drum. The pilot, a fifteen-year flight leader within the Democratic People's Republic of Korea's elite first strike squadron, pulled sharply back on the control yoke and the sleek death-deliverer nosed upward, its wings gradually swinging forward as the airspeed fell off. They would change only a few degrees, but their position would constantly insure that the pilot would be getting optimum performance from his aircraft. The copilot watched the bomb release point close.

The crew smiled in unison as they heard the air control chatter of South Korean F-16s being launched for the intercept. It was too late; they would be unable to intercept the Backfire in time. The most critical phase of the attack, the undetected approach, had been carried off with skill and no little daring, the short 120-kilometer run from their departure point covered in six and one-half minutes.

"Bomb away." With those words uttered dryly into the intercom, the pilot continued upward, pulling over into a tight Cuban-8 reversal, and dove once more for the rice fields north of Seoul, accelerating to his maximum escape speed. Beside himself with the glow of accomplishment, he listened to the futile directions and responses of the South Korean air control team desperately attempting to vector their F-16s for the intercept. The two confused fighters were over the center of the city when the twelve-megaton weapon detonated one thousand feet above the central business district. Without a doubt, the F-16 pilots found themselves being torn apart by the fireball and shock wave while, below, the city instantly cooked to ashes within a six-mile radius and 320,000 people entered eternity. One-half million immediately received lethal does of radiation, and all services to what remained of the city stopped.

The pilot wrestled with the delicate control forces that were necessary to keep the Backfire skimming the rice without plowing into the wet beds. He was confident that he was now below any probing radar waves as he scurried back toward his home base. The South Korean tactical radio net indicated that additional teams of interceptors had been launched. Then he heard them being destroyed as they entered North Korean airspace and the newly acquired Russian fire-sale MiG-31s assigned to protect the Backfire went about their tasks, as coolly and efficiently as the bomber crew had gone about theirs.

As the Backfire touched down, the tower notified the jubilant crew that North Korean regulars were pouring through the demilitarized zone and spreading south in two giant ground assaults that were splitting to bypass the ruins of Seoul. The few American forces along the border had been overrun as simply as a rapidly rising river covers the surrounding low country.

Shutting down his engines, the sweating Backfire pilot pulled off his black leather helmet and ran his gloved fingers through ruffled hair as he congratulated his crew.

Outside the fully articulated simulator, sitting at the control console, his instructor was waiting. "Perfect. Perfect mission, Colonel."

The pilot nodded. "We are ready. All we need are the operational weapons."

Yiechuan, People's Republic of China
Shortly after dawn

Chi Lin sat in front of his scope, the effects of his all night duty reflected in the puffy flesh under his eyes and the dry lips that he kept running his tongue over every few seconds. In his early fifties and despite the fact that he cared for his physical condition with daily exercises, he was weary as the end of his shift approached. But he had over the past years conditioned himself against such fatigue—primarily mental—and remained vigilant as he monitored the air traffic approaching and departing Yiechuan, most of it arriving from or destined for Beijing. It was not dense traffic; air traffic in China was never dense. There was no general aviation; the commercial transports of the national airlines were few in number and most flew limited schedules. The only exasperating factor was the military aircraft of the PRC air force that more or less regularly flew training missions within Chi Lin's sector of the Beijing Air Traffic Control Zone.

He coped well, however, with the unpredictable military flights and their habits of ignoring civilian traffic. The cocky pilots of the Air Force of the People's Liberation Army were confident that they had number one priority in the air, relying on the controllers sitting in the dark cells below to keep civilian traffic out of their way. To Chi Lin's credit, and that of his fellow controllers, the system worked reasonably well. He had never seen two blips at the same altitude merge, although it did sometimes happen. On those occasions, the sparse release of information routinely mentioned inclement weather as the cause of the civilian crash.

As Chi Lin watched his scope, the green phosphorescent blips slowly crisscrossing the large circular cathode ray tube, he saw two of the returns merge. There was no apprehension, as they were separated by over one thousand meters of altitude. He also watched as a third appeared, its path taking it between the other two as they separated. The stranger had appeared almost without warning, undoubtedly an unfiled military low-level mission that just happened to rise into Chi Lin's radar coverage at the point where the two civilian aircraft crossed. There were no other flight strips on Chi Lin's flight file board. The military jet just appeared and *swish!* it raced off the edge of his scope.

In an instant, Chi Lin realized that he had witnessed the solution to a very vexing problem, for Chi Lin was a San Francisco–born Chinese and an intelligence agent of the United States, planted in China a quarter century back, his ongoing mission to report on that country's capability to control air traffic with particular respect to military flight operations. A veteran and unreservedly trusted agent, he was also aware of a number of other intelligence operations taking place around Beijing and parts of northeastern China.

The crossing of the two airliners and the almost simultaneous passing of the military jet gave him a startling insight. He must contact his control as soon as he was off duty.

1

All in all, it was a tiring time.

A fall chill swept down the mountains and picked up the faint musty smell of leaves starting to decompose in the grass. The days were getting shorter. The clouds flowing eastward across the front range of the Rocky Mountains seemed to want to fade from bright white to dullish gray as they stretched over the high plains of Colorado. The highest mountain peaks themselves already wore thin white caps of early snow. Late September was a transitional time. The summer heat was gone but not unremembered, and on this particular morning there was the hint of winter cold.

For Joshua Dunne, it was a time of some regret. No longer in the military, he was just beginning his quest for a second career. Twenty-five years in the service had provided him with a comfortable retired pay, enough to live on if he watched his habits, but there was a drive to continue with creative thought and achievement. He was much too young to vegetate, his forty-fifth birthday still four months away; much too lonely as a widower and much too disgruntled with his difficulty in adjusting to the slower pace of civilian life. He had few responsibilities, no de-

5

manding ones. He passed his annual civilian flight physical examinations with ease, his six-foot, large-boned frame a solid base for his overall weight of 176 pounds. He had gone up one waist size during the past year, from thirty-four to thirty-six, but was taking steps to correct that. He just needed a more physically challenging existence.

The high-pitched jangle of his telephone startled him, and when he answered it, the voice on the other end startled him even more. "Captain? . . . Sheila Kohn."

In an instant, the vision of his former USS `Ford` shipmate—the talented, professional fellow naval officer who had been the officer in charge of the helicopter detachment aboard his ship—flashed into his mind as if it had been projected suddenly upon a large screen in vivid color. Lieutenant Sheila "Frosty" Kohn, chopper pilot extraordinaire, vivacious in a flight suit but all business. Silken auburn hair, skin as clear and pure as a baby's bottom and deep cobalt blue eyes that were as reflective of light as the purest of dark amethysts.

"Frosty," Dunne responded eagerly, "this is a surprise."

"It's good to hear your voice, Captain."

"Joshua, please. I'm out to pasture."

"I know. That's why I called."

"Oh?"

"Yes, sir. You free for dinner?"

Dunne was somewhat taken aback. "You're here . . . in Denver?"

"For the evening. You free?"

"Of course I am. Where would you like to meet?"

"Your turf, Joshua. You tell me."

Dunne's mind stalled for just a moment, faced with a sudden decision on where to eat. If he was to dine with Sheila Kohn, it should be somewhere special. Certainly quiet and with privacy for conversation. A place of exquisite food with comparable service. He would have to think.

"Let me pick you up. Seven okay? That'll give us time for a drink. Where are you?"

"Downtown, Brown Palace."

"Ah, first class."

"On official business," Kohn explained. "Great expense account. Seven it is. How shall I dress?"

"Colorado casual unless you want to go dancing."

Her laugh was as he remembered it. "Not this time. I have a proposition for you."

"You have my attention."

"Don't be late, sir. We have some talking to do."

Dunne shook his head, the movement an expression of the disbelief he had at the sudden return of Sheila Kohn into his life. It had been five years since he had last seen her, walking down the accommodation ladder of the *Ford* at the Pearl Harbor Naval Base after their harrowing experience with the Mid-Eastern terrorists. She had been a rock during that spontaneous operation and had literally saved his professional ass when it had come to the subsequent court-martial. It all came back and flashed through his mind in a matter of microseconds: the charges, the acquittal on one and conviction on the other, the tragic assassination of his wife, the presidential pardon, his restoration to duty. His retirement two years later. "I'll be there, Frosty."

The rest of his afternoon was completely shot as he recalled his time with Kohn. She had been flying helicopters then, SH-60F ASW Seahawks, and was the officer in charge of the chopper detachment aboard his ship. Now, Frosty Kohn was in Denver—and she had a proposition for him. That was intriguing. He shaved early and sat watching the five o'clock news in his skivvies, not really interested but it would make the final hours pass more quickly.

Promptly at seven, he used the house phone in the Brown Palace lobby to call Kohn's room.

"Yes? Joshua?" she answered, anticipating that it was he.

"On deck, or should I say in the lobby?"

"I'll be right down."

She had aged little, although there was an added pound or two nestled around the rib cage. She easily appeared ten years younger than her chronological age, which he suspected was in the late thirties. Her jeans were a little tighter than he had ever seen her wear but it was the style, not the hips. Her hips were perfect. Maybe she was loosening up a bit. She stepped off the elevator and held out her arms. As they hugged, Dunne recalled that they had never shared any physical contact before. Exchanging salutes had been their only acknowledgment of one another. She was warm and soft and let her form fit his; it was a much more intimate greeting than he had anticipated.

"It's really good to see you," he said. As they drew apart, he noticed something else. The rich color of her blue-green irises was still there, but there was a slight droop of the eyelids that seemed to reflect increased concentration rather than any beauty fault. It wasn't a squint, just a more concentrated focus. Then it hit him. Frosty Kohn had fighter pilots' eyes. Intense, wary, penetrating. She had been engaged in serious business since they had last served together—it was not a flattering change.

"Can we have the drink here?" she asked. "I didn't realize how cozy their bar is."

"Denver's finest. You know how to pick 'em, Sheila. Damn, it's good to see you."

They sat at a corner table. Kohn ordered white wine, he a Beefeater and tonic.

"Tell me about yourself," he asked. "What happened after you left the ship?"

"Back to the squadron at North Island. Finished my tour and got orders to Command and Staff Course at the Naval War College. Orders to J-3 on the Joint Staff, then a sudden switch to a special assignment. I'm still on it.''

"What kind of special assignment?''

Kohn sipped her wine. "It's really good to see you, Captain.''

"Joshua . . .''

"It's really good to see you—Joshua.''

"The assignment?''

A twinkle of mischief shot from Kohn's eyes as she let the tip of her tongue curl and slide briefly across her lips. On any other woman, the movement would have been interpreted as a come-on, but Dunne knew that Sheila "Frosty" Kohn added a new dimension to body language.

"In due time. Shall we talk about you?''

"Little to talk about.''

Kohn leaned forward and, like a child revealing a special secret, spoke softly. "You did your thing at War College and they shunted you off to an obscure joint billet at the North American Aerospace Defense Command down at Colorado Springs. As usual, you performed exceptionally well, but NORAD was dead-city for naval officers in those days. You got a belated promotion, but that was all.''

"I had the president's pardon, but the court-martial conviction was common knowledge. It went with me.''

"You did two years pushing papers and kowtowing to the boys in sky blue, then hung it up . . .''

Dunne sat back. "I wouldn't put it exactly that way.'' Kohn was telling *him* what he had done, answering her own question.

"You went back to aviation and got your civilian tickets, leased a Learjet 24 that was heading for the boneyard and now hire yourself out to private charters. Business is not so good, and if you didn't have that retirement pay, you'd be starving to death. No special friends at this point in your life. Your few acquaintances consider you a loner; they probably don't know the story of how Annie died.''

The mention of his deceased wife instantly sobered him.

"You seem to have kept pretty good track of me. Why?"

"Not me, Joshua. The man I work for. He is quite thorough and he wants you to join us."

"What's this all about, Frosty?"

Kohn looked around and seemed to decide the lounge was becoming too crowded. "Shall we go eat? Someplace with a secluded table, one where lovers can talk?"

Dunne could see that Kohn was enjoying the tease. "We're not lovers, Frosty," he ventured, confused.

Kohn took a final sip of her wine. The fighter pilots' eyes were fixed on his. "We're gonna be, Joshua. We're gonna be close as lovers, maybe closer." She stood and slung a small blue leather purse from her shoulder.

What the hell is going on? was all Joshua could say to himself. This was straitlaced, no-nonsense Lieutenant Sheila Kohn—or most probably a lieutenant commander by now?—and she was making a pass at *him*? He knew better and was more than a little anxious to find out why the subtle charade.

The drive into the foothills overlooking Denver took only twenty minutes, the evening rush hour having faded into the night. They didn't even make small talk, each for his or her own reason. Dunne left his Subaru station wagon with the valet and escorted Kohn into the High Mountain Chalet, a small but reasonably exclusive restaurant and lounge that was perched on a steep mountain slope facing the city and the eastern high plains beyond. A window wall gave every table a panoramic view of the city lights some thousand feet below the restaurant elevation. Their particular table was at the back of the candlelighted room but on a slightly elevated platform with several other tables, all of which were empty at the moment.

"Perfect," announced Kohn, savoring the view and noting they were isolated from the other occupants of the restaurant. Even the closest table was beyond earshot if their conversation was discreet. It would be.

"White wine and a gin and tonic." Dunne relayed their order to the server. "We'll order later."

"Right away, sir," the man responded. He was young, in his early twenties, and sported a neatly trimmed black beard. "My name is David and I will be serving you this evening." As he left, Dunne turned to Kohn.

"Should I be holding your hand or something?" He could tease as well as she, although this new relationship was still baffling to him.

Kohn let her eyes express her answer. Not just yet.

Their drinks came and they were alone again.

"Captain—Joshua—does the name Amin Mohamud Desird mean anything to you?"

"No."

"He is the man who was responsible for the death of your wife."

Dunne's eyes immediately moistened. "I'm listening."

"The two terrorists who actually made the attack, Jamal Hussein and Ahmad Libidi, were members of a very special elite squad of Mid-Eastern mercenaries, European-based men who will do anything, anywhere, to anybody for a price, although they prefer to strike first Jews, then Americans. They have no truly religious or patriotic motives; they just love to kill, and they use the Middle East tensions and the Islamic faith as their self-serving crutches. Amin has been so successful in leading the organization that he is being spoken of as the successor to the reputation of Abu Nidal, although his strategy and tactics often differ. He is the only known member of the group, so successful is the cover they use in their operations. And he is their control and sometimes the strategist for the cell's tactics."

"Hamas?" Dunne asked.

"They've worked with Hamas but are a little more worldwide-oriented. Think Pacific Rim."

Pacific Rim?

Their server, David, approached. Dunne halted him with,

"We'll order later; I'll give you a sign." The man obediently left.

Kohn continued, "The beast is getting into bigger and bigger things, Joshua, and at the moment is engaged in an activity that can be a very real threat to our national interests. He's working the Far East."

"I don't understand."

"He's gone worldwide. More threats, more money, more demand for his services."

Dunne lifted his drink in a silent toast before stating, "War College talk. You know that all of my security clearances lapsed with my retirement?"

"Yes, no matter. I can talk around that, especially since my mission is to recruit you."

"*Recruit* me?"

"I have a specific assignment with respect to Amin but it takes two people. Qualifications are low-key personalities, current flying skills, no living close relatives, and an overwhelming desire to kill Amin."

"You're a low-key personality? The number one naval aviatrix in the service?"

Kohn smiled. "In your eyes, perhaps. My reputation is within the navy; outside I'm just one of a flock of female military flyers. Anything happens to me, no big deal. Routine loss at sea."

Kohn's unexpected appearance in Denver began to take on an ominous tone. "Something going to happen to you, Frosty?" Dunne asked.

"I hope not, but if it does I would like to have you there—with me."

"Why exactly me?"

"Because the powers that be won't approve the mission with a female lead—and I won't follow anybody but you in this."

"That's chauvinistic, sexist—discriminatory."

"Not in my world at present. Our group has special responsibilities, and when we join we agree to a lot of things; discipline and command decisions go unquestioned.''

"I'm not sure I can operate like that. I never have, you know. I'm having trouble with this. Why me, or for that matter why you and me? There must be dozens of our kind to select from.''

"The main man wants me and, after getting a little bit of political direction from the top, he wants you.''

"And he is?''

"I can't tell you that, but I can take you to him.''

"He's presuming a lot. I'm to just take off and go with you? A command request out of the blue? I have obligations. My business.''

"You don't have a single charter, and the only obligation you have is a haircut, Tuesday. I called from my room and canceled the appointment.''

"I don't believe this.''

Kohn double-checked the nearby tables before continuing. "Wouldn't you like to come back and operate on the edge? Really contribute by flying one hell of a mission to bag Annie's killer, not to mention do your Uncle Samuel a big favor?''

"I hung up my wings early, remember? I haven't flown a military mission in years. I'm a retired frigate sailor, for God's sake.''

"You wore the same gold wings I do, and you jumped back in the air within a week of leaving active duty.''

"I fly a civilian Lear. That qualifies me for operational missions?''

"You're jet current. It's a matter of getting checked out in another airplane—and a couple other things.''

"What other things?'' Dunne asked.

"We meet the man first, but I can give you two quick teasers.''

"They better be pretty goddamned good.''

"You lead. I fly wing. We drive F-117Ns.''

"Stealth fighters? N-models?"

"Navy-configured so we can take off and land from the big gray boat."

Dunne was beginning to feel the first urgings that maybe he might be interested. "Let's order," he suggested. "Let me digest what you've said with a good meal and we'll see. This sounds like something I'd like to sleep on."

"Fair enough. But tomorrow morning when you wake up, we crank up your little overage executive turbojet and fly to Cajun country."

"Louisiana?" That was unexpected.

"The man we'll work for makes the best blackened redfish in New Orleans."

"We're going to work for a chef?"

"Not exactly, but he loves to cook and is quite good at it."

Damn it, Frosty, stop yanking my chain. Dunne raised his hand and summoned David, the bearded one.

2

Denver International Airport
The next morning

Dunne shoved the power levels forward and the spunky Learjet accelerated down runway one-seven-left just like the big boys. The cool morning air helped compensate for the mile-high elevation of the airport, and with a smooth rotation, Dunne eased the small jet into its element. Despite its age, it began to climb as if all the banshees from hell were chasing it.

"Not bad for an old-timer," commented Kohn.

"Me or the airplane?" Dunne mused as he rolled smoothly into a left bank for the new heading assigned by Departure Control and adjusted his power for climb. They were already passing through 11,000 feet en route to flight level 320 (32,000 feet). The Lear seemed to want to show that it had plenty of life left as it gobbled up the early morning cumulus like a child eating cotton candy, rapidly rising through the six-thousand-feet-thick broken layer that began a half mile up in the Denver skies.

"It's all yours," Dunne advised, patting his head.

"I don't know anything about this bird," Kohn protested but happily took the controls.

"We're cleared direct to Las Animas; climb to thirty-two thou, flight plan from there. Coffee's in the thermos. Relief tube's in the back. What else is there to know? You're either a flygirl or not. You plan on plunking my rear down into some skittish high performance fighter—if I sign up. Turnabout's fair play.''

Kohn rose to the challenge. "I can handle this toy.''

"Good. If you need me, I'll be in my quarters.'' Dunne reclined the back of his seat, leaned into it and closed his eyes.

"I'd really prefer two sets of eyeballs here,'' Kohn commented.

"Fighter jocks only use one. If we start to hit anything, yell. I'm a light sleeper.''

Kohn leveled at 32,000 feet, took a few minutes determining how to set the autopilot, engaged it and resumed her steady scan of the sky ahead.

Dunne was not really catching a catnap, although he had lain awake most of the night. He needed to consider what this trip to New Orleans meant. To begin with, he had the highest admiration for Kohn, and if she was involved in a special project he might very well want to be part of it. His brief sojourn into civilian life had been considerably less than satisfying. He loved the little Lear, although the more than 20,000 hours on the airframe were causing the airplane to squirm and squeak at certain speeds. It had been well cared for and, being an early model, it was unburdened with all sorts of mods and alterations and right now was scooting along nicely at 400 knots true airspeed. There were another ten thousand feet above that Dunne could utilize after they had burned some fuel and if the winds became more favorable. As it was, they would reach New Orleans two and a half hours after wheels-in-the-well at Denver. Not bad for an eighteen-year-old aluminum sky-scooter that had made some 15,000 landings, a number of them most probably more than a little bone-jarring.

Dunne eased an eyelid up and peeked at Kohn. She was

relaxed and her head was on the jet pilot swivel with periodic scans of the instrument panel. All pro.

As he wondered about the identity of "the man" she was taking him to meet, he recalled the circumstances that had bonded him to Sheila Kohn. Four years back, his frigate, the USS *Ford*, had accidentally encountered a Mid-Eastern terrorist freighter on a dark night two hundred miles south of Oahu in the midst of a building hurricane. Kohn had played an invaluable role as the helo driver attached to the *Ford* and had been one of the prime assets in Dunne's at-sea investigation and recommendation that he sink the ship before it could reach Oahu. There had been sensitive international ramifications, and the ultimate responsibility had been passed up the chain of command to the president as the service's commander in chief. That decision had been delayed by the several layers of civilian and military bureaucracy between the president and Dunne, so much so that Dunne had taken it upon himself to sink the ship that was flying the false colors of Greece and sporting the bogus name of *Salinika*. It had closed to within eleven miles of Waikiki. The bold act earned accolades from his military commanders and a presidential-directed court-martial for preempting the president's decision to sink the ship. It had been Kohn's testimony that had been a swinging point in the trial, although Dunne had been convicted on one count, a verdict later nullified by presidential pardon. She had also been present when they walked from the court building and vengeful terrorists attacked them, killing Dunne's wife, Annie. She had died in Kohn's arms while Dunne tried to shield them. Security guards quickly killed the attackers. It had been an unbelievably horrible, bloody scene, one that was engraved permanently in Dunne's mind and certainly in Kohn's as well.

Yes, Kohn was special to him. He owed her, and that was the primary factor in his decision to take a further look at her mysterious recruitment offer.

Thirty minutes after reclining his seat, he sat back up and unscrewed the top of the thermos. "You have any idea where we are?" he chided.

"On course, on schedule, and we should be in Great Falls, Montana, in another fifty-six minutes."

Dunne ignored the obvious needle. "That was a good snooze."

"Ha, I saw you eyeballing me. No trust?"

"I was just thinking about the *Salinika*. It ended my career. I meant to ask: I assume you made lieutenant commander?" He sipped the hot coffee.

"Just before I got orders to War College."

"Congratulations." *Lieutenant Commander Sheila Kohn, Commander Kohn; that had a nice ring to it.* "We've plenty of time left. Sure you don't want to fill me in more?"

Kohn looked at him, unsmiling. "We have to meet the man first."

Dunne shrugged and went back to his coffee.

The landing at New Orleans International was uneventful; the taxi ride to the French Quarter was something else. The Cuban driver spoke acceptable English but Dunne suspected he was faking his knowledge of the city when Kohn gave her directions. "French Quarter, Bourbon Street."

The driver picked up an awkwardly folded city street map and made a show of studying it, continuously turning it over while running one finger along various streets and muttering to himself.

"You *do* know the French Quarter?" Kohn asked, irritated.

"Not well, miss. I've only been here—I come from Miami last month—short time. But I find the way, no worry."

Kohn was in no mood to take the tourist tour around the historic part of the lowland city. There was no way you could drive a cab in New Orleans for more than ten minutes and not know where the French Quarter was. "Interstate ten takes you right to the French Quarter. Get off at exit two-thirty-six-A, Saint Philip's south to Bourbon. You know which way south is, right, towards Cuba.''

The driver sped north on Airport Road and swung easily into the eastbound traffic on the interstate, obviously ticked off that his ploy for a large fare was foiled. The late morning traffic was mostly outbound and they made good time, aided undoubtedly by the Cuban's practice of using his horn as a vital driving aid, second only to his accelerator. He appeared to have little knowledge of where his brake pedal was or its function, relying on intimidation to outmaneuver the other cars. Temporarily trapped on the inside lane, he cut across two lanes of traffic to make the exit. His turn indicator was apparently as foreign to him as his brakes, but this time his horn was drowned out by a half dozen others. He had to slow on the narrow St. Philip's street and they were immediately immersed in the fascinating but now somewhat seedy atmosphere of the *Vieux Carré*, the original settlement of New Orleans, bordered by Canal Street to the west, Rampart to the north, Esplanade Avenue to the east and the Mississippi River to the south. Seventy blocks of Spanish structures, contrary to its French origin, almost every house marked with narrow balconies embellished by wrought iron filigree railings. This had been the haunt of Jean Lafitte, the place where he and his brother, Philip, disposed of their contraband. On these streets passed early settlers seeking the advice and good grace of Marie Laveau, the most powerful of the early voodoo queens. Here, in compliance with her unlikely Catholic/Haitian mixture of faith, she had gone to Mass at the stately St. Louis Cathedral that dominated the north side of Jackson Square. Now, in the late '90s, fall tourists in tight shorts and loose, light sweaters were already strolling the district, and not all were on the sidewalks. Dunne hoped that at least the Cuban had some knowledge and reluctant respect for the term "vehicular homicide." As a last-ditch effort to increase his fare, the cabby turned right onto Dauphine rather than continuing another block to Bourbon.

"Hey, no tour today," Kohn objected. "Take the next left and then left onto Bourbon. We'll stop just beyond the Lafitte Blacksmith shop, on the left."

Dunne felt like kneeling and uttering a prayer of thanksgiving by the time the driver let them out before a tiny, hole-in-the-wall, open-air cafe. Then he read the sign: BLACKJACK'S. The short hairs on the back of his neck stood erect. It couldn't be.

Kohn led him through the closed dining area to a back door labeled PRIVATE and opened it without knocking. Across the room, sitting behind a weathered wooden desk amid paper clutter and several empty coffee cups sat the owner of Blackjack's Cajun Cafe—African-American, a good two hundred and fifty pounds with a wide expanse of white teeth arrayed in a shit-eating grin the size of a half-moon, hands tucked in his Levi's: Admiral John "Blackjack" Paterson, United States Navy, retired, former Commander in Chief, Pacific Fleet, and later Chief of Naval Operations and the man who had ordered Dunne's court-martial. He was also Annie's father, Dunne's father-in-law.

"You like redfish, Cajun style?" Blackjack asked, pulling an overly moist and well-chewed cigar butt from his mouth and ceremoniously dropping it into the circular file.

"I'll be a sonuvabitch" was all Dunne could say.

Kohn clapped her hands together. "This is great! You should see the expression on your face."

Dunne quickly stepped forward and grasped Blackjack's hand. "How is this? I've been writing to you in D.C., calling you occasionally, and your return mail carries the D.C. postmark." After a quick second thought, he exclaimed, "You're the man!"

Blackjack Paterson laughed so hard, the shirttail of his

plaid shirt pulled right out of the front of his Levi's. "Isn't modern technology wonderful?"

Dunne grabbed the chair in front of Blackjack's desk as Kohn pulled another from the wall. "You're a sight for sore eyes." There was a close bond between Dunne and Blackjack, father of the late Annie Paterson-Dunne, and although Blackjack had been responsible for Dunne's Pearl Harbor court-martial, it had been a deliberate benevolent act to avoid a presidential trial at the Pentagon—and considering all of the factors, things had worked out reasonably well. Paterson had insured that only combat-experienced officers had served on the court, and on the one count of which they were forced to find Dunne guilty, their sentence had revealed the true nature of their finding: a loss of one number on the promotion ladder and a one-dollar fine for a period of one month. The president had gotten the message and pardoned Dunne only a few days after.

Now there was a new president and obviously a new mission for Blackjack. Dunne was squirming in his pants, eager to find out the nature of Blackjack's assignment and what part he and Kohn would be playing. That he would play was now a foregone conclusion. This had to be something else.

Paterson pushed a button under the rim of his desk and Dunne heard two solid thunks as the entrance door was securely locked. Although the office was one hundred percent representative of a sloppy manager ensconced in a Cajun cafe, Dunne knew the walls were soundproofed and the space debugged, and he suspected that a complete set of state-of-the-art communication systems was nearby, perhaps even in the scratched desk or in the antique, weather-beaten pine chifforobe that stood slightly askew against one wall. What a cover. Coal-black Blackjack looked every bit the part, and Dunne, remembering the mouth-watering barbecues in Paterson's Georgetown backyard when Dunne was courting Annie, suspected the admiral was indeed the owner and chef at Blackjack's.

"You look well," Paterson commented.

"As do you, even with the stomach." Dunne had rarely kidded his father-in-law, but now seemed like an appropriate time.

"All for the sake of the role. Sort of suits me, actually."

"Well, I'm here," Dunne stated with obvious anticipation.

Paterson let his smile evaporate. "We can talk here for a minute. I have to determine if you're in with us before we get serious. I suspect Commander Kohn has given you only the sparsest of details."

"Only that she is on special assignment from the navy and, I assume, to you, whoever you are at the moment."

"What I say, stays here. I am the head of a special missions group that was organized right after the last national election. We're supported by the CIA and they provide us with intelligence. We report directly to the president—no in-betweens. I have open access to the Oval Office, and the White House chief of staff pees his britches every time I show up because he hasn't the faintest clue as to what I'm up to, nor does any of the White House staff."

"Who does know?" Dunne asked.

"The president and those *under* my command, plus three congressmen and you don't need to know who they are."

"No one in Central Intelligence?"

"The Director. Period. If I need something they can provide, I ask and they provide, no questions asked."

"Hard to believe."

"We don't exist on paper. We don't keep any records. We don't have any administrative organization. We operate on my initiative but with presidential approval for each mission, and we communicate with a codeword. Every major commander in the military, service or joint, knows that when they get a call with that identifiable codeword, they must respond. I talk directly to them; most of the time they have no idea who I am.''

"A single code word.''

"Determined by the date and certain other information. We have a small manual—that is not self-explanatory, I might add.''

"How do you get by the joint chiefs, and SECDEF?''

Paterson grinned. "Very carefully.''

"How large a group?''

"You don't need to know that.''

Dunne could understand. "What *do* I need to know?''

"At this point, only that what we do is sometimes outside of national and international law and would be considered by many unethical at best, illegal on occasion and immoral at worst. It's that way because the goddamned bad guys in this world are on the verge of taking over. I have handpicked every single member of the group, and our common bond is that we don't intend to see the United States of America go down the tubes just because well-intentioned Americans choose to fight the beasts of this planet with Marquis of Queensberry rules.''

"Sounds like you've been talking to Ollie North.''

"Our patron saint.''

"Does he know that?''

"He has no idea we exist; I used the comment in a figurative sense.''

"How could you even get something like this organized and staffed?''

"The president has a private black budget—no pun intended; how he got it I don't know. But it's there and he accounts to no one for it. It's basically mine.''

Dunne held up three fingers. "The three congressmen.''

"I didn't say that. You did.''

Dunne wanted to end the suspense. "I want in.''

"I figured as much. But there's more I have to tell you.''

"All right.''

"We're not melodramatic. We don't carry suicide capsules and that kind of stuff. But if any individual is found out, he will be disowned completely. We have no idea who you are or where you came from. If you possess any information about us beyond your own mission, and we take meticulous steps to see that doesn't happen, you are expendable. The fact that you're family doesn't affect that."

"I wouldn't expect it to. I'm curious."

"About what?"

"This sounds like a textbook company organization; why can't the spooks just handle it?"

"Too many people, too many bureaucrats, too much public exposure, too much decentralized control and, believe it or not, at the moment they're short of the right people without scruples."

"Which we don't have—this group, that is?"

"If you have, jump back in your little jet and starve to death in Colorado. I wouldn't like to see that."

"There have to be some limits."

Paterson nodded. "There are. We wouldn't kill the Pope, for instance, or rape the Queen Mother. We do have limits; I set them. One of the operating parameters is that you must have complete confidence in me. In return, I take one hundred percent of the responsibility if the worms start to crawl out of the can. Everyone else is just following orders."

"I'll need to be recalled?"

Paterson pulled open his center top desk drawer, retrieved a thin set of papers and handed them to Dunne. "You already have been."

Dunne glanced at the orders, folded them and stuck them in one of his flight jacket pockets. "You were pretty sure of yourself."

"Pretty sure of you."

Those folded pieces of paper in Dunne's jacket had immediately changed his world. He was once again Captain Joshua Dunne, U.S. Navy. It was a good feeling, and all of the uncertainties that he had as a struggling civilian charter pilot vanished. "Okay, what next?"

"We're sitting on top of one hell of a short fuse. Our window for the mission starts no more than ten days from now. In that time, you and Commander Kohn have to get to Nellis Air Force Base where a Patuxent test and development pilot is waiting to check the two of you out in the one-seventeen. From there, you and your airplanes will go by C-5 to Kunsan, South Korea. You'll fly aboard the *Lincoln*; she's heading for the East China Sea as we speak. You'll get your mission tactical briefing in Hong Kong."

"I do have some loose ends in Denver."

"What are they?"

"My airplane lease will have to be terminated. I have a young man who flies copilot with me. I owe him, and he'll have to be given a decent notice. My apartment and personal things."

"I'll take care of it. You keep the Lear until you reach Nellis. We'll terminate the lease and return the airplane. Give me your Denver pilot's name and address. We'll see he gets six months' termination pay. Your gear will be stored."

"I don't have any uniforms with me."

"You don't need any. You and Kohn will be going to Nellis and aboard ship as DOD civilian contract pilots. Outwardly, you will be on a nonmilitary special mission."

"Just one other thing," Dunne asked. "Why isn't Commander Kohn suitable to lead this mission? You know she's capable. Why pull me in?"

"With all due respect to Sheila, and she knows my opinion of her ability, she lacks the command experience to make the type of decisions that might have to be made. You handled the *Salinika* incident under extreme pressure. It was pretty goddamned delicate, if you recall. The current president made the decision. I made the suggestion at Sheila's request and he approved it."

"That's the whole story?"

"Whole story."

Dunne sat for a moment, speechless. Things had happened fast, almost too fast for him to follow in a logical manner. He wanted to question Paterson's rapid-fire briefing and assumptions, but he really didn't know what to ask at this point. He checked his watch. Just three hours and twenty-seven minutes earlier he had been rolling down the Denver runway.

Paterson placed both hands on his desktop and pushed himself up into a standing position. "I know. You've a million questions but you haven't the foggiest as to what they are. Not to worry. All things will be presented in due time. Right now, take a table in ole Blackjack's Cajun Cafe. I'm going to serve you an early lunch, the best blackened redfish in New Or-lee-oons, and you can take off for Nellis with the greatest spicy-hot feeling you ever had eating the lining right off your stomach." Paterson hit the desk button, and two thunks indicated that the office door was unlocked.

The fish was superb, too delicious to interrupt with conversation. They ate in silence, watching the tourists pass. Not as many Japanese as Dunne would have thought but, true to form, the few that strolled Bourbon Street were taking endless streams of pictures, the men smiling and posing against the buildings, the women with their feet planted in high fashion model style and leaning in doorways with embarrassed grins, trying unsuccessfully to squelch their giggles. The Japanese, thought Dunne, they're everywhere, but their shopping bags were not as filled as he had seen them back in the District.

Blackjack joined them for coffee, pointing to the CLOSED sign whenever any of the tourists started to venture inside.

"Aren't you pushing the cultural diversity thing," Dunne commented, "a black man serving Cajun food."

Blackjack grabbed one of the beignets he had brought from his tiny kitchen. "My great-great-granddaddy was

Acadian, my great-great-grandmama a slave; her genes won out."

"If that's your cover, you better count the 'greats' in your ancestry. The Acadians got here in the mid–seventeen hundreds, you know."

"Beignet?"

"Thanks." The delicate French doughnut, still warm from the fryer and dusted with powdered sugar, was the perfect complement to the thick black coffee. Dunne had two.

Blackjack allowed them to finish their coffee before suggesting, "Well, you better be on your way so I can haul in my paying customers."

Dunne and Kohn stood, and each in turn grasped the big, warm hand that conveyed Paterson's appreciation and trust.

"This has been a pleasant surprise; I hope I can say that a month from now," Dunne said.

"I'm just glad you've joined us. It's what you should be doing, not flailing about in the civilian world trying to play rent-a-pilot."

As they hailed a cab, Blackjack turned his sign around. Immediately a middle-aged foursome hurried inside and grabbed the prime table.

The taxi ride back to the airport was even more exciting, as there was the noon traffic to contend with and the driver was an apparent descendent of Laveau, the voodoo queen. As Dunne preceded Kohn from the cab, a young man, obviously military trying to pass as a civilian airplane mechanic, greeted him, but not by name. "The bird's all preflighted and topped off. I took the liberty of filing your flight plan, sir. Nellis operations has given you permission to land there. Here's a copy."

Dunne still didn't know a hell of a lot about Paterson's special group, but they were on top of every detail. All he and Kohn had to do was walk from the cab to the plane and strap in. The appropriate en route charts were already sorted and clipped to his kneeboard. Not a bad way to go. But then, anything commanded by Blackjack Paterson would be this way.

As Dunne pushed the start buttons and the two GE CJ610-8A turbojets whined into life, Kohn checked the flight plan. "We may be stretching the legs on this little bugger; what's our maximum range?"

"This is one of the first models. No wind, fifteen hundred." Dunne released the brakes and started his taxi.

"It's thirteen hundred to Las Vegas, plus a stone's throw to Nellis. We have an eight-knot tailwind component at thirty-five thousand."

Dunne had little confidence in the wind factor. A series of lows were between Dallas and Vegas. "Could be close. What's a midpoint?"

Kohn ran her finger down the list of navigational aids. "Albuquerque looks good, just to the north of our route."

"We'll check it there and refuel if it looks like a pucker."

"Sounds good." They had reached the takeoff runway. "All set?"

Kohn gave a cheery thumbs-up. "Let's go for it."

Once more the Lear roared down the runway, the twin voices of its small but powerful turbojets expressing themselves with confidence.

"Damn, this is fun," Kohn observed.

"Better than sex . . .."

Kohn laughed and shook her head. "That'll be the day."

The Lear rotated and Dunne sucked up the gear, keeping the nose down until the airspeed reached 240 knots. Then he pulled the nose up sharply into a three-G zoom climb. Kohn was forced down into her seat. "Ohhh, belay that last statement . . . ride 'em, cowboy!"

Kohn fiddled with the two omnidirectional navigational receivers, checked the number two DME (distance measuring equipment) and then announced, "We're on course. Albuquerque's fifty-six miles starboard; fuel's looking good. We've got a great tailwind component, thirty-two knots at present."

Dunne glanced over. "No sweat. We should make Nellis with plenty reserve." He reached down and grabbed his thermos from between the seats. "Coffee?"

"No, I'm fine. But I do have to pump bilges. You got it?"

"All mine. The female adapter's on the bulkhead by the relief tube."

Kohn returned several minutes later and strapped in.

"How do you feel about flying the one-seventeen?" Dunne asked.

"Same as you, probably. Excited. Anxious. I've never even seen one for real."

"Well, at least I'm one up on you there. They brought one into Peterson Air Force Base down at Colorado Springs for an open house. Mean machine. But I can't say I'm enthused about going operational with a checkout that is going to be pretty goddamned marginal at best. Four days is barely long enough to look at the pretty pictures in the pilot's operating manual."

Kohn nodded. "That part bothers me. This chance to get Amin must be extremely critical to take these kinds of risks. It's the way Blackjack works, but the short hairs on this one barely stick out above the skin."

"Everything points to a night mission; the one-seventeen just isn't used for daylight tasks. A night mission off the pointy end of the big gray boat with a minimum checkout can make a guy review his life insurance coverage in a hurry. Especially if we're expected to return at night. That will line the pooch up for screwin' if anything will. My last night trap was twelve years ago. This is crazy. And it's an attack airplane. What are we going after, I wonder? This is all kind of weird, isn't it? No one in their right mind would set this up as a conventional military action. We'll be violating all the sensible rules of preparation and mission planning. The NATOPS people will shit bricks if they even hear about this.''

"Second thoughts?" Kohn asked.

"No. You?"

"No. Apprehensive, maybe, for the same reasons you are. But we've trained all our professional lives for something like this.''

"You have," Dunne corrected her. "For the last year I've been driving the filthy rich around to party sites or pompous CEOs to meetings they're always late for. I've forgotten what a bank past forty-five degrees feels like.''

"Don't tell me you haven't had this scooter up on a wingtip.''

"Well . . ." Dunne grinned and shrugged before adding, "Not with any paying passengers.''

"My sources tell me you were a pretty good stick in your day.''

"There's another thing that's making my stomach rumble. Blackjack said the *Lincoln* is heading toward the East China Sea. What the hell's a camel-driver doing near the East China Sea?''

Kohn laughed. "True. But we get our final briefing in Hong Kong. What does that tell us?''

"Someone doesn't know their geography?''

"Could be, Joshua. Could be.''

Dunne knew the lighthearted chatter was just the aviators' way of disguising a real nervousness about what lay ahead. They obviously were being programmed for one hell of a one-flight mission with the probability of their return strictly secondary to the urgency and success of the mission itself. That was all right; the military often operated in that type of environment. But was this actually a military mission? Blackjack had stressed that they would be using a civilian cover. What would that be? When would they be told? Who would give that briefing? Where and when? In another hour and twenty minutes, they would be at Nellis.

3

Dunne eased the Lear along the white concrete tarmac, following the precise lead of the blue USAF FOLLOW ME pickup, and parked in front of base operations. A major wearing silver command pilot wings greeted him and Kohn as they stepped off the boarding door. "Welcome to Nellis, sir."

Dunne was not sure what was required of him, so he responded with an outstretched hand. "Thank you."

"Ma'am," added the major, greeting Kohn with equal cordiality. "I'm Major Willus. I'm to escort you to temporary living quarters. We have one for each of you. Your bags inside, sir?"

"We just have some carry-on," Dunne responded, feeling a bit stupid at his reply. What else would they have?

An Asian-American sergeant, also in the blue uniform of the day, climbed into the Lear and immediately reappeared with the two bags. He placed them in the trunk of the staff car as Major Willus held the rear door for Dunne and Kohn.

"The airplane . . ." Dunne started tentatively.

"All taken care of, sir."

Even as they drove off, USAF ground crewmen were

attaching a nose towbar to the Lear. Dunne took a long last look. It had been a good and faithful companion.

The two TLQs were side by side. The major carried Kohn's medium Samsonite while Dunne handled his own B-4 type. "Your keys, sir," the major said, handing Dunne a steel key on a black plastic tag labeled NELLIS 28. "Ma'am." He unlocked the door for Kohn and handed her a similar key. "Sir, you have a safe. The two packets inside are for you and the lady. This is the combination, sir, and you can reset it after the initial opening if you wish."

Dunne took the small brown envelope.

"The folders in each room describe base facilities and have all necessary phone numbers. The Officers' Open Mess serves dinner starting at seventeen hundred. Informal attire okay. You will have a briefing at nineteen hundred, in your room, sir. If there is anything you require, here is my duty phone number." The major handed each a business-size card that identified him as a member of the protocol office. "I have been instructed to tell you that your movements are restricted to the mess and your quarters until after your briefing. Have a nice evening, sir. Ma'am."

Dunne held out his hand again. "Thank you, Major."

Kohn visited her quarters briefly, then joined Dunne. He had opened the safe and placed the two manila envelopes on the small dining table. They were eight-by-eleven-inch government-type with TOP SECRET and NEED TO KNOW EYES ONLY stamped in red, inch-high letters. Each bore a serial number, but there was no receipt to be signed. Perhaps it was inside.

The quarters were standard USAF temporary living quarters with compact living area, bedroom, small kitchenette and bath. Two double beds were available with matching dresser and side tables, also an occasional chair under the lone bedroom window. The sofa bed and matching recliner in the living room were tastefully complemented by end tables, three-way lamps, a glass-topped coffee table and a recent model nineteen-inch TV with remote control. All of the furniture wood was mahogany-stained and contemporary in style. The kitchenette was chrome and blue with microwave, two-burner stove, stocked china and utensil cabinets, disposal and a small refrigerator. Dunne opened the reefer, glanced at the honor slip and quickly surveyed the pony bottles of various whiskeys, cans of beer and soda and the ample supply of nuts and chips.

"Beer?" he asked.

"Any wine?"

Yes, there it was, in the back of the bottle shelf. Splits. "White or red?"

"White, thank you."

Dunne set the wine and an ice-cold Bud on the table. He poured the Chablis into one of the full stock of wine and highball glasses and popped open his beer. "The Air Force knows how to live," he commented, taking a long swallow.

Kohn sat in one of the dining chairs, her attention on the envelopes. Dunne slid one to her and opened the other. Kohn slit hers open with a fingernail.

They both laid the contents in front of them as Dunne inventoried them aloud. "Base ID—for *Mister* Joshua Dunne—and a Lockheed employee identifier card, with picture, no less. I'm with the test and development division . . ."

"Me, too," Kohn interjected. "Flight test bureau."

Dunne ripped open the white business envelope. Inside was five hundred dollars in fifties and twenties, and a letter. It was obviously from Blackjack but not signed. It read:

Joshua and Sheila:

Place all material you have with you that identifies your service and/or rank in the safe. It will be picked up and saved for you. From this point on, do not refer to one another in a military manner. At 1900, you will be briefed on the first aspects of your mission. Enjoy your dinner. I will be in touch.

Dunne pulled his retired military ID and copy of orders to active duty. Kohn reached inside the blue purse and selected her military ID and a Visa card that carried her rank. "I'll feel undressed without this," she commented.

Dunne took them. "I assume your note is the same."

"Yes."

He placed the items in the safe and locked it.

They sat and enjoyed the beer and wine. Both were tired but not exhausted. The long day, almost eight hours of which had been spent in the confined cockpit of the Lear, had taken a toll on their muscles; the rapidity with which Blackjack had briefed them and then the rush to get to Nellis while some personal loose ends had been left hanging, had produced mental stress. Now they faced a briefing, the first of what they knew would be more detailed and demanding than the broad-brush provided by Blackjack.

Pilots love to fly; it's like making love. Total physical and mental concentration, pure satisfaction in mastery over the process, mutual feedback as the human acts and the machine reacts—heaven help you if the roles reverse—and a total sense of accomplishment when the engines shut down. Afterglow fits both activities quite well. But a full day of flying, even peacetime aviating, takes a lot out of you. There is the constant attention to the myriad of instruments, gauges and indicators; the head swivel so necessary whenever you are in an environment where two of you can close at over 1,000 miles an hour and, without control from the ground, the eyeball can fall short of providing enough lead time to avoid collision. Even among the coolest, there is stress, tension and concern. On the other side, there is the sheer ecstasy of freeing yourself from the two-dimensional travel on the surface of the planet, and the communion with nature's support system that envelops the earth and provides clouds and rains and winds to challenge your skills. Most of the time, it is friendly competition, but occasionally you are abruptly reminded that "it is not nice to try and fool Mother Nature." Then all of the orifices of your body assume the pucker position and you experience a concentration that is all-encompassing, all-consuming and all-demanding. You work yourself and your machine within a performance envelope that has ragged edges; step too close or outside those edges, even briefly, and all of the pleasantries of flight turn into the horror of unmitigated hell. When you finally work yourself back into the confines of that envelope, either by sheer perseverance or panic-driven instinct, you are a spent person—but fortunately one who is still alive, and *that* feeling is one of boundless exuberance, exhilaration, even disbelief at times.

The day in the Lear had not been that pronounced, but Dunne needed to just sit and drink his beer. His silence prompted Kohn to take the same opportunity.

After a while, she commented, "I'm going to freshen up before we eat. Give me a knock when you're ready."

"Will do." Dunne finished his beer and flopped on the bed. He had to stretch to reach the remote but managed to click on the early evening news. As usual, the world was going to hell in a handbasket. He hit the mute button and closed his eyes.

Dunne and Kohn were sitting in Dunne's quarters when promptly at nineteen hundred there was a knock on the door. Dunne opened it.

The man was probably in his late twenties, faint premature streaks of gray hair accenting the sides of a full head of black hair. It was cut long but squared across the back, and his sideburns were healthy and clipped off at the top of his ear lobes. Brown eyes had just a hint of mischief in them. He probably liked to laugh a lot, and his greeting supported that impression. "Hi, I'm Tony Delaney." He wore faded Levi's and a plaid, short-sleeved shirt.

"Come in. I'm Joshua Dunne; this is Sheila Kohn."

"I know." Delaney laid a thick, flexible leather carry-case on the table. "I'll be giving you your briefing this evening."

Dunne nodded. "Identification?"

Delaney chuckled. "Good, very good." He pulled out a card wallet and displayed his ID. Lieutenant Anthony J. Delaney, U.S. Navy. "Lieutenant commander selectee, actually," he announced with some pride.

"Congratulations," Kohn offered.

Delaney threw the carrycase on the sofa and sat at the table. "I'll be your checkout pilot. I'm a PAX graduate attached to a small training cadre sponsored by the air force's 4450th Tactical Group here at Nellis, although we do a lot of our work at a smaller facility, Groom Lake, just to the northwest of here. We also have a more expansive facility near Tonopah. My job has been to evaluate our two navy birds, N-models. As far as operational carrier aircraft, they're gull shit. So we have only the two and, while not suitable for routine bird farm operations by the average nasal radiator, they are great flying machines."

"What's their problem?" Kohn asked, scooting back in the sofa bed and kicking off her shoes.

"Cockpit visibility and no burners. They'll take a cat shot, but at max gross they're squirrelly. We'll get into that."

Oh, great, Dunne thought, *not good enough for the fleet but fine for us special ops folks who will still be riding the steam—at night, yet.*

"I'll go over your schedule, but we don't have it written down anywhere. I'll make sure you know where to go, when to go, and what to do. Tomorrow at oh-seven hundred it's life support. I'll pick you up in front of the mess. We'll get a refresher on the ejection seat and pressure chamber, and cover the cockpit life-support system. Then a quick flight over to Groom Lake for an introduction to the Sea Scorpion.''

"Sea Scorpion?'' Dunne queried.

"USAF called the one-seventeen the Scorpion early in the program, so the navy ordered the two prototypes under the contract name, Sea Scorpion.''

Kohn rubbed her feet together as if they were chilly. "We're going to be flying prototypes?''

"No, not exactly. They are proven Air Force birds with strengthened landing gear, a modification on the nosegear to take the catapult shuttle and a reworked hook for carrier ops. Boundary-layer control for slower landing speeds. I'll go over everything at the airplane. You folks work for Lockheed, so I assume you are generally familiar with the basic bird.''

"We know what it looks like,'' Dunne commented.

"Oh? Well, what kind of time do you have? In jets?''

"Sheila has over two thousand hours in F/A-18s, A-7s, and F-14s. She's also helo-qualified. I flew F-14s.'' Dunne did not care to go into his logbook any further. If Delaney knew his last jet time was in a Lear and his F-14 time consisted of 450 hours with one ejection and subsequent physical grounding, it might complicate matters.

"Ex-navy types. Good enough. The Stealth—Sea Scorpion—is a pussycat compared to those. But it is different, I kid you not.''

"How long will we be here?'' Kohn asked.

"You're programmed for four days. I hope you don't need a lot of sleep.''

"It'll take us that long to get by the writtens,'' Dunne muttered.

"You don't get the chance. The word to me is that you are two hotter-than-fresh-shit civilian specialists, excuse the French. I've been told to have you qualified to fly out of here in four days. No time for paperwork. Stick and rudder stuff plus Sidewinder weapons refresher. I'll do my best to see you get maximum exposure to the wiring diagrams and we'll cover basic emergencies, but that's about the size of it. Sounds to me like you two are going on a very exciting vacation somewhere.''

"How many flight hours?" Dunne asked.

"As many as we can get in. The first are tomorrow afternoon."

Kohn pulled her feet under her. "When do I get time for my housework?"

Delaney loved to chuckle. "I suspect, ma'am, that you haven't driven a vacuum cleaner over a rug in some time."

"Look, Tony," Dunne began. "Obviously, we have an almost impossible task here. You know it and we know it. We'll give you every drop of our blood, but we want to at least be exposed to everything you know about the bird. If we get saturated, we'll yell. Certainly, this is an unorthodox checkout, and we could very well bust up an airplane or worse. So don't cut us any slack. When we screw up, and we will, climb our asses then and there. I only ask one thing by the time we leave here. Either you say we're qualified to fly the airplane—not fight it, necessarily—or we're not. Just get us safe."

For the first time, Delaney had no smile. "I'm gonna do that, folks, or I'm not letting you have my airplanes."

Dunne remained just as serious. "I'm afraid you don't have any control over that, son."

"Then I better do my job. There're two operating manuals in the case, plus some test result papers on slow flight characteristics that you'll want to make love to tonight. Study 'em up to the point where you start to go stupid; then turn in, and I'll do my damnedest to see that tomorrow is not your last day on this earth."

"Fair enough," responded Kohn, reaching for the carrycase.

"I know you have questions, but believe me, just take this a step at a time and we'll get it done. One thing to give you comfort. On the outside, the Sea Scorpion is a state-of-the-art stealth machine, but inside she's basic Wright Brothers; you won't have any trouble with the cockpit. I promise to teach you to fly her, navy-style and safe, but what you do with her when you leave here is gonna be your own doin'. I can't help you much with that. I don't know the crazy bastards that talked you two into doing this but, with all due respect, they can't be any more suicidal than yourselves. You do realize what you're biting off?''

''More than you know, Tony,'' Dunne answered. On a personal basis, nothing was too risky if it meant bagging the man who had been responsible for Annie's death.

''Well, then, I'll pick you up at the club at oh-six-forty-five. You can pick up flight gear at the Life Support shack. Anything else you need to know tonight?''

Dunne held up a copy of the pilot's manual. ''I think we have all we can handle for one evening.''

Delaney's infectious grin signaled his agreement. ''See you on the morrow. G'nite, ma'am.''

Kohn was clutching her packet, ready to follow Delaney out the door. ''What say we get together before breakfast and compare notes?'' she asked Dunne.

''Good idea,'' answered Dunne. ''I'll come over at five.''

Kohn groaned. ''Oohhh; five-thirty? I have to put my face on.''

It was still dark outside when Dunne rapped lightly on Kohn's door. She was fully dressed but without her final makeup. She really didn't need it. For an awkward moment, Dunne stood admiring his partner, transfixed by her sensual, sleepy face and her mature natural beauty. It wouldn't be a bad face to wake up to. Kohn sensed his reaction and was flattered, although she tried not to show it. She had been hoping that one day he would see her as a woman rather than as an aviator but would rather die than reveal that she had been attracted to him when they first served together on board the *Ford*. Their shipboard contact had been occasional, strictly on a professional basis, and of course he had been married to a woman Kohn greatly admired. Now, with daily personal contact, she wondered if they would—or could—maintain that same distance. Maybe they didn't have to. Quickly, she put such unprofessional thoughts out of her mind, hoping he had not picked up any inadvertent signals. This was not the time; indeed, it could be the worst of times.

They sat at the dining table, their study packets in front of them. "One hell of an airplane," commented Kohn. "This is going to be a gas."

"I finally put it down at two A.M. Got through the whole thing twice and hit some sections several times. Tried to concentrate on emergency procedures."

"I spun in a little earlier. My eyes were seeing two words for every one in the manual. But I feel better. I think I'll be able to follow Delaney when he starts leading us through the airplane. I slept well and this morning I'm as anxious to get started as a new bride. I really feel good about it. How about you?"

"Much more confident. Seems like a straightforward airplane from the pilot's viewpoint. Systems are nothing new. Instrumentation a bit advanced over what I'm used to, but that should come quickly. I was afraid it was going to be so far ahead in concept I'd be uncomfortable with it at first. Not the case. The sophistication lies more in the exterior design concept. Airspeeds are in the Lear range, actually. Not a real fast bird."

"No. But in its role as a night attack Stealth, it doesn't have to be. Excuse me for a moment." Kohn left to finish her grooming but continued to talk from the bathroom area. "I'd still like to have more than four days."

"That's all we're going to get."

"What's your impression of Delaney?"

"Personable. Conscientious. Obviously a superior stick with Pax River quals. I suspect he's an early selectee. He looks like he's still in his teens. We'll see what kind of pro he is today."

"Take you back?"

"Ha! Yes, I suppose so. I wasn't bad in my day."

"Hey, the wonder years are not over yet." Kohn returned to the living/dining area. Her finishing touches had been subtle. No lipstick; that was taboo when undergoing oxygen retraining. She was definitely in her flygirl mode. "I'm starved."

Dunne watched with envy as Kohn stowed away a plate of scrambled eggs, hash browns, bacon, toast with jelly, a bran muffin, orange juice and coffee. If that was typical, he would sure like to have her metabolism. He kept in shape, but his breakfast was more typically one scrambled egg, a lightly buttered piece of toast, juice and black coffee.

No one seemed to take particular notice of them during breakfast, most of the others in flight gear preparing to do their own thing for the day. Several suntanned, gray-haired, retired couples were enjoying themselves, being back within the military community. Dunne wondered what the men were thinking, old warriors now confined to their memories and unable to shake the feeling that somehow, just by enjoying the same mess privileges as their modern counterparts, they were still part of the program. And, in a sense, they were. The current military pilots were all beneficiaries of techniques and tactics learned by those who had gone before them. The old-timers had flown the same type missions with less sophisticated means, engaged in aerial combat without such niceties as engine thrust that exceeded aircraft weight or navigational systems that automatically and continually told them where they were within feet of their actual position. In military air, each generation built upon the one before it. Dunne and Kohn used the same stick and rudder movements learned the hard way by pilots of the early Spads and Fokkers and Sopwith Camels. Perhaps that was one of the secrets that inspired such intense mutual admiration among military aviators: continuity. Each one could trace his aerial lineage back to an open cockpit, oil-splattered goggles and a long leather flying coat. Each had either around his neck or within his spirit a white silk scarf that streamed in the wind whenever he, and now she, flew.

Delaney was waiting with a staff car.

"Nice base," Kohn commented as she slid onto the rear seat.

Delaney responded, "Yes; good duty if you can stay away from the casinos."

Life support personnel were waiting in their spaces between two of the flight-line hangars, and they ushered Dunne and Kohn into the equipment issue room. Two neatly stacked piles of gear were on the counter, standard USAF flight gear, the only exception being the color of the flight suits and helmets. Black.

Dunne picked up one of the hard hats. "We'll look like Darth Vader in these." Lockers in the two dressing rooms were provided for their civilian clothes.

There was a mandatory brief lecture followed by a precise check of the fit of their masks and helmets. The air force would not compromise on any aspect of the life-support checkout if the subjects were going to fly out of Nellis. Kohn was pleased that her flight suit was the correct size, although it was a bit more baggy than the navy issue she was accustomed to. The high-G overpants would correct that.

A female captain, also in flight gear, joined them in the ejection-seat trainer room. The centerpiece was a fully functional ejection seat that sat submerged in a dummy fuselage, the seat's back mated to two high steel rails that rose ten feet above the fuselage. "I'm Mona Stith; I'll be supervising your checkout." Dunne noted that she wore flight surgeon's wings. "Who's first?"

Dunne climbed into the cockpit.

"Your weight, sir?" Stith asked.

"One-seventy-six."

The captain leaned over and adjusted a dial on the side of the trainer. She then leaned into the cockpit, checked Dunne's feet position and asked, "Any questions?"

"No. All set."

She backed away. "Face curtain, first time, sir."

Dunne reached up, keeping his elbows together as instructed and pulled down hard on the curtain handles.

Whhhoooopppppp! He was suspended in the seat, eight feet above the cockpit. *Tame compared to the real thing*, he thought, his actual ejection some years back coming to mind. It was an uncomfortable memory, for his rear-seater hadn't made it. He quickly erased the unwelcome recollection as the seat ratcheted back to its lowered position.

The captain checked him again and stepped back. "Thigh handles this time, sir. Keep your head back against the rest."

Dunne again pulled hard, this time on the twin yellow and black striped handles outside each thigh. Another smack on the rear and a jerky stop at the top.

Kohn replaced him.

Stith set the dial to Kohn's weight, explaining, "The real thing doesn't care how much you weigh. The boot in the ass is the same. No discrimination."

"That's nice," Kohn observed as she pulled the face curtain and shot herself to the top of the rails. There was no doubt in her mind that the drill gave only the barest hint of what it would feel like to be blasted out of a wildly gyrating airplane at several hundred knots.

As she started her second ride, the pull on the thigh handles failed to immediately activate the ejection charge and she inadvertently let her head go forward to check her hand position. Nothing wrong with them; the device belatedly fired and she felt a sharp pain in her neck as the seat blasted upward. She rubbed the spot as the seat lowered.

"I said keep that head back, ma'am," Stith fussed.

"The damned seat screwed up," an angry Kohn countered.

"It could do that in real life," Stith persisted.

Kohn nodded and gingerly turned her head from side to side. "Lesson learned. I should have known better."

The cylindrical atmospheric pressure chamber was in a room just off the open hangar area.

They entered and sat on one of the bench seats that were bolted along each side of the chamber. Captain Stith checked their oxygen mask fit and the intercom before directing that the door be closed. The three of them sat in silence as the air inside the chamber was pumped out until the altimeter read 35,000 feet.

Stith made some notations on her kneepad before asking, "This isn't your first time, I gather?"

Both shook their heads.

"We'll dispense with some of the Mickey Mouse games; just a reminder about anoxia: blue or purple fingernails, a slight euphoria, some confusion, and off into nighty-night land. Sound familiar?"

Kohn thought the captain sounded ticked off. Was it because she had let her head drop on her second ejection, or was the captain under pressure to get-'em-in, get-'em-checked and get-'em-out? Nevertheless, she answered in unison with Dunne. "Yes."

"All right; let's do the drop." Stith spoke into her microphone to the outside observer who immediately dumped the partial vacuum. A loud swish preceded an instant fog as the pressure returned to that of sea level and moisture condensed inside the chamber. There was just a tiny moment of disorientation as the explosive compression caused eardrums and sinuses to adjust.

Stith preceded them out of the chamber, and each was given a little white card with the date of their requalification stamped on it above the scrawling signature of the chief master sergeant who certified that they were now flyable.

By 0800, they were on the flight line but to their surprise were boarding a USAF C-21, the military equivalent of Dunne's Lear, although a later, improved model.

Delaney explained, "This will take us to Groom Lake and bring us back sometime tonight."

The VIP interior was considerably more plush than that of Dunne's tired airplane, and the coffee infinitely fresher. They reached Groom Lake in twenty minutes and were let out in front of one of a long line of hangars. They entered through the personnel door of one of the smaller ones and there it was, the coal black, triangular flying Frisbee, bathed in bright overhead lights and tended by three coveralled navy ground crewmen, one of whom immediately approached and checked their ID cards despite his obvious recognition of Delaney.

"Can we use your airplane for a few minutes?" asked Delaney.

"Sure, Lieutenant." The answer was to Delaney but the master chief petty officer's eyes were checking out Kohn, respectfully but thoroughly.

"Do I know you, Master Chief?" Kohn asked, disarming the veteran noncom with eye contact that clearly reflected her nickname. Dunne smiled as the traditional Frosty Kohn surfaced.

"No, ma'am. We've never had a female pilot in this hangar; not that we shouldn't, you understand."

Kohn let a tolerant smile emphasize her reply. "I understand."

Delaney began his walkaround as the three crewmen left. "This is Sea Scorpion number one, designated number five-zero-nine-one-one on the navy roster. The one next door is nine-one-two. The only radical difference from the USAF bird is the incorporation of the boundary-layer airflow system in the wings. Probably degrades the stealth characteristics a bit but not significantly, since the airflow slits are covered with RAM tape—radar absorbent material—prior to the mission. It blows off when the system is activated— usually. More about that later.''

"How about more about that now? We don't want to forget it,'' Kohn suggested.

"Once or twice the tape stayed on or tore off in irregular strips. We've got some new stuff with a different adhesive. You'll get to check it out. Not critical unless you're going aboard ship at night.''

Oh, that's great.

Delaney continued, "Wingspan forty-three feet, four inches. Production navy type would have had folding tips. Max gross, fifty-two thousand pounds with thirteen thousand fuel, four thousand in an internal weapons bay.''

"We know the stats; they're in the book,'' Dunne said. "Seven-G airframe, five-hundred sixty knots max at sea level, five-forty-five at thirty-five thousand. Four-fifty cruise. Combat radius, five hundred miles. We want the meat, Tony, the stuff that either isn't in the manual or is vague or incomplete.''

"No problem. Let's just walk around and I'll point out a few things that could use emphasis.''

They were at the radically sloped-down nose of the F-117N.

"First significant difference: in-flight refueling probe. The bird came originally with a receptacle for refueling from a boom. Standard air force technique. For navy use, since we use drogue and basket, the N-model has a retractable probe on top of the fuselage, just aft of the cockpit hatch.''

"Here on the nose, four air pressure sensing probes, one for each computer-controlled flight-control system. Good redundancy. Lose one, try and find a place to land, but no particular sweat. Lose two, get serious about landing; lose three and you have a problem. Not very probable. We've had no failures on the N-models.''

''I read about the first accident, April of eighty-two. That was a computer problem,'' Kohn interrupted.

''True, but not a failure per se. The aircraft has both elevons and ruddervators, multi-input flight control surfaces. The fly-by-wire systems were cross-wired; stick actually controlled ruddervator input, rudder-pedals the elevons. On takeoff, as soon as the controls became aerodynamically effective, all hell broke loose. The pilot had too little time to figure out what was going on before the airplane yawed and rotated itself into a self-destruct mode. Poor bastard was already dead but he didn't know it. Kept trying to correct yaw with what he thought was rudder input, but the pedals were actually feeding in stick signals. And vice versa. Didn't have a prayer. That won't happen again. And, as I said, it was not a failure of the system. Human error in the FBW assembly phase.''

Dunne reached out and stroked the fuselage surface.

''Completely covered with RAM. Used to be sheets, about the thickness of linoleum; now it's all painted on and all seams are sealed with tape or RAM paint prior to the mission.''

''She sits high,'' Kohn mentioned. The underside of the aircraft was completely flat, the fuselage humped and thick forward, tapered and thin at the rear where the two canted ruddervators were mounted.

''We refer to the flat rear as the platypus; you'll see the engine exhaust outlets when we walk around. Several feet long but only six inches high. The circular exhaust streams coming from the rear of the engines are diverted and channeled by a series of baffle plates and come out as wide gaseous ribbons. Very effective in attenuating the heat and hiding the hot parts of the engine. The whole airplane is really ingenious when it comes to design. All of the engine accessories are mounted on the bottom of the casing for easy ground access through the underside of the fuselage.''

"Looks like the flatiron my grandmother used to use out on the farm." Even though Dunne had seen the one at Colorado Springs, now that he was next to it, he could only marvel at the multifaceted top fuselage structure. No vertical plates; all were canted at least thirty degrees. It would be almost impossible for a ground radar to get the 180-degree angle it needed for maximum reflection unless it was directly underneath, and a low-flying, max-speed pass would provide that aspect for only a microsecond.

Dunne and Kohn moved the elevons and tested the ruddervators as they walked around the improbable-looking aircraft. Neither could resist the time-honored tradition of kicking the tires. Completely radical; modern jets were thought of in terms of curves and streamlined gussets. The F-117 had no curves, no less-than-sharp angle bends, no bubble canopy. Instead, the pilot sat well forward, encased in an angular structure that flowed along the top of the fuselage and provided five flat plates of glass for visibility, none of them rearward or downward.

The boarding ladder was sharply angled outward and down to avoid contact with any of the sharp edges of the fuselage. Kohn climbed into the cockpit.

"It's huge," she stated with disbelief. Indeed, her feminine frame was lost in the wide opening provided by the flat fuselage. "Feels great." She ran her scan about the cockpit and noted the standard arrangement of controls and consoles. The fact that controls and instrumentation had been taken from the F/A-18 made her feel more at home. Everything was clearly marked and highly visible, the various switches, gauges and levers arranged by systems and no more complicated than the F/A-18s and F-14s with which she was intimately familiar. Nor did the array look formidable to Dunne. More complicated than the little Lear, but still within his memory of the F-14. Kohn gave him the cockpit and he tried it on for size.. It *was* roomy, although a glance upward at the angular canopy suggested that there would not be an overabundance of head and helmet room once it was closed. Delaney ran over the cockpit items as he had with Kohn, explaining the purpose and method of activation of each.

Once back on the hangar deck, Delaney allowed them a few minutes for a final look, then directed, "We'll go to the simulator now. It's a procedural box only, no movement or scenery generation, but we can run through the start procedures, flight controls and system operations. In that respect, it's the real thing. You can dry-run a first flight. When you feel at home, we'll cover an area brief and go flying. How's that sound?"

"Like a shotgun wedding," mused Dunne.

"In a sense, I suppose that's what it is," Delaney added, his perpetual grin widening to the point where it appeared that the corners of his mouth would crack.

They had played in the simulator somewhat longer than anticipated, but it had been an excellent procedural training device and each had wanted to feel as familiar as possible with every control, switch and flight instrument. They had gobbled a flight-line box lunch while Delaney had given them the area brief and reviewed the radio control frequencies as well as call signs assigned to the Groom Lake facilities.

Now Dunne sat in the warmup spot for runway three-six-left, encased within the oddest looking airplane he had ever encountered and preparing to fly it for the first time. Delaney was in the spot ahead of him, and Kohn was strapped in the rear seat of the Northrup T-38 Talon that Delaney would fly as chase plane. It was a procedure that they would use for the first few flights, one flying the Sea Scorpion while the other sat in the chase aircraft and monitored the training flight. Delaney would check and advise airspeeds and maneuvers.

The compact Talon taxied onto the runway and sped down the centerline, its knife-thin wings slicing the hot desert air in their search for a lift component that would enable them to fly. Dunne watched it rotate, lift off and start a climbing left turn before the wheels were fully retracted. Delaney would come around and observe Dunne's takeoff. Less than a minute later, Dunne heard Delaney's call. "We're in position, niner-one-one." The tower immediately responded, "Niner-one-one, cleared for takeoff."

Dunne taxied into position and gave his instruments a last check. Plenty of runway ahead. The wind was right down the centerline. He had the best possible conditions. Then, why was that slight shiver of apprehension snaking up his spine? Probably because his ground checkout had fallen well short of that normally required for flight in the F-117. If he pranged the superexpensive flying machine, a lot of heads would be on the block.

What the hell, I can either hack it or I can't. Might as well find out now.

Taking a deep breath, he shoved his power levers forward, simultaneously pressing the mike button and announcing, "Rolling."

The acceleration was not quite what he expected, but it was positive and strong enough to press him back in his seat. Within moments, the Sea Scorpion was hungry for high sky and as soon as he rotated, it lifted off like a startled black swallow.

"You with me, Tony?" Dunne asked.

"Like a shadow, niner-one-one; like a shadow."

Dunne had entered the airman's world, and all earthly trials and tribulations, even pleasures, had vanished. In the next ninety minutes, he and the Sea Scorpion would go through an initial bonding process that was designed to establish a mutual respect between them. The machine would eagerly react to the intimate movements of its lover, and Dunne would experience the warm, solicitous response of the machine. Yes, indeed, damn all his preflight jitters, it was just like making love. . . .

4

Blackjack Paterson did not like to fly; he particularly did not like to fly civilian airlines, and he never flew at night or in bad weather if he could take a later flight. On this night, however, he found himself white-knuckled and strapped to his window seat aboard a Delta MD-80 as it held at 16,000 feet, twenty-three miles west of Dulles International. He had not wanted to fly to Dulles; he had booked this flight to Washington National, but some idiot had skidded off the operational runway there in heavy rain and the field was temporarily closed. The Delta captain had come on the cabin speaker and very casually announced that they had been diverted to the larger airport. Paterson was convinced a wing could fall off and the typical airline captain would announce to the passengers that there was "a minor mechanical problem." The MD-80 was going up and down like an aluminum yo-yo, and although the captain had announced earlier that Delta was offering its patient passengers drinks on the house, the flight attendants were restricted to their little jump seats.

Paterson's mouth was full of cotton balls and he found it impossible to just relax; he did try to convey that image to his seatmate, a female senior citizen who every few minutes was passing gas and muttering a barely audible "Excuse me." He was embarrassed for her but could not bring himself to change seats, despite the fact that there were several empties in nearby rows. It would have been too obvious and embarrassed the elderly lady further. He was sure that she had to be someone's nice little old grandmother. She had powerful intestinal muscles, however.

The captain's unhurried, deep baritone returned. "Ladies and gentlemen, we have been given an approach time and will be descending very shortly. We should be on the ground at four-eight past the hour. We apologize for the delay, and we do have a bus standing by to take to Washington National any passengers who may have flight connections there. Thank . . . excuse me . . ."

The MD-80 had encountered a downdraft and dropped like a clubbed cheetah. Paterson suspected that the captain had released the microphone to reach for something more solid. There was a chorus of gasps, and a baby started to cry. But Captain Calmness came back on the speaker. "Sorry about that, folks, it's a bit bumpy up here and I have requested a lower altitude . . . especially since we are now *at* a lower altitude . . ."

Nervous cabin laughter failed to cheer up Paterson.

". . . and air traffic control has granted our request. So please sit back and enjoy the rest of the flight."

Yes, about as much as early settlers had enjoyed Indian attacks, Paterson thought bitterly.

As they descended farther, the air did stabilize and the flight attendants made good the promise of complimentary drinks. Paterson had a double scotch, no ice. It helped.

He peered out the window and could see nothing, so he tried to interpret the different seat pressures and engine adjustments as the MD-80 continued down through the wet night. Obviously, the aircraft was banking and turning. He recognized the sound of the landing gear extension motors and the thunk as the wheels locked into position. That meant they were on final approach. *Thank God.* Then the high-pitched squeal of the flap electric motors—they sounded as if they were right underneath his seat—and the slight surge as if the MD-80 were encountering thicker air. That was normal; it just *felt* like the airplane was going over on its nose. He kept his face glued to the window. There! There was something, a white glow, some kind of ground lights. Now it was dark again, and abruptly the hypnotic silver flashing of the approach strobe lights lit the scud in which they were still engulfed. They had to be almost down. They were. The runway lights sped by the side, somewhat disconcerting white streaks that indicated they were about to touch down—or roll up into a gigantic red fireball. There was a short burst of power, the aircraft leveled for an instant and then Paterson felt the flare and heard the welcome *screech-creech* of tires contacting concrete. Immediately, all of the fluttering butterflies flew out of his stomach and nested at that secret place within his body from whence they would come next time he flew. The runway felt solid as the MD-80 slowed and began its taxi to the ramp. Now with the engine noises diminished, the passengers could hear how heavy the rain was; must be torrential from the way the fuselage was crying out in protest. A million tiny hammers pinging on the metal skin made conversation impossible.

As a final assault, the canvas closure of the debarking ramp leaked, and Paterson's head and shoulders were sprinkled as he stepped from the plane into the enclosure.

His limo was waiting and the coffee was steaming, just right for a cold, miserable evening around the nation's capital. Paterson flicked on the TV news; it was 10:00 P.M. and they were showing the crippled DC-9 that had landed too fast and too long at Washington National. No serious damage and no injuries. Oops! The limo suddenly swerved to avoid another vehicle, and hot coffee drenched Paterson's crotch.

By the time the limo reached the White House and the admiral was ushered into the chief of staff's office, Paterson was wet, cold, angry and fresh out of good will.

"Admiral, what happened?" asked the chief of staff, making a point of noticing Paterson's wet pants.

"Coffee spill."

"Oh, I was afraid that . . . oh, you know."

"That I'd pissed my pants? Don't you wish. Is he in?"

"He's been waiting. You're late, you know. He doesn't wait on many people. Must be your charisma. Go right in—please—there's no one else to see him this time of night. Everyone else tries to consider his schedule, you know."

Simple bastard, thought Paterson. How could the man be so close to the president? He had the personality of a peeled banana and was acutely short on couth. Yet there were outstanding people on the chief of staff's staff; how could they let him lead? The simpleton even parted his hair in the middle.

"Thank you," Paterson muttered as he entered the Oval Office.

The president rose from behind his desk and held out his hand. "John, thank you for coming, especially in this miserable weather. I know your aversion to flying under these conditions."

"Under *any* conditions," Paterson amplified, removing his soft suede battle jacket. He was one of the few people who didn't dress for a visit with the president.

Hot coffee was waiting and the president poured. "I needed an update. We have several things going with the Chinese, and this may be a particularly sensitive time. I know I could have called, but I wanted a face-to-face. How's the project going?"

Paterson took a swallow of his coffee, leaning over to insure that no drips added to his lower abdomen discomfort.

"Spilled the last cup," he explained. "Mister President, it is going well. We have the second pilot, just the one I wanted."

"Your son-in-law."

"Yes. He has a good feel for such things. We're all right at this point."

"Good, I would have been uncomfortable with the woman being the flight leader. I know she's a real professional, but this operation could suddenly go down and dirty. In that case, Dunne's command experience could be a saving grace."

An air-splitting clap of thunder shook the office windows. "A bit late for thunderstorms but it's been a goofy season," the president observed, rising to gaze onto the darkened Rose Garden.

Paterson waited for the real reason he had been summoned.

After a few minutes, the president turned and spoke. "John, is there any possibility your unit has been compromised?"

Paterson was not expecting *that* question. "There's always the possibility, but I am confident that it has not at this point. Why do you ask?"

"Just little things. Nothing to concern yourself with. I just needed to ask."

"In this business, Mister President, there are no little things."

"True enough." The president sat back down. "How confident are we of the Chinaman?"

"He's an American, sir. He's been on station for twenty-five years, so the director tells me."

"Yes, I know. It's just that I have this crazy thought bouncing around in my mental caution zone. What if this is a setup? What if the Chinese are waiting for us?"

"I've looked at this very carefully, sir, from all angles. To the best of our knowledge, Desird has never been to

China before. His mission appears legitimate. This is the first time we've had advance knowledge that he will be out of the Middle East. Besides, why would the Chinese want to set us up for something? I don't see any motive.''

"And the fact that we just happen to have an agent who knows Desird's itinerary?''

"I think you should be talking to the director if this is your concern. He's been my only source on the man.''

"You've built the whole operation on the Chinaman's proposal.''

"Yes. Mister President, I want Desird. He is a menace to world peace. He is dealing in weapons of mass destruction.''

"And the fact that he is one of those responsible for the death of your daughter has nothing to do with it?''

"It has a great deal to do with it, but it is not the prime motivating factor. I can't bring Annie back by killing Desird. I *can* possibly save thousands of innocents from being cooked alive—if we concede that Desird has a market for the detonators who will use them.''

"Oh, I have no doubt about that.''

"Mister President, my personal agony plays no part in my professional decisions. That could be fatal to any plan. Is that your real concern? Is that why you asked me to come tonight, so you could see my face when I answered that question?''

"Yes.''

Paterson sat back in his chair. "Mister President, if I don't have your complete trust, I must call this operation off.''

"I had to ask, John.''

"Yes, sir.''

"I understand.'' The president continued to watch the late evening rainfall. "Remember, when we were kids, how we loved the rain?'' he casually asked. "Those were precious days, John, when we were growing up together in the poorest section of north Memphis. How innocent we were.''

Blackjack smiled. ''White trash and the next-door nigger, that was us. Side by side on the most rundown street in the city, the last white house and the first black. Neither of us could get any lower than that.''

The president turned as if he had suddenly discovered a cure for cancer. ''Remember old Mrs. Larkin's apple tree? God, those were good apples. So damn moist, the sweet juice ran down the corners of your mouth, even when you were running like hell to get away from her stick—it was hickory, you know. If she had ever delivered a solid whack with that rod we'd still be wearing the scars.''

''We ran a lot from her.''

''But we got those apples—what were they? Yellow Delicious, I think.''

''A lot better than those we stole from the store.''

''Selfish old biddy,'' the president continued, ''a whole yard full of apple trees and she begrudged us the few we took, as if they were diamonds.''

''Didn't particularly care for us 'coloreds' either.''

''May she rest in peace. What do you think she would have thought if she knew that one day I'd be sitting here in the Oval Office and you would be wearing four navy stars on your pajamas?'' The president let his smile fade. ''What do you suppose she would think if she knew the business we're about on this night?''

''I don't know. I think maybe she would approve. She lost her husband and only son in World War Two but still flew the two gold-star flags in her window, even in forty-six. She loved this country, and I think she had an affection for us, actually. She knew we were always stealing her apples and you may remember that she never chased us until after we'd picked them.''

''We've come a long way, John.''

Paterson nodded. "So's the country. But there is so much more to do. I hope we make a difference."

"We will."

"I'm not sure she would approve of our methods."

The president's sigh was a weary one. "I don't either, John, but I am convinced we must do what we do. It's the only way left."

Paterson sat quietly in agreement.

The president started to sit down but stopped midway and let out a sharp "Damn!"

"Are you all right?" Concerned, Paterson walked around the desk and took the president's shoulders in his hands. "Should I call someone?"

"No, it's the lower back. Ever so often it locks up on me. Get around behind me."

Paterson moved behind his lifelong friend. The president leaned over farther and placed his hands on the top of his desk.

"Put your thumbs together on my spine, just above the belt, and when I say, push like hell . . . that's it . . . okay . . . push!"

Paterson could feel and even hear a snap.

"Oh, that's good, that's good . . . boy, what a catch."

"You need to have that looked at."

The president managed to sit. "The White House surgeon wants to cut on me but I don't like the thought of a knife anywhere near my spinal cord."

"So, dumb ass that you are, you just try and tolerate the pain."

The president chuckled. "You're the only person in the world who can call the President of the United States a dumb ass and make it sound like an affectionate term."

"It is, Mister President," Paterson said softly.

"Thanks, John. I'm okay now. Next time you're here, we'll set aside some time for dinner and a drink."

"And a good cigar?"

"A good cigar."

"Good night, Mister President."

The president seemed to be sitting more comfortably. "Goodnight, John. God bless America."

"And all her ships at sea." Paterson reached across the desk and clasped the president's hand. On the way out of the Oval Office, he spoke briefly to the chief of staff. "The president's having a back problem. You might want to check on him."

"Thank you, Admiral, I will."

Paterson hurried out into the rain and climbed quickly into his waiting limousine.

5

Tonopah Flight Test Range, Nevada
September 29, 5:45 P.M.

Joshua Dunne kept a steady three-G pull on the stick as he
sucked the Sea Scorpion up and over onto its back. He
stopped inverted, pegged the nose on the horizon and rolled
upright. The tight Immelmann, a vertical reversal of direction, was named after a World War I flyer and was a standard maneuver of acrobatic pilots. It also had a limited
combat purpose if you could catch your opponent by surprise, although that didn't happen too often in modern high-
speed, super-powered stand-off air engagements. Dunne
swung his head around and tried to see his right wingtip
despite the limited cockpit visibility. He couldn't quite
bring it into view, but he could see the number-two F-117N
tucked in as closely as it had been when he had started the
maneuver.

"Not bad for an old-timer; I like 'em a little tighter."
Kohn's verbal needle carried with it a tone of admiration.

The two were in the middle phases of their checkout,
Delaney having taken each of them through the basic phase
of flying the navy Stealth. Since that first visit to Groom
Lake yesterday morning, each had completed five training
missions out of the Tonopah Flight Test Center for a total

of approximately eleven hours. The concentrated syllabus was tiring, and Dunne felt as if he had been flying the blackbird all his life; there was at least that advantage. This was their first dual session and Delaney was somewhere near them in his T-38 as they flew tactical formation and became adjusted to each other's styles and peculiarities. It was time to change lead.

"You got it; I'll slide back," Dunne announced.

"Roger, you're clear," Kohn responded.

Dunne watched the right side as they exchanged lead, Kohn's aircraft moving forward. He held off her left wing and followed her through a series of gentle turns, then steeper ones that became reversals and finally into a wide sweeping aileron roll.

"Still there?" Kohn muttered.

"Like a coat of paint." Dunne had no trouble holding position. Kohn's lead was worthy of the Blue Angels: positive, smooth and confident. They were joined in an unusual aerial ballet, the female leading.

"Follow the leader . . ." Kohn teased as she rolled into a Split-S diving turn. Immediately she reversed it and began a series of closely coupled evasive maneuvers that forced Dunne to back off some but still stay in a satisfactory combat wing position. She wouldn't lose him, but she did try him. Like lovers, they were thrashing about on a huge bed of cumulus clouds, each reveling in his or her individual pleasures as they exercised complete mastery over their aircraft and, through the magnificent machines, over themselves. Four positive Gs and then two negative; body-slamming banks and rolls and quick-reaction decelerations. She gave him the same workout he had given her, maybe a bit more.

"Ooooooh . . . dirty dancin' if I ever saw it," Delaney commented.

Dunne was too crunched into his seat to reply, but with his peripheral vision he could see Delaney's T-38 following them through the maneuvers at a safe distance.

"Aerial foreplay . . ." Kohn managed as she tightened the turn.

Dunne watched his angle-of-attack indicator slip into the red zone. He would stall if he remained on the inside of the turn. A slight touch of the controls and he slid outside the turn, never varying more than a few feet in his station-keeping.

"Ready for the climax, skipper?" Kohn asked.

"I'm on your ass, Frosty . . ." Dunne could see Kohn jerk her head hard to look back at him off her right side. Even the green visor and tight oxygen mask could not hide the mischievous smile that Dunne knew was there.

Her voice returned, "I wouldn't touch *that* line . . ."

Her breakaway was too unexpected and violent to follow closely, but Dunne managed to hang on and get inside her turns to gradually start closing. For the next few minutes, she was turning him every which way but loose, and by the time he was back in position, she leveled and announced "I'm ready to go home if you are." Dunne was sweat-soaked and the airplane felt like an airborne eighteen-wheeler loaded with canned goods. The lady was good.

Delaney was all compliments during the debriefing. "You two take to each other like rum and Coke. You're not going to have any problems with the air work, whatever it turns out to be. Tonight we do some more night nav. Should be a piece of cake. I want a full hour of night bounce afterwards, with and without lights, with and without boundary control. Tomorrow, we review in-flight emergencies and evasive tactics along with attack countermeasures. Tomorrow night, it's FCLP—field carrier landing practice. We'll start at dusk so you can get into it gradually. Sorry I can't give you a pitching deck or rain showers, but don't wear your best skivvies. The Sea Scorpion will be showing you her dirty side."

"Sounds like fun," Kohn commented.

"Guar-an-God-damned-teed, but you've both been there before."

Dunne asked, "What about the last day, the day after tomorrow?"

"Live Sidewinder firing. Final night work. Then we break the birds down for transport, as I understand it. The C-5 will be here Thursday at noon."

It would be the fourth day.

Delaney had declined their invitation to have a nightcap at the club and the two sat at a side table, very weary and sipping diet Cokes. "You're a good stick, Frosty. You brought back my hemorrhoids today."

"Glad I could make an impression. You strained my bra a few times yourself. That airplane is something else, isn't it?"

"I was getting just the hint of a flutter before the stick-shaker came in. Did you?"

"No. Must be a difference in the two airplanes. Straight forward stalls. I don't like the lack of visibility. It's okay for land jocks with two miles of rock-steady runway, but on dark, rainy, bumpy nights I don't enjoy moving my head about and squinting to see the boat."

"Shouldn't be too bad; the HUD is beautiful."

Kohn had to agree. The heads-up display on the windshield was state of the art. "We'll get a feel tomorrow night."

"That we will." Dunne was not ready for the abrupt change in subjects.

"You have anyone—back in Denver?" Kohn asked cautiously.

"No, if I read the question correctly."

"You do. I was just curious, but I figured not with the way you threw your socks and shorts in a bag and let me take you to New Orleans."

Dunne sipped his cola. "You?"

"No, not now. Did have a thing going right after I left the *Ford*. Big dumb Swede from Wisconsin, but he wore a Tomcat like another layer of skin. Just when we were getting serious, he drove his bird into the spud locker of the *America*. Low, slow—and dumb."

"Sorry."

"No need. I later found out he had a wife and a pair of curtain climbers. That soured me, Joshua. I had held off for so long, and I thought he was the one."

"That happens."

"It won't happen to me any more. You were so fortunate to have had your Annie."

"Yes. I miss her."

Kohn stirred her Coke. "Aren't we a couple winners on this night?"

Dunne sat back in his chair. "Hey, no more of that. It's good to be with you, Frosty. We make a good team. Even Delaney is beginning to see that."

Kohn smiled over her glass. "I wonder how good we really are."

Dunne countered, "As good as we have to be."

Kohn let the silence linger for only a second. "Beddy-bye time. I'm bushed."

Crawling between the sheets, Kohn lay on her back and just enjoyed the opportunity to savor the afterglow of the hot shower and the contrasting stimulation of the cool linens. She was completely fatigued and it felt great. An honest feeling. The Sea Scorpion was a good airplane. Solid, responsive, forgiving of minor sins. She felt as if she had been flying on Dunne's wing for eternity. They were good together. In just a few short hours, she had already picked up the little, subtle movements that broadcast what he was going to do. A slight tilt of his head and she knew it would be a tight roll; by the time he cranked in full ailerons, she was starting her matching movement. They danced the skies like sparrows, each reacting to the other in breathtaking sweeps and turns and climbs and dives, a melody of movement that certified their mutual professionalism as airmen. If she were to go into combat, she could ask for no one better than Dunne to lead the way.

She wondered if that was where they were headed—combat. The F-117s were designed for attack, night attack. What would be their objective? And if it were an attack mission, why the air-to-air Sidewinders? The F-117 wasn't designed to take on opposing fighters. Bombers, maybe. But whose?

The night was full of questions, not the least of which was the mystery of the feeling that she also felt close to Dunne on a personal level. They had been shipmates before, of course, so a certain familiarity was to be expected. But this was more than that. Her respect for him as a senior officer and aviator led automatically to trust and confidence. But when they had said goodnight and he had dropped her at the door to her quarters, why had she hesitated before going in? It was just a moment, and she would not have been surprised if he had leaned over and given her a brotherly hug or a kiss on the cheek. That seemed like what he was going to do. But that wasn't where she wanted to be kissed. And that bothered her. They had just completed a full day of demanding physical and mental activity, trying themselves to the fullest and both completely engrossed in their profession. Yet, when he left her, she felt like a schoolgirl at the end of a prom date. That wasn't like Frosty Kohn. It was too damn feminine. She turned on her side and pulled her knees up. God, she was so deliciously tired.

Just on the other side of the wall, Dunne was drying himself. His shower had also felt great. He slipped on his pajama bottoms and sat on the small sofa, watching the late news and sipping a diet soda. They always tasted terrible, but he didn't need any more sugar. He was still hyped after the day's flying. The night bounce had gone particularly well. He liked to fly with Kohn. She was as aggressive as any man he had ever flown with. He had to smile when he thought of how she referred to the agile F-117s as sparrows. In Frosty's hands, they were more like hawks or falcons. Whatever their mission was to be, he had no worries about how they would work together.

The picture on the tube stopped registering; he could only see Kohn's face as it had appeared when they said goodnight. She seemed as if she were expecting him to kiss her. That wasn't like Frosty Kohn. It was a disturbing thought, not that a goodnight kiss would have been out of order. It would have been a natural thing, a sign between two close friends that each had appreciated the evening. The whole day, for that matter. But what concerned Dunne was that even such a kiss might have been just a step over the line that had to be maintained between them.

If she had been his male wingman, they very well could have high-fived one another or exchanged playful jabs. But what type of physical contact could a man and woman share without it being misinterpreted? A hug? *Fighter pilots don't hug one another, for Christ's sake.*

He flicked off the tube and rolled under the covers. All in all, it had been a good day.

The second full day of flying was almost a blur. Jump in the airplane; airwork, tactics and touch-and-goes; refuel, fly, eat, fly, refuel, fly. It was only after they entered the pattern for night FCLP that things slowed. This was precision flying at a high level.

They came over the numbers like Siamese twins joined wingtip to after-fuselage, and Kohn followed Dunne through the break to set up their carrier landing interval. Downwind at six hundred feet, 150 knots, boundary layer ON, landing check complete.

The flight deck simulation lights and the Fresnel lens and

optical landing system were positioned exactly as they would be on the *Lincoln*, and Delaney was in his LSO position. The only difference was that the runway was steady, no pitch or roll. Their ground speed would be higher than on actual carrier approaches, since the runway also failed to have any forward movement. On the plus side, there was no stack or island turbulence to deal with.

Dunne started his turn at 140 knots and played the maneuver to arrive on a short final at 130 knots, twenty knots slower than the non-modified F-117 requirements. He called "Ball" as soon as his wings were level and rode the invisible glide slope as if he were on rails. He would have nailed the number-three arresting wire had it actually been there; as it was, he boltered and lifted off to resume his pattern. Kohn followed him and landed in his tire tracks before continuing on and up into the night sky.

They came around again. Dunne was a twitch slow in correcting his low position fifty yards off the "ramp" and caught the simulated number-two wire. Okay, but not perfect. Kohn cloned her first approach.

By the time each had shot five landings, Delaney had come to the conclusion he was about as necessary as a chaperon at a senior citizens' dance. He gave each an unnecessary wave-off just to check their last minute reactions. Finally, after an hour of "three-wires," he began to pray for gusty winds. Conditions were just too good. At sea in the dark, coming down on a pitching deck would be different. But they had the basics and he could do no more.

"I'm going to bed," he announced facetiously. "You two godlike creatures can play out here all night if you want to. You must be cheating."

"Thank you, Paddles," teased Kohn. "It's nice to know you recognize class when you see it."

On their last pass, the two came in together and used the wide runway to execute a simultaneous landing—at the number-three wire spot, something that would never be attempted in the real world of carrier aviation.

They're not good; they're demented, Delaney concluded, not at all sure he was joking.

The next day's dawn came early. Dunne and Kohn watched it from 38,000 feet. The firing range was hot, and two KF-4 Phantom drones were out ahead at seventeen and twenty miles, crossing left to right. He would take the first. Since they were not maneuvering radically, radar acquisition was easy enough. He flicked on the MASTER ARMING switch, selected MISSILE and opened the bomb-bay doors. The Sidewinder racks automatically lowered to their firing position.

Eleven miles.

Using the heads-up display, he maneuvered to place the lead KF-4 in a locked-on position, and when the yellow cursor box began flashing he armed his first missile. The heat-seeking head immediately picked up the exhaust from the KF-4, and at six miles Dunne pressed the firing button. An off-bow shot was not the most favorable but the Sidewinder bolted from underneath the fuselage and zeroed in on the KF-4, leaving a slightly wavy ribbon of white cotton against the blue morning sky as it made minor tracking corrections. There was a flash and the KF-4 disintegrated. A second later, Kohn fired and her missile sped unerringly toward the second KF-4. It also disintegrated in a burst of brilliant white light, and then the sky was empty except for several trails of black smoke falling lazily earthward, burning debris that would join the remains of countless other targets now peppering the desert floor.

"All safe," Dunne reported as he swung around for the return to base. Kohn repeated the clearing command and joined on his left wing.

"Any problems?" Delaney asked, sweeping his T-38 under them and off to a high right wing position.

"Fish in a barrel," Dunne reported.

Kohn followed with "No problems."

"Let's take the other two home," Delaney instructed. He was satisfied, and the live-firing budget was tight. They would off-load the two remaining Sidewinders after landing.

Each of the two F-117s shot several touch and go landings and takeoffs before finally landing and taxiing to the ramp.

Kohn was standing on the concrete shaking the sweat from her hair by the time Dunne climbed down from the cockpit. Dunne pulled off his hard hat and used his sleeve to wipe his brow.

"That's gross," remarked Kohn, "soiling government issue with body fluids."

"Better than shaking off like a hot collie. Not very ladylike."

Delaney strode up. "Good shoot. Didn't see any sense in repeating that."

"It doesn't take a genius to fire Sidewinders," remarked Kohn, "especially against non-maneuvering targets. Speeding electrons do all the work."

"Well," agreed Delaney, "my job was to make sure you two knew the basics." He wiped the inside of his hard hat with a handkerchief. "I didn't think we'd get this far this fast."

"Thank you," Dunne replied. "We had a good instructor."

"Here, here," Kohn seconded.

"You two are the most natural military aviators I've ever flown with. I don't know who you really are, but I know who you've been. All navy and lots of it. You couldn't use a third on your trip to Disney World, could you?"

"You mean we've graduated?" Kohn asked.

"I can't show you anything else. Schedule what you'd like until noon tomorrow. That's when we break down the birds for transport."

Kohn glanced over at Dunne, her eyes obviously soliciting his preference.

"Low level night nav—VFR dead reckoning. Tonight. Wheels in the well at twenty-two hundred."

"I'll wear my good pearls," Kohn responded.

"I'll notify operations," Delaney offered. "Anything for the morning?"

"Nope. Tomorrow we sleep in. We'll be down for the loading operation."

"In that case," Delaney said, swelling his chest and sweeping his hard hat low in front of him as he bowed, "my job here is done."

"Thank you, Tony." Dunne offered his hand. As Delaney took it, Kohn wrapped an arm around the waist of each of the two men. "We wish you could join us. Three Musketeers. Whatever we do, you'll be part of it, Tony. Thanks."

Delaney made a last try. "You can't slip me a little hint?"

"We're just going to conduct further operational tests on the Sea Scorpion for our boss," Dunne answered.

"And the Pope's a Swedish dwarf who likes to dress in drag," countered Delaney.

"Could be," Kohn said.

"Good luck, shipmates."

Dunne and Kohn watched Delaney walk away. "Good man," commented Dunne.

"Cute, too."

"Yes, he is, in a sort of boyish way. . . ."

Kohn gave him a playful push toward the hangar. "Let's go work out our flight plan, Gramps."

"Captain Gramps to you, dear lady."

The two F-117Ns hugged the desert floor like snakes stalking mice, only the pair of Sea Scorpions were striving to keep at least five hundred feet between their black bellies and the sand. And on a dark, moonless night, that was not excessive.

"Ooooh!" murmured Kohn as she followed Dunne's quick climb to avoid a low knoll ahead that would have ruined their day had it remained unseen.

"I'm not sure we need any more of this shit," Dunne commented. They had been airborne for forty minutes and the constant stress of low level VFR night navigation was becoming a bit too much for his concern for safety. They had their sophisticated GPS systems to monitor exactly where they were at all times but were supposed to ignore the readout for the first hour. Then, a check could be made to see how accurately they had used their lap map and penlight routine. It was a technique long gone from serious consideration, but the Sea Scorpions had no terrain-following radar and there was a possibility that their mission, whatever it was, would call for such an ancient tactic.

"You okay?" Dunne asked with no little concern.

"No, but this is what we get the big bucks for," Kohn answered.

"Well, I say we cash it in. This is too damn squirrelly."

"Your idea, boss."

"Damn stupid idea. This kind of flying went away with fabric-covered wings. If it comes to this on the job, we'll just ad-lib it and hope for the best. I can't see a damned thing out of these little windows. Not down here at this speed."

"Concur."

Dunne zoomed up to fifteen thousand and headed back toward home plate. Kohn stayed tucked in.

"Don't you ever get tired of having one foot in my cockpit?" Dunne asked.

"This is the fleet, not the training command," Kohn answered quietly.

Dunne responded by pulling up and into a textbook perfect aileron roll. Halfway through, Kohn asked, "Are we upside down or rightside up?"

"What difference does it make?"

"None, I suppose. Do you realize people go all their lives and never get to do this? Sinful."

As they leveled, Dunne called, "Tonopah, nine-one-one, two for landing, twenty north."

"Cleared, runway three-six left. No reported traffic."

They broke over the numbers and taxied together to the spots in front of their hangars. Their ground crewmen were waiting.

"They're all yours," Dunne commented as he signed the flight/maintenance log. "No discrepancies."

By the time he and Kohn boarded the crew bus, the ground crew was starting to break down the aircraft for loading aboard the C-5 due next day at noon.

"I'm glad we quit early," Kohn commented. "That was antsy."

"Well, the bird does have its limitations. We may have been asking too much. You buying?"

Kohn held her watch up to catch some light. "Club's closed."

The bus dropped them at their quarters. Dunne left Kohn at her door with a simple "Goodnight." He was already thinking about the departure tomorrow for Kunsan. They'd ride the C-5 with their blackbirds. It would be a long and tiresome flight.

Kohn undressed and dropped on her bed without showering. She rarely did that, especially after a flight, but she had her first doubts about Dunne. The night VFR low-level training mission had been just plain dumb. They could have scattered themselves over several square miles of Nevada desert. It had been a long time since she had scared herself in an airplane.

6

Tokyo was drizzly. The steady, light rain had fallen for two days without any letup, and the gray skies forecast a maddening continuance.

Carrier Battle Group Three lay at anchor in Tokyo Bay, almost in the same spot where the *Missouri* and her escorts had dropped their hooks in 1945 to receive the formal Japanese surrender party. The flagship carrier, USS *Lincoln* (CVN-72), fresh out of a two-week upkeep period at one of the Yokosuka piers, was in the middle of her eleven-ship force: five cruisers, two of them nuclear powered; two guided missile destroyers; two ASW destroyers and two guided missile frigates. It was a quiet time and off-duty personnel were either ashore enjoying the sights and sounds of one of the world's largest metropolises—those who could afford it—or lounging on their respective ships. Many, despite their off-duty status, were catching up on cleaning their workspaces and gear. It was a sailor's lot. At sea, one became so accustomed to working around the clock that in-port leisure time still carried the urge to be doing *something*. Of course, there were a great number who had no trouble writing letters, playing cards or catching up on one of the most precious commodities aboard an operational warship: sleep.

Not Rear Admiral Joseph "Jumpin' Joe" Jefferson, COMCARBATGRPTHREE (Commander, Carrier Battle Group Three) and a direct descendent of *the* Thomas Jefferson. He was a long way from sleep, even if it was only 0926 on a rainy morning. Instead, he was on his hot line to Admiral John Decker, CINCPACFLT (Commander in Chief, Pacific Fleet), Jumpin' Joe's immediate operational commander.

Decker was not one to waste words, and he didn't on this occasion. "Joe, I know you're not going to like this, but Bob Páce, our nominee for the U.S. rep at the Tokyo naval talks, just died. Massive heart attack. The conference starts in two days, and Washington has ordered me to put you on temporary additional duty as our representative."

Jumpin' Joe was instantly antagonized. "Who ever heard of a battle group commander going on TDY when deployed? We can't do that."

"Yes, we can. You're going to the talks, your flagship is going to pay a port call on Hong Kong with whatever two escorts you decide upon—I'd suggest the cruisers—and your ASW group will exercise with a Japanese maritime self-defense force in the Inland Sea. Two weeks max. You can keep your flag ashore. Captain Tyler can be the officer in tactical command for the Hong Kong visit." Dave "Jocko" Tyler was the commanding officer of the *Lincoln*.

"This may be the last visit to Hong Kong while it's under British control. I would think we should have a flag officer in attendance. Why Hong Kong now, for Christ's sake? That's usually later on, before we redeploy."

"It's a Paterson operation, Joe. Presidential priority. You know the drill."

"That African-American—and I say that respectfully—has more clout now, being retired, than when he sat in your seat . . . sir."

"I'm faxing you the paperwork. It's all unclassified, just a change in deployment schedule. Routine."

"You just want me out of the way while Admiral Paterson does his thing. I can see how the admiral can work the deals to break up my battle group to exercise with the Japanese and get temporary custody of my flagship, but how in hell did he arrange the heart attack for Admiral Pace so that I'd be stuck here?"

"He doesn't have custody of your flagship, Joe. These are tough economic times and we suddenly found ourselves with three operational requirements, all of which obligate you and your people. There's no money to do it any other way."

"I don't suppose I can appeal to the Joint Chiefs?" Jefferson asked halfheartedly.

"Just so you send it through me for my endorsement." Decker was glad Jefferson could not see his grin. Jumpin' Joe liked to light fires, but this one wouldn't get past CINC-PACFLT, and Jumpin' Joe knew it.

Jumpin' Joe let his external sphincter muscle relax, wishing that the telephone could carry odors as well as sound. Then Admiral Decker would know exactly how he felt. "Aye, aye, sir."

"That's better. Enjoy yourself. Let your staff take over. There's nothing earthshaking in the wind. I'll get you back out to sea as soon as possible."

"A whole battle group, disbanded," Jefferson muttered.

"Temporarily," Decker added.

"It's quite a precedent," Jumpin' Joe continued, not quite able to give up.

"It's the times, Joe. Gotta go; we're short on communication funds also."

Jumpin' Joe returned to protocol. "Thank you, Admiral. I'll keep you posted on the talks."

As soon as he heard the line go dead, Jumpin' Joe buzzed for his chief of staff. As the four-striper entered, Jumpin'

Joe briefed him on the call and added, "I want the staff to stay here. We'll let Captain Tyler and the CAG have a free rein with the air wing. We can call it operational training in place or some other stupid goddamned thing."

"You're going to order the *Texas* and *California* to escort the *Lincoln*?"

"Yes, we'll let the small boys have the ASW task. At least they should profit from a period of intensified training."

"I'll get the necessary orders ready."

After the chief of staff left, Jumpin' Joe stormed out of his cabin and charged into Captain Tyler's in-port cabin.

Tyler, surprised, stood. "Admiral?"

"Sit down, Jocko; I just needed to walk off some energy."

Tyler could see that his immediate superior was about to burst at the seams. "Is there something I can do?"

"Yes, you can kick my dumb ass all the way to Guam for agreeing to take this job. We're not a battle group; we're an advanced training group. CINCPACFLT must have forgotten everything he should know about readiness."

Tyler knew the best tack to take was one of silence.

"You're to take the *Lincoln* to Hong Kong—another Paterson operation. I'm to sit here on shore and scope down sake with our Japanese allies. Admiral Pace died; I'm to replace him."

"I'm sorry to hear that—that Admiral Pace died; he was a good officer."

"Yes, well, he was a master of poor timing. I don't want to spend this cruise in dress canvas and cocktail parties. That's all these talks are. The Japanese bow and tell us what great tactical teachers we are; then they show us up in every goddamned joint exercise we have. Incidentally, you'll take the *Texas* and *California* with you. The rest of the group will play 'who's got the submarine?' with the Japanese in the Inland Sea."

"How long will our port call be?"

"Admiral Paterson will let you know. He's on some sort of super-classified schedule."

"I wish you were going with us, sir."

Jumpin' Joe's eyes lit up with memories of other Hong Kong visits. "Yes. You know, ever since my first visit as a boot ensign out of the academy aboard the old FDR, I've had a thing for those slit skirts. The Hong Kong Chinese women have the best-looking asses in all of Asia, and when I was a gold bar I jumped every one I could afford. Can't do *that* any more, but I can still look. It's hell having to be dignified and proper."

Tyler commented, "I'm certain the air wing will fill in for you, sir."

"Ha! That's for sure. Well, the paperwork is in the mill. I'm going to shift my flag ashore this evening." Jumpin' Joe stood and offered his hand. "Take care of the mini-armada, Jocko, and I'll see you when you get back."

"Thank you, Admiral."

7

The White House
October 1, 11:30 A.M.

"I hated to hold you over another day, Blackjack. I know you're anxious to get out to the *Lincoln*."

"I'm at your call, Mister President, but I do have a tight schedule."

"I understand. It's just that after you left last evening, I had a special briefing by Charlie Dobbs. He runs the Chinese Counterintelligence Section at Langley. The director sat in, of course, and some things were covered that prompted me to ask that you come over this morning. You'll miss your commercial flight, but I've arranged to provide you with government air back to New Orleans."

"Thank you, sir."

The president was sitting comfortably behind his desk in the Oval Office and continued his discussion without reference to any notes that were detectable by Blackjack. "You know, the present talks with the Chinese concern some major modifications of our trade agreement that are still being discussed—in closed committee, I might add. The Chinese have gotten wind of some of the changes that are not too favorable to them and are trying to sound tough, mostly to impress me since they know I already have some reservations about the content and they feel I may veto it. But I do support the language of the changes at this point.''

The puzzled look on Paterson's face was obviously preceding a question. The president held up a hand.

"Hear me out. The concern that the folks over at CIA have is how the Chinese got the information about the sensitive changes even before they've been discussed in full committee.''

"Wouldn't that be common knowledge at this point, at least within the committee staff?''

"No—or at least, it shouldn't be. The Senate chair had requested that the new provisions be kept classified until we could informally sound out the Chinese on certain issues. There was no military classification, just a Senate confidentiality that was almost immediately compromised.''

Blackjack grinned. "That's unusual?''

"In this case, yes. I don't want to go into detail; it's irrelevant to our discussion. The point I need to make with you is the thoroughness of Chinese intelligence in both the military and political arenas. The subject has a bearing on your present assignment.''

"And that is . . . ?''

"The Chinese intelligence system relies heavily on overseas Chinese, including those in this country.''

A caution flag climbed the pole in Paterson's brain. "Shades of pre–World War Two and the Japanese—and we were way off on that one. Practically all of the Nisei in this country were fiercely loyal to the United States.''

"The Chinese are a different breed in that respect.''

Paterson shrugged. "Perhaps.''

"In any event, the present friendly atmosphere could get a little sour. If that happens, we want to be sure we have the option to call your task off, even at the very last minute.''

"We always have that option, Mister President.''

"I know. I like your plan. As innovative and daring as

it is, it is almost foolproof from the standpoint of our planes' being detected. But if something *should* go wrong and we wind up with Dunne or Kohn or both in Chinese hands, along with the airplanes or parts thereof, the Chinese would have one powerful weapon to convince us to see that any changes to the trade agreement favor them. I have to weigh that admittedly outside chance against the desirability of getting Desird.''

''I would think that if we're detected, the trade agreement would be the least of our worries. If the Chinese wind up with either of our pilots or any parts of the airplanes, the international repercussions would be devastating. We've known that going into this.''

''I realize that. It's just that the atmosphere is a little more charged than it was when we set this task up.''

''Mister President, we are using two of the most sophisticated Stealth aircraft in the world. Our two pilots are professionals and fully qualified. Chinese radar surveillance is not the best, and there are gaps and inconsistencies in their coverage that we will be exploiting to the fullest. We have an in-country agent who will be exercising tactical control of the operation, and he has the authority to abort the mission at any time. Saddam Hussein never saw the Stealths electronically during Desert Storm. There is no reason to believe the Chinese will. Even if we fail to accomplish our task, there is every reason to believe that the aircraft will be recovered and the world will continue to turn with no one the wiser.''

''Nevertheless, we have our necks out a country mile on this one.''

''That's the nature of the business that you hired me for. We have to believe that this is the only chance we may have to get Desird for a long, long time. In that interim, he can raise holy hell along the entire Pacific Rim if our intelligence is anywhere near being right. And I believe it is.''

The president softly blew through pursed lips. "All right. I was just having second thoughts. I agree with you."

Paterson studied the president. The man seemed tired, as well he should be.

The president muttered, "This is a shitty job. Why anyone would want it is beyond me."

Paterson was unsure as to how to comment on the observation.

"Thanks, John," the president said. "A car is waiting to take you to Andrews. Good hunting."

"Thank you, Mister President." The two men exchanged warm handshakes and smiles.

A few minutes later, sitting in the back of the limo, Paterson ran the visit through his mind. It had been somewhat disjointed, the president starting off with remarks on Chinese intelligence procedures and then jumping to what would happen if the Chinese discovered the shootdown. What was the connection that the president seemed to want to make but had been unable to?

8

Twenty-two hours cooped up in the windowless passenger compartment of the C-5B Galaxy, with only brief leg-stretching fuel stops at Hickam and Guam, produced a fatigue that went beyond jet lag. Now Dunne and Kohn were aroused from their latest attempts at sleep by the announcement that they were letting down in their approach to the USAF Kunsan Air Base just seven miles south of the South Korean city of the same name. It was 0412, and they had lost a day crossing the International Date Line. The early morning was overcast, wet and most probably as cold as the proverbial witch's teat. Their aircraft were stuffed into the huge cargo compartment, outer wings and ruddervators removed and safely stowed in wooden racks. Placing two 55-foot-long fuselages within the 121-foot-long cargo bay had been quite a feat, only the removal of the ruddervators making it possible. Considering the wingless max width of the F-117Ns (just shy of seventeen feet), there was barely room within the 19-foot-wide cargo bay for the two fuselages, wing and ruddervator racks and several boxes of spare parts. Dunne figured the loadmasters must have used two giant shoehorns to accomplish the task. They had even sandwiched in two spare engines.

At the invitation of the aircraft commander, Kohn proceeded forward and stood on the flight deck as the giant cargo carrier began its letdown. Apparently they were descending through a massive warm front as the cloud cover was widespread and stratus in form, with little turbulence. The Galaxy broke through the ragged bottom of the cloud cover at four thousand feet. The pilot eased it into a wide turn over the western coastline to position himself for the landing at the Kunsan base. Kohn scanned as much of the area as she could, naturally curious about a country roughly the size of Indiana but home to over 44 million people, some 1,160 per square mile.

The port of Kunsan sat on the central coastal edge of the western plains and, from what Kohn could see by reflections from the moist fields to its east, the area was saturated and in part even flooded from the heavy rains. An irregular and jagged carpet of tiny lights, some of them moving and many of them colored, marked the major South Korean city, and to the south Kohn caught the rotating green and white beacon of the airfield. Even at this early hour, there was activity; she could see the running lights of several aircraft on the taxiways, and one was taking off. She was surprised but grateful that the aircraft commander allowed her to remain on the flight deck and observe the landing, a privilege that any pilot would enjoy. The young major placed the heavy Galaxy onto the wet runway with all of the care of a mother laying a sleeping baby into its crib. As they pulled off onto a taxiway, Kohn thanked the crew and returned to her seat.

"Sex has its privileges," Dunne remarked.

"The man was smooth. He knows his airplane."

"Felt good back here." Dunne began collecting his flight jacket and personal items that he had used during the long night, but one of the crewmen cautioned him. "Sir, would you remain strapped in until we hit the chocks?''

"Sure. Sorry." He should have known better.

An air force captain briefed them as they rode the passenger bus to the visiting officers quarters. "It is our understanding that you will be departing as soon as the aircraft are reassembled. Our maintenance people estimate ten hours from touchdown." Glancing at his watch, he continued, "That would be fifteen-thirty. Certainly, as DOD contract civilians, you have the run of the base. Would you like breakfast?"

"I just need some good sleep," Kohn replied.

Dunne agreed. "Why don't we plan on grabbing lunch at noon? That'll give us almost seven hours, and we need that if we're going flying." Turning to the captain, he amplified, "We should have a classified message waiting for us."

"Yes, sir, you do. The deputy chief of operations has it in his safe, and you can pick it up at any time."

"Can we swing by there now?"

"Yes, sir. I will have to wake him up. He's at his quarters."

"Don't you have a duty officer who has access to it?"

"No, sir. I'm sure the colonel won't mind."

Dunne could see no reason why the matter couldn't wait until they proceeded to the flight line. "No, that's not necessary. Please inform the colonel that we'll be at his office at fourteen-hundred."

"I'll have a car and driver at the VOQ at eleven-thirty if that's satisfactory," the captain offered.

"That'll be fine."

Dunne and Kohn sat opposite the deputy chief of operations as they read the message. There was no originator nor addressee, only the classification on the envelope: TOP SECRET.

AT 030600ZOCT LINCOLN WILL BE AT POSITION 125E 30N PIM 180/10. PROCEED LINCOLN DURING DARKNESS.

TACTICAL FREQUENCIES ATTACHED. CONTACT LINCOLN CALL SIGN *BIG MOTHER* 100 MILES OUT. FROM THIS POINT YOUR DESIGNATIONS *DARKSTAR ONE* AND *TWO*. DO NOT FILE FLIGHT PLAN. CLEARANCE WITH KUNSAN OPS ARRANGED. PATERSON SENDS.

After checking the frequencies and call signs sheet, Dunne placed the message back in the envelope, resealed it and wrote his initials across the flap, then handed it to the colonel. "Would you put this in your burn bag, please?"

"Certainly, Mister Dunne."

"We'll be departing this evening."

"Yes, *sir*. If there's anything you require, let me know." The colonel was obviously irritated at the special treatment he was required to give to the two Lockheed civilians. It was not proper procedure for military operations, and he had voiced his objections to the chief of operations. "This is not proper, sir," he had complained. "We receive two F-117s, reassemble them and two civilians fly them away with no flight plan and no knowledge on our part as to where they are going. How do we maintain flight following and SAR ability?"

"We don't" was the only reply received. "It's not our operation."

"Whose is it?"

"I don't know and I don't care to know. It's authorized."

After Dunne and Kohn left, the DCO locked his door and tore open the envelope. "The fucking navy!" he said aloud. *They're using two of our aircraft and our facilities for God knows what and we're not even given the courtesy of being informed.* He made a mental note to call his mentor back at air force headquarters. The general had a gigantic hard-on for special air ops that did not include the air force, and such information would be much appreciated, perhaps enough to get the deputy chief a silver star when the promotion board met next spring.

Dunne and Kohn spent the next few hours discussing the flight to the *Lincoln* and working up their flight plan. They ate an early dinner at the flight line snack bar, and a crew bus took them to their hangar.

By the time Dunne and Kohn arrived, Darkstars One and Two were completely reassembled and tucked back in the corner of the hangar—a pair of flat-black irregular shapes that had all of the menacing appearance of two black widow spiders trapped in the hold of their web and ready to pounce on any intruder. Both Dunne and Kohn were surprised to see the two navy ground crewmen from back at Tonopah as well as a USAF non-com who introduced himself. ''I'm Chief Master Sergeant Dunlap, air force liaison for this mission.''

''What mission?'' quietly queried Dunne.

Navy Master Chief Brown spoke up. ''Whatever, sir. Chief Dunlap knows more about the F-117 that any enlisted tech alive. He's been with the program since its inception. He holds the same clearances that we do, sir.''

Dunne did not like the development, although he could see Dunlap's value immediately. ''And those clearances are?''

''Direct from Admiral Paterson, sir.''

Kohn exchanged mildly surprised glances with Dunne before asking, ''What do you know about this mission?''

CMS Dunlap, obviously the leader of the team, responded ''Only that we will be going aboard a navy carrier to support whatever mission it is. We're concerned only with the readiness of the airplanes.''

"How the hell did you all get here so quickly? We came direct from Tonopah with very brief refueling stops en route."

Dunlap let his smile match those of the other two. "Special B-52 training mission, direct Tonopah to here."

Dunne shook his head. *Paterson, you old toad, are there any strings you can't pull?* "And how are you getting to the carrier?"

Dunlap continued, "Two navy Greyhounds are to pick us up after you depart." The Grumman C-2A Greyhounds were the largest COD— carrier onboard delivery—cargo aircraft operating with carrier forces. "We go in one, the second takes the spare parts, engine and other gear."

"From what carrier?"

"We won't know until they arrive, sir. We didn't need to know up to this point."

Dunne was pleased. One of his main concerns in addition to security had been maintenance personnel for the airplanes. He had just assumed that there were qualified navy personnel on the *Lincoln*. Obviously not. "They're en route?"

"As of forty minutes ago."

"Ops didn't seem to know about them."

Dunlap squeezed out another tight grin. "The United States Navy works in mysterious ways, sir. But I suspect you know that, sir." The senior air force non-com was fishing.

Dunne countered with "I know only what I need to know for this mission, Sergeant, and I suggest you curb any suspicions or speculations. Should I say more?"

"No, sir. We're looking forward to being part of it all, sir."

"Good. Miss Kohn and I are very pleased to have you on board."

"Thank you, sir. Would you like to inspect the aircraft now, sir?"

"Definitely."

Duncan accompanied Dunne as he went over every inch of Darkstar One, paying particular attention to the wing-fuselage seams, the RAM tapes and the ruddervator installations. Master Chief Brown assisted Kohn. Both pilots operated their flight controls, checking for the familiar responses they had become accustomed to back at Tonopah. Everything was in order.

"Let's roll 'em out and turn 'em up," Dunne ordered.

Dunlap suggested, "With your permission, sir, we'll open the hangar doors and keep them inside. There are a lot of prying eyes around here. I've taken the liberty of having two F-15s turned up at the same time just outside the other end of the hangar. They'll mask our ground checks."

"Good thought." Dunne could learn to like Duncan.

"We parked the C-5 just outside after the passengers disembarked. Then we used some of the larger base vehicles to mask the unloading. Very few, if any, base personnel know what we have in here. I figured no need to announce ourselves just yet."

"You ever thought about transferring to the navy, Chief?" Kohn asked lightly.

"No, ma'am. I like to feel grass between my toes and sleep in a bed that doesn't roll and pitch, although I am looking forward to this little cruise—I think."

"You'll love it. Clean sheets, ice cream and movies every night."

"Yes, ma'am."

After the turnup with engine and systems checks, Dunne and Kohn had their driver take them to ops, where they would check weather. As the car stopped and they stepped out, two U.S. Navy Greyhounds were taxiing in. Contrary to normal practice, they carried no aircraft carrier designations on their after-fuselages, and all squadron markings had been deleted.

*   *   *

Dunne and Kohn returned to base ops with their gear at sunset. The duty meteorologist gave them an update on the East China Sea weather. "This warm front extends south just about parallel the tip of the peninsula. It doesn't show any signs of weakening. Ceilings varying from three thousand feet here to probably one thousand in its southern extent. Rain throughout the area, but visibilities expected to stay above one mile at worst. If you want to give me your exact destination, I can be more precise."

Dunne could not do that. "A general brief is all we need. What's it like down near Hong Kong?" The last request had no significance; it was thrown in just to keep the meteorologist guessing.

"Much better. Scattered cumulus, bases at three thousand. Unlimited visibility. No surface winds to speak of."

"Thanks." With Kohn in tow, Dunne proceeded into the flight planning area, and they huddled over a table away from two other pilots preparing their plans.

"It's going to be pitch black when we reach the *Lincoln*," Kohn observed quietly. "Great conditions for our first actual trap aboard the boat."

"Wet deck, but the visibility doesn't sound bad and a decent ceiling. What do you have for en-route times?"

Leaning farther over the table to shield her charts and tables from prying eyes, Kohn briefed, "Takeoff at nineteen hundred. Advancing the PIM puts the *Lincoln* here. I figure five hundred eighty-seven miles. With climbout, winds at thirty-five thousand, we're looking at one-point-four." An hour and twenty four minutes. "We'll almost be on time for the evening movie."

"What do we have for alternates? I'd sure hate to bingo, but the weather could turn to worms."

"With the winds, best bet would be to return here. Barring that, we could make Taipei. Do you like Chinese?"

"On a cold night, it could be just the thing, but I prefer shipboard chow on this occasion."

"Thee and me," concluded Kohn. "Should be no sweat."

"Then let's do it."

The aircraft had been rolled out of the hangar. Dunlap and Brown were waiting. "They're topped off and ready to go," Dunlap reported.

Dunne noticed that several armed air force military police were stationed around the area but could see no one else. Red and blue cop lights were flashing from several military police cars back toward the road areas. Tight security. Very few people would observe their departure.

There was one, however. From the control tower, the DCO silently watched the two F-117Ns taxi to the duty runway. Their call came crisply from the tower speakers. "Kunsan, two for takeoff." No ID, no destination, no requests for routing.

The sergeant controller looked at the DCO for approval.

"Let 'em go."

The sergeant relayed, "Cleared for takeoff; no reported traffic. Advise remain below one-eight thousand until clear of any airways. Have a safe flight."

"Thank you, tower. Two rolling."

The DCO watched the aircraft accelerate into the darkness until only their running lights were visible. They pulled up and climbed seaward, the red, green and white lights dimming and finally vanishing.

The sergeant commented, "I wonder where they're heading . . . I certainly wish them well wherever it is."

The DCO nodded agreement. He was still pissed that the navy was getting some action that the air force could undoubtedly do much better, but the pilots were going in harm's way, through a dark night on important business for their country. With that in mind, he wished them well and even uttered a brief prayer for their success, although his only audible reply was a murmured "Crazy bastards." He hurried down the tower ladder to call his general and give him the takeoff time.

"Oooh, it's dark up here," Kohn commented. They had entered the overcast at 2,800 feet and were passing twelve thousand.

"We'll keep our lights on until we see what we have on top." *Actually*, Dunne thought, *there would be no need to turn them off.* There could very well be other aircraft over the East China Sea, and there would be no risk to their identity.

Three minutes later, they rose out of the cloud cover like vampires from a white satin coffin and were bathed in the relatively bright light of a full moon. "We'll level at thirty-two," Dunne announced.

"Roger." Kohn loosened her shoulder straps slightly and let her Sea Scorpion drift out to a more comfortable cruise position. She would have no trouble keeping the multifaceted silhouette of the lead aircraft in sight. What a weird airplane. From her side view, the fuselage started with a downcast pointed nose, thickened aft of the cockpit and then thinned into a long after-body that bled smoothly into the aft-canted swallowtail. Long and slim from the side, with a fat, angular middle. With the blending of the fuselage into the wide wingroot and no horizontal tailplanes, the F-117N was in effect a modification of the classic flying wing, the broad fuselage and ruler-flat bottom adding considerable lift.

The sky around them was a deep purple, and an unimaginable number of stars and planets peppered the purple with silver dots, ranging in size from pinpoints to bright Sirius in the eastern sky. Or was that Sirius? She didn't know. She knew the Dipper and Polaris, but they were behind her. It really didn't make any difference, her celestial ignorance. This was one of the joys of flight. Engulfed in an atmosphere she couldn't see, below a sky that held a trillion galaxies like the one her Earth revolved within. Could there be another human out there, somewhere, on a similar mission, looking for bad guys? Or maybe hers was the only universe where Man preyed upon Man.

A shooting star sliced the southern sky, adding a wisp of silver emphasis to the beauty of the night.

She and Dunne, encased in their tiny machines, if you looked at them on the scale of endless space, must be insignificant in the grand scheme of things. Was God watching them this very moment? She liked to think so. Would there be day and night in the afterlife? She let her thoughts ramble for a few minutes, then turned her thinking to more serious matters.

It was almost space-cold outside her warm cockpit, and the water below was near its winter low temperature. Despite the coziness of her warm cockpit, it would be one hell of a night to ditch. Just an expression, she thought. You didn't ditch a modern jet; you punched out and rode the nylon. She imagined the shock of being blasted upward into the rushing night air, tumbling until her seat separated, then being stabilized by the drogue chute and, almost immediately afterward, the blessed jerk of a filled canopy. And then that almost unbearable shock as you hit the water. . . .

A ripple of mild, clear air turbulence interrupted her thoughts. She glanced down at her GPS reading. The global positioning satellite system readout indicated a longitude of thirty-four degrees, nine minutes north. They must be abeam of the tip of the Korean peninsula, making good time.

Dunne also sat in peaceful silence, letting his scan alternate between the cockpit instruments and the vast sky around him. What was going to be their ultimate destination? North Korea was an obvious choice, but if that were the case why were they flying south? Despite his short-lived "retirement" he had tried to keep up with the international scene, and the recent acquisition of long-range SSMs made North Korea a much more formidable force to contend with. Their Rodong IIs had a reported range of nearly two thousand miles. If that were the case, all of Japan, a large chunk of east China and the island of Taiwan could all be reached.

If there were to be a strike against some other installation, in particular one that sheltered Desird, it could have originated much more simply within South Korea. But not nearly as securely. A land launch would give too many clues to such a mission. Timing could be compared and obvious conclusions drawn. A strike from the sea would reveal itself to no one. Yet they had not been checked out in the delivery of air-to-ground weapons, so there would be no ground strike in all probability. Air to air? That didn't make a lot of sense. Defense for other strike aircraft? No way. The F-117N was not designed, and lacked the capabilities, for such a task.

The People's Republic of China was off his starboard wing, some hundred miles or so. No reason to believe that was a factor, other than it should be something to stay away from. Paterson had been concerned with Chinese negotiations going on in Washington but that would be a normal caution with respect to any clandestine operation in this part of the world. Vietnam and the unstable Southeast Asia lay farther down the line. The carrier could take them anywhere.

There was an uneasy feeling in Dunne's stomach that this would be a bastard operation, using aircraft that had not been designed for such a mission out of the necessity for maximum stealth. That conjured up all sorts of horrible thoughts. But it was damned exciting, the kind of assignment the professional military pilot ached for.

He could see Kohn holding steady about twenty yards off his starboard side and slightly aft. They were riding the air ripples in unison, moving together like slow dancers who were comfortable in each other's arms and had been paired for some time. Gentle movements, just enough to break the monotony of transit flight.

Would the *Lincoln* have forward air surveillance in place, searching for the Sea Scorpions? It would be interesting to see if they ever received any radar return. With that thought in mind, Dunne was tempted to order retraction of their fuselage strobes for maximum stealth but they would be needed for visual pickup by the LSO during their approach to the carrier. Who would be the LSO? It was doubtful that he would be F-117N qualified. That added another twist to their arrival at the *Lincoln*. He and Kohn would be strictly on their own and could expect qualified assistance only if there were obvious flaws in their handling of the airplanes. Certainly a great way to start off the operational phase of the mission: night approach for their first actual F-117N carrier landing without a qualified LSO. Paterson must have lots of punch to get the navy to disregard some of its most sacred safety requirements. Maybe they had decided that with "air force" aircraft and "civilian" pilots, operational procedures were already compromised. Whatever.

The first lines of Canadian John Gillespie Magee's "High Flight" came to Kohn's mind: "Oh, I have slipped the surly bonds of Earth and danced the skies on laughter-silvered wings . . ." What perfect meter. Magee had spoken for every pilot who had ever lived, and as this particular pair raced across Asian skies, Kohn recited the poem in her mind until she reached the final phrases. On such a night, in such a sky, around such a place, the closing words must be spoken aloud. Indeed, at this moment, she "put out my hand and touched the face of God." There were few innocent moments left in the world; this had to be one of them. Man and machine in perfect harmony, together in the purity of the night sky. Her next thought was so completely out of character, it startled her. She wanted to have a baby.

They flew in silence for the next forty minutes, but the

quiet time quickly vanished with Dunne's call to the *Lincoln*. "Big Mother, Darkstar One, flight of two, one hundred miles north, angels three-two."

The reply from *Lincoln's* Air Traffic Control Center was instantaneous. "Roger, Darkstar. Squawk four-four-two-one, ident. Over."

"Four-four-two-one, ident." Reaching down on the right console, Dunne set in the 4421 code on his identification transponder and toggled the IDENT switch. Upon receiving a radar wave from the *Lincoln*, the unit would respond with a coded signal that would show up on the ship's air control radar scopes even though there would be no normal radar return.

"Roger, have you at niner-seven miles, bearing three-five-two. Understand you have Darkstar Two in tow."

"Affirmative."

"At your discretion, descend to and maintain angels ten. Call two-five miles out."

"Will do." Dunne checked his tactical aerial navigation receiver and verified the *Lincoln's* ID letters. The display indicated that he was ninety-one miles out. "Out of thirty-two for ten."

Kohn retarded her power levers and matched Dunne's gradual rate of descent.

"Flight quarters. Stand by to recover aircraft."

With the preparatory announcement, the quiet night of the *Lincoln* evaporated. Earlier, several hundred crewmen had walked the flight deck, bow to stern, meticulously checking for any foreign objects that might be injested into jet engines. Now, the standby SAR helicopter was readied. Primary Flight Control—PriFly, the glass-enclosed operational station of the Air Boss that protruded inboard from the ship's island superstructure and had a commanding view of the flight deck—was manned, and the small group of LSO personnel took their positions on the port aft corner of the flight deck. Crash and ship rescue personnel manned their stations.

Ten miles out, Dunne and Kohn were racing toward the ship at 400 knots, maintaining an altitude of eighteen hundred feet under a broken cloud base. Light rain, shifting winds. Both pilots held the *Lincoln* on their forward-looking-infrared-radar (FLIR), the warmth of the carrier easily conrasting with the coolness of the night rain and sea.

The *Lincoln* had turned to its recovery course and held a steady thirty knots. The atmospheric air flow across the flight deck combined with the ship's speed gave a comfortable thirty-eight knots of headwind for the landings, somewhat more than for normal flight operations; but the F-117Ns were an unknown breed, and a slower relative landing speed could produce a safer recovery condition. For the crewmen working the deck, however, it was a wet gale that called for constant caution. A slip near the edge of the deck and they could easily be blown over the side. Fortunately, there would be only the two inbound aircraft, and the number of men exposed to the elements would be minimal. In addition, the captain had already announced his intent to slow to fifteen knots as soon as the second aircraft was on board.

The two Sea Scorpions passed over the ship at eight hundred feet. Dunne broke sharply left, and Kohn followed ten seconds later. She would play her approach to arrive over the ramp fifty-five seconds after Dunne's trap. Normal interval was forty-five seconds, but here again the Sea Scorpion was an unknown breed when it came to night carrier landings. An additional ten seconds would give the deck crew extra time to direct Dunne clear of the canted-deck landing area.

The LSO watched the running lights of Darkstar One slow downwind as it dropped to six hundred feet. He could not see the actual airplane.

Dunne completed his landing check and activated the boundary layer control. He hit his abeam position at 140 knots, down and dirty, hook double-checked down. The tiny lights of the *Lincoln* appeared to be a thousand miles away although his position was perfect. All of the old night-recovery willies that he had known before came back, and he knew that could he measure them; his blood pressure and heart rate were reflecting the tension of the night. This was the ultimate in precise and demanding flight. No aviator ever took night carrier landings lightly.

He was on his base leg, and the big gray boat, black on this night, was off his port bow as he continued his turn. Visibility was hampered by the rain and patches of low scud. He didn't have a solid view of the approach light until three-quarter miles out. It was a comforting orange-red, and on each side two horizontal green rows extended to show he was cleared for his approach. They also provided the reference for flying the landing path. As long as the meatball was aligned with the bars, he was on the glide slope. If the ball rose, he was going high; if it fell, he was low.

"Darkstar One, Sea Scorpion, ball, two point seven," he reported, the last figures telling the ship he had three hours and forty-two minutes of fuel remaining. No problem there.

"Roger, ball," reported the LSO. He could clearly see Dunne's running lights as he stood braced against the wind that was swirling viciously around the steel windbreak behind him. He was holding the wave-off pistol grip in one hand and his handset in the other, his backup LSO and several other recorders bunched around him.

Positioned on the nose strut of the F-117N were three vertical lights, each aligned to give the LSO an indicator of the aircraft's AOA—angle of attack. The middle light, amber in color, would be visible to the LSO when the aircraft was on speed; if the upper light, red, were visible, the aircraft's speed would be too fast, and if the bottom light, green, were visible, the airspeed would be too slow. The lights also gave the LSO a positive indication that the landing gear was down on such a dark night.

Dunne was riding a steady amber light. "Looking good," the LSO radioed quietly. The sinister Sea Scorpion came aboard looking all the while like a giant bat emerging from the black cave of the night. It passed over the ramp and smacked down on the centerline, and the hook showered bright sparks as it scraped the steel deck and caught number-three wire. Perfect.

As was standard procedure, Dunne had advanced his throttles to full power at touchdown; in the event he had missed all four wires, he would have bolted forward to take off again and reenter the pattern for another approach. Such a bolter was not rare but tonight he caught the wire, and as it stopped him, he reduced his power to idle and was slowly pulled backward until the hook disengaged. A taxi signalman crossed his yellow-lighted wands to order BRAKES and then began to direct Dunne to a parking spot clear of the canted deck.

Kohn was on final one mile out, having dragged out her approach because of the low visibility.

The rain had increased but was still more of a nuisance than a hazard. At three-quarter miles, she called, "Darkstar Two, Sea Scorpion, ball, three point six," and adjusted her flight path to shift the landing ball upward a trace. She liked to ride a high ball in her initial approach, a personal trait that usually elicited a mild rebuke from her LSOs. She just felt she could detect variations on the glide path more readily that way. She always had the meatball centered by one-half mile.

The LSO had visual contact, and he heard the clear call from his backup LSO. "Clear deck! Gear set, four-zero-zero, Sea Scorpion." The 400 indicated the arresting gear was set to handle the estimated 40,000-pound landing weight of the F-117N. The LSO immediately responded to

Kohn's call with "Skoshi high, Two, check power . . . you're on . . . good . . ."

The voice had a familiar ring to it. *Delaney!* Their young Tonopah mentor, Tony Delaney, was bringing them in. What a comfort. But how on earth did he get here so fast? Kohn had no time to consider her last thought as the cockpit suddenly lit up with a bright red glow.

Fire warning light on number two engine! *Oh, sweet Jesus* . . . There were no other indications; her engine revolutions were holding steady, and her tailpipe temps were normal.

"Power, Two, power!" Delaney's call was urgent.

Distracted by the light, she had let her aircraft settle. She corrected smoothly with a touch of throttle but could not ignore the frightening light. The emergency could not have come at a more critical time. She was less than a hundred yards from the end of the carrier. Within the next few seconds she could easily lose control. Fighting panic, she slapped up her landing gear and added full power. There was no way she was going to ride a burning jet onto the flight deck.

Delaney, unaware of what was going on in the cockpit, saw only that the F-117N was rapidly rising above its proper glide path. He ordered, "Too high, too high, take it around!" He followed his verbal mandatory command with a squeeze of the waveoff pickle, and vertical rows of red lights glowed on each side of the ball.

Somewhat calmed by the realization that she was still in command of her aircraft and climbing to a more safe altitude for ejection, she reported, "I've got a fire warning light on number two."

Delaney and the others watched her pass low overhead. There was no outward indication of engine fire. "No sign here, Two," he reported.

Could it be the light? Delaney had told them back at Tonopah that there had been some false indications early on but that the lights had been rewired and the problem had disappeared. Everything else in the cockpit indicated normal operations. The engine was delivering full power. No vibrations. She had no visibility aft, but Delaney had reported that he could see nothing. Now his voice returned. "What are your intentions, Two?"

"I think it's the goddamned light," Kohn answered. "Everything else appears normal."

"Lifeguard is following inside your turn."

Kohn looked back over her left shoulder. The rescue chopper was between her and the ship and staying inside her flight path.

"I'm coming aboard, Big Mother. Deferred emergency." She *had* to do something about the light. Loosening her shoulder straps and leaning forward, she unscrewed the hold-down plate and twisted out the bulb. The cockpit was a much more calm place, despite the fact that if now she had a real engine fire she might not know it in time to punch out. Well, one crisis at a time. She would just monitor the number-two engine more closely the second time around.

As anticipated, there were no further signs of fire, and she brought Darkstar Two around and down to catch the three wire. Immediately, she was surrounded by the crash crew who instructed her to cut her engines as they inspected every inch of the Sea Scorpion. She quickly climbed down the egress ladder and, after insuring that there was indeed nothing wrong with her aircraft, she rode one of the low tow-tractors over to where Dunne was waiting.

Delaney met them both. "Some folks will do anything to get attention," he exclaimed as he shook Dunne's hand and enjoyed Kohn's unexpected hug.

"How did you get here?" asked Dunne.

"B-52 to Kunsan with your ground crew, F-14 to the ship. I was out of Kunsan before you arrived."

"Well, it's a big comfort to know you're with us on this," Kohn announced.

"Whatever *this* is," Delaney ventured.

"You know as much as we do at this point," Dunne countered.

The air boss approached. "Welcome aboard. I'm Commander Gilley."

"Joshua Dunne."

"Sheila Kohn."

"You were pretty cool up there, ma'am. Just a shorted light?"

"Apparently. The bird has had that problem in the past."

"Well, I can't compliment you enough."

"Thank you."

The air boss waved them toward the island structure. "A couple of the crew will show you to your quarters. We have a Mister Paterson occupying the flag cabin—the admiral's not with us on this trip. Mister Paterson would like you to join him for breakfast at oh-eight-hundred if that's satisfactory."

Is *everybody* in Paterson's unit on this ship? thought Dunne. And Paterson—was he taking over the duties of the battle group commander? There was no way he had that kind of clout.

They said their temporary farewells to Delaney and followed the two sailors into the red-lighted bowels of the *Lincoln*. Both were quartered in the forward officers country on the gallery deck, immediately under the "roof"—the flight deck. Kohn was assigned one of the cabins that had been prepared for female ship's officers, although there were none on board for this deployment. A small bag of personal clothing and toilet items lay on her bunk, including several blouses, slacks and a fresh black Nomex flight suit with F-117N and Lockheed logos as well as a name patch. After her shower, she put on a gray blouse and matching slacks. She placed the chain with her Lockheed

ID card around her neck. She had worn it since their arrival at Nellis.

Dunne had suggested that they meet in the wardroom for coffee before proceeding to breakfast with Paterson, and she made her way forward to the officers' mess. It was only 0630, but Dunne was waiting at one of the back tables. A few ship's company officers were at one of the other tables, and a scattering of off-duty pilots were at several others. Almost all glanced at her at least briefly as she entered the wardroom, and most greeted her with warm smiles of welcome. As she sat with Dunne, the commander who had been seated at the head of the ship's company table rose and joined them.

"I'm Commander Brill, executive officer. Welcome aboard."

"Thank you, Commander," Dunne replied.

"You're certainly welcome in this mess at any time, although I understand you will be taking most of your meals with Mister Paterson in the flag cabin. If there is anything you need or anything I can do for you, please let me know."

"We appreciate that, sir. Our needs will be quite minimal."

The exec nodded. "Well, the offer's there and we're very pleased to provide you with the support of the *Lincoln*." As he walked away, he wasn't sure that he wanted to know anything about the mission of the two Lockheed "civilians." Whatever it was, it sure as hell had a high priority and was cloaked in secrecy. The *Lincoln*, homeported in Japan, normally steamed with five cruisers, four destroyers and two frigates, not to mention an attack submarine that was routinely attached for operational control. She was home to Carrier Air Wing Eleven (CVW-11), a lethal strike and defense group of aircraft that included F/A-18 Hornets, F-14D Tomcats, A-6 Intruders and Prowlers, S-3B Vikings, and SH-60 Seahawks, the latter two types for anti-submarine warfare (ASW). A contingent of E-2C Hawkeyes provided airborne warning and control services.

On this night, the *Lincoln* was escorted by only two nuclear guided missile cruisers, the *California* and the *Texas*, while her other units were on joint exercises in Japan's Inland Sea with Japanese Maritime Self-Defense Forces. The Commander, Carrier Battle Group Three (COMCARBATGRPTHREE), Rear Admiral Joseph "Jumpin' Joe" Jefferson, was ashore in Tokyo attending a high-level strategic conference with U.S. and Japanese naval representatives. For all practical purposes, the *Lincoln* was cruising the East China Sea to exercise her air group and pay a last courtesy call at Hong Kong before it was relinquished by the British to the People's Republic of China. Such splitting of the battle group and operations at sea without the admiral was not a normal situation. But in the mid-'90s, a number of compromises had been made with standard operational practices and the exec, an ex-enlisted man with twenty-seven years of service, had long ago learned to roll with the punches, no matter how much he yearned for "the old navy."

"He seemed a little stiff," Dunne commented.

"I dunno. We are sort of intruders on the normal navy scene," Kohn replied.

Together, they enjoyed their coffee and the early morning routine of wardroom breakfast as the oncoming watch ate and the other officers prepared for the day's business.

A few minutes before eight, Dunne suggested, "Well, let's go see the man."

Paterson's cabin was forward on the same level. The marine sentry outside the flag cabin checked their ID, knocked lightly on the door and opened it.

Blackjack Paterson was standing across the room talking to a messman. Seeing Dunne and Kohn enter, he dismissed the sailor and walked to greet them. "Well, the first part's over. Glad to see you both. Have any problems getting aboard?''

Dunne knew it was an academic question. As critical as this mission was, Paterson had undoubtedly followed every moment of their arrival, most likely from the seclusion of the admiral's bridge. ''Not my favorite time of day to come aboard,'' Dunne commented, ''and Commander Kohn gave us a bit of a thrill.''

''Oh, yes, I heard.''

I'll bet you did, Dunne thought.

Kohn shrugged. ''That's why we get the big bucks.''

Paterson waved them to the breakfast table. ''I'm glad it went well.''

The messman entered with a pewter thermos of hot coffee and a liter-sized glass pitcher of orange juice. The three sat and gave their breakfast orders.

''What next?'' Dunne asked while Paterson poured coffee.

Paterson sipped his before replying, ''Hong Kong.''

When he said nothing further, Kohn asked, ''And?''

''The ship is programmed for a three-day stay, rest and relaxation. We'll anchor there day after tomorrow, about noon. En route, the air wing will exercise.''

A three-day stay in Hong Kong—and we busted our backs rushing through the checkout? Dunne was a bit peeved. ''We could have used another day at Tonopah.''

''No, you couldn't. The three days could be cut short, depending on a number of factors.''

''So what's our schedule?''

''Rooms are waiting for you and Kohn at the Regent Hotel, Kowloon. Your time is your own—as long as I know every minute where you are. When the time is right, we will have a strategic briefing on your mission.''

''At the hotel?''

''No. You'll get instructions.''

''What determines when the time is right?'' Kohn asked.

Paterson seemed reluctant to answer but did. "We'll be waiting on some arrivals from mainland China."

China? What would be the involvement of the Chinese? And Paterson had used the word "China" in the context of the People's Republic of China, not Taiwan.

"Can you fill us in on the mission?" Kohn asked. "I, for one, can't see any need to hold anything back at this point."

Paterson's dark eyes flashed for just a microsecond, as if he took offense at the question, but his answer was soft enough. "I understand, but you've been with me long enough to know how we operate. The need to know is just that, and for the moment you two don't need to know any more than that you will be required to execute your part of the mission in the Sea Scorpions. Immediately after the briefing, we'll put out to sea. There will be a tactical briefing at the proper time, and I assure you that all of your questions will be answered by that time. If you want to fly before then, either tomorrow or after we leave Hong Kong, there will be time."

"We can use some tanker practice, assuming the mission profile will require in-flight refueling."

The question obviously disturbed Paterson. "You didn't get that back at Tonopah?"

"We were scheduled to, but the tanker went down for mechanical problems. There was no other time to work it in."

"All right, tomorrow evening. I'll set it up so you get a couple practices before it gets dark and then a couple plug-ins at night."

"That'll work fine," Dunne answered. It would also be good for the airplanes. Nothing affected an aircraft's readiness like sitting still for too many days. All sorts of ass-twitching minor discrepancies seemed to crop up, and major ones weren't rare. Airplanes were meant to be flown.

The messman brought in their plates and set them down.

He freshened their coffee. "Anything else, sir?" he asked of Paterson.

"No, that's good. Thank you. We'll be fine."

As soon as the sailor left, Paterson continued, "I know you would like to be more informed at this point, but let me address what we're doing from the ship's standpoint. You two Lockheed pilots are going to evaluate some special equipment you have on board your aircraft. There is no special equipment in that sense, however. That's the cover. You're doing it in the East China Sea because the evaluation has to do with the analysis of Chinese and North Korean air defense radar capability. The ship's captain and the air wing commander are the only two who will be privy to the actual mission. Even those aircrews who fly in your support will not know. Believe me when I repeat that this is a damn sensitive operation. So sensitive that after your Hong Kong briefing you will be offered one last opportunity to turn it down—of course, I know you won't do that, but the president insisted."

"The president," Dunne repeated.

"Along with yours and mine, the presidential ass is on the line with this one. The one stipulation he put on the mission was that the pilots involved express confidence that it can be carried out and agree to the provisions without any reservations."

"By that, you mean the conditions that if something goes wrong, we're on our own?" Dunne asked.

"Yes, publicly the military will never acknowledge you ever existed."

"And just how, if we are compromised," Kohn interjected, "will you explain the use of two F-117s in unauthorized civilian hands?"

"The two aircraft were secretly based in South Korea and were hijacked."

Dunne threw up his hands. "That's ridiculous!"

Now it was Dunne's turn to be speared by Paterson's

dark eyes. ''If you come up with anything better, I sure as hell would like to know about it. The big risk in all this is my belief that nothing will go wrong, and I have given the president my assurances that the mission can be accomplished. If it does fail, the president and I take the fall and it'll be goddamned out in the open if our cover story breaks down.''

9

**Tsingdai Air Base, Beijing Military District
People's Republic of China
October 3, 2:00 P.M.**

Colonel Jin Fan of the 23rd Air Defense Regiment of the
Zhongkuo Shemin Taifang Tsunputai—Air Force of the
People's Liberation Army—was beside himself with anticipation as the tight three-plane formation of Ukrainian Su-
27s swept low across the airfield at near-sonic speed, the
sounds of their engines trying futilely to catch up with the
sleek ex–Soviet Union air superiority fighters.

The Tsingdai Air Base was the latest addition to the
modernization of the PRC's air defense system, and even
as the three Flanker-Bs broke sharply for their landing, construction crews were still working along the sides of two
of the five 5,000-meter runways. One pair of parallel landing strips was aligned with the direction of the prevalent
winds that normally flowed down from the high Inner Mongolian Plateau to the far west. Another pair crossed at forty-
five-degree angles to provide for the crosswinds that
frequently were part of winter storms, and a single right-
angle runway split the center of all four to allow for the
rare occasion when normal wind conditions were not present. Each reinforced concrete runway was equipped with

high-speed turnoffs that led to wide taxiways. They, in turn, provided easy access to either the operational and hangar areas or the multitude of dispersal revetments positioned around the inside perimeter of the air base.

Directly in the center of the one-hundred-and-twelve-square-kilometer complex, the five-story-high control tower sat on the top of a tapered, reinforced concrete column, a huge white golf tee of a structure that also supported a mini-forest of communication and navigational antennae. On the northwest corner of the field, three house-sized white fiberglass domes enclosed sophisticated air search and altitude-finding radars, and each primary runway offered an instrument landing system that provided for all-weather operation.

The air base, itself, sat in isolation from the villages to the north of Beijing, and those previously within fifty kilometers of the base had been leveled to provide the necessary security zone.

Colonel Fan, a Han Chinese whose father had been a pilot with the same fighter regiment and whose grandfather had fought alongside Mao's troops immediately after the Great War, was a lean, bronzed, muscular man who was perfectly proportioned. Thus, despite his diminutive five-foot-four height, he gave the impression of being a much larger air warrior. There were no shortcomings to his height or his 145-pound weight, for he fit a cockpit well and there was no fat to add to high-G discomfort.

A small military band was off to one side of where he stood in front of the operations building, and behind him were his three squadron commanders, all as eager as he to receive the trio of Sukhoi OKB fighters. The aircraft were the first of twenty-seven that had been purchased from the *Voyenne-Vozdushnyye Sily*—Air Force of the Ukraine—and while the PRC had been operating an even more advanced ex-Soviet interceptor, the MiG-31, the Flankers offered performance capabilities that would dovetail nicely into the varied tactical air requirements of air defense. Fan and two of his squadron leaders had already attended a transition course in the Ukraine, and after a short welcoming ceremony they would take the Flankers back into the air in a flyby that would symbolize the transfer of the first aircraft and those to come. Thus, Fan was outfitted in his flight gear, a rare departure from the protocol normally associated with ceremonial events.

The three Flankers taxied up in precise nose-to-tail formation and, on order from the flight commander, swung in unison to park wingtip-to-wingtip within ten feet of the smiling face of Fan and the small welcoming party, the drooping noses of the big fighters dipping with brake application as if to bow in greeting. Chinese ground crewmen hurriedly placed egress ladders in position; the pilots disembarked and paused a moment to form a line-abreast, then marched smartly across the short distance to face the Chinese and salute.

"Colonel, I am Major Vasily Utgoff and I present my respects, along with these three magnificent machines, to you and to the People's Republic of China."

Fan's enlisted translator conveyed the greeting in Mandarin Chinese, and Fan's reply in perfect Russian.

"Thank you, Comrade Major. I am Colonel Fan. On behalf of the People's Republic and the Twenty-Third Air Defense Regiment of the Air Force of the People's Liberation Army, I compliment you on your delivery of these three advance aircraft and welcome you to Tsingdai."

The Chinese contingent led the Ukrainians into a small conference room within the operations building, and the two pilot groups sat on opposite sides of a long table covered with red cotton cloth. Major Utgoff handed over a packet of logbooks and records.

"These are the documents for each aircraft, along with operational and service manuals. There are no outstanding discrepancies, and all equipment is operational. And, if you will, sir, this is the receipt for your signature of acceptance.''

Fan bowed slightly as he accepted the packet. *No wonder the revolution failed along with the Soviet Union,* he thought, being careful not to show the contempt he felt in his heart. All three Ukrainians were overweight and puffy in the face, obviously too indulgent of themselves. Their pressure suits barely constrained bodies that were ill-suited for high-speed aerial combat. A warrior should never allow himself to get into such a condition. Fan gave the receipts a cursory signature and slid them back across the table to Major Utgoff.

Bottles of mineral water sat on the table. Fan half-filled seven glasses and passed them to his pilots and the Ukrainians. Standing, he offered a toast. "May the friendship of the People's Republic of China with the Independent State of the Ukraine grow to the benefit of our people as the revolution continues.''

Despite the impolite reference to the ideals of Communism, a way of life all but abandoned in the Ukraine, Utgoff and his two pilots stood, lifted their glasses and responded, "To the people.''

Enlisted orderlies entered with steaming bowls of cabbage soup, plates of spicy meats and boiled bread, placing them before the Ukrainians. Several large bottles of Tsing Tao beer were also served.

"Nourish and refresh yourselves,'' Fan invited. "Tonight you will be our guests in Beijing, and it will be our honor to share with you the culture of Chairman Mao.'' Now that the transfer of the Su-27s had been completed, Fan was not overly concerned that the former brothers in the ideals of Marx and Lenin would take offense at his remarks. The Ukrainians seemed to ignore his comment and eagerly took to the food and beer. It had been a long flight from their air base near Mukacheve, and it had involved two in-flight refuelings. Their primary concern at the moment was the alleviation of their dehydration and the filling of their empty stomachs. Despite the fact that the cabbage soup was a world apart from that served in their country, it was not unpleasant, and the boiled bread had a heaviness that reminded them of their own as it sank into their stomachs with all of the consistency of billiard balls. If only the outside had been crusty instead of so moist.

"This is most filling, Colonel. We are in need of such a meal," Utgoff complimented. What he would like to have said was "This is garbage, Fan, but after six hours in the air, we would gladly eat fried dog if it were served." Inside, he winced. Perhaps the fried dog would come later. He and his pilots would be in China for another twenty-four hours.

The Chinese sipped mineral water while the Ukrainians ate, each side making casual remarks in a show of a companionship that actually did not exist. It was a necessary thing, and officers at such levels should not take it upon themselves to express their real feelings. Political correctness was not confined to the western countries. The Ukrainians sold their early Su-27 models because they were in desperate need of money. The Chinese eagerly purchased them, for they were sold at bargain prices and the sales included an abundance of spare parts and a condition that the Ukrainian technicians would train Chinese ground service personnel. But the association stopped there. The Ukrainians considered the mainland Chinese to be idiots who would most probably lose the aircraft in pilot-induced crashes. The Chinese considered the Ukrainians to be traitors to the revolution who would now sell their souls if that was required to fill their bellies.

Within a short while, an enlisted technician entered and spoke softly to Colonel Fan. Fan nodded and dismissed the man before standing. "Comrades, if you will excuse us, we will complete the most enjoyable climax to this exchange."

The Flankers had been fully serviced and the Ukrainian insignia painted over. In place were the red-star-and-bar insignias of the Air Force of the People's Liberation Army.

Fan and his pilots gave the three aircraft a careful walk-around, inspecting all the nooks and crannies within the wheel wells and paying careful attention to the control surfaces and inspection plates. The Su-27 was an impressive machine, over thirty tons in weight when fully loaded and outwardly quite similar to the American F-15 Eagle. The nose drooped a bit more and, in typical Soviet fashion, the airplane had a massive, heavy look.

The cockpit of the early B-model was less than state of the art, featuring the conventional dials and indicators of the postwar period that had since been replaced in later variants by cathode-ray tubes and vertical indicators. There was a well-designed HUD—heads-up display—and the Russian K-36DM zero/zero ejection seat could safely punch out the pilot even as the Flanker sat in its chocks.

Fan carefully avoided the protruding black and yellow ejection handles that would stick up between his legs once he was strapped in. His personal ground crewman placed a small pillow behind him in the small of his back. Everything within the cockpit was the same as it had been in the two-place Su-27UB trainer he had flown at Mukacheve. Fan felt right at home, and his juices were flowing.

The Chinese taxied out together, and Fan took the takeoff spot on the runway. There was little wind. Cleared for take-off, he advanced the throttles, pushing them deliberately past the afterburner detent, and felt the kick of over 54,000 pounds of thrust. He carried no external stores; thus the thrust easily exceeded his weight and he was propelled forward in an ever-increasing state of acceleration. After just 600 feet of ground roll, he eased the stick back, and at 750 feet the airplane departed Mother Earth. Fan pulled into a vertical climb and, fifty seconds later, he pushed over to level at 53,000 feet. A similarly loaded F-15, if one had taken off in company with him, would be some two thousand feet below him.

As prearranged, he and the other two pilots spent fifteen minutes in individual air work, familiarizing themselves with the single-seat Su-27. Then Fan called for joinup and led the formation in a supersonic dive toward the Tsingdai Air Base. They leveled at two thousand feet and reduced their speed to 750 kilometers per hour (468 knots).

"Tsingdai, this is Colonel Fan for flyby."

The sonic booms had already alerted everyone at Tsingdai, although they had originated high in the stratosphere and no damage was caused except for several cracked windows in classrooms on the far west side of the base.

Tsingdai tower replied, "Cleared for flyby, west to east. Do not descend below two hundred meters. No reported traffic."

Two hundred meters? Fan scornfully repeated to himself. The Manchu pussy in the tower would smell his afterburners when they dusted off the Ukrainians who were undoubtedly watching.

"Here they come," commented Major Utgoff, adding mentally, *the shitheads.*

Contrary to tower instructions, the Chinese came in from the north at one hundred meters, straight across the center of the field. They lifted momentarily to clear the tower, and just before reaching the operations building they cooked off their afterburners and pulled into a vertical climb.

Utgoff shook his head. "We apparently forgot to point out where the rudder pedals are to the right wingman." The number-two Flanker was woefully out of position and obviously struggling to match Fan's erratic lead. The skilled Ukrainians would have held a much tighter and more consistent position. "I give them ninety days and those three idiots will need replacement aircraft." Utgoff insured that his last remark was out of earshot of Fan's interpreter.

The Ukrainians continued to watch with interest as the three Su-27s landed. Utgoff was beginning to enjoy the show. Fan had undoubtedly wanted to impress the Ukrainians, but now his number-two man, the last to land, was coming in high and fast. "I can't believe that he is going to overshoot a five-thousand-meter runway," Utgoff said aside to one of his pilots as the Su-27 floated to a touchdown well past the halfway mark of the strip. The pilot immediately deployed the drag chute and stood on his brakes. The heat generated by the heavy braking caused the right main wheel to erupt into a yellow-orange flame, closely followed by smoke and licks of flame from the left gear.

The crash crew was much more proficient than the pilots. They had anticipated the extended landing and were on scene immediately. The hapless pilot was at least still on the runway, and he quickly jumped over the side as the crash crew enveloped the burning wheels with white foam, starving the flames of oxygen and putting out the fires.

Colonel Fan, egressing his aircraft in front of the Ukrainians, walked stiffly by them without commenting. Inside the operations building, he drafted an order and had a special courier take it to the headquarters of the 23rd Air Defense Regiment. Within twenty-four hours, the squadron commander who had just embarrassed the colonel and seriously damaged a brand-new acquisition would be on his way to a Tibetan communications station, his flying days over and his rank reduced to that of a lieutenant.

That evening, a very formal Colonel Fan escorted the Ukrainians to the Beijing Opera, where they were entertained by a cast of players who sang, danced, mimed and enthusiastically performed unbelievable acrobatics. When the house lights came on, Utgoff turned to thank their host, but an enlisted aide explained that Colonel Fan had left during the performance to attend to "urgent official business."

10

Joshua Dunne sat firmly strapped in Darkstar One, holding his brakes while the yellow shirts connected the shuttle arm of his nose landing gear to the catapult shuttle. Off to his right, Kohn was positioning Darkstar Two on the number-two catapult. Each had completed four dusk in-flight refueling hookups and an arrested landing back aboard the *Lincoln*. Now, as a dress rehearsal, they would blast off the bow of the *Lincoln* in the dark of night, rendezvous with the Grumman S-3 tanker, take on a token amount of fuel and return to the ship. It would be the last time they intended to fly prior to the actual mission.

All of the operational and safety checks had been completed, and Dunne turned on his running lights to signal the shooter that he was ready. During the moment it took for the shooter to give the signal to launch, Dunne swept his eyes over the interior of the cockpit. One last check of his control tab settings, for the launch would be hands-off, the success of the launch depending upon the settings of the tabs and the correct weight of the airplane set into the launch computer. With the two inputs, he would accelerate to 170 knots within 1.6 seconds and find himself over open water in a slightly nose-high, wing-level attitude. At that point he would unfold his right hand and grab the control stick while simultaneously releasing the throttle catapult bar and positioning his left hand on the throttles to insure proper throttle operation on the climbout.

There had been little light on the flight deck; now there was absolutely none, and he flew through the black void by concentrating on the HUD. The green translucent numbers, ladders and lines told him all he needed to know about the attitude and performance of the Sea Scorpion. He was passing one thousand feet when Kohn joined on his right side, and together they continued to climb.

The *Lincoln* was just clearing the southern edge of the strait between mainland China and Taiwan, the Chinese coast only fifty miles to the west. The carrier would be in the South China Sea for the recovery.

"Darkstar One, take angels three-zero, vector three-one-zero for Texaco. Over."

Dunne repeated back the instructions. They were high enough now to see pinpoints of light along the China coast, but they would remain far enough offshore to avoid concerning the PRC. U.S. operations in these waters were routine.

Somewhere within a fifty-mile radius, an air control Grumman E-2C Hawkeye was orbiting at angels 30—thirty thousand feet—providing not only routine radar and electronic surveillance for the *Lincoln* and her escorts but tactical control of the refueling operation. The Hawkeye held both the tanker S-3 and the two climbing F-117Ns. At one of the air control consoles, a female lieutenant would be conducting the intercept and monitoring the refueling.

"Darkstar," she called, "Texaco bearing three-one-two, forty. Over."

"Darkstar, roger." The numbers on the HUD indicated that Dunne and Kohn were passing 26,000 feet. They leveled at 30,000.

"Darkstar, vector three-two-two. Texaco ahead at twenty three, indicating two-five-zero knots."

Ten minutes later, Dunne had the tanker's lights and pulled up to plug into the port refueling basket. Kohn rode easily to his left. Reaching down for the probe switch, he set it on EXTEND. From the top of the fuselage, just a few inches behind the cockpit, a narrow door retracted and the refueling probe eased forward until Dunne could see its tip two feet ahead of the windscreen. The male navy-type probe had been installed in place of the standard USAF female receptacle formerly located in the same position on the USAF models. The hydraulically operated probe and its mechanism required a bit more space; consequently the F-117N carried fifty gallons less fuel in the fuselage than the F-117A, an amount not considered critical for most missions.

Dunne closed on the moonlit basket, a woven steel funnel at the end of a seventy-five-foot feed hose. Using gentle control movements and minute throttle adjustments, he placed his probe within the basket and eased it forward. The slight slackening of the feed hose indicated a good connection, and Dunne held his position.

"Passin' gas," Texaco reported.

For several minutes, Dunne watched his fuel quantity gauges indicate flow. Satisfied that everything was in order, he backed away. "Thanks, Texaco."

"It was good for me, Darkstar. But next time you have to buy me dinner first."

"That's a deal." Dunne slid away to starboard as Kohn approached the basket. She also plugged in on her first try, took on a thousand pounds and unplugged.

The two Sea Scorpions rejoined and dove back into the night. Dunne reported to their control Hawkeye. "Watchdog, exercise complete. Have Big Mother on the TACAN; verify one-nine-four, five-seven miles."

"Watchdog confirms. Do you desire vectors?"

"Negative; request permission to go over to Big Mother."

"Granted, Darkstar; have a pleasant evening."

Within the fuselage of the Hawkeye, the controller watched the IFF signal of the two Sea Scorpions close on the *Lincoln*. When they were still forty miles out, two strangers appeared from over the Chinese coast. "Where'd they come from?" she asked herself and began identification procedures. The *Lincoln* had nothing else in the air. They had to be bogies, strangers and possibly hostile, and clicking off Mach 1.7 at twenty thousand feet. The *Lincoln* undoubtedly also held them through the data links from the Hawkeye. The carrier combat center would have the same radar picture she had. But the two F-117Ns would not, and the two bogies were streaking right toward them. Could the bogies have radar contact or be under the direction of Chinese air defense controllers, and did *they* have contact? She reported to the *Lincoln* first. "Big Mother, Watchdog, bogies at two-five-five, sixty miles designated Bogie One and Bogie Two. Break. Darkstar One, Watchdog, did you copy? Over."

The ship replied, "Roger, Watchdog, launching standby CAP. Over to you on TAC Four." The ship always had two ready F-14s on five-minute alert whenever they were steaming this close to the PRC, and now the ready CAP—combat air patrol aircraft—were launched.

Dunne had switched to the ship's arrival control frequency. Consequently, he and Kohn heard nothing.

The Hawkeye controller picked up the two F-14s as they came off the catapults. "Digger One, vector two-four-five, take angels two-zero, buster. Over."

The F-14s would be climbing in burner to twenty thousand feet and then run their intercept at maximum speed.

Watching the situation from his vantage point in the *Lincoln*'s combat air control center, Blackjack Paterson watched the two unknowns closing fast on Dunne and

Kohn. He turned to the duty officer. "You think they have radar contact?"

"We don't; how could they have?"

Paterson was not happy. The F-117Ns should be invisible to any China-based radar, and the pair of strangers was too far out to have any return. They might possibly pick up a faint signal at five or six miles but not at thirty-five. Yet they were heading straight for the F-117Ns. He ordered the duty officer, "Have Darkstar take evasive action immediately."

The report of the two bogies had been relayed to the air wing commander along with the order to launch the CAP, and now the CAG stood beside Paterson. "I don't believe this," he muttered.

Everyone in the CACC listened as the Hawkeye directed the intercept. The F-14s had radar contact and were locked on with their Phoenix fire control systems. Each carried two of the long-range air-to-air missiles. Should the fire order be given, the two strangers were dead meat. But they had displayed no hostile intent and were over international waters.

The *Lincoln* issued a warning on the international guard frequencies. "Aircraft at twenty thousand feet, heading one-five-six, forty-eight miles off coast of People's Republic of China, you are entering air operations space of United States Navy battle group. Turn ninety degrees to either side of present course or you will be considered hostile. Identify yourselves. Over." The order had gone out in Chinese, delivered by an enlisted language specialist. He repeated the transmission in English.

The bogies were threatening to merge with the F-117Ns' IFF signals.

"Darkstar, turn right immediately, maximum descend to angels ten, reason: unidentified air traffic. Expedite!"

Instantly Dunne banked sharply right, cut back his power and dove for the deck. Kohn had also heard the transmission and followed closely. Suddenly, both aircraft were rocked by a sharp blast of air turbulence, and two black objects flashed overhead, their afterburners lighting up the night like high noon.

"Who are *they*?" Kohn asked, obviously startled.

Dunne was furious. "Big Mother, where did those come from? Why weren't we alerted sooner? We damn near had a midair up here!"

Paterson watched the bogies turn toward the coast. The F-14s were tracking them in firing position. He monitored the carrier's reply to Dunne.

"Darkstar, the two bogies are heading for the coastline. We had coverage, but events happened too quickly to warn you. Sorry about that."

"Sorry about that?" Dunne almost yelled into his mike. "Piss poor, Big Mother."

"Understand, Darkstar; you're Charlie for landing. Big Mother's base course one-seven-seven. The sky's all yours. Promise."

"It sure as hell better be."

Paterson was waiting in his cabin when Dunne and Kohn stormed in. They had resisted the urge to stop by the air control center and raise holy hell. First of all, they had received evasive orders in time—barely in time. Two, they allegedly were civilians, and butting heads with the air wing commander would not have endeared them to the top-ranking air officer. Third, the real problem wasn't that they had just escaped from a possible midair collision; it was that they may have been purposely intercepted. That would mean they were detected, and *that* was not good for their mission, whatever the hell it was. And that was exactly what Dunne wanted to ask Paterson. "Admiral, did you see what happened?"

"Yes." Paterson waved Dunne and Kohn to chairs. "I was in combat with the air wing commander. Those two bogies sprung up out of nowhere and were making better than one thousand knots. They closed on you within three minutes of initial detection.''

''Three minutes is a loooong time.''

''Yes, it is—from your standpoint. It caught everybody by surprise. The Hawkeye should not have released you from his control until you were in the pattern. You should not have asked him to.''

Dunne realized that was so. The fault wasn't all the ship's.

''The ship thought the Hawkeye was warning you; Hawkeye thought we had you. Situation screwup. Plenty of blame to go around.''

Dunne's sails suddenly lost most of their wind. ''I'm sorry. What really bothers me is, did they know we were there?''

''I don't think so. They were heading for the ship the instant they left the coast. So were you, and you were descending right through their twenty-thousand-foot cruise altitude. Your paths crossed. It was probably going to be a flyby to impress us and let us know that they know we're here. It wasn't a hostile move; it was an air traffic control problem.''

''You're convinced of that?''

''Certainly. Ask yourself, 'would they have tried to ram you if they were on a legitimate intercept?' They would have busted their ass—and yours—if you had not made that last-minute move.''

''It makes sense,'' Dunne weakly replied.

''Also, we sent them a warning message in Chinese on international distress. The instant they heard it, they turned and hauled ass for Mother China.''

''I hope that's the case,'' Kohn added.

''Look, we never held you on radar, nor did Watchdog. All air control was accomplished by means of your IFF return.''

''Shit, we broadcast the code in plain language.''

"Yes, but their equipment picks up their transponders, not ours. They only need to identify themselves."

"What do you figure they were?" Kohn asked.

"MiG-31s—possibly Su-27s. We know the Chinese have them, and they're capable of such speeds. Nothing else they have will do it."

"Maybe we should have had our radar reflectors installed," Dunne observed. The F-117 had provisions for a small rectangular reflector on top of its fuselage, normally used for safety purposes when flying U.S. airways. Such a device made the airplane radar-visible to air traffic controllers. It was never used on actual missions.

"No, I think not," Paterson decided. "The ship needed to work you without it, and our flying is done until the fun time comes up."

Dunne knew Paterson was right. Paterson was always right.

"So," Paterson continued, "join me for a bowl of ice cream? Cherry-vanilla. Right from the crew's galley. It's delicious."

And it was. Especially with chocolate syrup.

October 4, 8:20 A.M.

The bow of the *Lincoln* was aligned exactly with the center of the eastern passage into Victoria Harbor. Off to port, the eastern edge of Hong Kong Island was displaying the gold, silver and red rays of early dawn. They were reflecting from the windows of luxury houses peppering the Big Wave Bay area. Normally, one did not think of beaches when considering Hong Kong as a destination, but this eastern side, including the Shek-O strip, was a favorite spot for sun worshipers and water lovers. Wide, white stretches of sand led up to a beachside resort featuring kiosks, barbecue pits, lifeguards and changing rooms with showers and toilets. The shops and houses beyond the beach reached uphill in a cluster of painted stucco that gave Shek-O an almost Mediterranean aspect. Even now, in early October, the daily high temperatures were in the low eighties. Those living in the area were only a short underground ride from the center of the city. To starboard, the low purple hills of Mang Kung Uk peninsula rose just beyond the quiet waters of Junk Bay that, true to its name, provided a shallow anchorage for countless clusters of Chinese junks. Dead ahead but still some 14,000 yards away and across the world's most hospitable harbor, the principal runway of the Kai Tak International Airport jutted outward from Kowloon, an engineering marvel of reinforced concrete ribbon that had been laid on top of soil reclaimed from the harbor bottom and nearby hills. The entire harbor and airport were bathed in a thin white layer of early morning mist, and the hills around undoubtedly held a number of painters capturing the scene on raw silk with bamboo painting sticks, some with horsehair bristles, and sable brushes. If the *Lincoln* were to continue on course, it would drive right up onto the runway, but the American warship was moving at only seven knots and would slow even further to turn into the center of the harbor while still well clear of the end of the runway. At the far end of the landing strip, a giant Boeing 747 was settling toward the strip, a fat silver and blue condor, its nose raised and its multi-wheeled landing system reaching for the concrete. Another was climbing out, its low-roar fan-jets lifting it rapidly. By the time it passed over the *Lincoln*, it would be entering the base of the four-thousand-foot cloud layer.

The harbor, itself, was an almost indescribable teeming mass of traffic, to the casual observer a chaotic mixture of every known type of floating vessel. Literally, hundreds of sampans were crisscrossing the surface on their way to begin a thousand different chores; a half dozen ocean freighters and container ships were maneuvering to either make a pierside berth or thread their way out of the passage. Several would soon be abreast the *Lincoln* on their voyages to the ports of the world.

Passenger ferries, ranging from the small, sculled wooden flatboats of individual entrepreneurs to the large, green-and-white, familiar steel vessels of the Star Ferry Company, were winding their way among the other traffic, while two white-hulled cruise ships lay quietly alongside piers on the near side of the harbor. The port of Hong Kong, third in activity only to New York and San Francisco, was wide awake despite the early hour. There was not one square inch of settled water.

Several hundred sailors lined the flight deck of the impressive *Lincoln*, their dress whites providing a human gunwale around the flight deck of the giant carrier. The air wing aircraft were precisely arranged around the edges of the deck, their dominant gray color providing a more ominous tone to the general festive tone of the arriving warship.

Mount Parker, its peak trying mightily to touch the base of the low overcast, lay just abeam to port as the *Lincoln* squeezed through the narrowest part of the passage and began her slow swing port toward her anchorage.

On the bridge, the quartermasters checked progress by taking bearings on preselected fixed landmarks around the harbor, while precision radar within the darkened bowels of the ship's combat center backed up the visual sightings with their own radar fixes. There was a Chinese harbor pilot on board but, true to the traditions of every navy, the commanding officer was still responsible for the movement of the giant ship. At precisely the right spot, when all bearings were in agreement with the location of the assigned anchorage, the 97,000-ton warship lay dead in the water, released her bow anchor and let the current help set it firmly into the sandy soil of the harbor bottom. Then she set her second anchor for insurance against high winds. When properly secured, with enough chain-slack to allow her anchor flukes to grab a firm hold on the bottom, she would require over seven million square feet of harbor surface, roughly one-fifth of a square mile, to insure an unimpeded 360-degree swing.

Practically the entire perimeter of the harbor, broken only by the east and west entryways, was covered with piers, wharves, loading docks that featured cranes twenty stories high, and stretches of waterfront shops and high rises.

Dunne and Kohn had joined Paterson on the flag bridge during the entry into the harbor. All three had enjoyed the sights, sounds and odors of Hong Kong before, the admiral a veteran of over thirty visits while on active duty.

"Damn," uttered Paterson, "every time is like the first time. You just don't believe it until you see it."

"Awesome," Kohn added. "I don't know how they do it but look over there: they've found a spot for another high rise—and there. Some day the island will just sink."

Dunne shared their disbelief. "It's Asia's Oahu."

"No. Oahu's Honolulu-Waikiki area is a primitive, laid-back Polynesian village compared to this. Almost seven million people living within a thousand square kilometers." Paterson emphasized his comment with a wide swing of one arm. "What a loss to the Brits, the most industrious and effective capitalistic society in the world. It's the last outpost. The sun has finally set on the world's greatest empire."

Over the MC-1 general address system came the order, "Secure the special sea and anchor detail. The officer of the deck is shifting his watch to the quarterdeck. Liberty commences at zero-nine-hundred for all off-duty sections."

The whitehats manning the sides dissolved into a happy jumble of running, catcalling sailors, each intending to be the first man ashore. The slit-skirts of Kowloon were already adjusting their prices.

Paterson kept his eyes sweeping the harbor as he spoke. "At ten o'clock, one of the ship's choppers will take you two to Kai Tak customs. I have your passports with visas and some Hong Kong currency. Customs will pass you right through. Take overnight bags. You're on your own today if you want to do the tourist bit. Keep it low key. Take a cab to the Regent Hotel—''

"Oh—first class," Kohn interrupted.

Paterson continued, ''. . . we keep a suite there. You're already registered under Dunne.''

Kohn held up a finger for attention. ''I would prefer separate rooms.''

"The suite's not being used. Rooms run between twenty-three hundred and three-thousand Hong Kong, that's about four-fifty American. I'm certain that everything's booked. We're big boys and girls, I'm sure. There're separate bedrooms. And we do have some security measures installed in the suite. Things may start to get a bit dicey starting tomorrow morning.''

Dunne could not resist. ''Dicey?''

Paterson replied, ''Every major power in the world has agents in Hong Kong. They collide in the streets. Every Westerner is considered an opportunity until the Chinese spooks satisfy themselves that they're tailing tourists. As soon as you clear customs, a dozen agents will know your names, whom you work for and even that you rode the *Lincoln* into Victoria Harbor. That's why your cover has you as tech reps.''

"For Lockheed," Dunne added, although he didn't know why.

"The S-3s. Lockheed aircraft. Natural assignment.''

"Ship's personnel don't go through customs. It's all in the agreement with respect to visiting warships. They don't need passports for a short visit,'' Dunne continued. ''Why don't we go ashore in the liberty boats? Supposedly, we're under a DOD contract and should be afforded the same privileges.''

Paterson's body language telegraphed his dislike for being questioned. He rubbed one hand across the top of his head and exhaled through his lips. "Every boat that leaves this ship goes to a designated military landing. It's an open compound but staffed by shore patrol and civilian police. All of the dregs of Hong Kong society are waiting just beyond the gate. Both of you have been here before. You know that."

Dunne would not quit. "It still seems less conspicuous than landing at Kai Tak in a U.S. Navy helicopter."

Kohn could certainly agree.

Paterson put an end to the discussion with two words: "Trust me."

They could do that.

"Are you going to be joining us?" Dunne asked.

"No. Tomorrow morning, no later than eight, check with the front desk. You will have a message. We'll meet later."

Dunne thumbed through his passport. The last stamped page contained a visa to the People's Republic of China. "Whoa, what's this?" He held up the open page.

"Patience. Just read your mail when it comes."

Kohn checked hers. The same. "We *are* riding the boat out of here?" she questioned.

Paterson chuckled. "You're the only reason the boat is here. Now, get out of my sight for a while. The OOD will let you know when the chopper is ready."

Dunne and Kohn left Paterson on the bridge. On the way to their rooms, Kohn said, "We may not know what we're up to, yet, but I sure enjoy the perks. The Regent, a day off in Hong Kong. Fun money." She leafed through the stack of bills in one of the envelopes Paterson had given them. Her face fell. "Not enough for a visit to Mohan's. He could make me a great cashmere coat by this evening. Fooey."

"Too hot for cashmere."

"Not back in the States."

"Count your blessings," Dunne admonished, "You're

about to be wined and dined by a connoisseur of things Hong Kong.''

''At government expense,'' Kohn reminded.

''Only for the material things. I shall supply the ambiance from within my own resources.''

''And those are?''

''A raconteur's sleazy knowledge of this magnificent area and a naval officer's gracious manner when escorting a lady.''

''I'm not a lady; I'm a fighter pilot.''

''A *soft* fighter pilot, I must add.''

Kohn knew they were both faking the lighthearted patter, but Dunne's last remark could signal a new dimension to their relationship. If it was serious. *Please don't let it be.* It wasn't a silent prayer, just a reminder that she was feeling much too comfortable with the personal aspects of the mission.

The SH-60 Seahawk settled onto the Kai Tak pad as if it were landing on a bed of duck eggs. Dunne, Kohn and two of the *Lincoln's* officers were escorted into customs and passed through with only a cursory check of their passports. He and Kohn caught the first available taxi.

''The Regent,'' Dunne directed. The taxi worked south toward the tip of the Kowloon peninsula and the city proper, Tsimshatsui, pronounced ''Chim Sa Choy''—sharp sand point. As the taxi intercepted Salisbury Road, the perimeter throughway, the sunlit majesty of Victoria Harbor eased into view, superimposed against the unbelievable backdrop of the shiny steel and glass high-rises dominating the harbor side of Hong Kong Island.

''It sort of gives a whole new feeling to the word 'awesome,' doesn't it?'' Kohn ventured.

The Regent Hotel sat on the very tip of a small, man-made extension of the peninsula with an unencumbered view of the harbor and the great island beyond.

The desk clerk responded to Dunne's identification with

a sweeping smile of welcome. "Yes, Mister Dunne, your suite is ready. Do enjoy your stay with us." There were two keys in the envelope, and the suite was on the harbor side, tenth floor, just high enough to be above the street noises—had there been any. But the Regent had the prime location, and the bustle of Kowloon started well behind the hotel. To the east there was only one other hotel, the New World. To the west lay the modernistic buildings housing the Cultural Complex, the Planetarium and the Space Museum. From the suite, with its southern orientation, Kowloon could not even be seen.

Kohn walked directly to the glass wall that overlooked the harbor. "This is magnificent. What do you suppose Paterson pays for this on a year-round basis?"

"Not a penny. We are guests of the United States' taxpayers, and I suspect they expect us to earn our keep in such a place."

Kohn turned to look at Dunne. "I have a feeling we'll consider all this an underpayment after the briefing."

Dunne cocked his head in mild agreement.

"So! We enjoy." Kohn selected her bedroom, and Dunne knew she would be a few minutes freshening up. It was the universal trait of all females. He walked into his bedroom and placed his small bag on the bed. The decor, as in the great room, was contemporary Chinese with carved mahogany and teak furnishings, most black-lacquered to a depth of an eighth-inch and all set among red and gold walls that displayed watercolor-on-silk murals depicting harbor activity. The classic oriental brush strokes created masterpieces of design and composition. None were superfluous; instead, each was essential, but no more, to the depiction of ancient China. Two sets of floor-length drapes, one sheer, the other heavy and light-blocking, could be drawn across the glass wall. Traditional Chinese music played softly from concealed speakers, and it would have taken an electronic microscope to discern any dust. A subtle flower fragrance, possibly that of gardenias, completed the sensory experience.

The living area featured a curved sectional sofa, eight white leather units arranged together in an expansive semicircle facing the harbor. Behind the sofa, a narrow waist-table matched the curve but fell short of each end of the sofa by about a foot. The table supported two end-lamps and a solitary red stone Buddha that faced back toward the entry. Two low vases of assorted fresh flowers were to each side of the Buddha. Along the entry wall were several occasional chairs and, in an alcove, a wet bar.

Dunne sat in the center of the sofa and leaned over to the oval coffee table in front of him. There was a control unit with a number of buttons set into the marble top. He pushed the one marked TV. Ahead of him, a white screen dropped slowly from the ceiling, and behind the sofa a projection unit emerged from overhead. The sheer drapes closed, their weave softening the outside light, and the screen became alive with one of Hong Kong's TV channels. It was Oprah Winfrey, Chinese-dubbed. Dunne pushed the TV button a second time and everything returned to its stowage space. The wet bar had a more immediate attraction. He was stirring a Bloody Mary when Kohn returned. "What may I fix you?" he asked.

Kohn spun around on her heels, taking in all 360 degrees of the inside-outside view. Dunne fantasized that she was wearing a full skirt.

"Plain soda over a full glass of ice," she ordered. "Twist of lime, please. No straw."

Dunne had never seen her little-girl side before.

They sat on the sofa, sipping their drinks and letting their senses become completely seduced by the moment. "I could handle this," Kohn observed, drawing her legs under her.

"If only I could shake the feeling of being a calf undergoing fattening before the slaughter."

"Hey, that's an attitude I don't like."

Dunne laughed. "It does make you feel guilty, doesn't it?"

"No. That night arrival aboard the *Lincoln* paid for this. I don't feel guilty at all. The next time I may plow right into the ramp—but I will have lived." She raised her soda in a toast to the thought.

"Now, that's an attitude *I* don't like."

Kohn sobered. "Don't you ever think about things like that?"

"Of course. Every carrier jock carries with him the vision of the real world. But I don't *worry* about such things. If I did, I'd not be here. There's a difference between healthy concern and worry."

"And what's that?"

"Professionalism."

"True enough. I didn't mean to sound melodramatic. It just sounded appropriate, you know, the devil-may-care guise of us fighter pilots."

"Out of place in this day and age."

"Sadly, I agree with you. But you know, Joshua, I can't imagine myself doing anything other than military flying. I really love it. I love the exhilaration, the challenge, the accomplishment, the overall sense of doing something that not everyone wants to do, or can do. You must feel the same way."

"I did until the day I had to punch out and my rear-seater died."

"It wasn't your fault."

"You never quite believe that. You keep thinking that maybe there was something you could have done differently, something you could have anticipated. It adds a very serious dimension to flying."

"You seemed happy to go back to it—in the Lear."

"That was different. At times, that was fun."

"And this isn't?"

"Hell, in a sense it is. You know that. We're special people, Frosty, with more guts than brains in all probability."

"You didn't hesitate to sign up when we talked to the admiral."

"No. I have a lot of respect for him. If he said he needs me, I feel that he does. And I admit that the old juices are flowing. I just don't know how I'm going to feel when we find out just what we're going to do."

"We have one more right of refusal. But will it really make any difference?"

"I don't know. You're proud of what you do, Sheila, and I admire you for that. I've always been proud of what I've done. I love my country, and I still have a little-boy, wave-the-flag attitude in serving it. A lot of people think that is politically naive when it comes to special operations. And that's the area we're in, now. And I can't shake a certain feeling of self-doubt. What if I lose you on this mission? Two in a row for me."

Kohn did not like seeing Dunne depressed, and there was no reason for it—not yet, anyhow. "That's ridiculous. Whatever happens, even if it is the worst, I feel extremely confident on your wing. That's the nature of this life. Exposure. Accomplishment. Pride. I saw your character when you commanded the *Ford*. That was a test for any man. Besides, I talked you into this; it's not the other way around."

Dunne studied the remnants of his Bloody Mary. "Maybe I'm too old for this. This is a young man's work. Hell, the navy would never have let me strap on a jet if it hadn't been for Paterson. I don't even see how he did it."

"I've been involved in three operations for him, Joshua. He doesn't employ any young men, as you define them."

"Were they this type of operation?"

"I don't know. I don't know what this operation is. I do know that the admiral picks only the best, and the people he picks are those who are tailored for the job.''

"Do they all stay with him?"

"No. Several have left in my time. But they completed their assignments first.''

"How did Paterson feel about that?"

"No questions asked. They left with his good wishes.''

"He must have been concerned about security. One talker could have blown his operation.''

"Would you talk?" Kohn asked.

"No.''

"Do you feel you're the only person to have that kind of loyalty?''

"No, of course not.''

"End of discussion.''

Dunne agreed. He was probably just tired. They had flown late the previous night, talked long with Paterson and risen early to enjoy the entry into Hong Kong's harbor. "Well, why don't you decide what you want to do this afternoon and evening? I think I'm going to stretch out right here and enjoy the view, at least for a while.''

"What an old fud. I'm going shopping, and when I get back you'd best be in a better mood. We've one good day of liberty in this port, mate, and I intend to make the most of it. Then, Captain Dunne, my leader, it's party time!''

Dunne leaned back, placed his hands behind his head and let his eyes again roam the harbor. "Don't slam the door on your way out.''

Dunne was deep into his nap when Kohn returned.

"Wake up; time to mingle with the local populace!" Kohn emphasized her call with a clap of her hands.

Dunne sat up. "That was great. Best sleep I've had in a week. I need to brush my teeth.'' A small room-service cart was against one wall. On it was an empty coffee beaker and a small plate of half-eaten wheat toast.

"Before you do, take a look at this.'' Kohn was emptying two large shopping bags on the sofa. "Two silk blouses, three cashmere skirts and a sweater. My mission here is complete." She held the sweater across her chest. "Nice, huh?"

"You did that with house money?"

"Sure. You have enough to feed us."

The garments were nice, finely tailored of British wool and Chinese silk. "I don't suppose you bought me anything."

"I ran out of money."

"No credit cards?"

"We left those back at Nellis, remember?"

"Oh, yeah. I wonder why. Paterson has us using our own names."

Kohn shrugged. "He usually has a reason for everything he does. Go brush your teeth and let's hit the sights."

While Dunne was in the bathroom, Kohn called out, "Guess what? I was tailed all morning."

Dunne walked in, white foam in his mouth. "You sure?"

"Positive. I even rode the tube over to Hong Kong and back just to check. Chinese—as you might expect."

"Probably a routine surveillance. Paterson mentioned the possibility."

"He followed me all the way back to the hotel. I waited in the lobby until his cab drove up and he walked in."

"He knew you made him?"

"No, I was careful not to openly notice him."

"I wouldn't be overly concerned. Think this shirt is too wrinkled?"

Kohn wrinkled her nose. "Just because you slept in it?"

"I have a fresh one. I'll change."

Ten minutes later, they stepped from the elevator and crossed the lobby.

"See 'im?" Dunne asked quietly.

"No."

"Then either he was satisfied or someone else will pick

us up. We'll play it by ear. I think it was just a routine tail.''

The leisurely walk west past the Cultural Complex was an opportunity for Dunne to reintroduce himself to the sounds and smells of Victoria Harbor. The ride across to the island of Hong Kong on board the Star Ferry was a visual potpourri of water traffic and Hong Kong Chinese boat activity that had remained essentially the same for the last fifty years. In certain areas the harbor was practically paved with individual water taxis, all obeying some mysterious rules of the road that prevented what appeared to be the potential for scores of boat collisions just waiting to happen. Yet not even a gunwale was scratched as the boats passed within inches of one another. This was one place in the collection of world-class harbors where a pair of strong arms and a long sculling oar were definitely still in fashion.

Interspersed were the more modern hydrofoils, seemingly ignoring the slower traffic and counting on some unseen god to keep their way clear as they sped across the harbor.

The ferry was a lumbering green double-decker that crossed the harbor like a pregnant turtle, squatting deep in the water, its round bottom and blunt bow spreading white water ahead and beside it as it passed other traffic. The smallest craft rocked and pitched as they rode the wake, the standing scullers maintaining their balance as easily as one rode a bicycle on the streets of Kowloon.

The climbing sun had warmed the air and dissipated most of the cloud layer and now, at midday, was overhead and just a few degrees south. Human activity was at its apogee, and the streets and sidewalks of Hong Kong were covered with bumper-to-bumper traffic and shoulder-to-shoulder people, all in a hurry.

Dunne and Kohn took a pedicab to Stanley Street and disembarked in front of the Luk Yu restaurant, established in 1925 and remembered by Dunne as one of the premier dining spots in Central Hong Kong. Its four stories could seat 500 hungry patrons, and it was a favorite place for morning tea and dim sum, the delicious fried dumplings that came in a thousand varieties. The restaurant, named after the god of tea, had an ambiance that was still reminiscent of Hong Kong in the early colonial years, with lacquered chairs, mirrored cupboards, marble tables and even brass spittoons. Upon entering, Dunne and Kohn were directed to the third floor where a short, round waiter ushered them to a small table on the side overlooking Stanley Street and the bustling masses below. Brilliantly colored banners stretched below them, across from them and above them, many with one or two English words such as "Nikon" and "TV-VCRs" interspersed among the Chinese characters. One even sported the acronym RCA with its original listening-dog logo.

"We may have a slight problem here," Dunne advised, taking one of the two menus offered. There were no English translations of the dishes offered. "If I remember correctly, there are few if any waiters who speak English and, unlike many of the other places, they don't parade around the dishes for gringos like us to see and understand."

"Gringos?"

"You know what I mean. I don't know the Chinese equivalent."

Their waiter brought hot tea and stood by in anticipation of their order.

"You speak English?" Dunne asked.

The waiter shook his head, uttered "Ah" and held out his hand in a "wait" signal, fingers up and palm toward Dunne. Bowing and smiling, he hurried away only to return within the minute with a small girl by his side. She was perhaps eight and in Western dress, sweater and skirt. Her shiny black hair was square cut across the back, and dark brown eyes glistened with joy and innocence.

"I speak," she said without any hint of shyness. "You 'merican, yes?"

"Yes," Dunne replied. "Thank you. Many years ago I was here and had a dish—dim sum—with some kind of meat and cooked with tangerine peel. Do you still have it?"

"Oh, yes. All time, have dim sum. Is very good and favorite. My father will bring. For lady?"

Kohn looked at Dunne for help but the child interrupted, "I think maybe fried shrimp rolls, very delicious and will not crowd stomach. Best in all Hong Kong here. Very light and you do shopping later. Or maybe dim sum like gentleman? We have many kind."

Kohn smiled approval. "The shrimp rolls. They sound delicious."

The child translated the order to her father and he bowed rapidly several times before hurrying off.

"And now, a dining experience," Dunne declared, sitting back and patting his stomach.

"Dim sum and shrimp rolls? Okay for now, my leader, but I want some real chow for dinner."

"Chinese?"

"Of course, but the works. You know, soup, appetizer, a couple entrees, fortune cookies . . ."

"That you shall have. I know just the place."

Kohn lifted her cup of tea. "Salud."

11 ═══════════════════

Regent Hotel, Kowloon
October 5

Dunne stepped into the elevator at 7:45 A.M. and punched the lobby button. Kohn must still be asleep as there had been no noises coming from her bedroom area. No matter. He could check the front desk for the message from Paterson but was somewhat concerned that he had received no call, nor had the message light been flashing on the suite's master phone.

Initially he was alone, but on the fifth floor a young couple stepped in, dressed for exploring the area. Dunne judged them to be German by their speech, and they maintained polite smiles as the elevator reached the lobby and the doors slid open.

Kohn was waiting to board, looking refreshed in her gray jogging suit despite the dark stains of honest sweat around her neck. "Good morning, boss," she intoned, still breathing hard after her exercise. She stepped aside to talk to Dunne and the elevator doors closed. "It's great out there."

"I don't have running gear."

"Bought mine yesterday on my shopping spree. I really need my morning run, and it's been almost a week." Still mildly flushed from the increased blood flow, Kohn placed her hands on her hips and waited for Dunne's response. Standing there, her skin moist from the exertion, with no makeup and tousled hair struggling to climb out of her Adidas headband, she radiated the natural beauty that Dunne had first noticed back in Denver.

"Let me check the front desk and we'll go back up together."

Kohn nodded and resumed wiping her face with the small white hotel towel she had taken with her, oblivious to the stares of disapproval that several other people in the lobby cast her way. A female jock was not a common sight in the plush lobby of the Regent, although the hotel staff paid her no mind.

Dunne returned quickly. In one hand, he held a plain white envelope. "We'll open it in the suite."

The elevator doors opened and they stood aside as several people stepped out. Entering, Dunne pushed the number ten and CLOSE buttons.

"I had fun last night. Dinner was exquisite, and you aren't a bad dancer at all."

"It's been years. Neither Annie nor I were much for it, but I will confess it was nice. A nice crowd." There was no way Dunne would acknowledge how it had been with Kohn's body pressed against his.

Dunne let Kohn unlock their door with the key she had unswung from around her neck. Inside, he sat on the sofa. Kohn grabbed a tall glass of ice water from the wet bar and joined him as he was unfolding the message. He read it aloud. "There will be a tour group leaving the lobby at ten o'clock (China Travel Service Tours number one). You have been preregistered, and you can pick up your name tags and materials at the tour desk. You will need your passports. I will join you later. Paterson."

Dunne looked up. "Not exactly what I expected." He did recognize the CTS, China's official tour service.

Kohn had drained her water glass and was spiraling the ice around the inside of the glass in a vain effort to produce more melt. "Classic need-to-know Blackjack. The admiral never gives you any information prematurely." Lightly, she added, "All we need to know is that we're going on a tour." She tipped up the glass and sucked on the ice. "Well, I'll get changed. Had breakfast?"

"No."

"Why don't we order in? Coffee, orange juice and fruit for me."

"Why don't we hit the coffee shop? Maybe we can pick up our name tags early and a couple brochures. They'll tell us where we're going."

"Not as romantic as sitting there on the sofa and watching the harbor traffic, but probably a better idea." Kohn's words carried a hint of disappointment as she disappeared into her bedroom.

Dunne was not certain that they should be in any more romantic settings. They had sat on the sofa and unwound from the busy day when they returned last evening. They had shopped, toured, wined, dined and danced together and sipped Kahlua from the wet bar to close the evening. It was certainly well-stocked and there were no chits to be signed, so Dunne assumed Paterson was picking up the full tab. At one point, just before they retired, they had lowered the TV screen and caught the late news. Kohn had kicked off her shoes and sat in her favorite position, legs pulled under her, and their bodies had lightly touched as she squirmed into position. Dunne had been bothered by his reaction. It was like a mild but disturbing electrical shock, an instant awakening of desires he had not felt since well before Annie passed away, and he felt guilty. He had no right to feel that way. Not yet. Maybe when they had completed their assignment. Nevertheless, his admiration for Kohn had grown into genuine affection, stimulated in part by her professional but lighthearted manner, her give-and-take as they prepared themselves for what lay ahead. Then last night, the first warm feelings of desire, a natural evolution, perhaps, of their developing personal relationship. Had she deliberately triggered him? Was she expecting him to make a move? Did she want him to? He didn't want to believe that. Instead, he preferred to believe that she was just very comfortable with him. To that end, there had been many signs that she desired to maintain a professional senior-junior relationship. Still, she was not naive; she must know that their close relationship could generate other considerations and appreciations of one another. No, it would be best if he did not experience any more romantic settings with Frosty Kohn.

As they enjoyed their breakfast, Dunne perused the brochure he had picked up at the tour desk. They were going on a day trip to China via Macau. Their principal destination would be the village of Cuihengcun, the birthplace of Sun Yat-sen, the father of modern China—or so the brochure said. It was in the middle of the fertile Pearl River Delta, in Guangdong Province, bordering Macau. They would be traveling to Macau by hydrofoil, then bus across the border to Cuihengcun. That is why Paterson had instructed them to bring their passports. "We're going to mainland China," he announced quietly.

Kohn responded, "Five will get you ten the admiral'll be waiting for us."

"You think so?"

"Where else are we going?"

"We ride the hydrofoil to Macau, then take a bus across the border."

"We spend any time in Macau?"

"On the way back."

"Humf. How much time in each place?"

Dunne checked the time schedule on the back of the brochure. "Two hours for lunch at a village named Cuihengcun. Dinner later in Macau."

"We're due for the briefing. Yesterday was just the cushion in case the ship was delayed. Today has to be the day."

"I would agree with that, but why not here in Kowloon, or Hong Kong?"

"Because someone who will be attending the briefing doesn't want to come here—or can't come here."

"Chinese?"

"That would be a good bet. Traveling with the tour group is a great cover, very natural. We have any free time?"

Dunne scanned the schedule again. "Three hours in Macau."

"Then that's where I put my money."

Dunne was not that confident. The thought that they were very near to beginning their mission took him to a quick high. "Good; we've wasted enough time."

Kohn poured them both more coffee from the table decanter. "I doubt we've wasted a minute, really." She smiled as they made eye contact. "At least, I don't consider yesterday a total loss."

"It was fun, Sheila. I grant that. But I've been getting anxious. Paterson has been stressing that we're on a tight schedule. Despite that, to be frank, there were parts of yesterday that almost made me forget what we're here for."

Kohn went back to her last piece of fruit, a wedge of Asian pineapple. "I know what you mean. But I think it all starts today. Party time is over."

There were only eight other couples in the group. Their tour guide introduced herself while they were still in the hotel lobby. "Good morning. I am Sally Ling, and it is my pleasure to escort you today." The young woman wore the traditional high-necked cloth coat over black cotton slacks, an ensemble that failed to mask her small-breasted but curvaceous body. She had a pleasant lilt in her voice and, as with so many Hong Kong Chinese, her words were spoken with bits of high English clinging to the edges. "I see you all have your cameras, and I promise you that today will provide many memories to take back home with you.''

All but one of the couples appeared to be American, although most were older than Dunne and Kohn. The final couple was obviously Australian and considerable younger, possibly honeymooners judging from the way they clasped hands and rubbed against one another as the group left the lobby for the bus to the hydrofoil dock.

The swift craft had a cabin about the width of a DC-10, with similar seating—a pair of seats on each side and a four-seat row in the middle. There were fifteen rows, all occupied by the Regent group as well as groups from other hotels. As soon as the boat cleared the pier, it accelerated and rose on its hydrofoils, the white hull lifting clear of the water, the red area below the waterline riding in the spray. Banking smoothly, the boat rode the center of Victoria Harbor west toward Lantau Island, the largest among the 250 islands that make up the Hong Kong archipelago. A number of the smallest were mere rocks, but Lantau afforded more mountainous terrain than Hong Kong and was a popular holiday destination. The permanent population consisted of a mere twenty thousand people who were overrun every weekend by day-trippers and campers.

''Impressive piece of land,'' Kohn observed as they sped offshore at an exhilarating forty knots. ''Some day I would like to come back and really see this area—you know, travel to the New Territories and islands like Lantau there. I suspect it would be very quiet and restful.''

The hydrofoil banked right and headed for a narrow passage between the northern tip of Lantau and a tiny islet off the tip. Dunne and Kohn felt no tendency to lean as the skilled coxswain kept the turn smooth and consistent. The water surface was rippled with whitecaps from the westerly wind and there was a healthy chop to the waves, but the submerged hydrofoils maintained a steady depth and the hull was kept clear of any disturbances. The passengers were chattering among themselves and pointing to the various landmarks as they appeared, passed by and rapidly receded into the distance.

Like the rest, Dunne was thoroughly enjoying the ride. It had a jet feel to it, and the ventilation system was passing cool, clean air through the passenger compartment. "We're moving out," he commented. "This is some machine."

A cabin attendant slowly walked along the rows offering tea and cold liquid refreshments from a tray that she carried with no concern about their swift passage across the water. Kohn declined, but Dunne accepted a bottle of fruit-flavored mineral water. They passed close alongside a traditional junk, its sails stretched by the brisk breeze. Several children were waving from amidships, while on the high afterdeck a woman was tending a charcoal brazier. A half-clothed child clung to her side while another somewhat older child was throwing garbage over the transom.

"That's part of Hong Kong that will never change," Kohn observed.

"I hope not. Quite a contrast with this."

They raced around the western tip of the New Territories and headed across the mouth of Deep Bay toward Macau. As they entered the Outer Harbor and prepared to dock, Dunne checked his watch. "Sixty-three minutes; not bad."

Their shiny, air-conditioned CTS bus was waiting, its engine idling and entry door open. As soon as it was loaded, they began the run through Macau. The Portuguese enclave was a popular diversion, not only for tourists but for those who lived in Hong Kong. The tiny thirty-six-square-mile colony was a spot of Iberian culture, isolated but thriving mightily on the Chinese mainland. As soon as you set foot on the cobblestone streets, you were transported four centuries back in time, the streets lined with venerable banyan trees and a number of the Spanish-style churches founded as far back as 1557. The architecture could best be described as Sino-Iberian but modified by the peculiar styles of the Dutch, Moorish, Japanese and Spanish traders that had made Macau their destination since its founding.

The tour bus made its way through the town streets, Sally Ling pointing out the various landmarks. ". . . Mandarin Oriental Hotel, very nice place to stay . . . Jai Alai Stadium and entertainment center . . . Macau Forum for many events, including conferences and sports events. You can see grandstand for annual motorcar and motorcycle Grand Prix races . . ." It was a side of Macau that Dunne did not even know existed, his preconceived mental image being that of a somewhat behind-the-times area. Instead, Macau was a generous mixture of the new and old. The bus slowed for photographs as they passed the town square, reminiscent of those in Europe, and the municipal government building, the *Leal Senado* (Loyal Senate). They continued inland, passing a number of spruced-up buildings that reflected the colony's serious intent to renovate and upscale its older areas. Bright, unusual colors gave the buildings the look of a painter's palette, slightly off-tone pinks and reds, peppermint green, ochre and umber. Many of the street-side businesses sported mid-nineteenth-century facades with large multipaned windows that afforded views into the interiors of bakeries, beauty shops and multipurpose stores. As in Hong Kong and Kowloon, pedicabs mingled with taxis, and pedestrians strolled the sidewalks with a curiosity characteristic of overseas tourists. Still, the community had a more laid-back atmosphere than Hong Kong. Here, there was no frantic pace, no tunnel vision. The rich smells of Portuguese sausage, garlic, chilies and fish were present even inside the bus as it passed through the most crowded business area.

Near the colony limits, they passed through the *Portas do Cerco*, the stone gate that led to China. A steady stream of Chinese farmers was passing through the gate, carrying their produce to the Macau markets. Beyond the city proper, lush green mountains introduced the tourists to mainland China and were home to several monasteries, all with weathered red pagoda roofs that rose above the surrounding thick foliage. The small border station appeared and the bus stopped.

Two members of the border guard stationed themselves on each side of the entry door, and a customs official climbed aboard. He had a lean, undernourished look but smiled graciously and made small talk as he examined passports. Most he merely glanced at. Apparently the PRC was adopting a more hospitable bedside manner to its tourist trade.

He bowed slightly as he took Kohn's passport first, despite the fact that she was sitting in the window seat. "Welcome to the People's Republic of China, Miss Kohn. Is this your first visit?"

"Yes. I'm looking forward to it."

He flipped the passport closed, handed it back to Kohn with another polite bow and accepted Dunne's.

"You are also here on holiday, Mister Dunne?"

"Yes."

"May I ask your occupation?"

Dunne did not expect the question although it was routine enough for border crossings. He knew that he carried his Lockheed ID card in his wallet. "I am an engineer, aeronautical engineer."

The guard fingered through the passport and rechecked the photograph. "May I ask for whom?" His English was impeccable.

"Lockheed Aircraft Corporation. I do production follow-up studies on the DC-10." It was a spur of the moment reply, but it sounded good to Dunne.

"I see. Lockheed makes many fine aircraft, including the innovative Stealth attack plane, I believe."

The man's words were spoken without any change in tone or emphasis, but Dunne was hard pressed to maintain his posture and facial expression. Kohn had been looking out the window and continued doing so.

"Yes. It made quite a name for itself in the Gulf War."

"Do you work on the F-117, Mister Dunne?" The man was full of little surprises.

"No. I work strictly in the commercial aircraft division."

"I see. Please, enjoy your stay. Welcome to the People's Republic."

"Thank you."

The man's smile seemed genuine as he bowed and returned the passport. Within minutes he had finished his inspection and left the bus with an unexpected cheerful wave to the passengers.

As the bus pulled back onto the road, Kohn leaned over and spoke quietly. "What in all hell do you suppose that was about?"

"I don't know. When he said the word 'Stealth,' my whole body tensed. I couldn't stop it. I don't believe he noticed it, however. Boy, the temperature dropped."

"I felt just the opposite. In this seat, the temperature rose."

"We better mention this to Paterson when we see him."

"Definitely. It could just be one incredible coincidence. Maybe the guy's an aviation buff."

Dunne raised his eyebrows. "And maybe I'm the Queen Mum."

"You think Chinese intelligence?"

"God, I hope not. If so, they could be on to us."

"How could that happen?" Kohn asked.

Dunne pulled her over to him. As he kissed her lightly on the cheek, he whispered, "This bus could be bugged."

Kohn laughed as if he had said something humorous and resumed her quiet position at the window.

Within twenty minutes they were in Cuihengcun. Sally Ling announced, "We are here at the memorial square marking the location of the house that the great Sun Yat-sen built for his parents in 1866. Contrary to traditional Chinese geomancy, you can see the European-style verandahs that face west despite the fact that we are on the east beaches of this area. In that respect Sun Yat-sen was something of a rebel.''

Inside, the architecture was traditional with high ceilings, gilded carvings, plaques that honored Sun's ancestors and heavy blackwood furniture. In one of the small rooms there was a roofed Chinese marriage bed.

"Looks comfy," Kohn commented.

"You'll never know," Dunne responded.

"I have an instinct about such things."

Sally Ling concluded her guided tour of the house with, "As we exit to the patio of the Sun Yat-sen Museum, you will be met by your Chinese host who will take great pleasure in having you as guests for lunch. Afterward, please return to the museum, and the bus will depart exactly two hours from now."

Dunne and Kohn followed the others into the small garden area but were intercepted before they reached the museum next door.

"Mister Dunne? Miss Kohn?" The speaker was a middle-aged man of muscular build, wearing the traditional Chinese kimono and tasseled silk skull cap that covered the beginnings of his braided pigtail. It was as if he had just stepped out of a 1930s American movie. Without waiting for an answer, he continued, "I am Nim Chou. My house awaits your presence, and my wife has prepared a meal for us to enjoy. We have been looking forward to this honor."

Dunne and Kohn returned his bow and greeting and followed in his footsteps. His house was only a short walk north of the memorial, and he proudly encouraged them to enter. "Please, we are always anxious to visit with Americans."

The house was small as expected, built of hand-hewn wood skillfully joined together in tight walls and floors.

The roof was peaked but not in a pagoda style; it was more Western in design and capped with ochre clay tiles, a few of which needed replacing. Nim Chou led them through a tiny foyer into the main room. There, a wooden table was set and served by six high-backed chairs. Three were occupied, and the men stood as Kohn and Dunne entered. "Welcome to the People's Republic," a deep baritone voice intoned. The speaker was Admiral John "Blackjack" Paterson, U.S. Navy, retired.

"I figured," Dunne announced. Turning to Kohn, he added, "Pay me."

Kohn quickly extracted a fifty-yuan note from her pocket and slapped it into Dunne's hand. "I said it would be in Macau," she explained to Paterson.

As all sat, Nim Chou joined his wife in bringing in the food. Hot tea was already on the table. Soon the pots were surrounded by Cantonese specialties: a variety of dim sum, glistening fried dumplings with meat, vegetable and fish fillings; braised brisket of beef; crisp rolls of bean curd; sesame chicken and several large broiled carp, heads and eyes intact, lying on beds of fresh greens. Nim Chou exited the room with his wife, being careful to see that all entry doors were closed and locked.

Paterson made the introductions. "Nim Chou has provided us this house for several years. It is on the regular tourist circuit. His wife, incidentally, cooks Cantonese that one would die for, as you shall momentarily see. We are secure here." He addressed each of the other two men in turn. "This is Dong Sum, a civil worker at the air defense base near Changchun, approximately five hundred miles northeast of Beijing in the Jilin Military District. And this is Chi Lin, a senior air traffic controller and watch supervisor at the air traffic control center in Beijing. Both gentlemen are Chinese-Americans who have been serving our country here in the People's Republic for the past twenty-five years. Gentlemen, may I present Joshua Dunne and Sheila Kohn?''

''How do you do?'' responded Dunne, his words inter-mixed with Kohn's ''Good afternoon.''

Paterson continued, ''Mister Sum works in the opera-tional flight section of the base at Changchun as a sched-uling and operations clerk. Both he and Lin are valued members of our intelligence forces, and Lin is the originator of the strategy that has resulted in your assignment. I assure you that these gentlemen have devoted their lives to the interests of the United States and what they will now tell you is the result of considerable deliberations between themselves and subsequently with me.''

Dong Sum began, ''A few weeks ago, I learned that the Arab terrorist Amin Desird was coming to Changchun for the purpose of completing the purchase of three nuclear weapon detonators. He will act as courier for the transport of the devices out of China. We do not know his ultimate destination. What we do know is his estimated dates of arrival and departure at Changchun, his mode of transpor-tation, and his route to Beijing. Beyond that, we have no knowledge. It is obvious that the detonators are intended for sale to the highest bidder, Desird having become a ma-jor player in world terrorism, and if they do reach an ulti-mate buyer, we can only speculate as to the horror that can follow. Indeed, I should say, the horror that *will* follow.''

Dunne interrupted, ''China has no qualms about provid-ing the detonators?''

''That is not for me to speculate. There is a great deal of money involved. I have a secret wish that the detonators are flawed, but I do not see how we can count on that being the case. Double-crossing a man like Desird would seem to pose great risks.''

Dunne asked a second question. ''Detonators for what kind of devices?''

''Any type that uses fusion for the reaction. The detonators are the type used by the People's Republic primarily in air-delivered weapons, but they could just as well be installed in clandestine land weapons.''

"Thank you.''

"I have been in constant communication with Chi Lin since I learned of this, and we have been looking for some opportunity to affect Desird's mission. At this point, I should let Chi Lin say what happened next.''

Chi Lin bowed his head in response and took up the briefing, ''Our, that is the People's Republic of China's, air control network is not as sophisticated as that in the West, although it has been steadily improving in the past years. One problem we have is with the military, who are reluctant to place themselves completely in subjection to our control system. They prefer point-to-point flight as opposed to airways that may be of longer distance and result in increased fuel consumption. Directives have been issued by both civil and military authorities and the situation, as I have said, is getting better. Slowly. In any event, a few weeks ago while sitting at my scope I observed a near midair collision caused primarily by a military aircraft that suddenly popped up into my radar coverage. His return merged with that of a civil transport I was controlling. No harm was done, for different levels of flight were in use. But the incident generated a thought, and I relayed that thought first to Dong Sum. When he expressed confidence in my plan, I contacted my control in Beijing.'' Chi Lin looked at Paterson, wondering if he should continue. It was a proper move, for Paterson jumped into the discussion.

"Chi Lin has come up with one hell of a plan to assassinate Desird.''

Kohn smiled in anticipation of the response her question would elicit. "I thought we didn't do assassinations?''

Paterson seemed to take offense at the remark. "I believe I mentioned back in New Orleans that we wouldn't kill the

Pope. That was a facetious remark, of course. But I didn't rule out Desird.''

Kohn shrugged and deftly placed another piece of the carp on her plate, using the chopsticks with which she seemed quite competent.

Paterson continued, ''I'm going to give you the bottom line first and then let Chi Lin brief the overall plan. We're going to bag Desird's ass somewhere between Chengde and Beijing.''

To say that the remark caught Dunne and Kohn's attention would be the understatement of the Year of the Rat.

Dunne wondered aloud. ''Chengde?''

Paterson explained, ''It's on the airways from Changchun to Beijing.''

Dunne very slowly placed his chopsticks across the top rim of his plate. He had dropped the piece of braised beef when Paterson made the remark. ''We're going to fly into Chinese air space and attack Desird?''

Paterson smiled. He was enjoying the shock effect of his words. ''No, not *we*, exactly. *You* and Kohn are going to fly into Chinese airspace and bag Desird.''

The requirement for the F-117Ns was immediately obvious. Dunne asked, ''You want us to violate international law?''

Paterson snapped back, ''You think that son of a bitch, Desird, gives a rat's ass about international law?''

''No. But my contract says I fly for Uncle Sam, and penetrating the sovereign airspace of another country to deliberately kill someone is not what I've always thought of as the American Way.''

''The American Way is being threatened by a lot more than our simple little mission. In fact, it's to protect the American Way that we're even considering it.''

Dunne countered, ''Then the mission is not locked in concrete yet?''

"Not until you and Kohn agree that it is feasible. Whether it is moral or not is my concern."

"Tell us more," Dunne requested. "How exactly are we going to accomplish this mission impossible?"

Paterson deferred to Chi Lin.

"I have proposed to Admiral Paterson that we place an aircraft in position to intercept and destroy the aircraft that will be carrying Desird from Changchun to Beijing. He will have the detonators with him, of course."

"May I jump in here, please?" Kohn asked. Seeing no objections, she continued, "A thousand questions are vying for attention in my somewhat sophomoric mind; perhaps I can ask one of them? An air-to-air interception calls for control. Where will that come from?"

Chi Lin answered, "I will control you. I will place you into position to allow your own aircraft's detection systems to complete the final phase of the interception."

"And we're flying aircraft designed for ground attack."

Paterson interceded. "Primarily, but rigged for air to air. That's why you have Sidewinders, and the aircraft will handle those readily. Your target will be a non-evading transport type. I'm sure you understand the mission would not be possible without the stealth characteristics of the F-117."

"Let's back up," Dunne suggested. "How will we get into position? How will we be able to identify the target?"

Chi Lin seemed eager to continue. "First, let me say that the date for Desird's departure from the air base is established by a number of factors that will most probably remain firm . . ."

"Most probably . . ." Dunne repeated, obviously concerned.

"Let him go on," Paterson ordered.

"The route is known for it is a logistic flight that is scheduled every evening at the same time. I believe you would refer to such a flight as the Red-Eye Express. It is a routine flight and one that has established a reputation for consistency—a rarity, I must admit, in our system. The aircraft that is used is a very reliable machine. The military uses the flight regularly because of its dependability. Here is a picture.''

Dunne and Kohn studied the photograph as Chi Lin described the transport. ''It is a Xian Y-7, high-wing twin turboprop transport, easy to recognize from its upswept tail, high single vertical stabilizer and upturned winglets on the tips of its wings.''

''Chinese-built?'' Kohn asked.

''Yes, based originally upon a Russian design, the Antonov An-24, NATO code name 'Coke.' But the Xian-7 is an advancement over that design, converted by the Hong Kong Aircraft Engineering Company in 1985. There have been several other modifications, and technically the aircraft we will be targeting is a Xian Y7H-500. In the military configuration, it can carry thirty-eight troops or five-thousand five-hundred kilograms of cargo. The civil version can carry comparable loads.''

''One question comes immediately to mind,'' Dunne stated. ''You are going to control us—by radio, I assume. We don't speak Chinese, and English chatter on airborne frequencies will certainly alert somebody.''

Chi Lin went on. ''I will control you in Chinese through a simple system of numbers. All you have to learn is the Chinese pronunciation for the numbers one through zero.'' Chi Lin handed over a small JVC VHS camcorder. ''On the tape are fifteen minutes of typical tourist shots of Cuihengcun and Sun Yat-sen's house and memorial park. Then, among other things, there are the correct pronunciations of the numerals mentioned and a repetition of the control procedures we will be using with some examples. Control will be simple. You will be on a dedicated frequency, and your call will be Tsing Tao.'' Lin pronounced the word ''Ching Dow.''

"The coastal city farther south?" Dunne ventured.

"Also our most popular beer," corrected Chi Lin with a smile. "Any time I transmit three numbers, say two-one-zero, it will be a vector. Five or six numbers, bearing and distance to target. Two numbers, altitude in the angel code. If you need a repeat, merely respond with two twos, *èr-èr*. Simple, yes?"

"How about speeds?" Kohn asked.

"Good question; I should have mentioned it. Speed will be four numbers with the first number always being zero."

Dunne had to admit that the system was simple, yet ingenious. Nothing but numbers one to zero.

"Your call sign will only be used on initial contact or if there is difficulty during the process."

"What about your call?" Dunne asked.

"I will need no call. Anyone I hear on the circuit will have to be you."

Kohn rubbed her tongue across her lips to remove an errant piece of carp. "How will you track us?"

Paterson answered, "You will be flying civil airways, and your IFF codes are compatible with worldwide air control interrogators. You will be given the mission code in your preflight briefing."

It was obvious that considerable thought had been given to the plan and on the surface it did not sound inconceivable, but Dunne thought it time to spring the big question. "How about timing? This plan calls for us to be at a certain spot at a certain time in order to have you control the intercept, and that time depends upon a scheduled launch of the target aircraft—which can jolly well change no matter what you say about regularity. I don't have the full picture in mind or know how far away we will launch, but it's obvious that we don't have one hell of a lot of leeway."

"True," agreed Paterson, "but the concept in my mind is sound. The tactics need to be worked out, and obviously the timing. You and Kohn have that job, and it starts the moment we're back aboard the *Lincoln*. You will have to work out the route, fuel required, waypoints, the whole nine yards. What I want from you right now is the answer to my question 'Is it feasible?' and do you think you can pull it off?''

"What if we're detected well inside China?"

"That is the one assumption we must make. You won't be detected."

Kohn added, "There is one other question."

"And that is?"

"You said we have one final right of refusal. I submit that the timing required for the success of this mission is so critical that the odds against completion are pretty high, maybe too high for the risks involved. We could have mechanical problems while in Chinese airspace. Once we shoot down the aircraft, all hell will break loose, I would think."

Chi Lin responded, "No one will know the aircraft has been shot down. We have our share of aircraft accidents, and a midair with one of the cursed military is not unknown. Those we attribute to bad weather or pilot error. There will not be an extensive investigation of the wreckage and, at the altitude involved, the aircraft remains will be widely scattered. They will never be all recovered."

Paterson knew Dunne and Kohn were not yet convinced. "Look," he said, "I know we're reaching on this one and a number of things could go wrong, but I say, with your concurrence, that we launch and give it a try. We have the perfect airplane for the job and I say we have the odds when it comes to getting in, doing the deed, and hauling ass out. Sure, it's dicey. It's illegal. It depends upon a number of undependable factors. Timing must be perfect—perfect. That's why I wanted you two for the mission. I know how you both operate. You're perfectionists. You're experienced and you have the ability to weigh the possibilities of success as the situation develops. I have confidence in your judgment in the remote chance—at least, I believe it is remote—that something goes wrong.''

"You're asking a lot," Dunne stated.

"Remember what your wingman, there, always says."

"What is that?" Dunne asked.

"That's why you get the big bucks," Paterson stated with an ear to ear smile.

Kohn looked at Dunne. "I do say that a lot."

Dunne acquiesced. "All right. For now, I say it's a go. But if our mission profile doesn't seem to answer all the questions I know we'll have as we work this thing up, I reserve the right to abort."

"I can live with that," Paterson concluded, knowing that if Dunne concluded it could not be done, it couldn't be done. But he also knew that Dunne could not resist such a challenge and would give the scheme a very thorough mental checkout. That was all right; that's why he wanted Dunne. Mature judgment. Able to weigh the odds objectively.

Chi Lin reached across the table for Dunne's hand. "It will work, Mister Dunne. I assure you that we will be in control at our end. Dong Sum will confirm the takeoff date and time and Desird's presence aboard the aircraft. I will forward the information in time for you to launch and be in position, provided that you can depart from the carrier with no more than one hour and a half en route to the interception point."

Dunne had to smile at that requirement. The *Lincoln* would be dangerously close to mainland China. That would be a determination of the ship's captain and his operating restrictions. "We'll only get one shot," he declared. "The weather can't be a factor. If the Xian goes, we have to go."

"You have that capability," Chi Lin observed.

"Yes."

Chi Lin bowed to Kohn. "Good fortune go with you."

Kohn scanned the table. "Do we have the cookies? I'd like to read mine at this moment."

Chi Lin laughed. "Only almond cookies, this meal. You will have to make your own fortune."

"That's what I was afraid of."

Paterson thanked the two men, and they excused themselves. He sat back down as Kohn reached for another piece of the carp. "You really like that, don't you?" he observed.

"Out of this world. Everything is superb. I usually prefer Szechwan, but Cantonese has its merits. Besides, it's back to shipboard chow now. I may never get another meal like this—and the operative word is never, I might add."

Paterson poured himself more tea. "We're going to pull this off, you know?"

"No, I don't know," answered Dunne. "When do we go back aboard?"

"The ship sails at seventeen hundred."

Kohn gasped. "My God, we'll never make that!"

"No need to. The ship has to depart to get a leg on the trip north. She's leaving behind one of VS-29's Vikings. We'll meet in the morning. I have some things to do, and we'll fly out to the ship later. Tonight will give you two a chance to review what we've covered here and make a list of tactical requirements and considerations. Talk it over, weigh the pros and cons—and throw away the latter. Tomorrow night, I want your general plan in my cabin. After that you can complete your flight profile, and we can brief the ship's captain and the air wing commander. They're the only ones we're obligated to, as far as the specifics go."

Dunne and Kohn joined Paterson in thanking Nim Chou and his wife for the meal.

Paterson instructed, "You go on back to the museum; I'll be leaving shortly. When you get back to Macau, you might want to leave the tour unit and return to the hotel. You won't be able to do any detailed planning there, of course, but we need to start organizing our thoughts."

Dunne and Kohn did so and even walked through the collection of Sun Yat-sen artifacts, but nothing registered. Their minds were already on their assignment.

The bus departed twenty minutes later and stopped on the China side of the border with Macau.

"Why is this?" Dunne wondered aloud.

"It's a controlled society, Joshua. They have an interest in anyone who is leaving as well as arriving."

The same customs official boarded and began checking identities. When he came to Dunne, he noticed the camcorder. "I assume you were able to get some fine views of the house of Dr. Sun Yat-sen."

"I hope so."

"May I see the machine, please?"

Dunne handed over the camcorder without comment.

The official raised it to his eye and pushed the PLAY button. "I did not notice it when you passed through earlier."

"It was sitting between me and Miss Kohn, on the seat. I gave it no thought." *How much longer is he going to view the tape?*

The official pushed STOP and returned the camera. "You handle the instrument with skill. Your shots are almost of professional quality."

"Thank you. I've learned by trial and error."

"A good teacher—trial and error. Come back soon, Mister Dunne. And you also, Miss Kohn."

The Macau customs person did not even bother to board the bus, just waved the driver through.

Dunne scooted closer to Kohn, putting his arm around her shoulder. "That Chinese official paid too much attention to us," Dunne said in a whisper.

"I think he was just being thorough."

"I don't know. He managed to bring up the one-seventeen earlier. Now he goes right for the camcorder. It could have been a deliberate effort to intimidate us."

"Or simply a conscientious official doing his job. This is no time to go paranoid." Kohn picked up the camcorder and pretended to shoot the passing scenery. She didn't say it but she had the same concerns as Dunne. The Chinese didn't get a reputation for being inscrutable by accident.

The bus retraced its path through Macau, finally stopping at the Lou Lim Ieoc Garden, modeled on the old classic gardens of Soochow and set almost in the exact center of the Macau business area. Dunne spoke aside to Sally Ling. "I'm afraid that Miss Kohn and I will be leaving the tour here. She has what appears to be a migraine headache and has asked me to escort her back to Kowloon."

"Oh, I am so sorry, Miss Kohn," Sally Ling responded, placing a comforting hand on Kohn's shoulder. Then, turning back to Dunne, she continued, "If you hurry, there is a hydrofoil leaving in twenty minutes, and they will honor your return ticket. It has been a pleasure having you with the group."

Dunne hailed a pedicab as he spoke. "Thank you, Miss Ling."

Sally Ling turned to her group. "Please, enjoy the gardens. I must excuse myself for just a moment. I will rejoin you momentarily and we will have a short walking tour around central Macau."

She hurried to a nearby souvenir shop and asked permission to use the telephone.

It was early evening by the time Dunne and Kohn returned to their hotel. They grabbed a quick bite in the coffee shop and purchased some stationery in the gift shop, as well as a tour brochure that had a sketchy map of northern China on its back.

By seven they were seated in the living area before the great window wall. Dunne was trying to estimate distances on the brochure map while Kohn was making some calculations on the stationery.

Dunne was obviously frustrated. "What the hell can we do without any planning materials?"

"Concept," Kohn answered. "We may be able to come up with the concept. How close to mainland China can we expect the ship to be?"

"I don't know. I'm not sure they dare sail north or west of the Yellow Sea."

"What's there?"

Dunne slid closer to Kohn so she could share the map. "North Korea. Then to the west, the Gulf of Chihli. No way will the captain take the *Lincoln* into there."

"It's international water."

"It's a goddamned Chinese lake, surrounded on three sides by the PRC. It's big, three hundred by maybe a hundred and fifty miles wide, but the entrance from the Yellow Sea is only sixty miles across. The Chinese claim a hundred miles of territorial water off all their coasts. Washington would never authorize it."

"I wonder what their guidelines are?"

Dunne shrugged. "If we believe the admiral, Washington doesn't even know what we're about, except for the president. The *Lincoln* has some standard sailing orders, I'm sure, but you can bet your best bra they don't include anywhere north of the Yellow Sea."

Kohn made some finger measurements on the map. "That means refueling going in and coming out."

"I'd say that's a given."

"You think the *Lincoln* will have to stay south of the thirty-eighth parallel?"

"Yes."

Kohn walked her fingers over the map again. "We could be looking at a good five hundred miles minimum going in."

"And coming out."

"The air tanker boys are going to have their bare asses

hanging out in clearly North Korean or Chinese-claimed airspace. That doesn't look good.''

''Want something to drink?''

Kohn nodded without looking up from the crude map. ''This calls for scotch.''

''Up?''

''Two fingers, one cube.''

Dunne poured two and handed one to Kohn. Both sipped and sat back into the soft sofa.

''You know,'' Kohn ventured, ''another hundred and fifty miles and they could have launched this wild goose chase from South Korea.''

''And announced it to the whole world. Out where we'll be, the only observers will be fish and seabirds.''

''Commie fish and seabirds,'' Kohn amplified.

Dunne shook his head. ''I don't see what we can do tonight on this. We need access to the *Lincoln*'s flight planning facilities and intelligence.''

''Agreed. The overall plan's obvious. We launch, refuel, bag the bastard, refuel and recover. A piece of cake.''

The two matched smiles, their minds filled with the same thoughts. *A night launch, maybe in gawdawful weather and seas, refuel in the night sky, assuming the Gomers from North Korea or the Chinese don't take serious offense at such an operation taking place within their turf, evade the most concentrated early warning and anti-air defense net on the Chinese mainland, scoot around in Chinese airspace for up to an hour, bag Desird, then back across a network of SAMs and anti-air that must ring Beijing before another dark refueling—assuming the tankers would still be on station—and a night recovery aboard the* Lincoln—*maybe again in gawdawful weather. Miller time.*

Dunne repeated Kohn's expression. ''A piece of cake.''

Kohn stood and walked over by the window. ''I'd like another scotch.''

Dunne refreshed his as well.

Kohn sipped and commented, "This has to be the most beautiful view in the world."

Gray broken stratus was flowing in from behind them, from over the mainland, the wispy bottoms reflecting the millions of lights that adorned nighttime Hong Kong. An infinite variety of colors. Fast-moving silver streams met each other along the island's harborside roads, on the far side of the harbor. Organized clutters of lighted high-rise windows rose behind the traffic streams, the uppermost diffusing and finally disappearing as the low scud wrapped itself around the highest reaches of the tall buildings.

By contrast, the ever-present harbor traffic seemed to take no note of the weather. There was little wind, and the boats, junks, hydrofoils, ferries and ships moved with ageless consistency, a thousand floating vehicles crossing in the night, their red and green running lights aligning each to the other so they could pass safely and properly.

A light mist began to cloud the picture window.

Kohn sat back onto the sofa. Dunne sat beside her.

"Cozy . . ." Kohn muttered.

"Maybe even romantic," Dunne ventured. The scotch was releasing some inhibitions he had been trying to suppress. "You're very special, Sheila." The words sounded more awkward than he had intended. Too abrupt a change of pace.

Kohn was equally disturbed that she felt way too comfortable. "Oh?"

"I feel very confident in this with you. You're a good stick." Perhaps that would return the exchange back into one of professionalism.

"That makes me special? Every pilot on that ship is a good stick."

"That—and other things."

Kohn did not respond.

What the hell. The words seemed to pause on Dunne's lips before breaking free. "When Annie died in your arms back in the CINCPACFLT compound, I never saw such tenderness and sincerity. She should have died in my arms, but you gave her comfort. I'll always remember that.''

"You were busy, if I recall.''

Kohn's reminder brought back the vivid image of the charging terrorists and Dunne rising to Annie's defense just before the Marines had stopped the charge with a volley of M-16 fire. Still, Annie had been hit, and the picture of her lying in a pool of blood spreading across Kohn's white-uniformed lap would always be with him.

"Annie was the special person," Kohn spoke softly.

Dunne leaned forward and looked back at Kohn. "She's no longer a part of my life, Sheila.''

"She'll always be a part, Joshua.''

"No. She's part of my past. A very wonderful past. She liked you, and I think she would approve of us being together.''

"Joshua . . .''

"Let me finish. You've been a part of my life since the trial and that awful time. When you showed up in Denver, it was as if something was destined to happen. You stirred up all of the old feelings of comradeship and friendship and professional dependence and gratitude and . . .''

Kohn interrupted, "Joshua, I think maybe we should call it an evening . . .''

". . . And you triggered new emotions, Sheila, ones I could not have encouraged before. Then, when we were going through the checkout at Tonopah, I realized that we make one hell of a team. Our reactions with one another are instinctive.''

"We're professionals, Joshua. I'm not sure . . .''

"We're more than that, and I have been wanting to say so for some time.''

"Damn!'' Kohn stood and turned her back. "We can't let this happen now, Joshua. It just isn't the right time or place.''

"Don't try and tell me this is a surprise."

Kohn turned to face Dunne, her eyes moist. "Well, it is. I won't say I didn't think this could happen, but I just thought it could wait until we get back to the States. There will be time to look at things with more objectivity."

"Love is not objective."

"Don't say it, Joshua, if it's the scotch talking. Please."

"You feel it, too, Sheila. I know you do."

"I don't know what I feel at this moment. I'm not sure love is the operative word."

Dunne looked at his glass. There was a half inch remaining. He set it on the side table. "Sit down," he said. It was not spoken as a demand, just a plea.

Kohn's response was almost inaudible, "No. . . ."

Dunne jumped up and stopped her as she headed for her bedroom. She immediately turned and threw her arms around his neck. He pressed his lips to her forehead. "This had to happen, Sheila."

"I know."

October 6

Joshua Dunne opened his eyes with some effort. He had slept the deep, delicious sleep of sexual fatigue, and pressed against him was the unbelievably soft and warm body of Frosty Kohn. It was light outside, but the weak intensity indicated it was still early morning. A glance at his watch confirmed that it was 5:45 A.M. Carefully, he slipped away from Kohn, pulled on his shorts and walked into the living area.

"Good morning." Blackjack Paterson was seated in one of the wing chairs over by the window wall.

"Ah . . . good morning, Admiral." Dunne did not like the look on Paterson's face. It was about three miles past disapproval.

"I'm disappointed, Joshua."

"It's not your concern, Admiral."

Paterson pointed to the fresh pot of coffee on the bar. In retrospect, Dunne realized that was what had awakened him—the strong, enticing smell of fresh coffee.

"Everything you and Commander Kohn do is my concern."

"Only if it affects our mission, Admiral. This has no bearing on it."

"No? The holy shit it doesn't! You ever gone to bed with your wingman before?"

The question was too ridiculous to answer. Instead, Dunne poured himself a cup of coffee.

Paterson grimaced as he sipped his. It was cold. He had been holding it too long. Standing, he walked over and emptied it into the bar sink, then held his cup out. Dunne filled it.

"Would you like to put on some pants?"

Dunne hastily returned to the bedroom and emerged with trousers and undershirt added to his ensemble. "You knew this could happen," he accused.

"I was afraid it *might* happen. It was the only doubt I had about the mission. But I felt that you and Kohn were too professional to allow it to happen until later. I don't begrudge you wanting another companion. It's a natural thing. You're a young man. But I am disappointed. You should have waited."

"Annie's been gone over two years."

"That's not a consideration, Joshua. I think she'd approve."

"But you don't?"

"Not of the timing."

"We're not kids, Admiral. The situation was just too accommodating. We had to fall in love."

"Then it's not just hormones?"

A feminine voice spoke up behind them. "I believe I'm entitled to be a part of this conversation." Kohn had taken time only to lightly brush her hair and slip on her cotton kimono.

"Good morning, Sheila," Paterson said flatly.

"With all due respect, sir, I'm not sure I appreciate this invasion of our privacy."

"Understood. But you don't have any privacy as far as this mission goes. I stopped by to take you to the airport. The Viking will be ready at oh-eight-hundred."

Kohn softened. "I regret that it happened, Admiral, but I'm not sorry and I don't think it is any of your concern at this point."

"You and Joshua are in complete agreement on that, it seems. Well, I want you to understand that it damn well better not be my concern for the rest of the time we're on this mission. You both can see the potential for personal considerations to be present that were not here before. Damn, that's an awkward sentence. You know what I mean."

Seeing that neither Dunne nor Kohn was anxious to continue the conversation, Paterson added, "I'll wait downstairs. We have a car."

"It'll just take a few minutes for us to dress, Admiral," Kohn offered.

For just a brief moment, a flick of humor shone in Paterson's eyes. "All right—but there's no time for anything else."

Inwardly, Dunne and Kohn released collective sighs of relief. Things were not quite as bad as the admiral had tried to imply.

The ride out to the *Lincoln* was anything but comfortable. Cooped up in the rear of the Viking, strapped into crew seats, their only view of the outside through a couple of tiny porthole-like windows, Dunne and Kohn longed for the visibility of even the F-117N. This was no way to fly. The only consolation was the realization that Paterson was considerably more apprehensive. He sat stone quiet for the full fifty-five minutes it took to reach the *Lincoln*. Then the nose-high, slow approach, a bit of turbulence and the slam down onto the deck with deceleration that pressed them forward until the shoulder straps threatened to cut through their flight gear. The soft feel of the roll backward as the Viking, stopped by the arresting wire, was allowed to recoil slightly to release the wire caused the passengers to exchange smiles for the first time since they had left Kai Tak. Pilots definitely made the worst passengers—except possibly for black, retired, non-aviator four-stars.

Dunne stowed his gear in his stateroom and met Kohn in one of the squadron ready rooms that had been offered for their use. The VS-29 intelligence officer had provided them with charts and information on the PRC's and North Korea's air defense organizations and capabilities, the latter merely a confusion factor in the event that the young lieutenant tried to second-guess their mission.

Dunne ran off a copy of an air tactical map that covered northeast China, the Yellow Sea and the Korean Peninsula and spread it across a planning table. At that point, Paterson joined them. He placed a nine-by-twelve manila envelope on the map. "Here's the flight schedule information provided by Chi Lin. Desird's already at Changchun. He is scheduled to leave on the October ninth early morning run, just as Chi Lin briefed."

"We may have a time making a launch point by then," Dunne emphasized. Our preliminary thoughts indicate that the ship will have to be somewhere in the north section of the Yellow Sea. Even then, we're probably going to need refueling going and coming."

Paterson nodded. "Sea state's good all the way up. The captain has informed me that we can maintain thirty knots until tomorrow evening, no strain. I'd like a briefing this evening. The air wing commander as well as the captain will be present."

Kohn asked, "How far north will the captain be willing to go?"

"I don't know, but I would think he would not like to get too close to the thirty-eighth parallel."

"That's what we figured," Dunne added.

"I'll need to bounce the plan off the president one final time. Any reason I can't plan to do that after the briefing?"

"No, sir."

"Then I'll leave you two to your work. You can expect some tough questions from the captain and the CAG."

"We'll be ready."

"Any other thoughts at the moment?"

"No, sir."

"Nineteen hundred. Until then, if you need me, I'll be available. You have the ready room all day, and VS-29 will give you any help you need with planning material. Just be sure you don't let anything slip that could give them an idea of where we're going or what we're going to do. Incidentally, a PRC bomber overflew the ship before we arrived. I don't feel it was anything significant." Without further comment, Paterson departed. Kohn locked the ready room entry.

Dunne studied the material supplied by Chi Lin. Kohn peered over his shoulder. "Looks like fun, huh?"

"I don't know if it will be fun or not, but I think we can hack it if . . ."

"If what?"

"If the ship can be positioned where we want it; if Desird's airplane takes off as scheduled; *if* Chi Lin can get us into position for the intercept; *if* no one picks us up inbound . . ."

"I get the picture."

Dunne went back to the map. "Well, first things first; let's put in the major air defense radars and SAM sites."

Kohn called out the locations while Dunne plotted. "Major air defense radars at . . ."

"Just the ones on the east side of Beijing."

". . . at . . . ah . . . Baoding, Tianjin, Tangshan, Qin-huangdao and Chengde."

The plots formed an eastern semicircle with a radius of approximately eighty miles from Beijing.

"There's one more we should be concerned about."

"Where's that?"

"On the east side of the Gulf of Chihli, there's a main-land peninsula jutting southwest that separates the gulf from Korea Bay. Dalian is the city."

"I don't like that. How about right there to the south, on the Shandong Peninsula?"

"Radar, yes. On the tip at Yantai."

"We're going to have to go in over the Gulf of Chihli; that's obvious."

"Ready for the SAMs?"

Dunne selected a different color pencil. "Go ahead."

"All of the above except Dalian and Yantai."

"Did anyone ever tell you your nose is off center?"

"It is not!" Kohn protested.

"Sure it is; there's a twenty-degree bend in the bridge. From this angle you can see it." Dunne touched Kohn's nose with his pencil.

Kohn switched position. "That better?"

"Yeah, looks okay now. I never noticed it before."

"Well, don't notice it again, and we better get back to work."

Dunne grunted quietly. "Never made love to a woman with a crooked nose before."

"And you won't ever again until we're off this bird farm, so don't let your mind wander. Seriously, Joshua."

"Okay, so Beijing is ringed with air defense facilities. We expected that. Let's put in Desird's flight path." Dunne drew a line from Changchun to Beijing. It ran southwest. He carefully measured it. "Four hundred and forty nautical miles. Chi Lin said he'd like to shoot for Chengde as the point of interception. That's on course about ninety miles short of Beijing. What do the specs on his aircraft say for cruising speed?''

Kohn ran a finger down the spec sheet for the Xian Y-7 transport. ''Economical cruise at twenty thou, two-twenty-eight.''

''Knots?''

''Yes. Max cruise, two-fifty-eight.''

''Not much difference. We'll use the first figure.''

Dunne began entering data on a scratch pad. ''Takeoff time will be zero time. The airplane will be over Chengde at zero plus ninety minutes. We have to be there at the same time.''

''How close do you figure we can get the carrier?''

''God, I don't know. I would say about here.'' Dunne made a dot and drew a small circle around it. The spot was eighty miles west of Inchon, South Korea, and in the northernmost reaches of the Yellow Sea. ''For all practical purposes, we'll be in South Korean waters, actually. The captain should go for that. I don't believe he would buy anything farther north or west.''

Kohn took the ruler. ''That still puts us three hundred and sixty miles from Chengde.''

''Is that all? Are you sure?''

''See for yourself.''

Dunne grabbed the ruler and measured. ''Thank God for small favors. It's another hundred and twenty miles to Beijing—in case we have to play catch-up—and another three hundred and sixty, make that four hundred, back from Beijing. Total distance, eight hundred and eighty miles! We may not even have to refuel!'' Grabbing Kohn, he twirled her around in a clumsy waltz. ''We don't *have* to refuel, we don't *have* to refuel, we don't . . .''

''Whoa! We have to add a contingency amount of fuel for possible maneuvering and delays to get aboard the *Lin-*

coln. I don't want to arrive back here burning fumes. I've been there. Done that.''

"Okay, okay, so we set the tankers up for a rendezvous on the return leg only. That's a magnificent plus. They won't have to be hanging out there being painted by the Dalian and Yantai radars. That would be a sure givaway that something was up.''

Kohn let herself be held for a minute, then gently pushed away. ''That's the first good development we've seen. I just assumed we'd need the tankers going in.''

"Me, too. But figures don't lie. We can blast off this boat and not be detected until we set Desird's ass on fire. Things are looking up, Frosty Kohn. I think we have a Mission Possible here.''

12 ═══════════════════

Beijing
October 6, 8:20 A.M.

Zinyang Yang, Section Head of the Special Mission Intelligence Section of the Military Intelligence Department (MID) of the People's Liberation Army's General Staff Department (GSD), gazed pensively out the large picture window. Halfway up the twelve-story rectangular gray concrete building, his office faced south and his view encompassed a considerable chunk of the central part of Beijing. The area held such related government buildings as the Ministry of State Security (MSS) Branch Office, across from the stately Gugong Palace Museum, and two of a number of MSS Technical Surveillance Posts, one located in the government-run Palace Hotel and the other in the Beijing Hotel. Other MSS posts were located throughout Beijing, the only ones within his view being the Great Wall Hotel to the east and the Janguo Hotel to the southeast. Further to the south was the Ministry of Public Security Headquarters. Beijing was the controlling center of the PRC's intelligence community.

Yang's bureau-head office was responsible directly to the MID, also known as the Second Department of the Ministry of National Defense (MND), and Yang was known as the puzzle maker. Not from the standpoint of making puzzles; quite the contrary, his expertise, and that of those who worked under him, was in taking random but common-content intelligence, correlating it and producing a finished puzzle of what before had been only a series of apparently unrelated incidents. It was surprising, the amount of skill that thirty-three years in the bureau had given him. He was the recognized best at what he did.

The First Bureau was divided into five geographical divisions, the name of each division reflecting the major city within the division: Beijing, Shenyang, Shanghai, Guangzhou, and Nanjing.

The Guangzhou Division covered matters relative to the Hong Kong, Macau and Taiwan areas, and the papers back on Yang's desk referred to several minor matters that had been reported by operatives within the Hong Kong and Macau areas. They were part of routine reports, but something common to several of the reports had caught a staffer's eye and he had forwarded them to Yang for further analysis.

The first report covered the visit of the United States supercarrier USS *Lincoln* to the port of Hong Kong. Such visits were routine, although this could be one of the last before the British relinquished the colony to the PRC. One hundred and fifty-five years of British rule, the result of the Chinese defeat in the 1839 Opium Wars, would come to an end in just nine months. The report covered intelligence procured by the scores of shopkeepers, barmen, bargirls, prostitutes and taxi drivers—among others—all of whom attempted to draw information from the crews of visiting ships, whatever their nature or country of origin. The report indicated that several of the sailors from the American carrier had made reference to two Stealth aircraft being kept on board under tight security. The aircraft were being flown by civilian pilots as part of a Lockheed-sponsored operational test program. The very mention of the word Stealth was an instant red flag. The fact that they were on an aircraft carrier and presumedly were versions rigged for U.S. Navy use alone made the matter worthy of further probing.

Another report from agents on the staffs of one of the limousine taxi companies and of the Regent Hotel reported that two American civilians had been transported from the *Lincoln* via a navy helicopter to the Kai Tak International Airport and on to the Regent, where they were staying.

A third report, from one of the female agents who served as a tour guide for China Travel Service Tours, had reported that the two Americans, one male and one female, had taken Tour #1, which featured Macau and a brief border crossing to visit the village of Cuihengcun, a popular tourist stop. The same report indicated that the Americans had been hosted for lunch at the home of a local resident, Nim Chou. Three others had been present: a black American, probably in his sixties, and two middle-aged Chinese nationals, none of whom had been on the tour.

Yang cursed at the stupidity of the local agents in not identifying the two Chinese. As for Nim Chou, he was a respected villager, a tailor by trade and a fervent member of the Party. He and his wife often hosted American tourists and on occasion had reported to the local Party representative items that they had thought to be of interest. They never had been, however. Nevertheless, the presence of the older black American was particularly intriguing. Few blacks visited Macau, much less Cuihengcun.

Yang walked over to his computer station and pulled up a program called Jigsaw Two. Using material in the three reports, he started entering data, and after a few moments a statement appeared: VALID MATERIAL FOR POSSIBLE CORRELATION.

Yang selected AMPLIFY from the list of three options. Green lettering covered the screen: THERE IS A 35% POSSIBILITY THAT A CLANDESTINE AIR OPERATION IS BEING PLANNED FOR SKIES OVER OR NEAR THE PRC. OMEGA DATABASE SEARCH REVEALS NO PRIOR OPERATION OF

STEALTH AIRCRAFT ABOARD U.S. NAVY CARRIERS AL-THOUGH NAVY PROTOTYPE STUDIED IN LATE PHASES OF VE-HICLE DEVELOPMENT.

Yang entered: HOSTILE INTENT?

The reply was instantaneous: UNABLE TO DETERMINE DUE TO LACK OF SUFFICIENT INPUT. PROBABILITY TOO SMALL FOR MEASUREMENT.

What kind of response is that? Yang thought. *Sometimes the machines are as stupid as humans.*

The bureaucrats in the MND would expect more definite information. They wouldn't get any, not until there were any further developments. Yang ran the computer findings through a scrambler program, printed it and faxed the result to MND. Within minutes, a return fax ordered him to report to General Shangkun Sun, Head of Operational Intelligence in the MID and two administrative levels above Yang's office.

Yang hurried to the top floor and was immediately ush-ered into General Sun's office. Yang's immediate superior, Dr. Ning Li, civilian head of the First Bureau, was already present and directed Yang to a chair next to him. "I re-ceived the routine copy, Yang."

Yang was aware of that. Dr. Li received copies of every-thing that went out of Yang's office.

The general opened the discussion, leaning forward with his elbows resting on the glossy top of his ornately carved teakwood desk. It was completely clear of any matter ex-cept two multiline telephones—one deep red—and a Bic ballpoint pen, "What do you make of the reports?"

Yang could only repeat what the computer had declared. "Other than that, General, I have nothing further to offer."

"Where is the American carrier now?"

Yang was very glad he had checked before leaving his office. He had known that would be the general's first ques-tion. "It departed Hong Kong early last evening and is sailing north through the Taiwan Straits."

"To where?"

"I do not know, General."

"The presence of the two Stealth aircraft—that is most unusual, is it not?"

"It is the primary consideration that generated our interest."

"Doctor Li?"

"I have no further knowledge of the contents of the report."

General Sun made his own conclusion. "I suspect it is indeed routine operations. But why the Americans would choose our waters for any kind of operational development of new aircraft is of some concern, I suppose. I think maybe I will order overflights. I want the carrier to know we are aware of its presence. Assuming they proceed north of Taiwan, I will turn the matter over to the Beijing Military District." Pausing, he seemed to have second thoughts. "Or, perhaps, the matter may be of more concern to our comrades in the Korean People's Army Air Force than ours." The general spoke the name of his ideological Korean counterparts as if his mouth were full of dog dung. "If the Americans have any ulterior motive, I would suspect that any operations would be directed against them rather than us. The negotiations in Washington are such that this would be a poor time to conduct questionable aerial maneuvers. Nevertheless, I will turn the matter over to the military district commander. Thank you, thank both of you."

Tsingdai Air Base, Beijing Military District
October 6, 11:17 A.M.

Colonel Jin Fan reviewed the contingency plan forwarded to the 23rd Air Defense Regiment. It had originated at the headquarters of the Military Defense Department in Beijing, given priority down the chain of command until it came into the hands of Jin Fan. It really didn't call for immediate action, that being assigned to the Nanjing Military District, well to the south of Tsingdai. But eventually action could be required of Jin Fan's units, should the American carrier proceed north of thirty-five degrees north latitude.

Jin Fan would welcome—no, he would *relish*—an opportunity to go up against the Americans even if it were mock combat operations, each side trying to show the other its capabilities.

The first tasks would be routine surveillance, and he suspected that already the maritime patrol squadrons tasked at Guangzhou would be making overflights of the American warship.

The order indicated that the carrier, the USS *Lincoln*, was steaming north at a speed of advance of thirty knots. That would place the ship and its accompanying escorts at the thirty-fifth parallel about 0400 on the morning of October 7. That would be Jin Fan's H-hour, the time he would assume surveillance responsibilities.

It would be logical for him to employ the long-range Xian H-6 Badger bombers to show the flag of the PRC to the Americans, and he could do that with the 12th Strategic Bombing Squadron assigned temporarily to his air regiment. But he would bust a dim-sum-filled gut to be able to overfly the carrier force with his newly acquired Su-27As. That would be a flight he would personally lead, and he would pass low enough over the flight deck of the *Lincoln* to see the surprised faces of the Americans. Yes, indeed, they would smell the residue from his afterburners.

Jin Fan pushed the button on his intercom, and his deputy regimental commander answered, "Yes, Colonel?"

"I am going flying. Have the line prepare one of the Flankers for me, number two-two if it's available."

"What time, Colonel?"

"Give me a few minutes to complete some of this cursed

paperwork.'' Jin Fan glanced at the wall clock. "Twenty minutes.''

"The aircraft will be ready, Colonel.''

The cursed paperwork took thirty-five minutes, but by 3:00 P.M. Jin Fan was airborne and climbing east toward the Gulf of Chihli. He checked in with the military air defense identification zone monitors. "Dragon Fire, this is Tsingdai Two Two. I will be operating over Bo Hai [Chinese name for Gulf of Chihli] at altitudes between eight and fifteen thousand meters.''

"Tsingdai Two Two, we hold you. Display code one-one-one-seven while in area.''

"One-one-one-seven.''

Jin Fan took up a heading toward Inchon, South Korea, but he would not proceed beyond the portion of Korea Bay that was bordered by China. His communist compatriots from the northern part of the Korean Peninsula did not take kindly to anyone approaching their airspace, even their brothers from the vast mainland of China. No, his intent was to refresh himself on what the area looked like should the American carrier launch air strikes against Beijing. It was a fantasy thought, of course, but Jin Fan amused himself by diving and climbing and turning in imaginary combat with the F-14s and F/A-18s of the American navy. What glory there would be in such a defense of his homeland. Colonel Jin Fan, leading ace of the 23rd Air Defense Regiment, holder of the Order of Mao and Hero of the People's Republic! He placed a tiny white cloud in the center of his HUD and blasted another Hornet from the skies over Bo Hai.

Tiring of such play, Jin Fan called, "Dragon Fire, request you turn me over to Tianjin Control. I would like to practice an intercept.''

"Tsingdai Two Two, contact Tianjin, one-two-one-point-one.''

Jin Fan made his request and received an immediate

reply from Tianjin. "Tsingdai Two Two, the only target we hold is China Airlines Flight Three-Five from Baoding to Beijing."

"That will do nicely."

"Two Two, vector two-eight-five. Your speed, please?"

"One-zero-four-zero kilometers per hour."

"Maintain, Two Two."

Jin Fan changed his HUD from navigation to its air-to-air attack mode, and within seven minutes the controller had him within acquisition range of the airliner. "I have the target," Jin Fan reported.

"Cleared for simulated attack. Minimum approach distance, one thousand meters."

Jin Fan closed on his target, centered it until his missile guidance system had a firm lock-on, then pushed his FIRE button. The master arming switch was off, of course, so the deadly heat-seeking weapon did not fire. Jin Fan saw only an imaginary smoke trail and then an orange explosion as he downed another American jet.

The pilots of the transport leaped up against their restraining belts as Jin Fan passed below them with only seventy feet of clearance, pulling sharply up in front of them and executing a series of victory rolls.

"Idiot! Stupid dung-eating idiot!" the transport pilot cried out. "Report that military bastard to Beijing Center. I will kill the pig if we ever meet."

The copilot did as requested, knowing full well that nothing would come of his call. After all, there had been no collision—only a cabin full of panic-stricken passengers wearing soiled underwear.

13 ═══════════════════

Promptly at 1900, Dunne and Kohn were ushered into Paterson's cabin by the marine guard assigned to the admiral. Captain Dave "Jocko" Tyler, the skipper of the *Lincoln*, and Captain William "Walleye" Duke, commander of the carrier air wing (referred to as CAG in WW II tradition), were seated with Paterson at a green-felt-covered conference table. Tyler immediately struck Kohn as a miniature naval officer, one that you could set on your front lawn instead of the old prejudicial black jockey. Barely five-feet-four, the captain was as lean as a stalk of celery and tanned to the point where skin cancers were definitely in his future. He wore gold Naval Flight Officer wings above the left pocket of his khaki shirt, *real* gold wings that shone with their own glow instead of the standard GI-issue wings preferred by most flying officers. His record as a combat officer in the Persian Gulf War had given him command of a nuclear carrier, a highly prized billet only rarely assigned to nonpilots.

Walleye Duke, on the other hand, could have worn Jocko Tyler as an ornament on his belt buckle. Six-foot-two, pushing the maximum weight limit even for a four-striper,

Duke was a legend in the carrier navy. Four thousand hours in F-4s, F-14s and F/A-18s with over 1600 traps—Duke had done it all. He had two ejections under his belt, one from a wildly tumbling F-4 over the Inland Sea of Japan, the other from a wounded Desert Storm F/A-18 that managed to carry him back to his ship but sucked up the last drop of fuel when only 200 feet short of the number-one wire. It was after the second incident that Duke's left eye took on a mean outward cant whenever he became angry, thus his revised call sign "Walleye."

"Sit down," Paterson invited. There was no need for introductions; the five had talked on several occasions while the *Lincoln* had been en route to Hong Kong.

"Sirs," Dunne began, "Commander Kohn and I would like to give the bottom line first. We think we have a do-able mission here. There is only one main concern and that is the timing. It's a bitch. I'm sure you'll agree as we cover the tactics." Dunne spread his planning map on the table in such a way that the others could readily follow his briefing. First he pointed out the flight path of the Chinese transport carrying Desird from Changchun to Beijing. Placing a finger on Chengde, he added, "This is Chi Lin's recommended point of interception. Captain Tyler, we based our computations on the launch and recovery points being here, off Inchon."

Tyler mentally measured the distance. "Eighty miles offshore?"

"Yes, sir, in South Korean waters."

Tyler could see that there was ample steaming area for operating aircraft without infringing on the water north of the 38th parallel. "I don't see any problems."

Dunne continued, "We've based all of our times on the takeoff time of Desird's aircraft at Changchun. That'll be zero time. If our assumptions are correct, the target will reach Chengde at zero plus ninety minutes. Backing up the time and considering the distance of our route—" Dunne paused and traced the intended penetration route from the *Lincoln* to Chengde. "—and our no-wind speed, we will have to launch at zero plus thirty-six minutes."

Paterson interjected, "So we'll have about a half hour within which to get Chi Lin's report of the takeoff time before we have to launch?"

"Yes, sir. That's the first timing consideration. We do have some leeway. We computed our time en route at an economical cruise speed; we could punch it up if we're late getting the takeoff time, but not one hell of a lot."

Captain Duke added, "We'll have a Hawkeye airborne to receive Chi Lin's transmission and relay it to the ship."

Dunne went on. "In theory, we'll be vectored into position to make the intercept at Chengde. Realistically, we have about a thirty-minute window to complete the intercept before the transport starts letting down into Beijing. That's the second critical timing consideration."

Captain Tyler queried the CAG, "How's it look to you, Walleye?"

"Possible. I agree with Captain Dunne. It's a timing nightmare. There are so many variables, including the winds en route. Desird's launch time could certainly slip after we get Chi Lin's projection. Air traffic problems are possible between Changchun and Beijing, although I suspect there will be little traffic at that time of the night. Takeoff at Changchun should be at midnight, right?"

"Yes," Dunne replied, "it's a regularly scheduled red-eye logistic flight, five nights a week. At our briefing in Cuihengcun, Chi Lin reported that it's one of the few scheduled flights that routinely departs and arrives on time."

"Except for the night we fly," Walleye remarked, a sarcastic grin spreading across his massive face like the Trans-Siberian Railroad.

The others understood the significance of his comment: one of Murphy's Laws was that anything that can go wrong, will go wrong.

Walleye asked, "What's the total distance in and out?"

Kohn spoke for the first time. "Eight hundred and eighty miles."

"Refueling requirements?"

Dunne responded, "At first, we figured we could just squeeze by with our onboard fuel, but I don't think we want to just squeeze by on this type of mission. I know there's a real risk putting up tankers with all of the Chinese—and North Korean—radars around the area we'll be using. They might not buy a 'routine flight operations' explanation."

Tyler's interjection was low and slow. "That's for god-damned sure. They're going to be making noises about any flight operations in that part of the Yellow Sea. I assume we're counting on them not picking up the Sea Scorpions."

Paterson entered the discussion. "That's the premise. There's no reason for them to have any suspicions that we have Stealth aircraft on board."

Walleye Duke poured himself a glass of water from a chromed decanter on the table. "How about tactics going in?"

Dunne gave Kohn the go-ahead with a sideward glance her way.

"We'll fly best winds going in to conserve fuel. We anticipate the intercept will be in the twenty thousand feet altitude range. After the shoot, we go low and balls to the wall—as well as ovaries—coming out." Her last phrase brought grins but no comments.

"And you want tankers where?"

"Here." Dunne pointed to a small red dot above the thirty-eighth parallel, opposite the wide entry into Korea Bay.

Walleye's considerations intensified, "Shit, that's really letting it all hang out. The North Koreans will be on our asses for sure, and most probably the Chinese. We're really twisting the dragon's tail. This part, I do not like. I do not like it at all."

Dunne made his argument. "If we use tankers, that's the farthest away we can have them and be confident we can reach them. Move them back and we might as well not have them at all."

Kohn backed him. "They wouldn't have to be on station until we start back. In fact, if all goes well, they could launch at one-plus-forty-five. We both hit the refueling point at the same time, take ten minutes to top off—and we can do that while heading back toward the *Lincoln*—and all hands haul ass back aboard. Hell, I'm not sure the North Koreans can react fast enough to respond in time to intercept us, and I sincerely doubt the Chinese could reach us. If they challenge the tankers after we've refueled and gone, let them escort them out of their area of concern. There will be no cause for hostile action."

Walleye's left eye began to squint. "The North Koreans will be painting the tankers the moment they clear the bow of the *Lincoln*. Believe me, they run a first-class show. As for cause, they don't need any. Remember the Gomers that chopped up our man in the DMZ way back when. All it takes is one wild hair up some fighter jock's ass and we'll have the makings of another Gulf of Tonkin."

Tyler added his thoughts. "The North Koreans routinely monitor our flight operations when we're that far north, and they have interceptors on alert. They've come out before. The Chinese have major air bases at Dalian and Qingdao; both of those are within rapid response distances."

"How hard are you willing to squeeze those fuel tanks, commander?" Walleye asked.

Kohn bristled inside. *What kind of a wimp was the CAG? The whole point of carrier air was to go into harm's way. And why didn't he ask the question of Joshua? He was the flight leader and would be making the decisions.* "Until they squeak if we have to, sir, but I'd hate to lose our two birds for want of a quick drink. If need be, you can hold them on board until we start hollering."

"No, we won't shirk our side of this. You want tankers, you'll get tankers."

Kohn spoke a bit too quickly, "Neither the North Koreans nor the Chinese will pick us up."

Captain Duke's left eye went to full walleye position. "They sure as hell won't have any difficulty bagging our tankers if they take a mind to."

Kohn persisted, "Surely the tankers will have an escort."

Walleye didn't miss a beat. "*Surely.*"

Kohn knew it was time to backtrack. "I didn't think that one through, Captain. I apologize. I know the risks the tanker folks will be taking."

Paterson jumped in to defuse the situation. "That's why I wanted all of us to review the tactics involved, to iron out any differences of opinion. We have to be of one mind on this. We can't afford to have anything fall through the cracks. I'm sure Commander Kohn will more fully understand the situation when the detailed planning takes place."

Walleye was not pacified, "I thought this is the detailed planning."

"It is, sir," Dunne conceded, "and these are exactly the considerations we need to iron out."

Kohn was not happy with her slipup, but she was a lot more distressed at the tack the CAG had taken in responding to her remarks. These were all first-team players, and Walleye gave the impression that he considered female combatants one rung down the proficiency ladder. She had noticed it in the brief conversations they had had before. Despite that feeling, she would not let herself be intimidated. She deliberately reached in front of the CAG and grabbed the water decanter. "Excuse me, sir?"

Captain Tyler picked up the ball. "We can be on station by oh-four-hundred. That'll give us a day or so of routine flight operations to let the North Koreans get used to us before we have to launch the mission, assuming the date is still the ninth."

Paterson nodded. "At this point, it's locked in. I'll give the president a final briefing tonight. Chi Lin could contact us at any time, so I request we keep a Hawkeye airborne."

Walleye, his eyes almost normal, replied, "We'll have one airborne around the clock starting tomorrow morning."

"If I may, Captain," Paterson began, addressing his remarks to the CAG, "the aircrews need to know only their own roles in this, primarily the tanker crew. The actual mission—where we're going—is still beyond their need-to-know. If we can pull this off, no one beyond those of us in this compartment need be the wiser; I know we're all acutely aware of the sensitivity of what we're about. And I apologize for bringing it up again. I mean no offense. It's just that the president has taken some extraordinary steps to allow and approve this mission. It's gutsy, and I admire him for it."

"No problem," Walleye responded, "The air wing will do its part, Admiral."

It was the first time that Kohn had heard anyone refer to Paterson by his rank. But then, the ship's C.O. and the CAG had their necks on the line as well. They would have to know the identity and authority of the black man who was running the show.

"Well," Paterson decided, "if everybody's happy, I suggest we adjourn until the final prelaunch briefing. Captain, I assume you and Captain Duke will want to attend. We're using VS-29's ready room."

"Bridge business permitting. I think we're in good shape from the *Lincoln*'s standpoint."

Walleye led the others in rising. "Wonder which one of us will write the book down the line. Be one hell of a story. Unfortunately, I don't know a participle from a split infinitive. Maybe you'll ghost it for me, Commander Kohn?"

"It would be a pleasure, Captain." *When cows fly.*

Dunne and Kohn were the first to leave. "I think I triggered CAG. I didn't mean to," Kohn declared.

"He's just concerned about his people. That's the way he should be."

"Chauvinist."

"No, I don't think so. Just a pro—like you and me. You're overreacting. Women in love do that, you know."

Kohn stopped in place. Looking around to insure that they had some privacy, she hissed, "*That* is not an issue."

"Lighten up, Frosty."

"I'll show you Frosty if you keep on."

If there was one thing Dunne knew, it was when to shut up. Annie had taught him that.

"Come on; I'll buy you a cup of coffee." He steered a hesitant Kohn toward the wardroom.

Paterson checked his watch and converted the reading to Washington time. It would be 0636 and the president would be at breakfast, in all probability. That might be a good time to catch him, before the day's crowded schedule began. Paterson called the ship's communication center and asked for the duty officer. "This is Paterson. Patch me through to the White House on the scramble phone. The number is Flash One 393–1212. No tape."

"Aye, aye, sir." There was a short buzzing sound, a series of faint clicks and a voice requested, "One moment." That was normal. The president's discrete private line had only two outlets: one in the Oval Office, the other in his bedroom. He and the First Lady were probably just into their orange juice.

"Yes?"

Paterson recognized the president's voice but used their common code word to verify it. "Jambalaya?"

"Blackjack, what's up?"

"We had our briefing tonight, sir. It's a go for the morning of the ninth, our time."

"Anything unusual I should be aware of?"

"Yes, sir. The *Lincoln* will be on station approximately

eighty miles west of Inchon, but she won't have to go north of the thirty-eighth parallel.''

"Is that within her normal operating area for this deployment?'' The president knew that if it was not, the joint chiefs, CINCPAC and CINCPACFLT would have to know. That was too many people.

"Yes, sir.''

"Good. I want the word when it's over—and immediately if anything starts to unravel.''

"You'll have it, sir.''

"Good luck, Blackjack.''

"I don't count on luck, sir. I count on people, and we've got the best this time.''

"Then I'll keep a candle lit.''

"That would be nice.''

Blackjack heard the line go dead. So much for formalities.

Over at the command and control center in the Pentagon, the navy duty officer was reviewing the daily ship positions and intended movements. The *Lincoln* should be returning to Japan's Inland Sea after her port visit to Hong Kong. Instead, she was steaming north through the East China Sea, and her intended operating area for the eighth and ninth was in the Yellow Sea off Inchon. The battle group commander, Rear Admiral Jefferson, was still at the Tokyo conference, and only two escort ships were with the *Lincoln*: the cruisers *Texas* and *California*. That was not a normal situation. Battle groups deployed as a unit and steamed as a unit throughout the deployment. The duty officer called CINCPACFLT and asked to speak to the Deputy Chief of Staff (DCOS) for Operations. He was an Annapolis classmate, and the two frequently contacted one another whenever they needed an informal query answered. The DCOS came on the line. "I was sound asleep, Jason. What's up?''

The duty officer mentioned his concern. "Charlie, you know the *Lincoln* is steaming around in the China seas without her full complement of escorts."

"Yes, Admiral Jefferson is our rep at the Tokyo naval conference. The *Lincoln* was cleared for a port call to Hong Kong, along with the *Texas* and the *California*. The remainder of the task force is conducting joint training with the Japanese Maritime Defense Forces in the Inland Sea. It was all cleared with the CINC two weeks ago."

"Isn't that contrary to doctrine? Since when did we break up a battle group while deployed?"

"Since the budget-choppers got to us. We had three requirements: the naval conference, surface ASW ops with the Japanese, and a special requirement for the Hong Kong visit."

"What special requirement?"

"No need to be concerned, Jason; it's all legit."

Then why the hell aren't we aware of it? thought the duty officer. "Are the Joint Chiefs aware that they don't have a full battle group in Japanese waters?"

"Hell, Jason, that's in your area. You're on *their* staff. I'm sure they are. The CINC is in daily contact with them. You know all this. Why the questions?"

"Do you know that the *Lincoln* is steaming toward an operating area that is only eighty miles off Inchon?"

"That's within her area of responsibility."

"She'll be within North Korean and Chinese air strike coverage with inadequate air defense forces."

"We're not at war, Jason. I assume even you folks in the Pentagon know that."

"Well, the diversion is not in the original operation order. I can't pull up anything on the battle group's sailing orders that covers such a departure from standard operating procedures."

"Commander's prerogative. Admiral Jefferson has approved it and is fully aware of where the *Lincoln* is, twenty-four hours a day.''

The duty officer did not want to argue with a representative of the operational commander of the battle group. It would not be career-enhancing, even if Charlie was a classmate. ''Okay, Charlie, as long as you guys out there know what's going on. I just needed to check.''

''No problem. Say hello to Mary and the girls.''

''You bet. Thanks.'' The duty officer was not satisfied. He would see that the position and status of the *Lincoln* were included on the morning's Joint Chiefs of Staff briefing.

Dunne and Kohn sat at one of the back tables in the wardroom. The nightly movie was still in progress, some kind of action/adventure thriller set in the Congo and featuring a gray female gorilla named Amy. The mess attendants had kept the popcorn machine going, and the strong smell of the hot, buttered and generously salted white kernels overpowered even the coffee aroma. The audience was sparse, probably not more than twenty-five young fliers from the various squadrons and a foursome of ship's company flanking Commander Brill, the executive officer. The *Lincoln* was transiting an area of long, low swells and, despite her magnificent bulk, she was riding gently up and down. To the eyes, however, there was no movement of wardroom deck or bulkheads or overhead. This was in mild conflict with the hairs of the inner ear that detected even the slightest tilt of that organ with respect to the constant force of gravity.

''They could use a little more air in here,'' Kohn commented.

''Swells getting to you?''

''I can feel them. They must be considerable.''

''Would you rather have something cold to drink?''

Kohn pushed her coffee away. ''Yes, I think so.''

Dunne left and returned with two white mugs of a cherry-colored liquid and a glass of ice cubes. He dropped several into one of the cups before handing it to Kohn. "Tonight's flavor is cheery cherry."

The drink was slightly less flavorful and noticeably thinner than Kool Aid, but it was cold.

"Well, my staunch wingperson, we've got about fifty-two hours to fill in any gaps. You have one of the cards Chi Lin provided?" Dunne asked.

Kohn removed a three-by-five white filing card from her right shirt pocket and handed it to Dunne. "Test time?" she asked.

"Why not? I think I have the numbers down." The card listed the numerals from zero to nine, and across from each number was the Chinese pronunciation. "There's no way we'll get the inflections right. We'll have to watch the video for that."

Kohn reviewed the numerical code Chi Lin had proposed, "Okay, two numbers is altitude in thousands of feet; three numbers is vector direction; four with the first number zero is speed; and five or six numbers is bearing and distance. I'm ready."

"*Yao sān.*"

"Angels thirteen."

"*Dong sì wǔ dong.*"

"Four hundred and fifty knots."

"Very good. *Yao bá dong qí qí.*"

"Bearing one eight zero, distance seventy seven miles."

"*Èr èr.*"

"Two two."

"Gotcha. Two number twos means repeat transmission."

Kohn tilted her head slightly and looked down her nose at Dunne. "I knew that."

"Ha! No, you didn't! Miss Perfection screwed up."

"I did not. I was just giving you the literal translation."

"You know, this is a simple but very good system,"

Dunne commented. "Tell you what. From now to launch time, we use Chinese pronunciations whenever we have to use numbers. It'll sharpen us up. Okay?"

"*Yao dong sì.*"

"One zero four?"

"No, ten-four," Kohn corrected.

"Smart-ass."

Kohn had to hold down her giggle even though the movie was ending. "You ought to know."

"Aren't we being playful this evening?"

Kohn reached out and placed a hand over one of Dunne's. "Sorry; I just suddenly felt relaxed. I think I'll sleep tonight."

Dunne spoke softly as two officers sat down near them and started a game of gin rummy. "I've got a vacant upper in my room."

"Me on top and you on the bottom?"

"Variety is the spice of life."

"I think we both need a good night's rest. We're getting silly, and we're not about silly business on this cruise."

Dunne turned his hand over and grasped Kohn's. "I love you, Sheila. I wish I didn't, not in light of where we're going and what we're going to do, but I want you to remember that. Put it in the very back of your mind, right next to your visions of bright flowers and puppy dogs, little children and blue skies and stars. I know when we launch, neither of us will have time to think about it, and we shouldn't. But it'll be there, just in case we need it before we get back."

Kohn withdrew her hand. It didn't seem appropriate, even though they were civilians to the others in the wardroom. "Thank you, Joshua. That's very sweet."

The gentle rising and falling of the ship had a completely different effect once Kohn climbed into her bunk. The narrow shipboard bed, the nearness of the other bunk above her and the almost completely dark cabin—all combined to give her a warm, cozy feeling, almost as if she were back in the womb. She was very satisfied with her station in life, a respected military pilot who had been chosen for a special mission that would challenge all of her skills.

And her relationship with Joshua Dunne was as she had always imagined it: mutual respect and admiration and, now, mutual love. She tried to picture how life with him would be. Maybe back to Colorado; he could get another Lear and they could raise their children at the foot of the Rocky Mountains . . .

On that note, she fell asleep.

14 ═══════════════════

**USS _Lincoln,_ 80 miles west of Inchon
October 7, 7:20 A.M.**

With their planning largely completed, Dunne slept well, as did Kohn. They met in the wardroom at breakfast, Dunne just finishing his eggs as Kohn sat down. "Good morning," he said.

"Have you looked outside?"

"No."

"High thick cirrus. I talked with the weather guessers. There's one hell of a low pressure cell building over central China."

"We're two days away from launch."

Kohn took her coffee black as she commented, "That'll be just about right."

Dunne shrugged. "You pay your money and take your chances."

"Well, I was hoping we'd have something decent, at least back here for the recovery."

"That could still be the case."

Kohn started to reply, but the shrill whistle of a boat-swain's pipe came over the MC-1 speakers, and then a voice. "Now hear this; we have a Chinese overfly approaching; flight operations are in progress; no one allowed on flight deck except essential personnel—there may be photo opportunities on hanger deck. Overfly will be to port."

"Hey, let's take that in," Kohn suggested.

"Vulture's row will be wall-to-wall bodies."

"Hanger deck?"

"Same deal, I would think."

"Flag bridge should be clear."

Dunne pointed to a short stack of pancakes that one of the messmen had set in front of Kohn. "Let's just eat our breakfast."

"You're just not any fun this morning."

"You still rush outside to see airliners fly over?"

"Sometimes. This won't be an airliner."

"Your hotcakes are getting cold."

Five miles astern the *Lincoln*, the silver Xian H-6D Badger was approaching at five hundred feet altitude. The Chinese development of the 1960s Russian-built Tupolev TU-16, the H-6D was used primarily in a maritime patrol role but had the capability of carrying nuclear weapons when tasked with bombing missions. Under its swept-back wings, outboard of the two Wopen turbojets, hung two C-601 antiship missiles, wicked-looking bulbous units that featured delta wings and three tailplanes set around the main body at 120-degree angles. The inertia/radar-guided missiles were manufactured by the innocuous-sounding Chinese Precision Machinery Import and Export Corporation, and the modest 500-pound warhead could achieve significant damage if placed at the right spot on a warship, even one the size of the *Lincoln*. The six aircrewmen were at their battle stations.

Closely tucked under the tips of the Badger's wings, a pair of F/A-18 Hornets from the *Lincoln*'s air wing flew escort and, like attending remoras, matched every move of the Chinese aerial shark. In a gutsy response, the two twin-gun remotely controlled gun turrets of the Badger had their 23mm barrels aimed at the Hornets: the dorsal turret covered the port escort; the ventral turret aimed at the starboard.

"Now, let's don't piss these guys off too much, Charger. I've got a pair of cannon boresighted on my canopy," cautioned the right wingman.

"Me, too, Up-Chuck. You think they know how to work those things?"

"Like a pair of chopsticks."

The Badger was gradually descending.

"Hey, Charger, I'm taking sea spray. Shouldn't we go stepped-up?"

"They're trying to fly us into the water."

"Bastards." Up-Chuck's radar altimeter was reading eighty feet. The *Lincoln* was coming up on the starboard side. "Oh, shit . . ." The Badger was easing right. "This uncircumcised prick wants to fly me into the boat. Coming over to your wing."

Up-Chuck eased back, lifted fifty feet and then crossed behind the Badger to settle smoothly into position off his leader's left wing—stepped-up.

Charger rose to the occasion. "Let's see what color Chinese balls are." He moved his two-plane formation level with the Badger's left wingtip and placed his nose eight feet outboard of the red running light. The Badger could not turn left without risking a midair. The two F/A-18 pilots were not overly concerned; in such a tight formation, they would see any movement of the Badger before the large airplane could endanger them.

The pilot of the Badger had been snookered. He had been so concerned about trying to fly the starboard F/A-18 into dangerous proximity to the carrier, he had let himself get off heading. The stern of the *Lincoln* was less than a mile away, and he was heading right at it. At five hundred knots, closure would take less than eight seconds.

He had only one move left. He pulled up into a sharp climb and laid the Badger on its left side, intent on forcing the F/A-18s to scramble for their lives, but as he looked out and back they were sticking to his wingtip like superglue. Furious, he tightened his bank past ninety degrees as his copilot yelled, "Too steep, Wan!" The stall warning horn almost drowned out the copilot's frantic call.

The pilot immediately rolled his control wheel to the right and jammed his right foot forward, but it was too late. His left wing was no longer flying, the air rushing over it forced into worthless spirals and erratic whirls by the excessive angle of attack.

"Time to haul ass, Charger."

The two agile F/A-18s turned inside the Badger and pulled up to a safe altitude. The Badger slid downward. Its left wingtip sliced into the water, and the aircraft cartwheeled upside down into a great ball of orange flame and black smoke.

"Crash! Crash! Crash!" The MC-1 announcement froze the occupants of the wardroom.

"Dear God . . ." someone said.

Everyone rushed outside and headed for the hangar deck, except Dunne and Kohn. The admiral's bridge was closer and should be unoccupied. By the time they reached it and hurried out to the open wing on the port side, the site of the Badger's death was a half mile astern. Black smoke was still rising as flames burned fuel and oil layered on the surface of the sea. The *Lincoln*'s plane guard helicopter was hovering over the spot, just upwind of the smoke.

One of the ship's officers on vulture's row, the partially open passageway on the inboard side of the island, yelled up, "They went straight in."

Dunne could see two Hornets circling the area. "What was it? We were in the wardroom."

"Chinese Badger. The dumb shit was trying to impress us and spun it in."

Dunne became aware of another presence beside him. A large presence. "What was it?" Paterson asked, puffing heavily from his fast climb inside the island to the bridge.

"Badger," Kohn answered. "We were in the wardroom."

"Any survivors?"

Dunne shook his head. "I doubt it." The three watched the helicopter search the site; it remained fifty feet over the water and didn't lower any retrieval gear. If a survivor or even a body had been sighted, a rescueman would have jumped into the sea.

The deck bullhorn blared, "Stand by to recover aircraft."

The two F/A-18s were coming into the break.

At Paterson's invitation, Dunne and Kohn joined him in his cabin. All were drinking coffee and thinking of the Badger crewmen. The enlisted were most probably the same ages as the majority of the lower-rated flight deck personnel of the *Lincoln*—in their late teens, maybe early twenties.

"Kids," Paterson muttered. "We kill kids with these silly games. It's a goddamned shame. Somewhere over there on the mainland, a half dozen mothers are going to cry their eyes out tonight."

Kohn ventured, "You think they'll know by then? Is their military that responsive?"

"Probably not," Paterson conceded, "but they'll know eventually. It's the idea of the thing. I don't mind a bit going after some beast like Desird, but to lose good, promising young lives—theirs or ours—just to show the flag sometimes gets to me. I've lived with it for over forty years. That Badger pilot wanted to show us his stuff, and our Hornet jocks may have pressed him too hard."

Kohn was mildly surprised to see such sentimentality in

the old warhorse. It gave him another dimension—one that she liked. "Name of the game, Admiral. Sometimes we just try too hard."

"Well, there could be other repercussions. Captain Tyler will have to pass the word up the chain so the Chinese can be notified. What kind of interpretation they will put on such news can only be speculated. They knew he was out here, and I suspect that he called in when he started the flyby. I don't know if the ship warned him to stay clear or not. Ordinarily, they would, but I hope in this case they didn't."

"I don't follow you, Admiral," Dunne questioned.

"If the warning was monitored by the Chinese and then their airplane goes in the drink almost directly abeam the *Lincoln*, they just might get the idea that we shot him down."

"International incident," Kohn surmised.

"One that could force us to withdraw from this area before the ninth. Political forces could take over."

Dunne and Kohn both knew exactly what Paterson was thinking. If the *Lincoln* was forced off station, Desird would be departing Beijing with three nuclear weapon detonators in his possession.

Where was Tsingdai one-two-nine? The duty air defense controller at Quindao had been following the Badger as it had overflown the American carrier. The radar return had become intermittent when the H-6 had been twenty miles out from the ship, probably because the pilot was descending and had dropped below radar coverage. The aircraft carrier, *Lincoln*, had warned the aircraft not to approach within three miles; the controller had that transmission on his tape.

Now forty minutes had elapsed, and there was no aircraft return on his scope. For the next hour, he tried to raise the Badger on several frequencies, including international emergency. There had been no distress call. He would have to notify his watch supervisor.

"Ching Li, I have lost radar and radio contact with Tsingdai one-two-nine."

Within moments, the supervisor entered the dark control room. "When was your last contact?"

"Almost two hours ago. He was descending to overfly the American carrier *Lincoln* and its two escorts."

"And he has never reported in since then?"

"No. He was being escorted by two aircraft from the carrier. They merged into one target as he descended to approach the ships and then must have gone low below our coverage."

From the aircraft's call sign, the supervisor knew the base of the Badger's origin. "You better alert Tsingdai. I'm surprised we have maritime patrol aircraft there. It's an air defense base."

"The aircraft is on temporary assignment to the Twenty-Third Air Defense Regiment."

"Then notify them, and they can contact his parent squadron. We received no distress calls or signals?"

"No."

"It may be the pilot just decided to stay low and return to Tsingdai. They seem to feel we are no importance in following them. In any event, go ahead with the standard procedures for overdue aircraft."

Colonel Jin Fan adjusted the louvered shade on the window opposite his desk. The noon sun had been reflecting from the glass-covered top, making paperwork more of a chore than usual. As he reached for the next folder, his hot-line phone sprang to life and almost danced itself off the top of the glass.

"Colonel Fan."

His operational commander, the head of the Beijing Military District, was on the other end of the line. "We understand that Tsingdai one-two-nine has not returned to base.''

"Yes, sir, that is correct. He was due back almost two hours ago.''

"Well, Colonel, he won't be back. He was shot down by the American task force off Inchon.''

"What?''

"Quindao has reported that their last contact was at the point where our aircraft was starting a routine overfly of the American warships. The supervisor has a warning from the force, instructing our Badger to stay clear. Shortly thereafter, the aircraft disappeared from the scope.''

"And the Americans shot him down?''

"Of course. If he had some type of emergency, he would have reported it, would he not?''

"If he had time.''

"The matter has gone to the Central Committee. There will be a formal protest. Cancel all further reconnaissance overflights, but put your regiment on alert. I want a two-Flanker flight on runway alert with full squadron backup until further notice.''

"It will be so, sir.'' Jin Fan was elated. The stupid Americans had completely overstepped their authority. Not only were they sailing in PRC waters, they had actually committed an aggressive act. He now had eighteen of the promised twenty-six Ukrainian SU-27s plus his regular complement of six squadrons of Chengdu F-7s, advanced copies of the Soviet MiG-21s. Old but with modern instrumentation and modified to carry air-to-surface missiles, the Chengdus could make a name for themselves if called on. As for the runway alert, Jin Fan would see that he led such a flight if it were scrambled. The American F-14s and F/A-18s would be more than a match for the Chengdus, but the Ukrainian Su-27s could hold their own against anything in the sky.

Washington, D.C.
October 6, 2:15 P.M.

Secretary of State Barbara Hopkins received the ambassador from the People's Republic of China immediately. Bowing only slightly, the ambassador handed Hopkins a formal note. She read it and invited him to sit.

"I will stand. This is a matter of some urgency."

"Mister Ambassador, I have just been talking to the crisis room at the Pentagon. The report that our ships in the Yellow Sea shot down one of your aircraft is completely false. I have a videotape of the incident, relayed via satellite from the carrier *Lincoln* within the last hour."

Hopkins reached over and pushed the PLAY button on a VCR that serviced a large television monitor submerged within one wall of her office. The tape began with the Badger closing on the *Lincoln*'s stern. On the far side wing, two F/A-18s flew in close formation. "Our aircraft were escorting your bomber; standard procedure, as you well know."

The Badger passed up the port side of the *Lincoln*, then pulled up abruptly into a steep climbing turn until it was almost on its back. The two F/A-18s pulled out and away. The Badger seemed to sideslip until a wingtip hit the water and it tumbled and exploded. Hopkins pushed the STOP button and then ejected the tape.

The ambassador's expression did not change. "If anything, that proves that the fighters shot him down in cold blood."

"Here, show this to whomsoever you wish. Let them analyze it. The crash was the result of pilot error. That flyby was too low and too close. We would have been within our rights if we had decided to fire in self defense. We did not."

"I must insist that you convey to your president the demands of the People's Republic of China for a full apology and appropriate reparations, and have your warships vacate our territorial waters immediately."

"Mister Ambassador, our ships are in international waters. We do not recognize your one-hundred-mile claim. That is old business."

"Unreconciled business, Madam Secretary. Our claim is valid."

"We will not be bullied by a trumped-up incident. The *Lincoln* will remain in her legitimate operating area, and the next aircraft that attempts an overfly of an American battle group in those particular international waters will be considered hostile."

"Then, Madam Secretary, the United States must bear the responsibility for any response by my country. The trade agreement talks that we are engaged in promise real economic opportunity for the United States and the People's Republic. It would be a shame if some thoughtless act by one of your sea commanders preempted any further discussions of that pending agreement, one that I remind you is of great value to your country."

"And to yours."

"Yes."

"Good day, Mister Ambassador."

The Chinese official maintained his proper demeanor despite his fury at being summarily dismissed by the secretary of state, a woman no less. "I have been instructed to inform you that our Central Committee expects a reply from your president within twenty-four hours."

"Good *day*, Mister Ambassador."

Tokyo

Rear Ádmiral "Jumpin' Joe" Jefferson sat with his staff. "This changes things. I will have to pull out of the naval talks. Washington has a replacement on the way. How soon can we sail to rejoin the *Lincoln*?"

His chief of staff replied, "All ships have been notified of the situation. The surface ASW group that is with the

Japanese in the Inland Sea awaits your order to rejoin the *Lincoln*. We recommend you fly to your flagship. The air force has an aircraft on alert to take you to Kunsan. One of the *Lincoln*'s aircraft will be waiting there.''

"Make it so. I will go and tender my regrets to the host of the naval talks. Have CINCPAC and CINCPACFLT been informed of my intent?''

The chief of staff held out a clipboard. "For your release, Admiral.''

"Good. Let's get rolling.''

USS *Lincoln*

Paterson stood next to the captain's chair on the bridge of the *Lincoln*. Captain Tyler briefed him. "Admiral Jefferson and his staff will be rejoining us ASAP, and the other ships of the battle group are steaming to rendezvous with us here on station. The executive officer had turned his quarters over to you. I trust that will not be inconvenient.''

"Of course not. I am the admiral's guest. I fully understand. Is our mission threatened?''

"No. Business as usual. From now on, I will route all traffic by you. The Chinese are making loud noises, threatening to boycott the trade talks—also thinly veiled hints of military action.''

"Against us?''

"Just talk. They would be crazy to carry things that far. They need the trade agreement as much as we do. They're just moving to save face.''

Paterson was not that confident. And if his mission went sour, there could be a major confrontation. He would have to discuss that possibility with Rear Admiral Jefferson when he returned to his flagship.

As he stood by Tyler's chair, the closest thing to a throne in the United States military services, other thoughts were rushing through his mind. While the *Lincoln* had sufficient operating area at this time, the full battle group would find itself in restricted waters and very vulnerable to Chinese attack if the improbable came to pass. The PRC had a respectable submarine force, and a clandestine torpedo attack could well be under consideration by the Chinese if they really thought the *Lincoln* had shot down the Badger. And then there were the North Koreans, unlikely players in any game that developed from the current crisis, but they could not be ignored. They would welcome an opportunity to get in their licks at the United States. It would take a temporary reconciliation with the mainland Chinese, but under the proper circumstances that was not an impossibility. He wouldn't mention his thoughts to Tyler at the moment, but they would be a must when Jefferson arrived. Paterson also suspected the same thoughts were running around in the mind of Jocko Tyler. He was no man's fool. In fact, watching the feisty little four-striper in action would probably be quite a treat, along with Walleye Duke, the picture-book CAG, and Jumpin' Joe Jefferson, whom a lot of the right people thought was already on his way to the CNO's chair. If the Chinese wanted to take that trio on, Paterson figured they'd learn a completely new meaning for the old expression "tiger by the tail," and he would serve as a seaman under those three any day.

Kunsan, South Korea

The USAF C-21 Learjet had transited the five hundred miles from Tokyo in forty-five minutes, aided by a strong and unusual east-to-west tailwind. It was guided into position beside a waiting F-14 from the *Lincoln*. A multi-tailed, high-winged, twin turboprop Greyhound was parked just beyond the Tomcat. The large Grumman-built COD (carrier on-board delivery) aircraft would take the admiral's staff to the carrier.

"Got my flight gear?" Jefferson asked his aide.

"Yes, sir." The blond female lieutenant had hauled a crammed B-4 type bag off the Learjet and sat it at Jefferson's feet. He zipped it open and started suiting up. The jaygee F-14 driver assisted the admiral.

"Flight plan filed?" Jefferson asked, grunting as he pulled the flight suit up and over his shoulders.

"Yes, sir."

"Good. I'll drive. Any problems with that?"

The aide discreetly cast her eyes upward as the jaygee looked to her for guidance.

"No, sir."

"Don't grab your balls. I'm qualified and current." Jefferson double-checked his Velcro fittings and zippers as his aide handed him his helmet. It was all white and had a small American flag decal over each side, and on the front were two half-inch silver stars. Over the stars, in black one-inch-high letters, were two words "Jumpin' Joe." The admiral gave his staff a farewell wave as they approached the Greyhound and spoke a last time to his aide. "Paula, see you on board the *Lincoln*."

"Yes, sir, Admiral. Have a good flight."

Turning to his pilot, Jefferson gave him one last chance. "Would you rather go with her?"

The jaygee knew such a decision would end a beautiful budding career. He'd take his chances in the rear seat of the Tomcat. "No, sir." He climbed the boarding ladder and stooped over to climb into the cockpit. Jefferson was right behind him, and by the time the jaygee had his straps tight, the admiral had started the airplane and was motioning for the ground crewmen to pull the chocks. He gave a burst of power and the F-14 bolted forward as if it were an alert aircraft on a combat scramble. "You handle the radio," Jefferson said on the intercom. "I'll see if I can get this damn thing into the air. All buttoned up back there?"

"Yes, sir." The jaygee hurriedly requested taxi clearance, since they were already rolling, and then asked for their flight plan clearance. By the time he had rogered and cranked in the coordinates on the Global Positioning Satellite–based navigational system, Jefferson was pulling onto the active runway.

The tower was still giving climbout instructions as Jefferson cooked off the afterburners and released the brakes. He rotated and sucked up the gear as the Tomcat broke contact with the runway. They went supersonic as they passed five thousand feet and stayed at that speed until thirty miles from the *Lincoln*. At that point, Jefferson chopped his power, extended his speed brakes and smoothly executed a half dozen aileron rolls as they dropped to enter the landing pattern for the carrier. He leveled at one thousand feet, flew up the ship's wake until over the bow and broke sharply left. By the time he was downwind, he had his proper speed pegged, gear and hook down.

The jaygee's attitude had changed from sheer panic during the departure from Kunsan to mild shock as the admiral turned on final and called the ball in a slightly unorthodox manner. "Tomcat, ball, Jumpin' Joe, one plus thirty."

"Five knots fast," the jaygee called, one of his duties as rear-seater to closely monitor airspeed during approaches.

"You get to be my age, son, and you carry a little extra for deteriorating reflexes."

The jaygee wished he were in Philadelphia. Nevertheless, the airspeed needle dropped five knots and stayed right on speed during the remainder of the approach. A perfect number-three wire pass, and as they followed the plane director into their park position, Jefferson opened the canopy and adjusted his seat height.

Eight yellow-shirts, plane handlers, took positions as side boys in front of the deplaning ladder. As the engine spooled down and Jefferson unstrapped himself, the flight deck bullhorn carried the sound of four-bells, then the boatswain's whistle followed by the traditional "Commander, Carrier Battle Group Three, arriving."

The side boys held their salute as Jefferson passed through their ranks, his hard hat still on so he could return the salute.

Captains Tyler and Duke greeted him first. "Welcome back aboard, Admiral," Tyler said. Duke handed Jefferson a cold can of Pepsi as he repeated the salutation. Whenever Jumpin' Joe Jefferson climbed out of an airplane after an operational flight as pilot, somebody better be on hand with a Pepsi. It was such a trademark with him that there were rumors he was getting a fee from the cola company. Not true, of course, but it added color, and Jefferson liked color.

"Good to be back . . . ah! Admiral Paterson . . ." Jefferson saluted and reached out for Paterson's hand. Several of the nearby crew raised their eyebrows as they heard the greeting. They knew the big black man was somebody important, but the official word was that he was nonmilitary, like the two Stealth pilots. There would be some interesting mess deck conversations later on.

"Good to see you again, Admiral. I'd like to present Joshua Dunne and Sheila Kohn."

"Our two Lockheed civilians, I gather," Jefferson responded, rolling his tongue around in his cheek. "I want to talk to you two. Admiral, if you would, sir, give me time to pump bilges and slip into something comfortable, and let's get together in my cabin."

Paterson nodded consent.

"Jocko, Walleye, can you join us?"

The two captains assured him they would be there.

Rear Admiral Jumpin' Joe Jefferson, fighter pilot extraordinaire and carrier battle group commander, upended his Pepsi while he strode rapidly across the flight deck as if on a personal mission from God and disappeared into the island hatch, closely followed by the marine assigned as his personal guard.

"So that's Jumpin' Joe Jefferson," remarked Kohn.

Patterson chuckled. "That he is. Every navy should have one—but only one."

Jefferson had changed to work khakis, although a green foul-weather jacket was slung across the back of his chair at his conference table. "Sir," he began, addressing Paterson, "my presence back aboard doesn't change anything concerning your mission, but I would like to make sure the command situation meets with your concurrence. It's a bit unusual to have a retired four-star on board with authority of the president to direct this battle group."

"Joe, I understand. I have no official command authority here. I have no official navy orders. I am not on active duty. Therefore, I certainly defer to you as the commander of the battle group. I do have responsibility for the special mission, but in a manner of speaking it is at the convenience of the U.S. Navy."

"Thank you, sir. I just wanted to make sure we're driving the same train. The situation with the Badger crash has turned into a real donnybrook. There could be some hostile action as a result, either covertly or overtly. If there is, I intend to kick some Chinese ass. I hope you're comfortable with that, Admiral."

"I've already reserved a box seat."

"Great! Now, if something does develop along those lines, I hope you will feel free to give me any advice and counsel you deem appropriate. I may not take it, since the ultimate responsibility for the conduct and safety of this battle group is mine, but I sincerely solicit it. I'm a great fan of yours, Admiral, and your experience and leadership could be of value to us, command relationships aside."

Paterson responded, "Thank you, Joe. I appreciate that. I'll stay out of your way, but I'm not shy. I will speak up if I think I can be of any help."

"Thank you, sir. Now, about this Desird thing. Is it on

track?'' Jefferson obviously was addressing his question to Dunne.

''Yes, sir. We have confirmed the date and time of his flight. Our tactical planning is complete except for the final briefing. It's down to a matter of timing and luck, I suppose.''

''Don't like the word 'luck.' Commander Kohn, I've heard some nice things about you. It's a pleasure to meet you in person and have an opportunity to observe you in action.''

''Thank you, Admiral.''

''I have a terrific aide, Lieutenant Paula Crommelin. Comes from a long line of distinguished naval officers. She's everything I want in an aide—bright, responsive, has a wealth of initiative and takes care of me as if I have Alzheimer's. You'll like her. There's only two things. She wears too much makeup and uses some kind of perfume that makes me want to grab her and break into a tango. Now, that's not fair to us old studs. I can't say anything in today's navy. Maybe you could sort of give her a little advice and counsel—and if you're touchy about this sexual harassment thing, these other four naval officers will swear I never said a word to you.''

Kohn was completely won over by Jefferson's personality. ''Admiral, I'd be pleased to be of any assistance.'' Her broad smile confirmed her acquiescence.

''She's just a young lady. You understand what I'm saying.''

''Yes, sir, I do.''

''Thank you. Now, let's get back to the mainland Chinese. Jocko, I think we better assume that they'll be up to something. How long before we have the other ships in formation?''

''They've only been underway for a couple hours as you know, Admiral, but with good seas and weather, they project arrival by tomorrow afternoon.''

"All right; as soon as my staff gets on board we can start functioning the way we should. Until then, Walleye, I want some increased ASW protection."

"We can set that up immediately. We already have minimum coverage, although with just the *Texas* and the *California* we're vulnerable."

"How good are our VS and HS people?"

"Well-trained and lots of experienced personnel."

"They'll have to hold the fort until the surface units arrive. They may have to modify their search patterns to avoid getting too close to the coastal areas. Meanwhile, our main task remains the same. Hold in this area until Admiral Paterson's unit can accomplish their mission. At that point, I'll have no qualms about sailing south to relieve some of the tension. Meanwhile, we must hope and pray the Chinese don't do anything irrational."

15 ━━━━━━━━━━━━━━

Colonel Jin Fan was pleased. His request for a routine surveillance flight by the alert Flanker flight over the Gulf of Chihli had been approved. If he had stated his real purpose, he would have been reprimanded and grounded. But Fan was an ardent disciple of the revolution, not a mere figurehead like the fat generals who determined military policy based exclusively on political purposes. They had not the courage for what Fan would have proposed. There was a time for debate and a time for action. Let them debate the cause of the loss of the Badger until the Great Wall fell; it was no mystery to Fan. The Americans had had their way for the last fifty-five years, at first deserving it as they pulled the world out of World War II with their tremendous economical and industrial base. But they had been no match for Mao, their first losing effort being their futile attempt to shore up those forces who opposed the revolution. Even when obviously defeated in their political support of Chiang Kai-shek, they attempted to salvage their integrity by the recognition of Taiwan as Nationalist China—a stupid phrase—while it was, in fact, a dissident province of the PRC. Fan could never understand why the PRC allowed

216

it to exist, and now in the late '90s, the United States, depleted by economical woes and moral decadence, would think twice before honoring its commitment to the Taiwanese. Maybe now was the time to test that resolve, to show the imperialists a hint of what the military forces of the PRC had become: a much more modern force manned by patriots like Fan who on this day intended to make a point. He would play an active role in the deteriorating politico-military situation between the PRC and the United States. With one stroke, he would avenge his comrades who died in the Badger incident and end the trade talks that were already an impediment to the growth of the PRC's economy. China's market was the world, particularly the emerging nations of the Pacific Rim, not the near-bankrupt Americans.

Even now, in their declining days as a world power, they were resisting any demands that their naval forces withdraw to the south, probably because they felt so superior and so smug with their state-of-the-art carrier air forces. Well, they needed to see the red star and bar insignia of the Air Force of the People's Liberation Army emblazoned on the sides and wings of a pair of Su-27 Flankers; that would cause them to have second thoughts.

He led his wingman into the partly cloudy sky over Beijing and turned southeast toward Bo Hai—the Gulf of Chihli. The pair of ex-Soviet air superiority fighters leveled at 13,000 meters, a fuel-efficient altitude that would swiftly take them to the Yellow Sea. To add credence to what he had reported as an advanced patrol exercise, he had arranged for an air-to-air refueling over the tip of the Bandao Peninsula. The southward jut of land marked the north side of the entrance to Bo Hai and was a mere 360 kilometers from the position of the American carrier—200 nautical miles.

"Tiger Two," Fan called to his wingman, "when we reach the refueling point, you will refuel first." Fan intended to have absolutely full tanks when the final phase of his plan began.

"Tiger Two, acknowledged."

Within minutes, Fan was picking up the tanker's position transmitter. The modified Ilyushin Il-28 Beagle was one of only a few airborne tankers, the PRC concentrating on fighter and strike force modernization; at the moment, it was dead ahead at seventy-five kilometers, altitude 12,000 meters. Fan raised his gloved right hand and gave a descend signal to his wingman. As they leveled at the tanker's altitude, Fan reported, "Skyfuel, this is Tiger Flight, distance twenty-six kilometers."

"Tiger Flight, my refueling course is one hundred and sixty degrees."

Watchdog entered a standard rate 180-degree left turn to complete another circuit of his on-station pattern along the thirty-eighth parallel equidistant from the Chinese and North Korean coastlines. Five thousand feet overhead, a pair of Tomcats was flying cover.

At the center console within the darkened crew compartment of the E-2C Hawkeye, air controller Amy Swayze reported two contacts to the airborne CICO. "I have two bogies, bearing three-zero-zero degrees, one hundred and twenty miles, altitude thirty-eight thousand. Phil, can you give me a better picture? There's a lot of clutter on the scope."

Radar operator/technician Phil Burrows checked his tuning and brilliance settings.

"Their course is one-two-zero," Swayze added.

The CICO responded, "Designate Bogies One and Two."

Within the CIC compartment of the *Lincoln*, the contacts were automatically relayed, displayed and designated by digital downlink from the Hawkeye.

"I have another contact over the tip of the Bandao

Peninsula, left hand turn, thirty-eight thousand. Bogies One and Two seem to be merging with him,'' Swayze reported.

"Designate new contact Bogie Three." The CICO watched the contacts on his scope.

"Bogie Three steady on course one-six-zero."

The three air surveillance and control crewmen watched Bogie Three for another five minutes before it split into three separate returns, the two smaller taking a course directly toward the Hawkeye. "Refueling operation," the CICO said quietly. "They may be intending to look us over."

Swayze reported, "Bogies One and Two closing, eighty miles."

The CICO alerted his air cover, "Topcap, we have a pair of bogies bearing three-zero-zero, eight-zero miles, closing. Vector one-two-zero, angels forty."

"Topcap, one-two-zero, angels forty."

Colonel Jin Fan glanced back at his wingman who was riding comfortably off his right wing. He also looked around at the developing weather. There had been light rain and a noticeable temperature drop back at Tsingdai, prompting his weather briefer to forecast frontal weather for their return. Ahead, over the northernmost reaches of the Yellow Sea, there was a lower overcast with tops probably at five to six thousand meters. He wouldn't be able to see the carrier, and he mentally weighed the consequences if he took his flight underneath the cloud cover.

"Tiger Leader, we're under radar surveillance."

Jin Fan cursed to himself. He had been so engrossed in his thoughts of the carrier, the faint buzz in his headset had come unnoticed. His flight was definitely being tracked by air search radar, most probably from the carrier. Good; he wanted his presence known.

"Fire control radar, tracking!" Tiger Two called, then immediately added, "We're under attack!"

"No. We'll hold this course." Jin Fan was confident that they were not under attack. That would be a stupid mistake by the Americans. An intercept, yes. That was expected, and even as he congratulated himself for planning such a flight, he and his wingman were rocked by the two F-14s that flashed by, one on each side. Jin Fan called the controller at Yantai and set the second phase of his plan into action. "Tiger Flight under attack! Taking defensive action."

The Tomcats had pulled up into loops and came up behind the two Flankers. They eased into positions until Jin Fan was leading a four-plane formation. A voice came up on the international distress frequency. "Flanker Flight, this is Topcat One. If you read English, switch to frequency two-two-six-point-one."

Jin Fan and his wingman were proficient in English. That was necessary for his plan. Fan replied, "This is Tiger Leader. Good afternoon."

"Tiger Leader, you are approaching an American battle group. Request you remain clear; flight operations are in progress."

"Strange," Jin Fan replied, "it appears to me that there is no United States flag painted on the Yellow Sea." Jin Fan gave a descend hand signal to his wingman and they started down. The F-14s held their position.

"What are your intentions, Tiger Flight?"

"To carry out my orders. Is it not the same with you?"

"Be advised, Tiger Flight, an overflight of the battle group will be considered a hostile act."

The two Flankers were dropping fast, ten thousand feet per minute. "Congratulations, Topcat, you and your wingman fly a commendable parade position. This could be a historic day, could it not? Two aircraft from the Air Force of the People's Liberation Army leading two American naval fighters in a salute to your battle group. I will try and provide a smooth lead.''

"Tiger Flight, we are cleared to engage."

"As are we, Topcat, but such a move would seem foolish. You and your battle group are in Chinese airspace and waters. We would be justified in whatever hostile act we choose. But as a gesture of peace and an appeal to your better judgment, our intention is to salute the brave seamen and airmen of Carrier Battle Group Three. You have joined us in what I would think could be a show of mutual courtesy. Beijing is aware that I and my comrade are making only a surveillance pass and would react instantly should American forces take hostile action. You, yourselves, perform such maneuvers over waters in all parts of the world, and they are universally recognized as nonhostile.''

"Your call, Tiger Flight."

"It is that, Topcat."

The formation dropped out of the bottom of the cloud layer. The USS *Lincoln* lay dead ahead at twenty-five miles.

Both the Hawkeye and the *Lincoln* had followed the frequency switch and had monitored the transmissions of the mixed formation. Admiral Jefferson, most of his staff, Walleye Duke and Paterson were all monitoring the situation in the ship's CIC spaces. The ship's CICO was keeping Jocko Tyler advised as the captain remained on the bridge.

"We may have a couple of cowboys here," Jumpin' Joe declared.

Walleye agreed. "They're damned determined to overfly us. I recommend we launch the alert CAP." A pair of manned F/A-18 Hornets was in position on the ship's numbers one and two catapults.

Jumpin' Joe disagreed. "No; the F-14s can handle the situation. I don't believe those two commies are foolish enough to commit suicide. They're just trying to rattle our cages by showing off their new airplanes. We've had reports that they have several squadrons of them and are acquiring more from the Ukrainians. Let 'em crow a bit. In fact, let's pull a switch and welcome them to our airspace, but be specific. They're to make the pass along the port side no lower than five hundred feet and no closer than one mile when they pass abeam.''

"They'll be thinking in metric, Admiral," advised the air controller assigned to Jumpin' Joe.

"Okay, translate; can you do that?"

"Yes, sir."

"What if they violate the order?" Walleye asked. "The rules of engagement we're under specify fire only if fired upon."

"I just changed 'em," Jumpin' Joe declared. "Tell the Tomcats that if the Flankers deviate one quarter of an inch, splash the sonsuvbitches."

Jin Fan heard the instructions relayed by his escort leader. "Tiger Flight will comply," he responded. That was exactly what he wanted. He spoke briefly to his wingman in Chinese.

The formation approached the *Lincoln* well within the parameters set by the Commander, Battle Group Three.

Jumpin' Joe motioned for the others to follow him. "Let's go up on the bridge and take a look at these new airplanes the Chinks want us to see so badly."

The flag bridge was manned with talkers and lookouts. Jumpin' Joe and the others took their positions on the port open wing. Dunne and Kohn were a level lower on vulture's row, which was full as usual.

"Now there's a sight to see," Jumpin' Joe observed. The F-14s had closed to within a few feet of the Flankers, and the fingertip formation rode as if the four pilots were members of some international flight demonstration team. "We're taping this, aren't we, Walleye?"

"Yes, sir."

The formation was exactly abeam of the *Lincoln*. Jin Fan knew the moment had come. *Observe, former world leaders, the agility and daring of the new Air Force of the People's Liberation Army.* "Stand by . . ." he ordered in Chinese, ". . . execute!"

Paterson was the first to cry out. "Sweet Jesus, look at that!"

The two Flankers, racing along at well over three hundred knots, had abruptly jerked their noses into the air until they actually passed the vertical and tilted slightly backward. Simultaneously, the pair had lit off their afterburners. It was the classic Cobra maneuver that Soviet pilots had used to astound Western observers at the Paris Air Show just a few years back. Any other aircraft would have experienced a high-speed stall and spun in on the spot. Caught by surprise, the two F-14s shot ahead as the Flankers stood on their tails, held against the force of gravity by the 55,000 pounds of combined thrust from their twin Saturn AL-31F turbofan engines.

Then, by brute force, the Flankers climbed out of their vertical nose position to level flight. The Tomcats were in a maximum-G turn, frantically trying to get back into position to resume their escort duties. They would never have executed such a maneuver if it had been a combat situation, for the Flankers, at an extremely low speed, were turning inside them.

"Oh, God, no . . ." Jumpin' Joe prayed as two pairs of short-range AA-8 Aphid missiles erupted from under the wings of the Flankers.

Wrapped tightly in their ninety-degree banks, the broad topside view of the Tomcats presented a perfect target for the radar-homing Aphids. The Americans had no time to react, and the solid-rocket-propelled air-to-air weapons smashed into the Tomcats at Mach 3. The two swing-wing fighters disintegrated.

Even as Jumpin' Joe was calling, "Launch the CAP!" the two ready Hornets were catapulted off the bow of the *Lincoln*, the angry sounds of their turbojets roaring for vengeance. The second tier of duty aviators who had been standing on the flight deck next to their airplanes, watching the flyby, was already climbing into the cockpits.

The two Flankers were going straight up and disappeared into the cloud cover.

"Save those goddamned tapes!" Jumpin' Joe ordered just as the bridge of the *Lincoln* passed the word "General quarters! General quarters! All hands man their battle stations. This is no drill. I say again, this is no drill."

"Pass those orders to the *Texas* and *California*," Jumpin' Joe directed, already out of sight as he left the flag bridge for CIC.

Charger and Up-Chuck had been sitting in their catapult-positioned aircraft, tightly strapped in, their necks twisted as they tried to watch the flyby. Charger had a terrible intuitive feeling as he saw the Flankers go vertical. "Start your engines, Up-Chuck!" he had ordered, simultaneously giving his plane director his hand signal that he was spooling up. It seemed a lifetime before all of the necessary checks and launch routines had been accomplished. The catapult officer swung his arm forward and down as Charger saluted to initiate the launch. Both planes were in the air and climbing before Jumpin' Joe's launch command even reached the flight deck.

The air defense Hawkeye was tracking the Flankers as they streaked for the Chinese mainland.

Amy Swayze picked up the Hornets as they shot off the bow and gave them their first vector. "Crossbow One, vector two-seven-zero, buster, bandits at two-seven-zero, three-five miles, angels thirty.''

"Two-seven-zero, Crossbow Flight passing angels twelve." Charger began his acquisition search. The Flankers were Mach 2.3 speedsters and easily capable of 50,000 feet. The Hornet could pull Mach 1.8 on a good day, maybe a skosh more if it was angry, and these were two very mad Hornets. Maybe Charger and Up-Chuck would never catch the Flankers, but they didn't need to. Between them, they carried four AIM-7 Sparrow III air-to-air medium range missiles.

As they passed through 30,000 feet, both Hornets had acquired the Flankers on their fire-control radar. They would have to shoot before their targets opened to fifty-three miles, the Sparrow's maximum acquisition range.

"I've got a lock!" Up-Chuck jubilantly declared, and the twelve-foot, eight-inch diameter weapon blasted forward from under his port wing.

Charger was desperately trying to line up the green acquisition and lock symbols on his HUD. There! He fired his first missile as Up-Chuck fired his second. Then Charger fired his second. The Flankers were almost fifty miles ahead, but at Mach 4 the Sparrows would close in a matter of a minute or so. Once locked on, as they now were, their semi-active radar guidance system was a bitch to counter. Both pilots had reported "Fox One" as they fired, the voice signal that they had launched the weapons.

Jin Fan heard the irritating headphone buzz indicating that he and his wingman were under radar-guided missile attack. "Chaff!" he called, and the two Flankers spewed forth a cloud of shiny metal foil strips as they cranked over into a tight diving turn.

Too late. Three Sparrows went after the chaff; the remaining one smashed into Jin Fan's Flanker, and the debris cut his wingman into a thousand pieces.

*   *   *

Jumpin' Joe heard the splash reports with no change of expression. Bagging the Flankers would not bring back the Tomcat aviators. The Hawkeye reported, "All bogies destroyed; sky clear." For the first time since the Flankers had gone vertical, the battle group commander had an opportunity to try and come up with a reason why the Chinese had attacked in full view of the ships of his command. He asked his operations officer, "CINCPAC and CINC-PACFLT all brought up to date?"

"And the Joint Chiefs," his ops boss answered.

"What the hell will happen next?" Jumpin' Joe asked, more to himself than anyone else. "This is the second time the Chinese have shit all over themselves. Still, it's hard for me to think this attack was ordered." His eyes sought Paterson's. "Sir, I think we need to talk. Your two people, also."

Paterson, Dunne and Kohn followed Jumpin' Joe into a corner of the combat information center where they could speak with relative privacy.

"No sonuvabitch Chinese bastard is going to run me out of these waters or goad me into responding to this type attack with an air strike of my own. We wouldn't know what to hit, even if Washington would condone a strike." Jumpin' Joe's raspy voice was reminiscent of George C. Scott's Patton. "The question is, if the Chinese detect your little foray into their airspace, will they interpret it as a strike on the mainland? God knows where that would lead. I know Desird is a high-priority target and I would like to see the fucker dead as much as you, but I have my first doubts about allowing the mission."

Paterson kept his voice low. "It's your call, Admiral. The situation has changed, I grant you that. I would like an opportunity to get some guidance from the president. He feels even more strongly about this than I. We really don't know what the political situation is back in Washington.''

''That's reasonable,'' Jumpin' Joe declared. ''The rest of the battle group will be with us tomorrow afternoon. I'll feel much better then.''

Paterson asked, ''Joshua, would you like to add anything? Sheila?''

Dunne took the informal tone as sincerity on the part of Paterson in asking for his and Kohn's input. ''We've gone through a lot to get here and frankly, sirs, I would like to do what we've set out to do. I recognize the delicacy of the matter, but it was extremely sensitive before. The stealth qualities of our aircraft have not changed. The probabilities of us completing the task are unchanged.''

''Commander Kohn?'' Jumpin' Joe asked.

''I agree with Joshua, and in my mind by tomorrow night we're either going to be in a full-fledged combat situation or the Chinese will have come to their senses, particularly when they view the tape of the Flanker attack. Of course, if they *ordered* the attack, that's something else.''

Paterson added, ''It was completely unprovoked. The world will see that, and I think we, the United States, have the advantage now. If the Chinese want to gain an edge on the trade talks, they've chosen the wrong method. Consequently, I think the attack was independent of Beijing. If that is the case, I don't see that we are in any different position than we were two days ago. I think that the possibility of three nuclear detonators loose in the world is still justification to go with tomorrow night's mission, and that is the way I would like to present it to the president.''

Jumpin' Joe nodded. ''I can live with that assessment, as long as the president goes along with it. I would prefer he pass his decision, if that is what it is, down the chain of command rather than me passing it up.''

"Thank all of you," Paterson said. "I'll see if I can reach the president. Under the circumstances, he may feel he has to discuss the issue with a few more people. I don't know. But that alone could jeopardize further activities of our special group."

Jumpin' Joe held up a finger of caution. "One final reminder. We've a second ticklish area here. We have a carrier battle group on a legitimate deployment but responding to special presidential directives that have been bypassing most of the normal chain of command. While such a setup is the president's prerogative as commander in chief, I think it is a very dangerous one from the standpoint of future relationships between him and the military. With reference to your remark, Admiral, I would like to legitimize the clandestine part of this cruise. I think the president should call together his top advisers and key members of the Congress and brief them on our plan to assassinate Desird. And that's exactly what it is: an assassination."

"And if the media gets wind of it?" Paterson posed.

"We can all start looking for new jobs in the civilian sector. But I still think we must approach the president on such a disclosure. There is the matter of security, and maybe we can't operate any more in the dark. Now is the time to find out. We either have the ability and the guts to protect this country—and, in this case, the world—or we don't. And if a handful of the highest civilian and military authorities in this country can't keep such a secret as this, a top secret mission of the highest order, then we're bogged down in more of a moral morass than I thought."

"I'll discuss the subject with the president."

"Thank you, Admiral Paterson. I know I approached you when I arrived from Tokyo on where we stood with respect to my responsibilities to this battle group and your presence. Now I seem to be getting into your area. I don't mean it to sound that way."

"No problem, Joe. I have a lot of respect and confidence in your insights. It's proper that we have this discussion."

"Well, I'll speak with Captain Tyler and tell him what we're about. Perhaps we could get together after you've had the chance to talk to the president. And I suspect CINCPACFLT will be burning my ear any time now. My quarters at dinner, unless the damned Chinese decide to stage another flyby."

16

The secretary of state rose as the ambassador from the People's Republic of China entered her office. "Good morning, Mister Ambassador. It is good of you to respond to my request so promptly."

"Good morning, Madam Secretary."

"Mister Ambassador, there has been another incident in the Yellow Sea, the second within eight hours, and this one is much more serious. I called you as soon as I was alerted. Two fighter aircraft from your base at Tsingdai made an authorized overfly of the USS *Lincoln*. As they passed abeam our carrier, escorted by two F-14 Tomcats from the air wing, they suddenly and without any provocation shot down our aircraft—in full view of personnel on our ships in the area. We immediately launched our ready combat air patrol fighters, and they destroyed the two agressors.

"As before, the flyby incident was videotaped, and I expect a copy of the relayed tape any moment. The aircraft have been identified as Su-27s."

"You say they were on an authorized flyby?"

"Yes; they at first refused to comply with our warning to stay out of the operating carrier's airspace, and the officer in tactical command, wanting to avoid any confrontation, authorized the flyby with certain very definitive restrictions.''

''I am puzzled and extremely disturbed. I have no word of this incident.''

''That is probably because our forces notified us immediately, and the president has directed me to speak with you so that you may inform your government as to what has happened. I suspect that, since your aircraft are overdue, your authorities are already investigating the matter, but we believe they are not aware of the loss of their aircraft.''

The ambassador was clearly confused.

''Here is the formal complaint from my government to the People's Republic of China.'' The secretary handed over a large white envelope just as an aide entered with a videotape.

''Would you care to sit?''

''Yes, thank you.'' The ambassador's face had resumed its normally inscrutable expression.

The two, along with the aide, watched the tape in silence. Then it was extracted and handed to the ambassador.

''We have our copy?'' the secretary questioned.

''Yes, ma'am,'' the aide replied. He walked quietly out of the room.

''Madam Secretary, I can only convey this communique and tape to my superiors. May I speak off the record?''

Barbara Hopkins pressed a button on her internal communications unit. ''The tape is off, Mister Zhoy.''

The ambassador's eyes were trying desperately to convey his regrets. ''I do not know what is going on. Clearly, this attack was not provoked, and I am convinced that the crash of the Badger was just an unfortunate accident. This will destroy the trade talks. I will deliver the tape and bring you my government's reply. Then I will make one final request.''

"Yes?"

"I will ask for political asylum for me and my wife."

It was the last thing Hopkins had expected. Zhoy had been a firm, proper and enthusiastic representative of the PRC. "I can only say that I would be quite receptive to such a request."

"Thank you. Is that all, Madam Secretary?"

"Yes, Mister Ambassador."

After the ambassador withdrew, Barbara Hopkins had one of her aides bring a cup of green tea. Her thought processes seemed to be more orderly when she sipped and enjoyed the warmth and flavor of the oriental beverage. She leaned back in her chair and let the supple brown leather caress her back. Zhoy's request for asylum was a shocker. She had always pictured him as a staunch supporter of the revolutionary process.

17 ━━━━━━━━━━━━━━━

White House
October 7, 10:00 P.M.

The president rarely consulted directly with the chairman
of the Joint Chiefs of Staff (CJCS), preferring to follow the
more standard procedure of discussing an issue with the
secretary of defense (SECDEF) and then having the secretary solicit any necessary JCS inputs. But this was a late-
night exception. Even so, the SECDEF was present, as was
the president's foreign policy advisor, Raymond Gaia, and
the secretary of state, Barbara Hopkins.

"What I want to do here," the president began, "is to
keep this situation as low-key as possible. By that, I mean
with respect to the overt actions we take. The press has the
story, and the visual media will be running program after
program on the shootdowns that occurred yesterday in the
Yellow Sea. That's why I preferred to keep this meeting
small. I don't believe the situation calls for a crisis response—not yet."

"Mister President," the secretary of state interjected, "I
would agree with that approach. Ambassador Zhoy is confused over the two incidents. I'm not sure his superiors are
any clearer on why they happened. There's no diplomatic

233

pressure from the PRC, despite their public announcements.''

"Do you think the trade agreement talks are down the tubes?"

"No, sir. I believe the Chinese want the talks to end and the shootdowns could give them an excuse, except for the videotape. The Flankers clearly instituted an attack. Our actions were just a response. If anyone should call off the trade talks, it would be us.''

"And I don't want to do that yet. That would put the ball too squarely in their court.''

The CJCS added, "We have a deployment dilemma as well. Do we pull the *Lincoln* and her escorts south, which would be in effect a retreat, or leave her where she is and risk another confrontation?''

The president knew he would not recall the *Lincoln*. His last conversation with Admiral Paterson had revealed that tomorrow morning, Washington time, the strike against Desird would take place. He was too close to that personal goal to back off. Just a few more hours was all he needed. He could see that the CJCS was harboring similar thoughts, despite the fact that he had laid the options on the table. "No. To pull back would be a show of weakness. We must continue to insist on our right to operate in those waters. They don't belong to the PRC no matter how loudly they insist on recognition of their one-hundred-mile territorial sea limit. Perhaps the one question we really need to address is, do they intend any military action, however foolish?''

"I don't think so," said the secretary of state.

"Nor do I,'' the CJSC added. "I strongly suspect that the leader of the Flanker flight was a renegade, some sort of radical thinker who thought it was time to show us what they were capable of.''

"He sure as hell didn't think it through with a pair of

Hornets sitting on catapults at the ready," SECDEF observed.

The CJCS added, "He probably thought they could outrun any of our naval fighters."

"They could, but not the missiles."

The president suggested, "I think the *Lincoln* responded with a very high degree of professionalism. There might be some awards in order."

"I think not, Mister President," SECDEF responded. "They were doing their job, and the two Hornets were doing theirs. Both the ship and the pilots performed superbly, but we would have expected them to. It's what they're trained to do. I don't see any particular heroics involved."

"I would second that thought," the CJCS agreed. "Let's don't build this up by decorating anyone."

"Then what we're saying," the president concluded, "is business as usual, and let Barbara be our feeler. If Zhoy begins to deliver a harsher response, then we look at it again. Meanwhile, I expect an apology from the Chinese."

"Zhoy has the formal demand, sir."

"Thank you for coming on short notice. I know several of you were involved in other matters that could suffer from this interruption. I just needed your input. General Jackson, would you remain for a moment?"

"Certainly, sir."

The others left.

"I want to talk to Admiral Paterson one last time. I'd like you to be here."

Northern Yellow Sea
October 8, 11:00 A.M.

The *Lincoln* was exercising her air wing in routine training. A secondary purpose was a show of force to whosoever might be watching. Blackjack Paterson was observing on the flag bridge when the president's call came over the scramble satellite connection.

"Blackjack, I just finished meeting with SECDEF, Barbara Hopkins, Raymond Gaia and General Jackson. The general's with me here, now. Is it still a go?"

"Yes, Mister President. At the moment, the pilots are drawing some extra flight equipment that we decided might be prudent."

"Such as?"

"Primarily, exposure suits. One of the fighter squadrons on board has extras. The water temperature at these latitudes is quite low."

"Well, I hope neither one of them has to swim home."

"Just a precaution, sir, and navy regulations."

"Do you have a launch time?"

"No, sir. That will come from Dong Sum. We'll launch thirty-six minutes after Desird is in the air."

"I want to know the minute the planes are back on board. We may want Admiral Jefferson to sail south."

"I understand."

"Are the other ships of the battle group with you?"

"They'll be on station by mid-afternoon."

"Good."

Paterson shifted the handset to his other ear. "I am confident we are as ready as can be."

"Please relate this conversation to Admiral Jefferson and explain to him that it was not my intent to bypass the normal chain of command."

"I'm certain he understands, sir."

"Well, good hunting, old friend."

"Thank you, Mister President."

Frosty Kohn fastened the final Velcro fittings of the rubberized exposure suit. It was a state-of-the-art design, a far cry from the early suits that fit like a balloon and were extremely uncomfortable. The thin, resilient garment was worn under the normal flight suit and anti-G trousers and featured watertight neck and wrist cuffs. The special fabric could breathe air while keeping out water for comfort while in the cockpit. The flight/survival vest and the shoulder-holstered standard-issue 9mm were the outermost garments. Kohn checked the fit. "I'll lose twenty pounds before we get back, wearing this thing." Tiny beads of perspiration were already starting to appear on her forehead despite the advertised breathability of the exposure undergarment.

Dunne was struggling into his own garment. "You punch out over these waters and you'll be singing the praises of the folks who designed these things. I remember the older ones."

Kohn was removing the suit and folding it for later use. Dunne removed his. "Thanks for the loan of the dry goods," he said to the VF-124 pilot who was assisting him and Kohn with the fitting and the inevitable paperwork.

"Just sign here for the suits, Mister Dunne."

Dunne scribled his signature on the receipt. "What happens if I don't bring this back?" he joked.

"Well, if you were military, we'd dock your pay record," the pilot said facetiously, "but since you're not, I guess we could cross them off to public relations. Sure you can't use another pilot? On your 'operational evaluation' flight, that is?"

"We don't have any more airplanes—just the two."

"Oh, I can get an airplane, sir."

Dunne studied the young man's face. It was mature beyond his years, and his eyes reflected several years of expertise gained by flying off carriers on dark and stormy nights. The air wing was well stocked with such men, and Dunne had to admit that practically every one of them could do the job he and Kohn were to do, with equal if not more grace. But that was not the way such games were played. "Maybe next time," he answered.

"Have fun, sir."

"Always do."

The ready room was two decks up and forward. Entering it, Kohn flopped down on one of the front-row chairs directly under an overhead air blower. The warm air did little to erase the hot discomfort of the exposure suit residue.

Dunne spread their planning chart across a briefing table. "Shall we go over it one last time?"

"I can fly the mission in my sleep. In fact, I may just do that if I don't get some sack time before we go. It's going to be a long night."

Dunne studied the chart for a few more minutes before folding it and stuffing it into his planning packet. He sat next to Kohn. "Any reservations?"

Kohn stretched as she tried to stifle a yawn. It didn't work. "No. I'll just be glad when it's over."

"The admiral has our briefing set for midnight. He hopes to have Desird's takeoff time confirmed while we brief."

"The timing nightmare begins . . ."

"I think we're ready. That gives us plenty of time for chow and some Zs. It's early lunch hour. Shall we do it?"

Kohn had let the back of her chair recline. "I could stay right here."

Dunne leaned over. The kiss was as light as falling snow but definitely of a different temperature. "Come on, wingperson; I'll treat you to a *Lincoln*-burger and tuck you in."

"I can tuck myself in."

"It won't be as much fun. I'm a good tucker."

Kohn pushed Dunne away and raised herself from the briefing chair. "This conversation is straying from the professional—and this is not proper ready-room conduct."

"That's right. We should be playing grab-ass and reading *Playboy*."

"You *are* from the old school."

"Those were the days, m'dear, when men were men and the ship's store was not stocked with feminine hygiene products, all the heads had urinals and there was not a copy of *Cosmopolitan* to be found in the fleet.''

Kohn playfully shoved her way past Dunne and stepped into the passageway. ''One more remark like that and I'll file harassment charges—and tonight you'll be flying on *my* wing!''

''All the way to the ends of the earth . . .'' Looking around to be sure they were alone, Dunne lowered his voice and continued, ''. . . or at least to Chengde and back.''

The happy moment dissolved.

18

The USS *Lincoln*, home away from home to some five thousand souls, steamed north through waters claimed by at least three nations. The PRC and North Korea, with their insistence that all waters within one hundred miles of their coasts belonged to them as territorial waters, actually had overlapping claims to the salt water flowing under the keel of the 97,000-ton warship. The United States, among others, said no way. This was international water, accessible to all without restrictions. The argument was political for the moment and of no consequence, except that it gave the two communist countries an excuse for denouncing one of the major naval operations of their most significant free-world opponent. Both had filed formal complaints with the United Nations as well as Washington.

The *Lincoln*, if she had a soul on this cold night, could care less. She was in the middle of a battle group formation that carried more firepower than all of the ships of World War II.

Six thousand yards, three nautical miles out from her, patrolling in concert with the carrier, were the guided missile cruisers *Texas* and *California*. The reach of their weap-

240

ons alone was over the entire land mass of North Korea and, in the other direction, into China as far as Mongolia.

Beyond the cruisers, at five miles from the guide-carrier and arranged in a predetermined tactical circle, were the other nine ships of the full battle group, swift destroyers and frigates that swung back and forth patrolling with textbook precision, ever listening for undersea threats, ever vigilant for airborne intruders.

The battle group was a chunk of American military power, far at sea but connected with the motherland by data links and memory chips that made communications as instantaneous as if the ships were anchored in the Potomac River opposite the Washington Mall. Such a powerful force was not easily intimidated on this cold, wet night.

With a potent air strike force of over eighty aircraft, a long-range sea-to-land attack capability and an anti-submarine armada that included ASROC missile/torpedoes and homing torpedoes carried aboard ASW helicopters that sought their quarry with dipping sonar and magnetic anomaly detection devices, the battle group represented the mightiest rapid-deployable, sea-based fighting force ever fielded by the United States.

Overhead in black skies, air wing aircraft provided vigilance and protection around the clock and now, in a battle condition, aircraft were constantly being launched and retrieved as they went about their combat air patrol missions.

There was no higher degree of aeronautical skill anywhere in the world than in the cockpits of the Hawkeyes, Tomcats and Hornets as they were shot off the bow of the *Lincoln* into turbulent skies and then returned to the rolling, pitching deck, breaking out of the swirling low clouds when only a few seconds from touchdown. The growling ASW SH-60F Seahawks were matching the fixed wings in skill and determination as they lifted from the flight deck into the wet gloom and went about their sub-hunting business.

There was a matching skill among those personnel who

served on the flight deck, spotting, launching and recovering the aircraft with movements so practiced and exact that their activity was known as the Flight Deck Dance, a precise choreography of guidance and service that demanded nothing less than perfection. If you slipped up, someone would die, possibly you.

There simply was not a parallel activity in all of military aviation, and so close to the edge did the pilots and flight officers, crewmen and flight deck dancers operate that even in routine, peaceable operations, one or more of them would commit that fatal mistake. If the odds were infallible, then someone could very well die on this night.

Tonight was one of the more demanding nights. Rough seas were rolling and pitching the *Lincoln* as if she were made of cork and wood instead of steel. By comparison, her smallest escorts, the destroyers and frigates, were rubber rafts shooting the rapids on the Colorado River.

Low, graveyard-gray clouds were passing swiftly overhead, driven by peripheral winds of a tight low pressure cell over Beijing, their bottoms so ragged that plumes of visible moisture were reaching down and wisping across the flight deck, gossamer ghosts of the Yellow Sea. Falling rain, mixed with snow, washed down the *Lincoln* and turned flight deck shoes into snowboards.

Eighty miles to the east lay the site of MacArthur's great Korean War coup, the amphibious landing at Inchon; eighty miles to the west, the coastline of mainland China.

Eighty miles to the north, the skies were being patrolled by medium-range bombers of the North Korean Air Force and, within the past six hours, similar aircraft from the People's Republic of China had been conducting similar operations. They were used to one another, but not to the racetrack patterns flown by the Hawkeyes of the *Lincoln* who were using the thirty-eighth parallel as the limit of their northern swing.

At Yiangdai, north of Beijing, Chinese pilots were sitting

in closed cockpits, their groundcrewmen squatting under the wings of the poised Fulcrums and Flankers, seeking refuge from the driving rain. Despite the unfavorable conditions, they could be airborne in two minutes, should they receive a scramble order.

It was the kind of night when you could bare your sleeve, raise your arm into the air and *feel* tension. What was the other fellow up to? Those aboard the *Lincoln* felt it, although they weren't sure just who the other fellow was. Those aboard the bombers to the north felt it, and those on the ready pads at Yiangdai felt it.

Inside the *Lincoln* it was certainly warmer and drier, but there was no escaping the surging and rolling movements of the ship, and a few of the crew had yet to fully acquire their sea legs. Therefore, midnight rations were left largely untouched. Off-duty old salts were having no problems, however. The lifers, as the short-timers liked to call them, were chewing on giant, make-it-yourself sandwiches and consuming large white mugs of coffee, a fluid that rivaled jet fuel in its rate of consumption. They would laughingly hassle the queasy for a while and then hit their bunks for a good night's sleep, being rocked back and forth by their sea-mother.

Dunne and Kohn had slept almost six hours, then consumed a modest dinner of sliced roast beef, a small baked potato and mixed vegetables. No need to load the system down for six hours of flying, but nourishment was a must.

Promptly at 2300, Paterson joined them in the ready room. "Desird should be departing on time." Lacking anything else to do, he flipped over a desk calendar to October 9. The date was only one hour away. "You two all rested?"

"I slept like a baby," Kohn replied. Like Dunne, she was suited up and ready.

"We picked one hell of a night," Dunne observed. "I walked up to the flag bridge, had a cup of coffee with the admiral. He's really a pisser, so hyper that I had to remind him to come in out of the rain before he caught double pneumonia. He wanted to watch recoveries and was giving his own grade to each pilot as he came aboard. His foul weather jacket was soaked, and it had ice on the collar. You know what he said? 'We should be flying seaplanes tonight.' I'd have to agree. The flight deck looks more like a flight lake and is fast becoming the flight deck ski run. The snow is trying to stick. A few degrees colder and you can just shove us over the side.''

"All right; I have some last-minute data for you." Paterson passed each of them a small three-by-five card. "Your primary and backup frequencies for comm with Chi Lin. Transponder settings. You have airway charts for backup?"

Dunne pointed to his flight packet.

"Good. I don't know what good it could do you, but on the card are three contacts: one in Beijing, one in Chengde and one in Tianjin. If you have to punch out and can make it to one of those cities, they can get you back to Hong Kong. Extra long shot, but possible. Now, if the weather will cooperate. . . .''

As if on cue, the ship's meteorologist knocked and entered. "Good evening, everyone," he intoned. Placing a printout of the latest satellite weather on the briefing wall, he began. "I must modestly admit that what you have outside tonight is exactly what I forecast.''

Neither Dunne, Kohn nor Paterson was impressed with the statement. The man seemed proud of the lousiest weather this side of a Mongolian monsoon. But then, he wasn't going flying.

"You have given me a request for a rather broad area briefing. If you would like to be more specific, I might be able to give you a more accurate picture where you're going. It's difficult to concentrate on any one area when you're given a request that runs from Central China clear across to Japan.''

"A broad brush will do," Paterson said, his impatience showing.

"Yes. Well, I hope you're going to China, for the weather there is the best of the lot. Over Beijing, for example, they have a six-thousand-foot ceiling with light rain. Broken layers up to thirty-five thousand. Winds aloft, westerlies from ten to twenty knots. I could go into specific altitudes if you like."

Paterson waved aside the suggestion. The man was fishing for their destination, and it was of no concern to him.

"Here, we have the worst of it: low ceilings, strong variable winds, rain, snow, and sleet." He spoke the last three words as if he had invented the conditions. "Tops at thirty-one thousand. Forecast for your return at six plus hours, little change."

I must have done something very bad in my youth to deserve this, thought Kohn.

"Somewhat higher ceilings to the east. North Korea has cold dry air at the moment, broken clouds three to twelve thousand feet. Winds northeasterly. I'm really uncomfortable with such a broad brush approach. . . ." The man, a balding, tall, thin commander, addressed his discomfort toward Paterson. "I don't feel I'm serving a useful purpose here. You people can see the satellite photo as well as I, and the front that's over us right now. The weather is typical for such activity this time of year."

Paterson nodded. "I'm sure it is and we thank you for your concern. It's really all we need."

The man looked around as if expecting other comments.

"Thank you very much," Dunne added.

"Yes, thank you," Kohn agreed.

"Have a safe flight." The last words were spoken as the commander left the room. He had obviously wasted his time.

Paterson held up a hand, "Would you ask Lieutenant Delaney to come in, please?"

It was good to see their Tonopah mentor again.

"Hi." Delaney took his place before them, beside Paterson. "You folks really like to tick off the gods, don't you. I know you have to go, but if my opinion was asked I would say, 'Abort, abort, abort.' "

"The word is not in my vocabulary," Kohn teased.

"I know. For flag and country. Well, if anybody is so crazy and at the same time so dedicated, it has to be you two. I've kept the airplanes on the hangar deck out of the weather. There's really no icing problem yet, and we can deice if we have to before you launch. But the flight deck is slippery as snot on a piece of fiberglass. I recommend you let the tractors tow you into position on the cats. Taxiing would be far too hazardous."

That sounded like a good thought.

"On the return, let's keep it standard. Just fly the approach; I'll keep you posted on deck conditions. If they're the same as now, or worse, once you're stopped stay on the binders until we get a tow hooked up, and we'll bring you back down to the hangar deck. The ship just recovered a CAP flight of F-14s and it wasn't too bad. Looks shitty, and is, but flyable. If it really turns to garbage and you have to bingo, I would recommend Kunsan. We can advise them that you're on the way. With your concurrence, Admiral?"

"In extremis. And in that case, Joshua, you and Kohn hole up and fly back out when it's better."

"Sounds good to me," Dunne answered.

Delaney's forced smile seemed to say, "You're in for one hell of a night," but he allowed his mouth to voice only, "Well, you two have a good flight. I'll be waiting for you."

Kohn spoke for both of them. "Thanks, Tony, and we'll be looking for you!"

Paterson half-sat on the briefing table. "I want you both to know that I'm confident you'll pull this off. You're two of my favorite people and, professionally, two of the best I've ever served with. Joshua, we pulled you back without so much as a thank you. I want to rectify that now.''

"That's not necessary, Admiral.''

"Yes, it is. As for your personal lives, I apologize for coming on perhaps a bit too strong. As Delaney mentioned, the airplanes are still on the hangar deck. I'd like you to be in the cockpits by quarter past. I'm going to CIC and wait for Dong Sum's takeoff report. That way, you'll have a few moments here for any . . . ah . . . final briefing you want to give each other. See you on the hangar deck.''

Before Dunne could respond, Kohn rose and approached Paterson. "Thank you for understanding, Admiral.''

Paterson took one of her hands, leaned over and kissed her on the cheek. "You give 'em hell tonight, Frosty.''

"Yes, sir.''

Paterson shook Dunne's hand just before he left. "This one's for Annie.''

Dunne glanced at his watch and picked up his flight packet. "We best go preflight.''

Kohn put her arms around his waist and lifted her face to his. "For a moment, let's just be a man and a woman.''

"We are that.''

"I love you, Joshua, and I'm very proud to be with you tonight.''

They kissed. There was no passion, just a feeling of intimacy so intense it almost transcended the human level. It was as if from the beginning of time they had been destined to arrive at this point in their existence, when the two of them would be going hand in hand deep into harm's way. All of their lives had been spent preparing for this and, although it was a subconscious thought, they both realized each would gladly die for the other—in a very real sense.

They reluctantly let go of one another.

Kohn grabbed her hard hat from one of the briefing chairs. "Now, let's go kick some Arab ass.''

*   *   *

The two Sea Scorpions were nested in a back corner of the hangar deck, black bats in a bat cave. Navy Master Chief Brown and air force Chief Master Sergeant Dunlap, wearing foul weather gear over their plane-captain-brown shirts, were standing in front of their respective aircraft. Four marines were keeping other personnel well clear of the F-117Ns and, as Dunne and Kohn approached, a khaki-clad lieutenant came out of the dim light to meet them. A silver cross caught the light from the overhead fixtures and glistened on the collar of his shirt.

"Chaplain," Dunne greeted. Like Kohn, he was wearing red goggles to allow his eyes to adapt to the night darkness.

"Please, just a moment. I would like you to have something. I'm Father Nick."

Kohn could see the name tag on his shirt, and it confirmed the chaplain's preferred address. No last name, although she suspected it was Nicholas.

The priest placed a small pewter medallion in Dunne's hand. "This is the medal of Saint Joseph Cupertino."

"I'm not Catholic, Father."

"Saint Joe doesn't care. You see, he's the patron saint of naval aviators. It's your gold wings that are important to him."

Dunne examined the round medallion. On one side it had navy wings imprinted with the saint's name above them. Below, along the curved edge, it read, "Protect our pilots."

On the other side was the figure of a Franciscan monk, suspended among clouds and holding forth a large cross. Around the edge were the words "The Lord opened His wings and lifted him up and bore him in His arms."

Father Nick grinned. "He was one of our saints who could levitate." He handed another medallion to Kohn. "It's said that he really loved to fly—in his own way."

"Thank you, Chaplain." Kohn placed the medal in one of her flight vest compartments.

"Saint Joe will be with you tonight, and don't hesitate to call on him. He's an equal-opportunity saint."

Dunne and Kohn offered their hands, and as they continued to their aircraft, Father Nick raised his right hand in a small blessing.

"That was nice," Kohn said.

"I bet if Saint Joe knew where we are going, he would have stayed in Father Nick's pocket."

"He knows."

The two plane captains greeted their pilots and walked with them as they conducted their preflight inspections of the airplanes. Bomb bays were open, and the weapons trapezes were lowered in their FIRE positions, each holding a pair of heat-seeking air-to-air AIM-9M Sidewinder missiles. The nine-and-a-half-foot-long, five-inch-diameter weapons would be propelled at Mach 2.5 by the burning of their solid rocket fuel, and their infrared passive homing would allow them to detect and streak toward the heat of the Xian's turboprop exhaust with the accuracy of a Robin Hood arrow. All Dunne and Kohn would have to do would be to place their Sea Scorpions within ten miles of the target.

Dunne started his walkaround, as did Kohn on her aircraft. They checked carefully for any fluid leaks, the security of all inspection panels, the integrity of the flight surfaces. Both stuck their heads into the wheel wells and looked for any sign of malfunction: rubbed hydraulic lines, frayed electrical cable bundles, tightness of lock nuts and safety wires. All was in order, and they finished their checks by examining the Sidewinders and condition of the bomb bays.

Dunne reminded Kohn, "Admiral Paterson wanted us to be in the cockpits by a quarter after the hour. It's almost that." Even as he spoke, Paterson came striding across the hangar deck. He motioned for them to join him by one of the aircraft. ''We just got confirmation. Desird was airborne at three past the hour. We're on.''

''That would make our launch at thirty-nine after,'' Kohn added. ''We better mount up.'' Getting raised to the hangar deck, being positioned and starting up could eat away almost all of the remaining time.

Paterson hurried away as Dunne and Kohn headed for their boarding ladders.

CMS Dunlap assisted Dunne in getting strapped in.

''Thanks, Sergeant,'' Dunne said as he prepared to pull on his hard hat.

''Safe flight, sir.''

For the first time Dunne realized how many personnel had congregated on the hangar deck. They had stood in almost absolute silence while he and Kohn had inspected their aircraft. Now a number were waving, and an equal group were clapping their hands in encouragement. A few had made fists and were moving their arms forward in a gesture of ''Go! . . . Go! . . . Go!'' It was an unexpected and moving show of support, and Dunne waved his hand in response. They were all telling him that he and Kohn were truly members of the *Lincoln* battle group. Hell, they knew the Sea Scorpions were going to launch on an extremely critical mission. You didn't fly on a night like this unless it was a mission you couldn't abort.

The low tow tractor started him forward as soon as he gave the thumbs-up, and as the Sea Scorpion was positioned on the unprotected deck edge elevator, he closed the canopy to keep out the rain and wet snow. Still, the cold penetrated the airtight cockpit, and Dunne watched with some discomfort as slush began to build up on the bottom of his windscreen.

The elevator stopped and the tow slowly pulled him into position on the number-three catapult, on the port side of the waist launching area. Dunne wiped the inside of his windows to remove the condensation of his breath and could see Kohn being positioned on number four, just to his right. The plane director, bracing himself on the wet deck to the left of the cockpit, raised his left hand, forefinger extended, and began a rotating motion with his right hand. Dunne was cleared to start his number-one engine.

The surge of power brought welcome heat into the cockpit, and air flow cleared away the condensation. Dunne secured his oxygen mask tightly against his face and double-checked all his harness fittings.

Manning PriFly, the primary flight control station of the *Lincoln*, the air boss and his crew watched the evolution of the launch. PriFly was actually the control tower of the flight deck and also a place of authority for directing and insuring the safety of all launches and recoveries. The multi-windowed compartment jutted out from the island over a portion of the flight deck, giving everyone inside an unobstructed view of operations.

The air boss came up on the launch frequency. "Darkstar Flight, this is Big Mother. We're all going with you on this one."

"We appreciate that," Dunne replied. "Be sure and leave the lights on for us."

"Just like Motel Six."

The assistant air boss, with "Mini-boss" stenciled across the back of his yellow jersey, wondered out loud, "I wonder what they're paying those two. Whatever it is, it isn't enough."

"My guess is that they're getting union wages just like you and me."

"You can't get civilians to do this for what they pay us."

The air boss laughed out loud. "You just fall off the strawberry truck? Those two are as navy as you and I."

"The word is they're Lockheed operational test pilots."

"Uh-huh. Jumpin' Joe called the black honcho 'Admiral'

when he arrived on board yesterday. Everybody on the flight deck heard it. Now if the number-one man is an admiral, you can bet those two night drivers wear navy blue and wings of gold. Something very special is going on tonight, and they don't intend to come back with those Sidewinders. They're going hunting for someone or something very big. And it's airborne.''

Paterson was also watching the spotting of the two Stealth aircraft from his vantage point on the flag bridge with Admiral Jefferson and the admiral's aide, Lieutenant Crommelin. Launch would be at thirty-nine minutes past midnight—four minutes from now.

"Damn," uttered Jumpin' Joe, "I wish I was going with them. They're riding the edge of the envelope tonight, and that is where it's all at. How about you, Lieutenant; wouldn't you give one of your ovaries to be out there in that cockpit?"

"With all due respect, Admiral, I'm not sure I have that kind of expertise yet."

"Well, you'll get it. When you're through baby-sitting me, I intend to get you into the hottest cockpit available. You want a career in naval aviation, VF is the way to go. Y'know, Admiral Paterson, this young lady already has fifteen hundred hours in A-sixes."

Paterson would have preferred that Jumpin' Joe not use his rank. He spoke into the rear admiral's ear. "Joe, why don't you just call me 'Blackjack'?"

"Oh, yeah. Forgot. No harm done. Crommelin is the soul of discretion. I'll fix it with her."

Paterson wondered if Jumpin' Joe would also fix it with the other members of the battle group staff who were on the bridge. At least the mission had not been compromised—even Jumpin' Joe knew enough to keep quiet about that.

Walleye Duke joined them.

"How's it look, CAG?" asked Jumpin' Joe.

"I was just down in combat air control; Watchdog is on station and waiting for them. Except for that batch of Badgers up north, assuming that's what they are, they have the night to themselves. What's their first waypoint?"

"Dalian," Paterson answered.

"Right into Chinese radar coverage. That's guts ball."

"Dunne wanted to test the defenses right away. If Dalian doesn't pick them up, no one else will. They have both standard and Doppler radar there. I think it's smart. If they are detected, they can turn around and come back here and we can claim navigational error. But the bottom line is that those two Sea Scorpions will be invisible to whatever radar the Chinese light off."

Walleye peered up at the falling rain and snow. "This weather will help. All this moisture will degrade their older stuff."

"You all set for the return?" Jefferson asked.

"Yes, sir. We'll replace Watchdog at oh-one-hundred, and relief for the Tomcat cover. The tankers will be spotted and ready after that."

"Captain Tyler has the plan?"

"Fully informed."

"Thanks, Walleye." Jefferson turned to his chief of staff. "I would like the battle group to go to general quarters at oh-one-hundred. If we do trigger the Chinese, anything could happen. I don't want any surprises."

"Aye, aye, sir."

October 9, 12:39 A.M.

Time to go. Dunne turned on his running lights to signal that all of his checks were complete and he was ready for launch. Kohn did the same on catapult four.

The catapult officer received his final thumbs-up from his launch personnel. He faced forward, swung his right arm over his head and squatted as he continued the energetic swing until his hand was on the flight deck. *Launch!*

Dunne was pressed back into his seat as the F-117N was hurled off the bow at an airspeed of 170 knots. He kept his eyes on the green numbers and attitude indicators of his HUD; there was absolutely nothing else to see. He was in a bottle of black drawing ink. The Sea Scorpion wallowed for a moment as it grabbed the night air; Dunne adjusted the nose attitude and slapped up his landing gear. A minor nose adjustment gave him max climb, and he eased five degrees left of his launch heading. Kohn would be ten seconds behind him and swinging five degrees right on her climb. The divergent headings would keep them separated until Watchdog, the duty Hawkeye, could assist them in their rendezvous. Both had entered the base of the rainclouds at three hundred feet, only one hundred and forty feet above the level of the flight deck. The E-2C could not pick them up on radar, so contact would be by their transponder codes. Consequently, tracking would not be precise enough to affect the rendezvous while climbing through the clouds.

"Watchdog has Darkstars One and Two airborne. Continue climb to angels three-two. Darkstar Two, come left five degrees." The Hawkeye controller had determined that there was sufficient clearance between the two Sea Scorpions, and they could remain parallel for the remainder of their climb.

"Roger, Two." Kohn adjusted her heading. The ride was much smoother than she had anticipated. From the patterns forming and then dissipating on her windscreen, the moisture was almost exclusively snow now. That would soon change to ice as she climbed, but they would not be in the white stuff long enough to make any difference. Already she was passing through 25,000 feet. Less than a minute later, she topped out at 32,600 and could instantly see Dunne's running lights approximately one mile to her left.

"I have a visual on One," she reported and began to ease over for the rendezvous.

Dunne watched her close and, as she settled into position off his right wing, he made a gentle turn to their first heading. "Let's go dark, Frosty."

Simultaneously, the two black Sea Scorpions turned off all lights. There was a quarter moon; that helped a bit.

"Thanks for the assist, Watchdog; we're dark."

The air controller already knew. He not only had heard Dunne's order to Kohn; the transponder signals had disappeared from his scope. As far as his radar knew, there were no airplanes out there.

His eyes fully adjusted to the night, Dunne could see Kohn riding easily off his wing, the dark angular outline just visible in the faint moonlight.

One hundred and forty miles ahead, the Chinese air intercept controller manning the air search scope at Dalian yawned. He had been watching the Hawkeye in its racetrack pattern for the last hour. That must be as boring a job as his. He and the crew of the American airplane must be the only ones awake at this ungodly hour.

19 ⟞⟞⟞⟞⟞⟞⟞⟞⟞

Northern Yellow Sea
October 9, 1:05 A.M.

Five hundred feet below the surface, the water was calm.
Wind and swell had little effect on the Chinese-built Han
class submarine. The nuclear-powered *Shandong* and her
three sister ships were the pride of the PRC navy, and like
the others she was an attack boat, her weapons load including torpedoes with nuclear warheads. Fat and cigar-
shaped, she was the counterpart of Western attack boats,
and the Chinese had excelled in producing a quiet submarine with a twenty-five-knot-plus submerged speed. Her underwater duration was limited only by the endurance of the
crew and, like U.S. ballistic missile submarines, six months
under the surface was no particular hardship. By American
standards, her living quarters were adequate; by Chinese
standards, she was an underwater cruise ship.

Her commanding officer, Captain Pi Jiechi, a submariner
with twenty-two years of service, was a strong political
advocate of the Communist cause and a tactician of some
skill, having been trained by the Soviets. Over his bunk in
the tiny compartment reserved for the commanding officer,
he kept a small photo of his wife and their one allotted
child, a son, taped to the bulkhead. The only other photo-

graph was a wallet-sized picture of his father, an infantry-man who had been killed chasing the American marines in South Korea during their retreat from the Chosin reservoir. For that reason, he harbored no love for American naval forces.

The command and conning center was spacious by sub-marine standards and Jiechi was surrounded by his watchs-tanders, all of whom gave the same dedication to their ship as he. The pressure compartment featured an array of com-puter monitors, cathode-ray tubes, keyboards and an as-sortment of warning and status lights, as well as diving and surfacing controls. Some would introduce seawater into special voids, while others would release compressed air to vacate the voids of seawater and allow the submarine to surface. The helmsman sat at a console with a control wheel not unlike that of large aircraft, although more sturdy in construction. The planesman sat next to him, and behind both the officer of the watch hovered, all the while gazing about with constant supervision of his watchstanders. At the moment, the *Shandong* was at neutral buoyancy with no forward speed, and it was listening.

After a long period of time, the sonar operator announced quietly, "Propeller noises, faint, forward quadrant."

"One ping," the captain ordered.

Ping! . . . . *PING*! The return *ping* was at a slightly higher pitch. "Range one-five-thousand meters, up Doppler."

"Periscope depth," the captain directed. "Ahead, one third."

The *Shandong* rose and eased forward at five knots.

"Periscope depth," the officer of the watch announced.

"All stop, up scope." Short, pudgy Jiechi hooked his arms over the hand controls and began a slow sweep of the surface. The heavy sea obstructed his visibility, and he did not know that Carrier Battle Group Three was at general quarters and running dark. Consequently, he could see nothing. But he did know he was in the vicinity of the *Lincoln* force, and he carried, in his log, orders that would involve a unique contact with the Americans. First, he must let them know that he was there.

"Range?"

Ping! . . . . *PING*! "One-three thousand four hundred meters."

He needed his radar. "Antenna depth, steerageway only."

The submarine rose until the waves were crashing across the exposed radar antenna, its screws turning over only fast enough to give the boat effective rudder control. Jiechi leaned over the radar operator to better see the scope. It was on a fifteen-kilometer range, and several surface targets were at the outer edges of the coverage, dead ahead.

"Ah! Probably destroyers. Periscope depth."

The *Shandong* settled down into the sea with only three feet of its periscope showing. The sea return from the white-capped waves should mask it on the Americans' scopes. Jiechi's pulse increased. He was a cocky sea carp preparing to take on a school of great white sharks.

The USS *John Paul Jones* (DDG-53) was the first to report. "Intermittent surface radar contact, bearing three-two-two degrees, fifteen thousand four hundred yards." The combat information center on the *Lincoln* received the report seconds later. The CICO reported the contact to Captain Tyler on the bridge and Admiral Jefferson, who was in his sea cabin. The admiral immediately took his station in CIC. The contact was already on the master viewing screen and, by data link, the *Lincoln* would be seeing the same picture as that on the *John Paul Jones*. The contact was at the moment lost, but it carried a designation as possible submarine.

The *Jones*, its skipper the officer in tactical command (OTC) of the sub hunt, was conducting an aggressive acquisition search in concert with the two ships on her flanks.

"Have they launched the chopper?" Jumpin' Joe asked.

"No, sir," answered the CICO. "I suspect they want to wait and see if they can acquire it by sonar and start a track. It's pretty rough for a chopper launch."

"Smart thinking," Jumpin' Joe agreed.

The *Jones* had sonar contact. There was positive identification as a large submarine, probably nuclear powered.

"What's he up to?" Jumpin' Joe wondered aloud. The submarine was not taking any great pains to avoid detection.

"Ruffle our feathers, I expect, Admiral."

"Good on-the-job training for our boys."

The *Jones* and the other two ships had the contact boxed and were in complete command of the situation. The submarine was turning slowly starboard away from the battle group.

"Looks like he's got the message," Jumpin' Joe murmured to himself.

The *Shandong* leveled at six hundred feet as the *Jones* passed overhead. Jiechi consulted his water density and temperature charts. "Take her to eight hundred feet, all engines stop. Quiet on the boat." Along with the others, he listened to the sonar pulses hitting his hull and rebounding back toward the destroyers. Several minutes after the sub had begun to hover at eight hundred feet, the intensity of the pings decreased. "We're below the layer," he announced with some satisfaction. The high-pitched pulses were still hitting his hull, but they were attenuated by the sudden temperature change of the water level at seven hundred feet and they decreased more as they rebounded. The destroyers in all probability had lost him. Now to give the Americans a thrill they would never expect. It would be a perfect night.

20

This was the part of any mission that Dunne did not like, the time spent getting from point A to point B. With the aircraft computers doing all the work, the pilot had little to do, physically. The F-117N's navigational system, utilizing the satellites of the Global Positioning System (GPS), would take him unerringly along the route he had programmed into the device. The automatic pilot would use the guidance signals from the navigation system to keep the Sea Scorpion on a precise course much more accurately than any human could. Dozens of sensors were monitoring the airplane's engines, systems and avionics, and any malfunction would be instantly displayed on the instrument panel warning indicators. Five flight-control computers were constantly monitoring the F-117N's attitude, making adjustments and corrections to the flight controls to produce a smooth progress through the night sky. Without them, a human pilot would find the aircraft uncontrollable.

The technology was not without disadvantages. With little to do, the pilot could become complacent. Should an acute emergency arise, his reaction time could be lengthened, and even a second or two's delay in a catastrophic failure response could mean the difference between life and death.

Dunne did not intend for that to happen. He constantly scanned his HUD and instrument panels, keeping mental track of fuel consumed and distance flown. He also kept his head on a swivel neck, checking the skies around him. That was instinctive to any military pilot. From time to time, he would squirm around enough to check on Kohn. Her steady position was like a security blanket; he was not alone. He reviewed the tactics they would be using once they gained contact with Desird's plane. He reviewed the techniques required to fire his weapons and execute his escape path. He and Kohn had had precious little training time back at Tonopah. They had made it all count, but flying and fighting the F-117 was not quite second nature—at least not to him. He felt confident he could handle whatever occurred, but it would take more conscious thought than that required of a seasoned and current combat pilot.

There were occasional breaks in the clouds despite their five-mile depth, and through one ahead, Dunne could see the pinpoint lights of the Bandao Peninsula, his first landfall on mainland China. At the tip was the city of Dalian and somewhere near it was a radar eye, sweeping the sky around Dalian to a distance of a hundred miles or more. If Dalian could detect the Sea Scorpions, it would have been able to do so for the last half hour at least. Dunne and Kohn would already have been intercepted and escorted out of Chinese airspace. The fact that they had not was a source of considerable comfort. To Chinese electronic eyes, the two black intruders were invisible.

He continued his scan of his instruments and the sky. If his purpose were not so sinister, it would be a pleasant night to fly, despite the tension of the launch.

Annie had always liked to fly with him at night. She said the canopy of stars reminded her of the minute place humans filled in the galaxy. He had agreed with her comment that it was an experience in humility. Now he felt that she was with him on this night, and her memory brought back the horror of her death. He tried to stop the emerging mental picture but it was too strong, too much a part of the rest of his life. Thirty-six thousand feet above the entrance to the Gulf of Chihli, it came again.

Annie was on his right arm, his military lawyer, Commander David Soto, and his star witness, Lieutenant Commander Sheila Kohn, behind as they walked outside from the building where his court-martial had just ended. Somewhere in the distance, he could hear a car's racing engine and the faint squeal of tires. Some idiot was begging to attract the attention of the base police. The sky overhead was the same shimmering blue that it was on every day over Oahu, and around the immediate area, a few sailors were going about their business. The world had still been turning at that moment. "Well," he had said to Annie, trying to be lighthearted, "I could buy you a piece of candy." The white ANDY'S CANDIES truck was parked just opposite the place of the court-martial, and the driver was crossing the street toward them, his tray of candy bars swung from around his neck.

At that precise moment, time slowed to a crawl and Dunne would forever remember each second for the rest of his life. When about twenty feet away, the candy man dropped his tray and shouted, "Allahu Akbar! God is great!" His hand reached down into the top of one trouser leg and withdrew a rusty machete. "Die, devil!" he shouted, his face contorted with hate. He began to run toward Dunne. All eyes were on the man, all wide with horror and anticipation of what was about to be—and all the others were too far away to intercept the assassin. Dunne grabbed Annie and started to push her behind him. He heard the first shot. It came from his left.

"Allahu Akbar!" Ahmad Libidi, the other of the two assassins sent by Desird, shouted just before he raised his

*weapon. He was no more than fifteen feet to the left of
Dunne but just as he squeezed the trigger, he was struck
by a vicious body blow.*

*Dunne felt a sharp sting across the back of his neck and
then heard the sickening impact of a bullet striking flesh.
He turned to see Annie with her mouth open, the left side
of her head a mass of blood, bone and ripped skin.*

*A volley of gunfire erupted as Dunne threw Annie to the
ground. To his left, Libidi fell when the two FBI agents
emptied their guns into his head and body. A car careened
into the curb and two men jumped out, one in the uniform
of the Honolulu Police Department.*

*Dunne looked up. Incredibly, the machete man was still
coming, as the gunfire had been concentrated on Libidi.
Dunne let go of Annie, and when Jamal Hussein was only
a few feet away, Dunne dove straight forward under the
vicious arc of the machete and made a textbook ankle-
tackle of his assailant. The two men rolled twice and Dunne
sprang to his feet—Hussein had been quicker. He was only
three feet away with his machete raised. That was the position in which he died. The two marine guards blasted his
chest at point-blank range.*

*Annie! Dunne rushed back to her. Kohn was sitting on
the ground, cradling his wife's head in her lap, Annie's
vivid red blood saturating Kohn's white uniform trousers
and shirt.*

Dunne raised his visor and wiped away the tears. That
was stupid, allowing himself to be so distracted. He glanced
back at Kohn and spoke on his interplane scramble circuit.
"How you doing, wingperson?"

"A-okay, fearless leader."

Tsingdai Air Base
October 9, 1:20 A.M.

Major Wu Chiang eased back on the control stick of his
MiG-29 and the fighter rotated into its takeoff attitude. So

rapidly did the airspeed advance, Chiang had to pull the nose even higher to keep from exceeding his maximum gear-down speed before he could slap up the landing gear lever. His wingman matched his movements, and together they climbed at a seventy-degree angle to seven thousand meters. Why they had been assigned to escort the red-eye flight from Changchun to Beijing was a mystery to the two pilots. All they had been briefed on was that they would be an escort flight and they were to "keep their eyes open." What kind of a tactical briefing was that for a pair of professional military pilots?

Chiang also had to silently chuckle as he realized that the Xian Y-7 transport would be chugging along at only about 450 kilometers per hour, and Chiang was a man who liked speed. Four hundred and fifty kilometers per hour was more like his taxi speed, he reasoned, enjoying the exaggeration. Oh, well, at such a cruise at seven thousand meters he would be saving on fuel, that was for certain.

The weather didn't seem to be improving, and they were mostly in the wet clouds as the Beijing GCI controller vectored them toward their interception. The Xian showed up early on their fire control radar and shortly thereafter on the passive infrared (IR) search scope. Chiang confirmed that he had the right target. "Beijing control, I hold the target at three-six-zero relative, twelve miles."

"This is Beijing. That is correct."

"Beijing, we can provide our own station-keeping from this point on."

"This is Beijing. I understand and will monitor your flight. Beijing out."

Chiang could not visually detect the Xian because of the cloud cover but would have no difficulty maintaining IR contact. The two turboprop engines of the transport were putting out so much heat, his scope looked like he was following the sun. He decided to climb to ten thousand meters for even better fuel economy. The look-down capabilities of both the IR and radar systems would keep the transport on both scopes.

Through breaks in the clouds, he observed a clutter of ground lights. Checking his navigation readout, he determined the lights to be the town of Fuxin, just to the south of the Changchun/Beijing airways. The Xian had another eighty minutes to go before it would reach Beijing. Then Chiang and his wingman could return to Tsingdai and crawl between warm quilts for a late sleep-in.

Dunne was pleasantly surprised at the large clearing of clouds over the Gulf of Chihli. Their next waypoint was the city of Qinhuangdao, on the coast across the gulf, and there they would pick up the airways to Chengde. Not that they needed the airways navigational systems; their own GPS system would keep them on track, but the airways would provide a backup system, and Dunne liked backup systems. He spoke briefly to Kohn. ''Almost clear skies through here.''

''I'm being painted by every radar in China. How about you?''

''The same, but if the engineers were right, none of the signals are bouncing back to where they came from.''

''Ha! It must be working or we'd have plenty of company by now.''

The multifaceted design of the Sea Scorpions was performing as advertised, aided by the radar-absorbing paint.

''Okay, no more interplane unless in emergency.'' Dunne doubted that their scrambled conversation would be heard, unless some detection station was scanning their frequency band. Even so, they would not be understood nor would the noises resemble English transmissions. But from this point on, the only one they needed to talk to was Chi Lin. In another fifteen minutes, Dunne would check in with the Chinese controller.

* * *

Aboard the *Lincoln*, Paterson was on the flag bridge with Admiral Jefferson. They were in contact with the ship's CIC by interphone, and the admiral's chief of staff was on the other end.

"They should be about halfway to the intercept by now," Paterson observed quietly.

"Yes, I would think so."

The running lights of an aircraft came out of the gray gloom astern of the carrier.

"That should be the Hawkeye," Jumpin' Joe observed, squeezing against a port-side window in an attempt to see through the rain. "These lads are earning their flight pay tonight."

The Hawkeye materialized, a great gray phantom, its huge radar disk on top of the fuselage still spinning slowly. It crossed the transom of the carrier and without changing attitude slammed onto the flight deck, its engines roaring in the event it didn't catch a wire. But it did—number three. Just like the fighter boys. It had completed six hours on station, and now fresh eyes and ears were just south of the thirty-eighth parallel waiting for the Sea Scorpions to return.

Jumpin' Joe picked up his handset to CIC. "What's the latest on the submarine?" he asked.

"No further contact, Admiral."

"Thank you."

"Gone?" Paterson asked.

"I don't know about gone, but no one holds him. The *John Paul Jones* threw over a couple hand grenades when they passed over his last position. They might have convinced him to go play somewhere else."

"Funny, isn't it? Here we are with a state-of-the-art battle group equipped with high-tech sensors that can practically track a sea bass at a thousand-foot depth, and the guy just disappears. We should have held him longer than that."

"That depends upon his skill as well as ours. If it's a

nuke boat, we've got our work cut out for us. He'll be back. They're trying to put the screws to us."

"So, you figure it's Chinese?" Paterson asked.

"My first choice, but Chinese or North Korean, he's added another dimension to tonight." Jumpin' Joe scanned the seas around the *Lincoln*. Where was the bastard? At the moment, he was just a nuisance. Jumpin' Joe had no intention of letting him become more than that. That could call for some aggressive tracking. "You know, the PRC has several of its new Han-class nuclear-powered boats in commission. I would bet my private parts that one is steaming in this area."

"I understand they have four."

"That's the figure I have, and they're quiet sonsuvbitches. We'll have a different problem on our hands if one of those babies decides to pull our chains. They carry nuke torpedoes. That would sure ruin our goddamned night, wouldn't it?"

"This is hardly the situation where anything like that could occur."

"True enough, unless the skipper carries the same perverted genes as those Flanker pilots who decided on their own form of self-destruction. The world is full of crazies."

"More the reason we're going after Desird."

Jumpin' Joe turned and eyeballed Paterson. "Exactly. Those detonators could become a much bigger threat if they get outside of China."

Paterson knew Jefferson was familiar with the mission. He had to be. But Paterson didn't realize that Jumpin' Joe knew about the detonators. That was beyond his need-to-know. No big deal, but someone had talked a bit too much.

The skipper of the *Shandong* had worked his way around to the west of the American force, and now it was time to reappear. "Surface! Full speed ahead."

"Surface, Captain?" The OOW asked.

"That was my command, was it not?"

"Yes, sir."

The *Shandong* surfaced within ten thousand yards of the frigate USS *Gary*. His position was no surprise, as the frigate had picked him up the moment he left his safe depth and increased the speed of his propellers. In fact, the *Gary* was bearing down on him fast.

"Turn on all running lights," Jiechi commanded. His comrades on watch suddenly began to doubt the sanity of their commanding officer.

The captain of the *Gary* could not believe what he was seeing: a large, apparently nuclear-powered submarine surfacing well within the battle group formation. And it wasn't an American boat.

Rear Admiral Joseph "Jumpin' Joe" Jefferson heard the contact report and then the amplifying report with disbelief. "He must be in trouble."

In answer to Jefferson's query, the *Gary* reported, "Big Mother, he doesn't seem to be in any distress. The open conning tower bridge is manned, his running lights are on and he's making twenty-five knots along our base course."

The *Lincoln* and her battle group were making fifteen knots and preparing to reverse course as they were within thirty thousand yards of the thirty-eighth parallel. There was no reason to approach any closer.

Jefferson, Paterson and the flag bridge watch had all rushed to the open port wing. One level down, Captain Tyler and his OOD had taken a similar position.

The call from CIC to the flag bridge came as no surprise. "Contact is Chinese Han-class nuclear attack boat. Its present course will take it five hundred yards off our port side."

"Now, what in the hell is he thinking? Combat, get that lad that talked Chinese to the aircraft on this circuit."

"He's standing by here now, Admiral."

Jefferson could see the running lights of the intruder closing from astern. The *Gary* and her sister frigate, the *Ingraham*, were escorting the submarine. Jefferson selected the ship's bridge circuit and talked to Tyler. "Jocko, let's turn our lights on. This guy knows where we are. I want to make sure he realizes *what* we are."

Within moments, the *Lincoln*'s running lights and flight deck floodlights were on.

"Admiral, we have a call from the submarine on our TACONE [Tactical One] frequency. He's speaking English and asking for you, sir."

"By name?"

"Yes, sir."

"Well, that's really no surprise. Patch him up here." The names of U.S. battle group commanders were common knowledge within foreign intelligence communities.

"Done, sir."

Jefferson took the handset. "Unidentified submarine, this is the USS *Lincoln*, flagship of American Carrier Battle Group Three."

The reply was prompt. "Yes, this is People's Republic of China attack submarine *Shandong*. Captain Pi Jiechi speaking. I wish to talk to Admiral Jefferson."

Jumpin' Joe did not like to have someone upstage him. "Captain Jiechi, this is Admiral Jefferson. You are endangering yourself as well as the ships of my command by your irresponsible action. Your presence is a hazard to navigation, as this force is preparing to reverse course. You have no authority to penetrate this formation. It is a dangerous and very careless action."

"With respect, Admiral, you will find our station-keeping ability equal to that of your own ships. We pose no threat to navigation or safe passage even though you are in violation of our coastal waters."

Jumpin' Joe was close to coming unglued. "Who the hell does this bastard think he is?"

Paterson grinned. "I'd say he thinks he is one skilled and bold commander, and he is showing every sign of being just that."

Jumpin' Joe fumed. "He's got jade balls, that's for sure. How did he know we wouldn't consider his approach a hostile action and sink his ass?"

"We're not at war with the PRC. He made a point of surfacing and showing lights to make certain we would not consider him hostile."

Jefferson could only wonder what the other ship commanders were thinking. A foreign submarine had penetrated their defenses and surfaced almost at the carrier. In fact, the *Shandong* was now almost abeam the *Lincoln* at about two hundred yards' distance. Jumpin' Joe Jefferson would be the laughingstock of the U.S. Navy. But what action could he have taken? His rules of engagement as promulgated by CINCPACFLT prohibited him from taking any defensive action unless there was a clear hostile threat—and there had been none.

"Captain Jiechi," Jefferson said, "you are still alive only because the U.S. Navy wills it so. We have no desire to be a party to an international incident that would do discredit to both our nations."

"It has not been my intent to embarrass you, Admiral. These are our waters. You are the intruder, and since no state of hostilities exists, our actions are limited. Otherwise, I assure you, you would be transferring your flag to another ship in this formation—one that would be still afloat."

"You arrogant bastard," Jefferson cursed, his Jumpin' Joe personality returning. Nevertheless, he made sure he was not speaking over the communications link to the *Shandong*.

Paterson had to speak up. "Joe, this guy has pulled our tail, but good. We could not have attacked him without provocation. He knew that and knows it now."

Jefferson knew Paterson was right. "Captain Jiechi, I

must request that you stay on the surface and exit this formation. As a seaman, you know that your presence is jeopardizing the maneuverability of this force.''

"I shall be pleased to do that, Admiral. I believe the *Shandong* has demonstrated the determination of the People's Republic of China to assert our national will. I leave with my respects to you and your battle group.''

"My compliments to you, Captain Jiechi. I must add that should you approach this battle group again, it will be considered a hostile act.''

"That is a reasonable attitude, Admiral, for if I do approach you, it *will* be a hostile act.''

Jefferson watched the *Shandong* veer to port and head for open water beyond the limits of the battle group, his two frigates keeping station only fifty yards from the sub.

Down on the ship's bridge, Captain Tyler spoke to a relieved bridge watch. "I bet the old man's pissing blood.'' Then he called the flag bridge and suggested, "Admiral, recommend we darken ship.''

"Yes, I agree. Admiral Paterson, I'm going down to my battle station in CIC, and I'm going to order this battle group to attack any vessel that approaches us without identification and our permission.''

"Are you sure you want to do that, Joe?''

"What would you do, Admiral?''

"Roll with the punch, I think. If that Captain Jiechi had any hostile intent, we would be one or two ships short by now. I think it was a political move—a very risky one, but it worked.''

"I'll give your words some consideration.'' Jefferson started down an inside ladder for his battle station.

Paterson stayed on the bridge and let his eyes roam the night as he considered the events of the day. Wars had started over less serious encounters. He wondered under what orders the commanding officer of the *Shandong* was sailing. Surely they did not include taking on an entire battle group. Or were there more submarines out there, invisible to the eye and beyond sonar range or hiding under a thermal layer? The frigates and destroyers had their work to do this night, and a launch of S-3s would seem to be in order. Even as the last thought meandered through his mind, Paterson could see a pair of the S-3 Vikings being readied for launch. They would hunt and track the *Shandong* and her comrades far beyond the limits of the surface ships. Carrier Battle Group Three personnel had had their last good night's sleep for a while.

21

Cuihengcun, Guangzhou Province
October 9, 1:32 A.M.

"Wife . . . wife . . . wake up."

Nim Chou gently shook his wife. What a shame. This was one of the few nights she had been sleeping well. Even the low knock on their front door had failed to wake her. Chou had immediately heard it; his ears never slept.

"What is it?" she finally asked, obviously irritated at such an early morning wake-up.

"Get up. We must get dressed."

She forced her eyes open and turned to look at him. "What do you mean, we must get dressed? What is it?"

"We have no time to talk. Put on some clothes; we will take nothing but our papers and what money we have."

His wife was now fully awake. "What is happening? Where are we going?"

"Woman, I said get some clothes on. Please, do it now. I will explain as we travel."

"Travel?"

Nim Chou was losing patience but could understand his wife's confusion. He kissed her forehead and said, "We must go to Hong Kong. It is not safe here any more. We have little time."

273

"At this time of night? How will we get across the border into Macau?"

"That is why we must bring our money, all of it. Anything you have hidden for special purposes, that must go with us as well."

While his wife dressed, Nim Chou made ready their bicycles. It was a long ride to the Portas do Cerco, the stone gate that led into the Portuguese colony. It would be closed, but with the proper "offering" it could be opened for a moment.

Now convinced of the urgency, Chou's wife joined him outside and handed him a small stack of yuan notes. "It's all I have."

"It will do, along with what I have."

With a sad look backward at their home for the last twenty-two years, they pedaled off into the night. The road was practically deserted. No one traveled this time of night except for the few overindustrious farmers who wished to be waiting at the gate when dawn came and the gate opened. They would get the best stalls in Macau.

Nim Chou figured that since he and his wife had no heavy items to carry, they should pass most of the farmers and pushcarts from the Cuihengcun area.

It would be a long ride, twenty-eight kilometers—three hours if they could maintain a steady pace. The road was in good condition, and the last portion of the trip would be downhill. They could make very good time then.

"You said you would tell me," Nim Chou's wife reminded him.

Riding close to her, Nim Chou began, "We have done a service to the Americans for many years. Now it is at an end. While you were sleeping, a messenger came and told me that just before dawn the police would be coming for us."

"Messenger? What kind of messenger? I heard nothing."

"You were sleeping as soundly as an owl at high noon. As for the messenger, it was a friend."

Nim Chou's wife picked up the pace in protest. "You never tell me anything. All these years, I have worked with you."

"It has been better that you do not know too much."

"Well, I think I am entitled now."

"When we get to Hong Kong. First, I must get some critical information to Admiral Paterson. I can do that from Macau, as we have agents there with the proper equipment."

"Agents? Has the American been using us for some illegal purpose? You told me they were only holding business meetings."

"Shut up, woman, and pedal."

22

Bo Hai (Gulf of Chihli)
October 9, 1:35 A.M.

The two Sea Scorpions were now completely submerged within Chinese airspace, surrounded on all four sides by mainland China except for the narrow sixty-mile-wide entrance from the Yellow Sea to the Gulf of Chihli. That was behind them, one hundred and twenty miles to the southeast. Chengde was one hundred miles ahead, the coastal city of Qinhuangdao only ten. There was no noticeable change in the weather; the winds had held pretty much as predicted, and fuel consumption was as forecast. Their mission was on track.

For Dunne, there was still a disturbing feeling. He and Kohn had no legal right to be there. As for moral right, he would penetrate the airspace of hell to get a shot at Desird. That thought eased his conscience, although a lifetime of belief in the integrity of his country was being challenged. The United States of America did not do things like this. Or, at least, not on this scale. Such acts were more properly the responsibilities of agencies like the CIA, and they in most cases would have used in-country nationals and, of necessity, completely different tactics. But worldwide terrorism had changed the rules. You couldn't engage in a street fight without pulling out all the stops. The establishment of such a special group with almost unlimited power to select and attack targets on an international scale, headed by a retired four-star admiral, must have been a difficult decision for the president. The bottom line for Dunne was that he believed in the necessity for the group—although the revelation of its existence to the general public would create a worldwide scandal. Still, at this moment he was proud to be a part of it. International terrorism had to be stopped, and the only way to stop it was to send the message that such purveyors of indiscriminate death and destruction could expect a relentless pursuit and a non-compromising reprisal. They would be hunted and tracked down wherever they went. That was his mission on this night, and he wondered if Kohn had similar mixed feelings.

He double-checked his frequency setting for communication with Chi Lin and set his transponder on the code specified in Chi Lin's written briefing notes. Almost immediately, he heard a faint "Tsingdao, Tsingdao." It was Chi Lin's way of saying that he was on the frequency and ready to control the intercept.

Dunne answered, "Tsingdao, Tsingdao."

Chi Lin responded with the target aircraft's relative bearing and distance from Dunne, "Dong-sān-dong, jiǔ-èr." Five numbers: zero-three-zero, nine-two. Desird's aircraft was thirty degrees to the right at a range of ninety-two miles. That should be about right.

Chi Lin followed with vector instructions. "Sān-dong-wǔ." Fly heading three-zero-five.

Dunne made the slight five degree heading correction.

Chi Lin added the final command for the preliminary stages of the intercept, "Èr dong." Take angels two-zero. That would be twenty thousand feet; the transport must be at about seven thousand meters altitude.

Dunne began his descent.

*   *   *

Major Wu Chiang and his wingman were also receiving intercept instructions. "Tsingdai Leader, descend to seven thousand meters and take position fifteen kilometers behind target aircraft."

Wu Chiang flipped down the special visor that featured a pair of bug-eyed night turrets. The light amplification within the special viewing units would enable him to see the faintest of objects in the night darkness. There were drawbacks: in-cockpit visibility could be confusing, and there was a very narrow field of vision. Nevertheless, he began his descent.

Dunne was searching the skies, his head cocked around to his left when the flash came. It was only an instant, and when he swung his head back around to check his instruments, everything was normal. But there had been a momentary sharp glow, as if a cockpit warning light had flashed. He checked his engine gauges. Normal. Hydraulic pressures, electrical systems, flight-control computers. All normal. Had it been his imagination? No. For the next few minutes he increased the frequency of his instrument scan, and gradually he began to think it was some sort of outside influence. There was lightning off to the north. It could have been a reflection from the red plastic that covered the lights on his warning panel. The explanation did not satisfy him, but it was all he had to work with at the moment. He glanced back at Kohn. She was there, steady as a shadow.

He also recalled Tony Delaney's comment that in the early prototypes, a warning light would occasionally malfunction, and there was the incident of Kohn's false light as she prepared to come aboard the *Lincoln* on their flight from Kunsan.

"Dong-dong-wŭ, bā dong." Chi Lin was updating the relative position of the target aircraft: zero-zero-five, eight zero. The Xian Y-7 was five degrees right at eighty miles.

It would be crossing their path from right to left on its final leg to Beijing. Dunne slowly increased his speed. The Sea Scorpions had no radar, their only sensors infrared. Chi Lin would have to place him and Kohn within ten miles of the target aircraft before they could acquire the transport. Now at max speed, Dunne and Kohn had a 250-knot rate of closure.

"Èr-bā-dong." Vector two-eight-zero.

The first signs of apprehension began, a slight tightening of his stomach muscles. That vector would take the two Sea Scorpions to the west of Chengde. The interception was behind schedule. The computer-generated map on his right multifunction display (MFD) confirmed his evaluation of the progress of the intercept. The MFD would not be showing the position of the target, as it had no sensor input, but the transport's position could be estimated from Chi Lin's information and directions. Dunne made a quick mental calculation; interception would be on the Chengde-Beijing leg of the transport's flight, probably about sixty miles east of Beijing. That would not give them a great deal of time to execute the attack. Assuming the Xian Y-7 would begin its descent thirty miles out, Dunne and Kohn would have less than eight minutes to visually identify their target and fire.

Chi Lin's next call confirmed Dunne's calculations, "Èr-sì-dong." Vector two-four-zero degrees. That was the airways heading. As Dunne rolled out on his new heading, Chi Lin followed with the bearing and distance to the target, "Sān-liù-dong, sān-wǔ." Dead ahead at thirty-five miles.

The Sea Scorpion had two infrared detection systems: one looking forward, FLIR, and one capable of looking down, DLIR. They were designed to give the pilot a constant infrared picture of his target as he approached for a bombing or air-to-ground missile attack. The airplane had never been intended to be used as a fighter despite its F designation. Only the FLIR sensor would be used for this air-to-air operation, and its reliable range against an air-borne target was stated to be twenty-five miles, depending upon the amount of heat generated by the target. Back at Tonopah, Dunne had consistently detected Tony Delaney's T-38 at that range. Whether the two turbo-engine exhausts of the Xian Y-7 would generate as much heat as that coming from a T-38 tailpipe was yet to be determined. The large square infrared target acquisition and tracking display was at the top of the instrument panel, just below the HUD and flanked by the two MFDs. At the moment, it showed no heat pickup, no target.

"Sān-liǔ-dong, èr-bā." Dead ahead, twenty-eight miles.

There! A thermal image began to appear, the bright glow of the turboprop engines and exhaust and then a gradual filling out of the transport's outline.

Dunne and Kohn were still in the clouds although there were numerous breaks. He glanced back at Kohn, unable to see through the shielded and darkened canopy. Did she have the same picture? He did not want to break radio silence but felt it imperative. "Two, this is One. Tallyho."

"One, Two, tallyho." Kohn also held their target.

The transport should be making around 250 knots. Dunne slowed and began a more gradual closing rate, judging the distance to the target by the increase in the size of the thermal image. Now it was just a matter of positive identification and the attack.

The image was definitely that of a twin-engined, high-winged aircraft with a single vertical stabilizer. There was no way to determine if the engines were conventional or turboprop, but from the intensity of the return, the latter was certainly feasible. Dunne searched for the winglets, the small vertical wingtip extensions. They would be the coolest part of the aircraft structure, and with the intermittent cloud cover causing some attenuation of the heat return, they might not show up.

Whomp! Whomp! Two muffled explosions shook

Dunne's aircraft, and the fire warning light for his right engine filled the dark cockpit with a bright red glow. His heart rate went into overdrive as he saw the tailpipe temperature of his right engine increase into the red-lined danger zone. He shut it down and punched the fire extinguisher button for that engine. Despite his fight against panic, he held his position on the target. *Thank you, God*, he prayed as the fire warning light went out. He had also lost two of his flight-control computers.

"Mayday! Frosty, I have to abort. Your target."

"Joshua, what is it?"

"Lost number-two engine and two flight computers. Returning to home plate, Frosty. I've got warning lights all over the cockpit."

Kohn went numb. She didn't even have time to respond before Dunne's Sea Scorpion peeled off to the left and disappeared below and behind her. There was no time to call him again. She was only a few miles behind the target; in fact, within moments she was in a break of the clouds and could see the transport's running lights and red strobe. All of her professionalism and experience kept her thoughts foremost on her mission. She had so many things to do in such a short time. But even as she closed Desird's aircraft, a thousand unanswered thoughts were trying to distract her. What had gone wrong? Had there been any warning? If so, why hadn't Dunne called her sooner? Oh, dear God, she loved him so.

Wu Chiang was curious. He held the red-eye flight on his radar, which he had left in search mode. It was fifteen kilometers ahead of him. But for the briefest of moments, there had appeared a very faint target just seven kilometers behind the Xian Y-7. It was too definite to be a fluke of the atmosphere or some sort of skipping return. At the same time there had been a faint thermal response on his passive IR search scope.

He called his GCI controller. "Beijing, possible target ahead, range eight kilometers."

"Tsingdai, I show only China Airways Flight zero-one at fourteen kilometers."

There were no further indications on Chiang's scopes. He began to close slowly, and within a few minutes a vague form appeared outside his windscreen. If anything, it was wedge-shaped. He adjusted the fit of his night-viewers and the object became more sharply focused, but it was still too far away to be identified.

Kohn eased forward until she was below the after-fuselage of the Xian Y-7. Puzzled, she studied the paint scheme. It wasn't military. She moved out to the right where she could get a better view. The aircraft was gray or possibly white, which would show as gray in the dim light of night. There were two dark decorative stripes that started at the nose, possibly red or maroon. They ran back along the fuselage to pass under the wing and sweep up the vertical stabilizer. There were some large letters on the fin and rudder, Y-7 . . . something. She moved into a stepped-up position where she could see the top of the transport. On the right wing was the designation: B-3499. That was a Chinese civil registry number. The Y-7 wasn't military; it was a civilian flight!

She tried to recall the briefings. She couldn't remember anyone actually stating that the transport would be military. She had just assumed it would be.

The interior cabin lights could be seen through the fuselage windows, but there was no possibility that anyone inside could see the black wedge-shaped form riding just a few feet away.

Kohn began to let her aircraft drift back. She needed to open to her minimum firing range.

New factors began to race around in her mind. The Y-7 had a passenger capacity of eighty persons. That would be Desird plus seventy-nine civilians, innocent Chinese who were most probably farmers, merchants, mothers, pregnant women and children on their way to Beijing and forced to take the least desirable flight because of the savings to their meager purses. The children were most probably asleep, nestled in their mothers laps and wrapped in their special blankets. The pregnant women would be extremely uncomfortable, wishing the flight would soon be over. Some of the merchants would be old men, reluctant to travel at this late time in their lives but doing so out of necessity to remain productive, or perhaps on their way to visit grandchildren.

And she was going to kill them all? Just to remove a parasite like Desird? Would such a thing have any bearing on easing Dunne's grief for Annie's death? Even if so, was Desird's death worth the lives of the others? Why hadn't Paterson told them they would be downing a civilian airliner? Maybe he didn't know. Certainly, Chi Lin should have known.

Kohn was in position. She activated her master arming switch and opened the bomb-bay doors. The weapons trapeze lowered and the two deadly Sidewinders got their first sniff of the cold night air.

She *had* to fire. She and Dunne had come all this way. They had volunteered for this mission. An entire battle group had been diverted just to support them. By killing Desird, she would be saving an unknown number of lives, certainly more than eighty. The three nuclear detonators could result in millions of deaths. There was precedent: the atom bombs of World War II had been dropped to save lives despite the certain knowledge that the weapons would be killing innocent women and children. But that was all-out, kill-or-be-killed war. Even now, the morality of the act was still being debated.

There were other factors. She had lost her flight leader

and lover. There was no way of knowing if Dunne were still in the air. At best, he may have ejected and would soon be in the hands of the Chinese—if he survived the ejection. Should that effort be wasted?

She selected one of the Sidewinders, and immediately a pulsating tone in her headset told her that the heat-seeking electronic eye of the missile had locked onto the hot exhausts of the Y-7. It would start its decent into Beijing any second now. She would have to destroy it before then or the explosion could be seen from the ground. It would be much better here in the clouds, where the only evidence would be the pieces of the airplane falling to earth. And pieces of bodies. Little pieces of little bodies. Little pieces of bodies not yet born.

Her right hand was wrapped around the control stick, her forefinger positioned over the FIRE button. *God, give me strength to make the right decision*, she prayed.

Her finger refused to move. She couldn't kill children, born or unborn. Or women and old men. Yet, she recalled once more, in every war innocents were sacrificed for the common good. *Oh, God*, she thought, *would a male warrior have such thoughts?*

If she aborted, what would it say about females in combat? That they were less decisive? Less capable? Less "macho"? Did she have a responsibility to her sister warriors to show that females were fully as combative as males? Was that even a pertinent question?

Ahead, just six miles from eternity, the transport droned on and the babies slept.

To hell with it! Kohn turned off the master arming switch and set the bomb-bay doors on CLOSE. The death of Desird was not worth the lives of the innocents. No matter what Paterson might say. No matter what Dunne might think, if she ever saw him again. No matter what the battle group commander or the whole goddamned United States Navy might say because she had aborted the mission. She had taken an oath to defend her country against enemies within and without. But she was the one who had to live with her conscience, and she was not a baby killer, nor was her country.

She rolled the Sea Scorpion over on its side and started down. Their egress plan had called for a low-level, max speed profile until over the Gulf of Chihli, then a climb to mate with the refueling S-3.

What was wrong? The F-117N seemed sluggish. Had she been too absorbed in her intercept to have noticed it before? The airplane was responding to her control inputs, but there seemed to be excessive drag and a low key vibration. She checked her instrument panels. What the . . . ? She had forgotten to close her bomb-bay doors. That was not like her. Wait . . . no, she hadn't. The switch was set to CLOSE but the position light indicated they were open. She recycled the control. The OPEN light stayed on, and she could still feel the slight drag and vibration. Kohn checked the circuit breaker. Normal, not popped. Again she tried. They would not close.

Her speed would not be affected to any great extent, and the doors were designed to withstand a high-speed bombing run. Fuel consumption would be a little higher due to the drag, but she should have plenty to reach the refueling point.

Shit! She estimated the dimensions of the doors to be fifteen by three feet. She had forty-five square feet of vertical metal hanging below her fuselage as well as the Sidewinders and trapeze. The doors and bomb bay had been designed to reduce radar reflections even when open, but the configuration could not be as efficient as a clean airplane. From the right angle, radar return would light up a scope like a mini-flare! She was no longer flying a Stealth aircraft; she was flying a barn door! And there were a half dozen air search radars between her and the Yellow Sea, four hundred miles away.

* * *

Wu Chiang had lost his night-vision target. It had quickly rolled away and disappeared from his field of vision. What was the thing?

The Beijing GCI controller now had an unidentified target. It was intermittent, but when it showed, it was strong. He called Chiang. "Tsingdai, this is Beijing. I have unidentified target bearing one-four-zero degrees your position, twenty kilometers. Vector one-four-zero for intercept."

Perhaps this is why we were assigned escort tonight, thought Chiang. "Beijing, what is speed of target?"

"Tsingdai, target speed is six hundred and twenty kilometers per hour."

Chiang signaled his wingman, and the two MiG-29s went into afterburner as they started down for the intercept. The target must be the object he had briefly seen.

Paterson reached across in front of Jumpin' Joe and grabbed the coffee pot. "More?" he asked. Jumpin' Joe held up his cup. The *Lincoln*'s combat information center was relatively quiet. Only the surveillance and early warning Hawkeye and its two-Tomcat combat air patrol were in the air, and information between the units was by silent data-link.

The watchstanders were alert but tired. The Sea Scorpions had launched almost two hours ago.

Desird should be a dead man by now, Paterson thought. He would not be confident, however, until they knew Dunne and Kohn were on the way out. The refueling S-3 Viking would be launching in twenty minutes. He could see that Jumpin' Joe Jefferson was antsy.

"Damn! I hate the waiting," Jumpin' Joe exclaimed.

"We should hear from them soon," Paterson said.

"Drink coffee and wait. That's been eighty-five percent of my naval career. Those two stellar performers of yours could be in deep kimchi if anything goes wrong. Us, too, for that matter.''

"They're the best.''

Joshua Dunne had recovered from his initial fright. His airplane was still in the air, and he had control. His GPS navigational system was functioning. At the moment, he was passing over the gulf coastal city of Tianjin. He really didn't need the GPS system to tell him that. He was maintaining his altitude at five hundred feet by radar altimeter, and he had decent visibility below the clouds. Tianjin was lit like a Christmas tree, so bright he feared that the lights might actually reach up and make him visible to someone on the ground. But at this time of night, who would be out looking up at a rainstorm? He should be well under radar coverage. Even if he were not, they would not detect him. He passed over Tianjin at 530 knots and in a matter of a few seconds was over the dark waters of the Gulf of Chihli. One hundred and eighty miles ahead was Yantai, on the point of the Shandong Peninsula; then it was the open water of the Yellow Sea, his refueling rendezvous and a hot meal on the *Lincoln*. Kohn should have iced Desird by this time and be a half hour or so behind him.

Wu Chiang didn't hold a thing on his sensors despite the GCI controller's statement that the unidentified target was ahead at ten miles. What Chiang didn't know was that his angle on the open bomb-bay doors of Kohn's aircraft was from dead astern and the slim, faceted edges of the open doors provided no radar return. The Beijing radar had a different angle.

He continued on despite the lack of contact and his two-thousand-foot altitude. The target was descending and still in thin clouds.

Ayeeeee! A wedge-shaped dark form appeared straight ahead, and he shot past it before he had time to react. It had seemed like a sure collision; there had been no time for him to even react. Mere fortune had decreed that his flight path was off to one side of the target.

Kohn let out a yell of surprise as she was jolted by the shock of the two MiGs passing her left side. She caught the forms and running lights and was unsure as to what they were, but she knew one thing: *she had been intercepted!* Those damned doors. With desperation, she tried once more to close them. No luck. Why hadn't her defense sensors picked up the radar of the interceptors?

She started a series of jinking right, holding the heading for a few minutes, then jinking left, then holding, then right again. She couldn't go any lower as she was uncertain of the terrain elevation, and despite her radar altimeter a sudden rise could cause her to impact the ground if she were below her self-imposed five hundred feet.

Could the near midair been the result of a random encounter? No. Not at such a low altitude. Well, the game was on. She knew it had been too quiet.

Chiang and his wingman were being vectored for another approach, and he had reduced their speed to a more reasonable closure rate. Purely by happenstance, his intercept angle was from the starboard quarter of Kohn's Sea Scorpion, and his radar picked up the open bomb-bay doors. It was a faint target, but workable. He maneuvered to place his weapons acquisition circle on the return, and then he got a lock! He raised his night-vision viewer now that he had radar contact.

Kohn's headset buzzed like it had been invaded by a swarm of angry bees. Someone had a radar lock on her. She released a bundle of chaff, and the hundreds of slender thin aluminum strips spread out into a silver cloud just as Chiang fired his AA-2 Atoll short-range air-to-air missile. The semi-active radar homing guidance system switched to the higher density chaff strips as Kohn banked sharply right and pulled up into a vertical climb. At the first buzz, she had turned on her master arming switch and selected a Side-winder. Now she twisted and turned, trying to get a return from an aggressor who could be anywhere around her. On her back and starting a roll to the upright position, she received an audible signal from her weapon that it was de-tecting a strong thermal signal. She fired, and the Side-winder blasted away from its trapeze rack and disappeared into the gloom ahead. There was a sudden burst of reflected light.

Chiang flinched as his wingman disintegrated. What was he up against? Suddenly, a horrible thought flashed through his mind. Could their target have been a comrade? He had fired instinctively, without a release from Beijing. Natu-rally, the target would have returned fire. His career could be ruined, but he had an out. He could claim that his wing-man had fired first, without Chiang's permission. But he also could use the return fire to justify his continued attack. "Beijing," he called, "request vector for new intercept."

"Tsingdai, I have lost contact. Contact Tianjin GCI this frequency."

Wu Chiang cursed and directed his call to the new con-troller. "Tianjin, this is Tsingdai Flight, request vectors to intercept."

Tianjin was almost ninety degrees off Kohn's heading, and the open bomb-bay doors hung at right angles to the Chinese radar. "Tsingdai, target is ahead at fifty-five kilo-meters, vector two-three-eight."

Chiang held the heading, but once more he was paralleling Kohn's course and the rear edges of the bomb bay doors gave him no target. *How could that be?* he won-dered. His radar was operative. His FLIR was working. Once more he flew by Kohn without ever seeing her or holding her on any of his sensors.

Tianjin called again. "Tsingdai, you have overrun your target."

Chiang was almost clipping the waves. "Is the target still low?" he asked.

"I hold target at four hundred meters altitude."

He should have acquired it when approaching. "Request vectors," he said with some disgust.

Kohn felt that being in the base of clouds added additional protection, not just from the standpoint of eye visibility but from an IR search as well. She mentally thanked the designer of the F-117 for his cunning in routing the exhaust through a wide baffled slit that ran along each side of the platypus after-fuselage. It was so diffused by the time it exited that there was little thermal signature, and a pursuer would have to be practically on top of her to get any indications. She was unaware that Chiang had overflown her, although she did get a brief radar warning from her sensor. She needed to complicate the next attack. She zoomed to 6,000 feet and reversed direction. After three minutes, she again reversed direction and headed for the deck. Breaking out at eight hundred feet, she realized she was over the gulf and could rely on her radar altimeter to keep her free of the water. She descended until it read two hundred feet. She was close aboard Tianjin and should be below radar coverage.

Joshua Dunne watched with disbelief as another of his flight-control computers failed. Too vividly, he recalled Tony Delaney's words in the early stages of their checkout: ". . . four computer-controlled flight-control systems. Good redundancy. Lose one, try and find a place to land, but no particular sweat. Lose two, get serious about landing; lose three and you have a problem. Not very probable. We've had no failures on the N-models."

Well, my young friend, we sure as hell have one now,

Dunne thought. He was down to one computer, and the F-117N was a fly-by-wire airplane with no manual connections between the cockpit controls and the flight-control surfaces. Delaney had been right about one thing. He did have a problem.

There was every good chance that the remaining computer would fail. Dunne tightened his harness until it was cutting his thighs and shoulders. He was almost across the gulf. It was time to see if he could reach Watchdog. The Hawkeye would be in its high racetrack pattern and could receive Dunne's scrambled message. "Watchdog, this is Darkstar One. Mayday. Do you copy? Over."

The controller's voice was a deep baritone and it radiated confidence. Why not? He wasn't having the emergency. "Darkstar One, I believe we hold you. Squawk four-four-one-one."

Dunne set his transponder on the assigned frequency as Watchdog continued, "What is the nature of your emergency?"

"I've lost my number-two engine and three-fourths of my flight-control computer system. The airplane is still flyable, but I anticipate an ejection."

"Roger, we hold you, Darkstar One. Is Darkstar Two in company?"

"Negative. She should be approximately two hundred miles west of my position. Over."

"Continue on course as long as you can, Darkstar. We have alerted Big Mother, and she is launching escort helicopters."

"Thank you, Watchdog. Will keep you advised." Dunne knew he would never make it to the refueling point. He was already getting a sluggish response to some of his control inputs. He climbed to three thousand feet. That would be a safe ejection altitude and would also give him some time to perhaps steer his chute to a preferred landing spot. In all probability, he was going to arrive unannounced somewhere on the Shandong Peninsula. There was a chance he could eject offshore where the choppers could pick him up, provided they dared come that close to Chinese territory. That was a big unknown to him.

The clouds were still solid, and he was flying through snow. For some reason, he remembered the medallion Father Nick had given him. He had exhausted all other avenues of hope. Maybe Saint Joseph Cupertino was standing by. "If you are," prayed Dunne, "I'd sure appreciate being levitated long enough to reach the Yellow Sea. I won't be greedy and ask more than that, but I sure would appreciate another one hundred miles."

Back aboard the *Lincoln*, Paterson and company received the news with both elation and alarm. Dunne was in radio contact and proceeding toward the refueling point, but his aircraft was severely damaged. Two levels above on the roof, a pair of Seahawk helicopters was preparing to launch.

"He has to make it to open water," Jumpin' Joe declared. We can't pick him up if he goes down on the mainland."

"I wonder where Kohn is," Paterson stated. "Why is Dunne so far ahead of her?"

Walleye Duke answered, "Right after the initial call, Darkstar One indicated his wingman was about two hundred miles behind him." All communications were being patched by Watchdog to the *Lincoln*.

"They must have made it in and out without detection. Damn good show for that."

PriFly called. "Rescue One and Two airborne."

CAG read Jefferson's thoughts and responded to the air boss, "Have them proceed west and stand by five-zero miles off the coast."

"They've switched over to Watchdog for control."

"We'll have Watchdog inform them."

CAG carried out the order. "We can control them from here if you like, Admiral."

"No, let's stay with standard procedure. No time for me to be sticking my nose in this." He turned and watched the large viewing screen. The two helicopters were already twenty miles west and streaking for their assigned station.

Kohn was halfway across the Gulf of Chihli, and there were no further indications of any pursuit. She had switched her radio to the refueling frequency and gave a tentative call. "Texaco, Darkstar Two, do you read? Over."

No answer. She was too far out, or else the S-3 wasn't on station yet. Her present course would take her out the center of the eastern entrance to the gulf. She tried Watchdog.

"Watchdog, this is Darkstar Two. Over."

"Loud and clear, Darkstar Two. Squawk four-four-one-two. Ident. Over."

Kohn did as instructed.

"We hold you one hundred ninety miles west, low."

"I concur; any word on Darkstar One?"

"Affirmative." Watchdog did not consider it prudent to give Dunne's position. "He's returning to Big Mother."

Joshua was alive! Kohn let out a shriek of joy and executed a quick roll. Unbelievable. She had figured him for lost. The world was once again a happy place. *Oh, Joshua, Joshua!*

Dunne was passing over the Shandong Peninsula, disregarding the refueling point. His hope was to get as close to the *Lincoln* as possible before ejecting. Suddenly, he realized he was not going to make it. His last flight-control computer failed, and the Sea Scorpion began a series of uncontrolled rolls and vertical displacements. He was thrown against his restraining harness with unbelievable force, and the inside of the cockpit was a blur. "Mayday!

Ejection!'' was all he could shout before pulling up the yellow and black handles on the outside of each thigh. The canopy exploded away from the Sea Scorpion, and a split second later Dunne was blasted upward—or was it upward? He had no clues as to his attitude. He was thrown into a rapid tumble, his body squeezed into his seat by the force of the five-hundred-knot relative wind. His mask ripped away from his face but was still attached to the oxygen hose, and it flapped violently across his chest.

Some semblance of order returned with the deployment of his drogue chute. The seat separated and the main canopy blossomed. There was one final, violent jerk and he was oscillating below a full steerable canopy. Now to drop out of the cloud cover and see what was below him.

Kohn was still one hundred and fifty miles away from the refueling point. Her evasive actions had caused her fuel consumption to rise, and while she figured she would make the tanker, it would be close.

The return of the buzzing in her earphones was like a bad dream. Her pursuer was someone with unbelievable perseverance. The fact that her sensors were picking up radar signals didn't necessarily mean she was detected, but there was still that strong possibility that her open bomb-bay doors were once more betraying her. She rolled hard right, doubled back on herself for three minutes and then soared upward. The tankers would be at thirty thousand. If something was chasing her, she would suck them up to where the combat air patrol Tomcats could detect the aggressor and employ their long-range Phoenix missiles without closing Chinese airspace. ''Watchdog,'' she called, ''Darkstar One. I'm being pursued by a hostile. Climbing to angels thirty.''

''Roger, Darkstar, we hold a bogie thirty miles west of your position, parallel course. Are you certain he's hostile?''

"Affirmative; I have been under attack on two separate occasions. My bomb-bay doors are stuck open and he can detect me from certain angles, I'm sure." *Come on, guys, help me out here.*

"Roger, target designated Bandit One and passed to CAP. They will engage."

Paterson was watching the developing situation on the main viewing screen. Kohn was showing an IFF signal but no radar return. Thirty miles behind, a clear radar target, Bandit One, was closing on her. One of the Tomcats had left station over the Hawkeye and was racing toward Kohn's position.

Admiral Jefferson gave permission for the shoot. "Watchdog, this is Big Mother. Advise CAP they are cleared to engage."

"Roger, Big Mother, understand cleared to engage."

Lieutenant "Bobbie Joe" Gifford, Naval Flight Officer, radar intercept officer (RIO) in Skystrike One, reported to his pilot, Lieutenant Tom "Gator" Gore, "I have Darkstar Two clear of firing area . . . Phoenix locked on Bandit One. Let's nail his ass, Bobbie Joe."

Nestled tightly against the underbelly of Skystrike One, four long-range Phoenix AAMs were poised for launch; outboard but still within the area of the fuselage hung a pair of medium-range Sparrows, formidable air intercept missiles, and just beyond them two Sidewinders for close-in air combat. The Tomcat could simultaneously engage four separate targets with its Phoenix fire-control system, and one of the missiles was firmly locked on Wu Chiang's MiG-29.

Bobbie Joe's Georgia drawl did not soften his deadly serious words. "Take him out, Gator boy."

The RIO reached forward and pushed the red FIRE button

on the lower left side of his instrument panel with a No-mex-gloved forefinger.

The Phoenix dropped clear of the aircraft, and its Rocketdyne solid-propellant rocket motor ignited with sufficient force to drive the half-ton weapon upward to 81,000 feet, its initial cruise altitude. The stubby, one-foot-diameter by thirteen-foot-long missile accelerated to Mach 5 under the guidance of the host aircraft's Doppler radar, its path unerringly maintained by an onboard autopilot that fed movement signals to the guidance vanes.

Ninety seconds later, the missile's own active radar began painting the target and the Phoenix entered its terminal phase, roaring down to the MiG's altitude. The 132-pound continuous-rod warhead could be detonated by impact or by any one of a series of proximity fuses.

Major Wu Chiang's body stiffened as the warning buzzing sounded in his earphones. He was under attack by a weapon with radar guidance! *From where?* He held no targets. *From which direction was it coming?* He had rolled almost forty degrees to his right and was reaching for the chaff release button when the Phoenix warhead uncoiled and sliced him and his MiG into several hundred pieces.

"Gotcha!" exclaimed Gator as he triggered his circuit to Watchdog. "Watchdog, splash Bogie One; returning to station."

"Damned good shoot," muttered Jumpin' Joe Jefferson, raising his coffee mug toward the viewing screen. His eyes were now on the refueling S-3 arriving on station and Kohn approaching from the west. "You're home free, young lady."

Paterson was more concerned by Dunne's situation. Where had he landed?

As if Watchdog had been reading his thoughts, the Hawkeye reported, "We have a successful ejection and landing. Pilot reports position as thirty-seven degrees, two minutes, twelve seconds north latitude; one hundred twenty-two degrees, five minutes, five seconds east longitude.''

Dunne's flight vest had contained both his emergency radio and his individual GPS navigation receiver. A marvel of space technology, the triangular position readout was accurate to within thirteen feet of the receiver's position.

''Chart! Who has a chart?'' Paterson asked loudly. One of the watchstanders opened a wide drawer from the chart cabinet and handed Paterson a chart of the east China coast. Together with Jumpin' Joe, Paterson made a circle around a penciled dot. Looking up, he said with some despair, ''He's right on the eastern tip of an outcropping of the Shandong Peninsula. Shit, he's on the mainland.'' The determination was both a disappointment and a relief: Dunne was beyond a legal rescue attempt, but he wasn't in the cold water of the Yellow Sea. ''What do we do now?''

Jumpin' Joe smiled his best shit-eating grin. ''We go get him,'' he said.

''Big, big risk, Joe.''

''Fuckit. He's one of our people, and at this stage of the game we're not going to leave him to the CHICOMS. Look, the weather's stinkin' ass-bad. It's doubtful anyone saw his ejection or his landing. If they had, they'd have been there waiting for him. If we're lucky, the airplane went into the water. We've got two choppers within twenty minutes of his position. They stay right in the sea spray and go in and get him. The closest radar is at Yantai, across the tip of the peninsula, and there's hilly terrain between them and Dunne; between them and the choppers. They'll never pick 'em up.''

Walleye relayed Jumpin' Joe's decision to Watchdog, who passed it on to the two Seahawks.

''Thanks, Admiral,'' Paterson said to Jumpin' Joe. ''You're getting a workout tonight.''

''Beats hell out of kissing ass back at the naval confer-

ence.'' Rear Admiral Joseph ''Jumpin' Joe'' Jefferson,
Commander Carrier Battle Group Three, stuck a cigar in
his mouth but stopped short of lighting it. Rolling it around
with his tongue, he found a comfortable spot and clamped
it with his teeth.

Dunne finished burying his chute and harness. He had a
''Roger'' for his position report from Watchdog. He was
on the rocky beach of a tiny jut of land that was attached
to the mainland and had climbed to the top of a small knoll.
He could see no lights. Apparently the area was far from
any village or even a house. The brush inland was thick
and thorny, almost impassable, but would provide excellent
cover should he have to remain during the coming day. He
swallowed generously from one of his two small plastic
bottles of water and then held the open container up to the
rain. He had little to do; he would replenish the vital fluid.

He was certain that recovery operations were underway,
but would the admiral authorize a pickup on the mainland?
He decided to wait another hour, and if there were no signs
of a chopper, he would give Watchdog a call. He was cold
but not wet next to his skin, the exposure suit providing
him protection. It was almost unbearably tight, however,
and uncomfortable now that he was walking around in it.
There was no way he could dry his flight suit or equipment
vest. His hard hat provided some protection from the rain,
and squeezed under some heavy brush he could at least
maintain his status quo. He checked his 9mm automatic,
making sure it was dry and loaded with a full clip.

Kohn had the S-3 in sight and began her approach. The
refueling basket was streamed from the refueling package
hanging from the Viking's left wing, and the two aircraft
were in clear air above the storm.

Positive and gentle control was the order of the night as
Kohn brought her Sea Scorpion slowly ahead. The refueling

probe had been extended and it stuck out above and beyond the canopy, where she had a clear view of the tip. On the first try she was overanxious, and her probe slipped off the outside of the basket. *Calm down*, she advised herself. She had backed off a few yards and now began her second approach, playing the F-117's controls as a virtuoso would finger and stroke a Stradivarius. The probe entered the mouth of the basket squarely in the middle. She rammed it home into the receptacle at the bottom of the funnel-shaped steel basket and watched with relief as her fuel quantity gauges began to rise after almost three hours of falling. She would not need full tanks to reach the *Lincoln*, but after the wild things that had already happened to her, she would feel more comfortable with all the resources at her command. She could dump fuel to get down to maximum landing weight. Surely they had conducted tests on landing with the bomb-bay doors open, although probably not in the carrier mode where the touchdown would be much more harsh. Delaney had mentioned no restrictions, nor had the flight manuals.

All tanks read full. "Thanks, Texaco," she said, then, as her probe cleared the basket, "I'm free."

She dropped away and headed for the *Lincoln*.

Rescue One and Two skimmed the night waves. The pickup point lay dead ahead at eleven miles. Primarily antisubmarine warfare (ASW) vehicles, they carried little protection against any attack from the ground or the air. The indefinite line of rocky beach meeting confused water appeared out of the gloom ahead. Their target, Joshua Dunne, should be huddling some fifty yards beyond the water's edge.

"There, that light!" said Rescue One's copilot, Lieutenant Junior Grade Timothy "Birdman" Brown.

His aircraft commander, Lieutenant Paul "Beaver" Dunsworth, nodded his head as he zeroed in on the waving flashlight beam being swung around in an attempt to reveal the flora of the area. The rough scrub oak and thorny groundcover could be seen, especially after Rescue One illuminated the area with its landing lights, and just off to the right a soaked and waving figure was directing the chopper toward him. "We'll have to swing him in; I don't see any decent landing area."

Behind the pilots, their crewman had rigged the hoist and was leaning out into the slipstream, trying to penetrate the falling rain with goggle-shielded eyes.

Rescue Two took a position aft and to the left of the lead helicopter.

Dunne reached up and grabbed the large rubber and nylon sling, pulled it over his head and fixed the loop against his lower back. Then he wrapped his arms around the front of the sling and held up a thumb. The crewman reeled him in like a snagged trout. As Dunne was raised to the level of the Seahawk, the crewman reached out, wrapped an arm around Dunne's waist and pulled him into the chopper.

"You guys are the most beautiful sight I have ever seen," Dunne said, hugging the crewman.

Dunsworth had just started a wide swing to the left and was lowering the nose of the Seahawk to accelerate when a shouted warning from Rescue Two came over their tactical frequency.

"Beaver! Watch it! We've got. . . ." He never heard the remainder of the sentence, as a bone-jarring explosion took off his tail rotor and fifteen feet of his after-fuselage. A covey of eight unguided rockets had saturated the air around his empennage, and one had scored a direct hit. The Seahawk started a wild swing to the right and its nose plunged downward. Dunne, not yet strapped in, was hurled through the open hatch, but fortunately the Seahawk was over open water and less than fifteen feet in the air. He entered the water on his back and touched bottom before rebounding to the surface.

A pair of ancient, piston-engined PRC Harbin Z-5 helicopters had come around the east point of the peninsula and completely surprised the Americans. Armed with two canisters, each containing eight unguided rockets, and a 12.7mm machine gun under the nose, the obsolete troop carriers had used surprise to their maximum advantage. Now they attempted to get into firing position on Rescue Two, but it was no match. The second Seahawk carried only four weapons, two light-weight anti-submarine torpedoes and two AGM-119B Penguin anti-ship missiles. However, with twin turboshaft engines and all-weather instrumentation, the Seahawk easily positioned itself behind the closest Z-5.

"Now what the shit do we do?" the copilot asked.

"Arm the Penguins!" answered the pilot, a ruddy-faced lieutenant commander who had over five thousand hours in rotary-wing aircraft.

"They're anti-ship."

"They're infrared, and that bastard has hot exhausts."

The second Z-5 had zoomed into the clouds, probably thinking that the American choppers had air-to-air weapons.

The first Z-5 was more gutsy and was trying to turn inside the Seahawk in order to bring his rockets or machine gun to bear. The Seahawk, with a veteran pilot at its controls, was a hawk lining up a sparrow. It was a point-blank shot, and the Penguin's heat-seeking nose could care less that it was excited by a piston-driven aircraft engine instead of the heat signature of a surface vessel.

The Penguin erupted from Rescue Two, driven by an inertia guidance system. Immediately the infrared homing took over, and the weapon crashed through the frantically maneuvering Z-5. It didn't explode, probably because it had insufficient flight time to arm, but its mass was enough to tear the helicopter into two pieces. The Z-5 fell into the sea.

Rescue Two hovered over the spot where its leader had crashed in a ball of fire.

"Nobody got out of that," said the crewman behind the pilots.

"Wait! Over there!"

A figure was struggling to stay afloat only twenty yards beyond the port bow of the chopper. The pilot moved his hover to over the man, and his crewman lowered the sling. It hit the water beside the exhausted survivor but the man could not grab it.

"I'm going over the side," the crewman said and jumped into the water. The copilot left his seat and manned the hoist.

"Keep a sharp lookout for that other chopper," the pilot yelled. He was already eyeballing the air around him. The ceiling was less than three hundred feet, and the second Z-5 could pop out at any second.

The crewman was holding the man's head above the water and paddling for the sling when the second Z-5 did make another appearance. It came from the north once more and was turning toward Rescue Two.

"Oh, shit!" The Seahawk pilot lifted straight up into the clouds. "We'll have to wait until he leaves."

The Seahawk crewman started for the shore, pulling Dunne behind him. The Z-5 had passed almost directly overhead but in the darkness would have had difficulty in sighting the two men. They reached the shore and took shelter under some overgrowth that hung down into the water. Dunne had regained consciousness. "Where are we?"

"It's okay. They can't see us."

Dunne had regained enough strength to turn around and face his rescuer. "Thanks. I'm Joshua Dunne."

"Charlie Price. Feel strong enough to climb up the bank?"

"I think so. I was just winded from the fall."

"You're lucky. God, I'm cold. We need to get out of the water."

"Any of the others get out?"

"I don't think so."

Dunne took time to grab several deep breaths. "Then I guess it's just you and me."

"Darkstar Two, you are cleared for your approach. Present weather, two-hundred-foot ceiling, visibility one-half mile in falling snow. We have a wet deck. No other flight operations in progress." The clearance from the carrier's air traffic control center (CATCC) was small comfort to Kohn. The Sea Scorpion was not equipped with the automatic carrier landing system.

"Roger, Big Mother. I am jettisoning my remaining weapon. Cannot close my bomb-bay doors."

"No problem, Two." The voice belonged to Tony Delaney. "We're ready for you. Call three miles out."

Kohn would make an approach using the familiar ILS system: over the carrier, outbound for ten miles while letting down to one thousand feet, a teardrop reversal and interception of the centerline and glide slope until she had a visual ball. She had burned enough fuel to be within her maximum landing weight and began her descent. The Sea Scorpion was a stable instrument aircraft despite the early press reports that had named it the "Wobblin' Goblin" after some nameless "Pentagon spokesman" had declared the unique design difficult to fly at slow speeds.

Ten miles out, she executed her teardrop reversal and headed back toward the carrier. Correcting for right drift, she had the centerline pegged at nine miles and at seven miles started down the glide slope.

"We hold you six miles on centerline and glide slope," Delaney reported, "Double-check your landing gear and hook down and locked, landing check complete."

After over four hours of flight on a stormy night, the tension of her decision to abort the shootdown, the encounter with the unknown CHICOM fighter and the trauma of the possible loss of Joshua Dunne, Kohn now faced the most precise requirement of her mission. At three miles, she had the cross-lines of her ILS indicator steady on the center of the small, round instrument. At one mile, she was at three hundred feet and still in the clouds. At three-quarters of a mile, Delaney reported, "Paddles." He could see the faint outline of her aircraft. She could see nothing. At one-half mile, the welcome deep orange of the meatball shone through the night. She had only a moment to call, "Sea Scorpion, Kohn, ball, two-point-niner." It was centered exactly on the row of horizontal green lights that stretched on each side of it. It stayed that way until she slammed down on the roof of the *Lincoln* and the number-three wire brought her to a halt. A yellow-shirt appeared and gave her the signal to hold brakes. Then, after wheel chocks had been put in place, she heard Delaney instruct her, "Okay, ma'am, shut it down. We'll tow you to the hangar deck."

Kohn kept the canopy closed as she was pulled over the white, slushy flight deck to the deck-edge elevator and lowered to the hangar deck. As soon as she was parked, she opened the canopy, an egress ladder was placed in position and the first figure to greet her was Master Chief Brown. "Welcome back, ma'am. It's great to see you." He assisted her out of the cockpit, and at the foot of the ladder she was met by Admiral Jefferson, CAG, and Blackjack Paterson. Around her, the personnel of the *Lincoln* stood in respectful silence, and she fought tears as she gave them a salute and then a raised hand-clasp.

"Damned good show, Commander," Jumpin' Joe said, pumping her hand. CAG reached around and patted her shoulders. Paterson opened his arms and she walked into them. "God, it's good to have you back," Paterson said.

"Joshua?" Kohn queried. "How's Joshua?"

Paterson guided her after Jefferson and the CAG as they started across the hangar deck. "Let's debrief in the admiral's cabin. I'll fill you in."

Kohn insisted, "Where's Joshua? He did make it?"

Paterson wanted to take her hand but decided he would keep everything on a professional level while within view of the crew. "We think he's all right. Wait just a few more minutes."

Jumpin' Joe's messman had hot coffee and pastries on the conference table. After all had sat and Kohn had had time to collect herself and swallow some of the coffee, Paterson asked, "Did you get Desird?"

Kohn looked as squarely as she could into Paterson's eyes. "No, sir. Joshua had aborted just before we got contact. I pulled a visual check on the transport. You didn't tell us it would be civilian."

Paterson matched the surprised look on Jefferson's face. "We didn't know. We assumed it would be military."

"Well, it wasn't, and I couldn't shoot down a planeload of innocent people. I'm sorry; I just couldn't. We haven't sunk to that level, have we, Admiral?"

Paterson seemed to understand. "I can't fault you for going with your conscience. This was a long shot from the beginning. There were some things I guess Chi Lin didn't tell us. We'll get another shot at Desird somewhere down the line." Inside, Paterson could only wonder what effect Kohn's decision would have on the unit. From the president on down, everyone had gone to great lengths to set up and execute the operation, and now they were in a very precarious position with one of the pilots still stranded on the mainland.

"Please, where is Joshua?"

"For the moment, he is safe on the mainland. On an isolated section of the east coast, actually, but we have a serious problem."

"What kind of problem?"

"We sent a pair of Seahawks to pull him out. Somehow, the Chinese know he's there and sent two army choppers to investigate. They surprised our people and shot down one of the Seahawks. The other is still on station, using cloud cover to escape detection."

Jumpin' Joe called CIC. "What is the position of Rescue Two?"

"Holding twenty miles offshore, Admiral."

"Well," decided Paterson, "I guess we can postpone the rest of this debriefing until we can get Joshua out of there."

Walleye interrupted. "We've got another pair of choppers ready to go, and I'd like to send a couple of Tomcats to give them some cover, Admiral."

"No," Kohn protested. "My airplane is ready to go. Refuel it and give me two more Sidewinders. I'll fly cover."

Paterson did not like the idea. "You're beat and your airplane is not ready to go. You can't close the bomb-bay doors, remember?"

"I'll still have more stealth than a pair of F-14s. I can fly with the doors open. They tried for almost two hours to find me and couldn't get a decent interception."

Jumpin' Joe backed up Paterson. "No. From here on out, it's a battle group operation and I'm not going to expose you to any more risks. We have people trained to handle any contingency, even one like this goddamned donny-brook. The F-14s can stand off the beach for fifty miles or more and provide cover without violating Chinese airspace. They'll be perfect for the job. Walleye, you and I need to think this through. Admiral Paterson, you're welcome to join us; we'd appreciate your input."

Paterson tried to comfort Kohn. Jumpin' Joe was right. "Sheila," he said, "I want you to get some rest. I promise I'll call you as soon as anything develops."

Kohn did not want any rest, but she knew when she was

being dismissed. "Thank you, Admiral. I'll try." It was the navy way: you made your best argument, and when you were overruled, you saluted with a hearty "Aye, aye, sir." She left for her stateroom.

"Gentlemen," Jumpin' Joe began, "they've got us by the short hairs. If we leave Dunne there, he'll be found. They'll have proof positive that we violated their airspace with deliberate intent. And with modern drugs, Dunne will tell them everything they need to know. On the other hand, any further excursions into China, even a few feet onto the beach, can have some very serious ramifications."

Neither Paterson nor Walleye wanted to interrupt Jumpin' Joe as he continued to think aloud. "We've lost two Tomcats and a Seahawk; they've lost two Flankers, a pair of MiGs, the Badger, and a helicopter that would have been dead of old age soon. Quite a tally for a peacetime incident. I'm going to talk to CINCPACFLT and give him our options. My recommendation will be to make one more try to get Dunne. If he concurs, Walleye, we'll do it your way. If he objects, we'll do it anyhow. I'd just as soon go out of this man's navy knowing I did all I could for one of our own. But I need to give the CINC the courtesy of the right of refusal. Admiral Paterson?"

"I can always use a good man in my cafe in New Orleans. You know how to wait tables, Joe?"

"No, but I can beat the hell out of a banjo if you keep me in swamp water."

The three planners were interrupted by a message from the CICO. "Admiral, Rescue Two reports he was driven away from the scene by a Chinese chopper. He left a crewman in the water with the Darkstar pilot."

"What are his intentions?"

"He's using cloud cover to evade and intends to return to the scene when and if it's clear."

"Very well; instruct him to hold any further action until

we get him some help. Tell him it's on the way."

"Will do, Admiral."

"Okay, Walleye, that cinches it. Start the ball rolling. I'll talk to CINCPACFLT."

23

Admiral John Decker, Commander in Chief, Pacific Fleet, was about to leave his office for a meeting with CINC-PACOM when his command and control center requested his presence. "It's Rear Admiral Jefferson, sir," the command duty officer had informed him. Good. Decker had been up since early morning, following up on the previous day's inquiries from the Joint Chiefs concerning the activities of Jefferson's battle group. The state department had already received several formal complaints from the PRC about the battle group, whom they were accusing of violating Chinese air- and sea-space as well as being responsible for the loss of three military aircraft. The morning papers in Honolulu, both the *Honolulu Advertiser* and the *Star Bulletin*, had carried Associated Press stories about confrontations between the Americans and the Chinese in the Yellow Sea, and several editorials had accused the United States of baiting the Chinese to gain advantages in the mainland trade talks. It took only a few minutes for Decker to reach his command center and pick up the scramble handset. "Yes, Joe?"

"Sir, we have a bucket of worms out here, but things are under control . . ."

Decker listened impassively as Jumpin' Joe briefed him on the current situation. The Paterson operation was a bust. The main concern now was the two men stranded on the east coast of the Shandong Peninsula. "We have to get them out," Decker immediately decided.

"Yes, sir, that's my intent. I wanted to brief you first since this is getting to be a pretty deep operation."

"Listen, Joe, you go in after them. Nothing overly aggressive, understand. I'm sure the Joint Chiefs will buy the plan—besides, before I can brief them and get a response, you should have the mission completed—or we'll be at war with China. We'll use the same cover we had planned for the Paterson operation. Besides, we have the Chinese on the hook for their Flanker assault on your battle group. I'm informed that they're looking for a way to get out of that, and they just may backpedal with respect to giving you any more opposition to the rescue. I'll talk to CINCPACOM and we'll get the word up the line to the president so he can be prepared."

"Thank you, Admiral."

"Joe?"

"Yes, sir?"

"Good luck—and don't make us look bad."

"You know me, Admiral."

"That's what I said."

Decker briefed his immediate superior, Admiral Hugh Donley, Commander in Chief, Pacific Command. The two were Naval Academy classmates, Donley only twelve numbers senior to Decker. The Joint Chiefs received Donley's briefing within the hour and informed him that they would immediately brief the secretary of defense and the president.

"That'll take the rest of the day," Decker commented. "At least it's still a go."

Both senior officers knew that by the time the matter had received the attention of the president and his advisors, Jefferson would either have pulled off the rescue or gotten them into an irreversible conflict with China.

Consequently, they were surprised when the chairman of the Joint Chiefs returned Decker's call only ninety minutes later. Decker's eyebrows did a little forehead dance as the chairman advised him, "The president says go get them."

For once, everyone in the chain of command was in complete agreement.

The president used his private line to call his secretary of state. "Barbara, contact Ambassador Zhoy at his chancery and bring him over to the Oval Office. A command performance."

"We've been in contact all morning, Mister President; I'm sure we can be there within the half hour."

They arrived in twenty-three minutes. The president briefed Ambassador Zhoy and asked for comment.

"I have been in constant contact with Premier Xiang. He is most anxious to defuse what has become a dangerous and embarrassing situation. However, he is adamant that he will not tolerate any action that results in further conflict with our military."

"Is he willing to return our two men by diplomatic means, with no publicity?"

"That would not be his desire. The media would surely descend on such a story and there would be much explaining to do—on both sides of this regrettable incident."

"Can he call off any military interference with our recovery operations?"

"The units stationed on the Shandong Peninsula are mostly conscripts and would not understand the political necessity for ceasing operations. They are from peasant stock and very patriotic. Certainly, we will contact the regional commander and give him the premier's orders not to interfere. Communications are sometimes difficult in that region and, like your military forces, we have a layered chain of command.''

The president studied Zhoy. You could never get a straight answer from the man. "I would think that with modern technology, it would be merely a matter of picking up a phone or handset.''

"The People's Republic is modernizing its military as quickly as our economic situation allows.''

The president did not like to be tied to the end of a yo-yo string. "I'm confident that Premier Xiang and I want the same thing in this matter.''

"Yes, Mr. President. I shall contact him immediately.''

Premier Xiang listened to his ambassador to the United States with considerable interest. He was aware of the circumstances surrounding the loss of the Badger and the two Flankers but had yet to learn of the loss of the MiGs in their ill-fated pursuit of Kohn. Nor had he been informed of the presence of two Americans on the isolated coastal spot of the Shandong Peninsula. He was concerned about the direction the trade talks were taking and for that reason he was not disturbed that Ambassador Zhoy had called him so early in the morning. If anything, the situation concerning the American battle group in the Yellow Sea should be defused or at least placed in a perspective where the Chinese were the injured party. Already several of his heady military commanders had brought the situation close to a major conflict. The problem was, how could he do so in a face-saving manner? The military, operating out of bases near Yantai, could already have forces on the way to capture the Americans, and communications with troops in the field were not always efficient. "I will have General Tong order the regional commander to recall any forces engaged in tracking down the Americans," he informed his ambassador. "Assure the president of that. However, this particular situation is not of our making, and if there is an unfortunate end to this violation of our territory, the American government must shoulder that responsibility.''

''Thank you, Comrade Xiang. I will convey your response within the hour.''

Premier Xiang was confident that he had acted with the best interests of the PRC in mind. He had satisfied his ambassador, who would satisfy the American president, but Xiang had no intention of having his senior military commander order the Shandong regional commander—or anyone else, for that matter—to allow the intruding Americans to be rescued. Far from that; he knew the Americans would most probably resist any attempt to capture them, and that would undoubtedly result in their deaths. That would be appropriate justice, and Xiang could return the bodies with a great show of regret and considerable chastisement to the Americans for such a flagrant violation of Chinese sovereignty.

24

Dunne and Charlie Price were literally freezing to death
despite the fact that both wore exposure suits under their
soaked flight gear. They had managed to crawl out of the
water, but their immediate need was warmth. Hypothermia
could be only minutes away. Also, Dunne could tell by the
increasing pain in his rib cage that the fall from the stricken
Seahawk had done more than just taken the wind out of
him for a short period. His whole chest and right side were
extremely sensitive to his touch.

"I haven't seen any lights anywhere," Dunne said. "We
need to get warm, but I don't think we should light a fire,
not yet." Dawn was still several hours away and if the
Chinese helicopter returned, a fire would lead them right to
him and Charlie Price.

"Come on; let's work our way into the brush. That'll
knock off some of the wind." Dunne could see Price beginning to shiver violently. The rough coastal foliage did
offer some shelter, but they needed to have more. Dunne
knelt and began scooping some of the wet sand. It became
dry about six inches down. "Dig. We need to dig a
trench."

314

Price joined him, and they were able to scoop away enough of the sand to form a long ditch.

"We need to go down at least two feet," Dunne instructed. While Price continued digging, Dunne gathered an armload of broken branches with leaves still attached, although, like everything else around them, they were soaked. As soon as the hole was ready, he told Price, "Give me your flight suit and lie down in there." Dunne also removed his flight vest and outer flying suit and placed the garments at the head of the trench next to the gathered branches. He lay down beside Price. "Now, pull the sand over you. Get as much of the dry stuff as you can and keep your body pressed against me. We need to combine our body warmth." Soon the two were covered up to their chests. Dunne arranged the dead wood around and over their heads and then, after several attempts, was able to flip his flight suit on top of the crude wood shelter. Price joined him in covering the rest of their bodies with sand until only their faces were showing.

Out of the wind and insulated by several inches of more or less dry sand, they began to warm one another. "This is great," Price exclaimed. "Where did you learn this?"

Dunne chuckled. "Right here. Our only chance is to get out of the wind chill and keep our body temperature from falling. These exposure suits have kept our skin reasonably dry, and now the sand will insulate us from the cold. If it doesn't start raining again, our flight suits may dry some as soon as it's daylight. We can check where we are then, and maybe find some kind of shelter until our choppers come back."

"You think the Chinese will come?"

"Yes. But this is one hell of an area to search. I doubt that any foot patrols can reach us before mid-morning. By that time, we could be out of here."

They lay in silence for a while until Dunne cautioned, "Don't go to sleep." They were still subject to hypothermia from their previous exposure to the frigid water and cold air. At least, however, they could conserve some strength. Dunne had some meat bars and candy as well as the two plastic containers of water in his flight vest. "You have any provisions in your flight vest?" he asked.

"Candy bars."

Good. Their immediate needs were taken care of. Dunne felt Price beginning to shiver again. He tried to get more of his body in contact with the young sailor, but the weight of the sand kept them practically immobile. "Don't go to sleep, Price."

"I'm really tired, sir."

"No. You have to stay awake." Dunne would have to keep the air crewman talking. "How old are you? Where you from?"

"Nineteen. San Diego. Sure ... wish I was ... there now."

Nineteen. Most of Price's contemporaries were probably enjoying a comfortable Southern California winter, sunning and chasing young women while the teenaged sailor was a combatant in an undeclared war and in danger of freezing to death on an isolated stretch of beach in eastern China. The *Lincoln* was manned and operated by thousands of teenage sailors like Price, along with the more seasoned hands. They were just kids but very responsible, maturing men and women. *God bless 'em,* Dunne prayed. Maybe the United States would survive after all.

At first light, Dunne began to dig himself out. Price had stopped shivering but had dozed off despite Dunne's efforts to keep him awake. He left Price in the sand and walked to a low dune some fifty feet to the west. As he stood on top, he suddenly saw white smoke. It was coming from what appeared to be a mud and thatch hut a quarter mile away. Smoke meant fire, and fire meant warmth. He ran back to Price. "Price, get up. Come on!"

Price dug himself out and both grabbed their flight gear. Dunne checked his service automatic and made sure it had stayed dry and clean. The skies were still overcast but the rain had stopped, and there was no sign of ground or air activity.

Cautiously, they approached the hut, staying low and using the foliage for cover. An old man, bent with age and bundled in thick cotton quilt clothes, was outside, walking with some difficulty toward a small outhouse-type structure. He entered and closed the door.

"Come on," Dunne ordered. They ran the last few yards and stood against the door of the hut, listening. Someone else was inside moving around, in all probability the old man's wife.

Dunne drew his weapon and opened the door.

The elderly woman, wrinkled and bent, was stirring something in a wok. She looked up, startled, and turned to face them. Her eyes darted from side to side as if looking for her husband but, realizing that she was alone, she crossed her hands on her bust and started a series of bows.

"Do you speak English?" Dunne asked.

From her reply, it was obvious that she did not.

Dunne lowered his weapon. Shaking his head, he tried to reassure the frightened lady. "It's all right. We won't harm you."

The woman had no idea as to what Dunne was saying.

"The man is coming back," Charlie Price warned.

Dunne and Price stood behind the door as the man entered, then stepped forward as he closed it. He was as frightened as his wife and immediately went to her side. The couple were harmless.

Dunne made a show of holstering his weapon, then held up both hands to show he had no harmful intent. The Chinese knew he and Price were Caucasians but probably had no idea as to their nationality.

Dunne pointed to the cooking fire and gave an exaggerated shiver. A knowing light came into the woman's eyes, and she urged them to warm themselves. Seeing that probably he and his wife were in no immediate danger, the man offered chairs; they had only two beside a small homemade table. Dunne and Price pulled the chairs by the fire, and the woman poured steaming water over a smattering of green tea leaves in the bottom of two cups. She offered them with a cautious smile.

"Thank you, thank you," responded Dunne, trying to appear as nonthreatening as he could.

The woman went back to her wok, poured in a tiny bit of oil and added some vegetables that looked like sliced turnips and carrots. From a covered box on the floor of the hut she withdrew a large, dressed fish and chopped it with a cleaver until it was a pile of bite-sized pieces. She dropped them into the wok, stirred for several minutes and filled two bowls with the mixture, handing one to Dunne, the other to Price.

Dunne made motions that he and Price would share, but the woman shook her head and reached into the wok with large bamboo chopsticks to serve her husband and herself. Then she placed a portion of steamed rice in each of their bowls.

The stir-fried meal was filling and hot, and the two Americans eagerly ate all that had been set before them.

As all sipped tea, Dunne pulled off his wristwatch and offered it to the old man, who vehemently refused it. Dunne insisted, and the Chinese finally accepted it with a wide grin and several jerky bows.

Charlie Price offered his candy bars to the woman, who took them without hesitation, smiling broadly and running her tongue across a smattering of decayed teeth, a few with silver caps.

The man gathered the soaked flight suits and hung them across a string that ran behind the firepit.

"Should we tell them who we are?" Price asked.

"No. This is all very unexpected and confusing to them, although they may realize that we are airmen." Dunne accepted a second cup of tea, as did Price, but when Dunne stood to adjust their drying flight gear he winced from the pain in his rib cage. The woman immediately came to him and began a gentle probing. Dunne answered with a series of grunts, the loudest ones at the sites of the most severe pain.

"Ah!" the woman exclaimed and held up a hand to indicate that Dunne should stay where he was. From the far side of the hut, the woman retrieved a long piece of cotton cloth and tore it into strips, then tied the strips to produce one long piece of material. She held her arms high to indicate to Dunne that he should do the same. As Dunne lifted them, the woman passed the strip of cloth behind Dunne's upper back, looped it once to secure the end and tightly wrapped his upper body. It hurt at first, but as the woman adjusted it to even the pressure there was a noticeable relief from the pain. Dunne could not resist reaching out and hugging the gracious lady. The woman responded with an embarrassed giggle and sought the side of her husband.

"I think we've found some new friends," Dunne commented.

"They're wonderful, and I don't think they're scared any more."

The woman picked up a small, wooden-framed picture from a low chest and showed it to Price, pointing with a finger to first the picture and then to the young airman's face. She said something in Chinese to her husband, who heartily agreed with whatever she was saying. The photograph was that of a young Chinese man about the same age as Price. He wore a PRC army uniform.

Dunne could think of no other way of showing his approval other than by clapping his hands and nodding his head. With a small bow, the woman acknowledged the gesture and returned the picture to its place.

"Her son?" asked Price.

"No. I think maybe a grandson. It's a recent picture." Dunne started to elaborate but stopped and cocked his head. "Hear that?" he asked.

"Choppers!" Price answered and headed for the door. He cautiously opened it only partway before exclaiming, "Seahawks!"

The two Americans quickly gathered their gear, and Dunne gave his meat bars and candy to the old couple before rushing out of the hut. He and Price pulled on their still-wet gear as they ran to a clearing behind the hut.

The two Seahawks obviously had them in sight and started a wide swing to approach the clearing into the wind.

"Hey!" Charlie Price shouted. "Look at their fuselage markings!"

The helicopters were devoid of any U.S. Navy markings and instead wore the red bar and star insignia of the PRC military. Dunne stopped abruptly. "Back to the hut!"

"No!" Price answered, "They're Seahawks. They have to be from the *Lincoln*."

There was sufficient light to clearly see the two helicopters; there was no mistaking their make, and the Chinese did not fly Seahawks. That, Dunne knew for a fact. At that moment, a series of shots rang out behind them and Price collapsed, clutching his left leg. Dunne dropped to the ground, rolled and drew his weapon. Far on the other side of the hut, several running figures were raising rifles and firing. "Army troops!" Dunne called as he squirmed over to Price. The sailor had an upper leg wound, but it was not bleeding profusely. Dunne fired off three quick shots before the downwash from the first Seahawk covered him with loose grass and dirt. It was touching down almost on top of him and the wounded Price. The other helicopter swept overhead and flew sideways toward the soldiers, the crewman in the open door firing rapidly with a semiautomatic rifle and tossing grenades. The Chinese troops were scattering, some of them falling as they were hit by the rifle fire or grenade shrapnel.

Dunne started to rise but was jerked to his feet by strong arms, assisted to the Seahawk and unceremoniously tossed through the open hatch. The crewman ran away and within moments returned with Price. The Seahawk lifted into the air even as the crewman was climbing on board. He immediately picked up an M-16 and began firing at the Chinese. It took only seconds for the helicopters to escape the ground fire and head out to sea.

"What's with the insignia?" Dunne asked as he strapped in.

The crewman laughed. "CAG's idea. He figured anyone living out here would not recognize the type of chopper but would know the U.S. insignia, so he ordered us to paint over everything. Good thing we didn't hit any rainstorms, as it's water-based paint."

The crewman had spoken even as he was tying a cloth tightly above Price's leg wound. He was one of Price's squadronmates. "Shit, Charlie, how'd you fall off Rescue One?"

"He didn't fall; he jumped in after me," Dunne answered.

"Always trying for the headlines, aren't you, Charlie?"

Price looked reasonably comfortable. "Why don't you shut up and give us some water. Can't you see I'm now a wounded veteran?"

"No way; we're not at war, shipmate."

"Those Chink soldiers were."

The crewman broke out a water jug and filled two paper cups. To Dunne, it was the coldest, clearest, best-tasting water he had ever swallowed. He took a last glance back at the shoreline but could no longer see the hut. Could one of the soldiers have been the young man in the old woman's picture? He hoped not.

"Big Mother, this is Watchdog, over."

"Go ahead, Watchdog."

"Rescue One advises operation completed. Two personnel picked up, one with minor bullet wound in left leg. ETA oh-eight-two-six local."

"They're on the way back," a jubilant Paterson shouted. Everyone else in CIC applauded.

"That's the way it's supposed to go," declared Jumpin' Joe.

Sheila Kohn felt as if she had just come down to check under the Christmas tree and all of her requests had been granted. Never had she uttered a more sincere silent prayer. *Thank you.*

The air controller on board Watchdog had strong returns from the two Seahawks as they raced across the Yellow Sea toward the *Lincoln*, but now there seemed to be another problem. Two rapidly moving targets appeared from over the entrance to the Gulf of Chihli, and from their heading changes it appeared they were being vectored to intercept the rescue helicopters.

"Radar contact, two bogies bearing two-eight-five degrees, one hundred twenty-six miles. Designate Bogies One and Two."

Watchdog's radar picture and transmission were received in the *Lincoln* combat information center. Paterson and Jumpin' Joe had left for the flag bridge, intending to wait for the rescue unit to arrive, and they were immediately notified.

"Roger, combat," Jumpin' Joe answered. "How far away from our choppers are they?"

"One hundred and sixty miles, Admiral."

"Closing speed?"

"Roughly three hundred knots, sir."

"Thirty minutes," Jumpin' Joe calculated aloud. "Consider them hostile if they cross the parallel; in fact, designate them hostile now."

"Will do, sir . . . Watchdog designates both targets as Bandits One and Two."

Jumpin' Joe spoke to Paterson. "Will this night ever end?"

"If they're on an intercept, Joe, they must be under the controller at Yantai. Our choppers should be under his radar coverage in another fifteen minutes, assuming they stay low."

Jumpin' Joe concurred, then spoke again to CIC. "The Tomcats on station with Watchdog are cleared to engage if the bandits fly south of the thirty-eighth parallel."

"Combat, aye, sir."

"Digger One, do you hold Bandits One and Two?"

"Affirmative, Watchdog."

"Digger One, Big Mother advises you are clear to engage if bandits cross the thirty-eighth parallel to the south."

"Understand cleared to engage. We have positive Phoenix contact this time."

The two F-14s left their racetrack patrol pattern and headed toward their targets. They were already within lock-on and firing range. If the bandits did turn south, it would be a tail chase, but there was plenty of time to intercept.

"Two, this is One. Let's swing around aft of them and see if showing the flag makes an impression."

"Roger, Two."

In burner, the Tomcats would close the bandits within a matter of a few minutes. The question was whether the GCI controller at Yantai would pick them up and warn the two Chinese aircraft.

"Digger One, bandits are at angels thirty."

The Tomcats dropped to the bandits' altitude and took

position dead astern. "They're not taking any evasive action," Digger One reported. "You suppose they're sleeping on the job?"

"If so, they may never wake up. I figure forty miles to the parallel."

"Switch to Sparrows."

The RIO in each Digger aircraft moved his weapons selector switch to the medium range air-to-air missiles.

Still confused as to why the Chinese had made no evasive moves, the Tomcats slid into close position on the bandits. They were Chengdu-J-7 interceptors, Chinese versions of the MiG-21 Fishbed, a mid-1960s design. Obsolete, they carried no defensive sensors, and these particular two carried only droppable fuel tanks on their external hardpoints. Their only armament would be twin 30mm cannon with only sixty rounds per gun.

"These guys must be brain-dead if they think they're going to get our choppers with cannon," Digger One said to his RIO. He was flying on the left wing of the leader and still had not been observed! Finally, the Chengdu pilot looked back to his left and the airplane did a little jump as its driver saw the Tomcats. Immediately, the two Chengdus began a right turn and headed back for the Gulf of Chihli. Apparently they were not suicidal.

"Admiral, the bandits have headed back toward the mainland. Watchdog reports the Tomcats made a positive ID. They are Chengdu-7 interceptors, Chinese MiG-21s."

"Ha! They figured no contest, I suspect," Jumpin' Joe declared.

The air boss reported, "Rescues One and Two, thirty miles out, Admiral."

"Well," Jumpin' Joe said to Paterson, "let's go down and roll out the red carpet for your son-in-law and that lad with the leg wound."

Sheila Kohn was already on the flight deck, standing by the island.

"There they are!" Kohn said, pointing to the low-flying Seahawks. The second took position behind his leader, and in tandem they approached from the port side of the *Lincoln* and touched down on the canted deck under the direction of a pair of yellowshirts.

The medics had a basket litter ready for Price, and he came off first to the shouts and applause of his shipmates. Then Joshua Dunne dropped to the flight deck and saluted Jumpin' Joe as the admiral came forward, his smile reaching almost to his ears. "Welcome back, Joshua, welcome back."

Dunne gave Paterson a salute and then a brief hug to Frosty Kohn. He knew they dare not kiss as it would take the crew an hour to pry them apart.

"Sheila, you just look great," Dunne muttered as Tony Delaney reached around him and patted Dunne's shoulders.

"You two sure know how to keep a guy on edge," Delaney declared.

"You brought us back, Tony. Without your checkout, it would have been a different story," Dunne complimented.

Jumpin' Joe ushered them all into the island and to the flag bridge. Delaney had excused himself, conscious of the fact that he would not be included in the debrief. Captain Tyler and the CAG were waiting.

"Did your airplane go into the water?" was Paterson's first question.

"It must have," Dunne answered. "With the wind that blew me southwest toward the coast, I must have punched out well over the water."

"Do you think the soldiers identified you? By nationality, that is."

"I doubt it. We spent some time with an older couple in the hut. I don't think they knew where we came from, although they probably knew we were speaking English despite the fact that they couldn't understand us.'' Dunne used the pause to ask the question uppermost in his mind. "Did you get Desird?''

"No,'' Kohn replied flatly. "It was a civilian airplane; I couldn't do it.''

There was an awkward silence before Paterson said, "We'll get another chance.''

Kohn could feel the agony within Dunne's heart. He had wanted Desird. But she was pleased that a greater morality had prevailed. He realized that, also. "You did right, Sheila.''

"All right,'' Paterson said. "We're all tired, and you two need some rest. Joshua, I want the flight surgeon to check you out.''

"I'm fine.''

"Let him take a quick look, just so I'll feel better. I have to call the president, and he'll want some kind of written report. Let's get together on that this evening, after dinner—my cabin. The XO has given me his quarters.'' Turning to Captain Tyler, Jumpin' Joe and Walleye, he continued, "Would you like to join us?''

Jumpin' Joe replied for them all. "We have some duties we need to address. Jocko, I think we can turn south and resume normal operations in accordance with our OPLAN. There's no need for us to be involved in your report, Admiral Paterson. I assume you have no more surprises for us.''

Paterson grinned. "No, Admiral, and we thank you— and the ship, Captain Tyler, and of course the air wing, Walleye. I think all of the excitement is over.''

"Our pleasure, sir,'' Walleye responded.

"Come on, fearless flight leader, I'll walk you down to sick bay.'' Kohn led the way off the flag bridge.

As they made their way through the various passageways and down several ladders, Dunne and Kohn walked as closely together as they dared.

25

The White House
October 8, 10:00 P.M.

President Matthew Laughton Perry strode down the red-carpeted hallway to the White House press room, followed by his chief of staff. Perry took his position behind the podium and waved the assembled press corps into their seats.

"Ladies and gentlemen, I have a short statement, and then I will answer a few questions."

He waited a moment while tape recorders and notebooks were positioned. Clearing his throat, he began, "On October sixth, our date, a maritime reconnaissance aircraft of the People's Republic of China overflew one of our carrier battle groups that has been operating in the Yellow Sea while our forces were conducting routine operations in international waters. Regrettably, the PRC aircraft crashed while passing abeam of the battle group's flagship, the aircraft carrier USS *Lincoln*. The entire incident was videotaped by navy photographers aboard the *Lincoln*, and it clearly shows that the cause of the accident was pilot error on behalf of the Chinese crew. The Chinese have accused us of shooting down the aircraft.

"A copy of the tape has been provided to the PRC embassy, and it will be released to you after this press conference.

"Later on that same day, and I remind you that it was October seventh in that part of the world, a pair of Su-27 Flankers, purchased from the Republic of Ukraine and belonging to the PRC, approached our naval battle group and, despite our warnings to remain clear, they descended and began their own overflight of our ships at a very low altitude. They were escorted by two F-14D Tomcats from the *Lincoln*'s air wing. As they drew abreast of the *Lincoln*, the Su-27s executed a radical aggressive maneuver and without any provocation attacked and shot down our two Tomcats with air-to-air missiles. That action was also videotaped."

The press room began to hum with whispered comments and a shuffling of positions.

"The battle group commander immediately launched the ready combat air patrol aircraft, and in subsequent action they destroyed the Chinese aircraft.

"We have filed a formal protest with the People's Republic of China, and I have requested an immediate convening of the United Nations Security Council.

"I will now take questions."

There was a confused flurry of hands and voices before the president recognized one of the reporters. "Yes?"

"Mister President, were our aircrews lost?"

"Yes. We are withholding their names pending notification of next of kin."

The president skipped around the room as more questions came in rapid order.

"Just where were our ships? Could you be more specific?"

"In the Yellow Sea, approximately eighty miles west of Inchon."

"What is the current situation there?"

"Our forces are continuing routine operations with increased vigilance, of course. We have informed the PRC that any further incursion of the airspace around the battle group will be considered as a hostile action, and intruders will be engaged.''

"Sir, have there been any further acts of aggression by the Chinese?"

"No, although a Han-class submarine, operating on the surface, did interfere with the safe navigation of the battle group by steaming through the formation. It was a reckless and irresponsible act, and we have included that violation of the international rules of the road in our protest to the PRC.''

"Is that a nuclear ship, Mister President?"

"Yes, it is an SSN nuclear attack boat."

"What action did we take, sir?"

"The submarine was detected as it approached the force, and since it was on the surface it was not considered a threat. Two of the battle group frigates escorted the submarine out of the area."

"What about the trade talks, Mister President?"

"We have suspended further talks until we receive a response to our protest from the PRC."

"Are they scuttled?"

"No, I think not. Beijing has given us a preliminary reply that indicates the attack by the two Su-27s was the action of an irresponsible maverick senior pilot."

"Who is the battle group commander, sir?"

"Rear Admiral Joseph Jefferson."

From the rear of the room came a exclamation. "Jesus, not Jumpin' Joe? The Chinese are really in deep kimchi now."

The president hushed the laughter with raised hands. "Admiral Jefferson is one of our most experienced combat officers and is acting under the guidance of the secretary of defense and the Joint Chiefs."

"What do you figure his surrender terms are, sir?"

Again, the president had to wait until the laughter subsided. "I have every confidence that the admiral will handle this delicate situation with all of the tact and diplomacy called for. It is a serious incident, but early indications are that it does not demonstrate any aggressive intent by the government of the People's Republic of China. They are understandably concerned about our operations so close to their territorial waters, but neither the accidental crash of their reconnaissance aircraft nor the attack by the two fighters is considered to be a deliberately hostile move by the PRC."

"Then why are we requesting a meeting of the UN Security Council?"

"To open another avenue of discussion with the PRC and to demonstrate that we take this incident most seriously and consider it a threat to the success of the trade talks—which have been going well, I might remind you."

"Mister President . . ."

"Thank you, thank you." The president turned and walked away while questions were still being shouted after him.

"Very well done, Mister President," complimented the chief of staff as they reentered the Oval Office.

"Well, we'll have to wait and see how the media reports it. Are the tapes being distributed?"

"Yes, sir; the press secretary is handling them."

"Thank you, Bob. Give me a few minutes before Senator Alexander."

"Certainly, sir."

President Perry sat at his desk and began dunking a tea bag in a cup of hot water. It had been a long day. A thousand thoughts were fighting for priority within his mind. He had to arrange them in some priority. First would have to be contact with Paterson. Desird should have been taken care of by now. With all of the Chinese screaming about violation of their territorial waters, there had been no mention of airspace violation. That should be a good sign. Paterson's people must have completed their mission undetected.

He tried the tea. Too weak. Back in went the bag.

He had to smile when he thought of the press's reaction to his revelation of Jumpin' Joe Jefferson as the on-scene commander. The man had a reputation for positive, uninhibited action and was a skilled leader and consummate sea warrior, having cut his battle teeth as a young junior grade lieutenant in the skies over Vietnam. Carrier Battle Group Three could not be in better hands.

26 ═══════════════════════════

Dunne was already present when Kohn arrived at Paterson's cabin. The small conference table was set for dinner with a white linen cloth and the ship's china and silverware.

"Come in. Did you get some rest?"

"Yes, Admiral, I did. I usually don't sleep that soundly during the day."

Paterson handed Dunne a small glass of pineapple juice. "Pretend it's bourbon," he said. "You had a rough night. I was just telling Joshua that I talked with Walleye. The squadron skippers have hard jobs writing letters to the next of kin. Six pilots and a crewman among the two Tomcats and the Seahawk that fell to the rocket attack. Jumpin' Joe was concerned that some of the helicopter crew might have survived, but after talking to you and Price, there was no way."

"It exploded on contact. Lucky I hadn't strapped in yet," observed Dunne.

Paterson made a final remark before changing the subject. "I suspect Washington will ask the Chinese to return the bodies when this thing is all settled. It's a shame we didn't recover any of the Badger crew. So much for that.

"I'm having the food brought up from the general mess; it's turkey and dressing, one of my favorites. The admiral offered me his cook, but standard navy chow normally satisfies me on these occasions. I trust you will enjoy it, also."

"I slept through lunch," Dunne admitted. "I'm hungry enough to eat a horse—or should I say a seahorse?"

"You'd have to eat a lot of those," Kohn commented.

"Shall we sit?" Paterson asked. Two messmen were preparing to serve from a small steam table brought to the cabin for the occasion. Paterson dismissed them as soon as their plates were full.

The meal was excellent; the *Lincoln*, despite its enormous size and requirement to feed five thousand men four meals a day, had a reputation as a good feeder.

Paterson was quiet at first, allowing his guests time to enjoy the meal. As he passed the coffee decanter, he said, "I talked with the president a couple hours ago. He doesn't have any particular heartburn over the fact that we failed to bag Desird. I'll elaborate on that in a minute, but first I wanted to ask you two: are you still interested in staying with my group?"

Dunne answered first. "I'd like to stay until we get Desird."

Kohn followed with "Yes, sir, I would."

"Well, I don't know if we'll get another crack at the bastard or not. Certainly, if the opportunity is there. Incidentally, you may have noticed that we've turned to the south. Jumpin' Joe figured it might help defuse the situation."

Kohn asked, "Did we ever regain contact with the submarine?"

"As a matter of fact, we did. Two of the destroyers worked him for about an hour and he was gone. Noisy bastard. Apparently we had no trouble tracking him."

"Did the president say how the diplomatic scene is going?"

"Yes, the Chinese are making angry noises, as you might suspect, but with the videotapes being shown all over the world, they have no substantive argument."

Dunne poured a spot of cream into his coffee and added a half teaspoon of sugar. "I wonder what the status of my encounter with the army back on the coast is. The reports should have reached Beijing by now."

"I don't know. We may have to wait that one out for a while. It'll be obvious to Beijing that we went in there and pulled out our people, but I don't think they know how you got there. It's a matter of whether the GCI people that controlled the MiGs can convince Beijing that there was really anything out there. The pilots are dead. With every passing hour, it appears more and more likely that Darkstar One is sitting on the bottom of the Yellow Sea. I really believe we got away with it—except for one thing."

Dunne and Kohn looked expectantly at Paterson. He seemed to be pausing for dramatic effect. His words came out slowly. "Amin Desird was not on the airplane."

Absolute silence greeted his announcement. *Not on the airplane?* Finally, Dunne repeated his thought aloud. "*Not* on the airplane?"

"It was a setup, just like the president suggested to me a week ago."

Kohn carefully folded her napkin and placed it beside her plate. "This was all a drill?"

"No, it was worth all the effort we put into it; it's just that we were suckered."

"Desird never came to pick up any detonators?"

"No, Sheila. The whole scheme was orchestrated by Chinese counterintelligence. Dong Sum was a double agent, and Chi Lin was his unknowing accomplice."

"How do we know all this?" Dunne asked.

"I received the information from Nim Chou less than an hour ago. I haven't told the president about this development yet."

"I can't believe it," Kohn said with noticeable disgust.

"Believe it," Paterson assured her. "Nim Chou was alerted by a fellow agent early this morning, about the time you were deciding whether or not you wanted to take out the transport. He and his wife made it to Macau—pedaled their bicycles twenty-eight kilometers and bribed the border guards. He contacted the ship through our usual channels."

"You indicated Chi Lin was not in on the plan?"

"Chi Lin was arrested by Chinese counterintelligence while conducting your intercept."

"I wondered why he suddenly stopped giving data; I just assumed he figured we had made contact," Dunne observed.

"I imagine he is with his ancestors by now, and I can only hope our network in China survives. I have my own people outside the CIA."

Dunne asked, "If the Chinese set this all up, why haven't they been making accusations?"

"Because you could not bring yourself to shoot down a planeload of civilians, which is exactly what they wanted us to do. They don't have any evidence to show the world."

Dunne continued, "They thought they could detect and destroy our Sea Scorpions? They would have to have that evidence also."

"Originally, when the plan was formatted, they figured we'd use Hornets on a low-level, pop-up attack. Possibly F-14s. We would figure we could do that if we had the element of surprise. I suspect that they felt they could still bag one of you if they had fighters on the scene with the transport. They just didn't realize how effective the Stealth design is. If your bomb-bay doors hadn't stuck open, Sheila, they would never have had a crack at you. As it was, they can claim *something* was in their airspace but have nothing to show what it was. Checkmate."

"Why would they set up such a thing?" Kohn asked.

"The trade talks. They wanted to put us at a disadvantage. Blackmail."

"You think they knew Desird was that important to us?" Dunne questioned.

"He made the perfect target. World's number-one terrorist, hated by all civilized governments."

"Incredible," Dunne mused. "They were risking major conflict, especially with the Flanker attack and the submarine show of force."

"That was all coincidental, I suspect," Paterson said.

"So what do we do now?" asked Kohn.

Paterson scooted back his chair. "Your Tony Delaney will fly the remaining F-117N to Kunsan, where it will be taken back to Tonopah by C-5. You can go along if you wish, or I can arrange for the ship to fly you to Seoul and then commercial back to the States. I have some unfinished business in Tokyo. I'll be back at the cafe by the fifteenth. Why don't you two join me there? I may have something of interest for you."

Dunne stood. "*This* has been an interesting experience, Admiral. I don't see how we can top it."

"Well, you two have earned a few days off. I suspect you want to discuss your personal relationship, perhaps even make plans. Incidentally, which one of you will write the book?" Paterson asked.

Dunne chuckled. "It would make one hell of a story."

"All I ask is that you wait a few years and make it fiction. No real names," cautioned Paterson, just in case Dunne was tempted.

"We could dedicate it to Annie," Kohn said, slipping her hand into Dunne's.

"She'd like that. That's a nice thought."

Electrifying Thrillers by
Ryne Douglas Pearson

"A gifted high-tech specialist . . .
with mind-boggling expertise"
Kirkus Reviews

CAPITOL PUNISHMENT
72228-3/$5.99 US/$7.99 Can

Bodies litter the street in L.A.—victims of a lethal chemi-
cal killer unleashed by an American monster who has
decreed that the government, too, must die.

OCTOBER'S GHOST
72227-5/$5.99 US/$7.99 Can

Thirty-five years after the Cuban Missile Crisis, an
attempted coup breaks out against an aging Castro. He
aims a nuclear missile at a major city to force the United
States to become his ally against his enemies.

THUNDER ONE
(previously published as *Cloudburst*)
72037-X/$5.50 US/$6.50 Can

The President of the United States is assassinated in a Los
Angeles street, while half a world away, an American
plane and its passengers are taken hostage. The terrorist
war has hit home with a vengeance.

STUART WOODS

The *New York Times* Bestselling Author

GRASS ROOTS
71169-/ $6.50 US/ $8.50 Can

When the nation's most influential senator
succumbs to a stroke, his brilliant chief aide
runs in his stead, tackling scandal, the governor
of Georgia and a white supremacist
organization that would rather see him
dead than in office.

Don't miss these other page-turners from
Stuart Woods

WHITE CARGO   70783-7/ $6.50 US/ $8.50 Can
A father searches for his kidnapped daughter in the
drug-soaked Colombian underworld.

DEEP LIE   70266-5/ $6.50 US/ $8.50 Can
At a secret Baltic submarine base, a renegade Soviet
commander prepares a plan so outrageous that it just
might work.

UNDER THE LAKE   70519-2/ $6.50 US/ $8.50 Can

CHIEFS   70347-5/ $6.50 US/ $8.50 Can

RUN BEFORE THE WIND

70507-9/ $6.50 US/ $8.50 Can